Meg Hutchinson left school at fifteen and didn't return to education until she was thirty-three, when she entered Teacher Training College and studied for her degree in the evenings. She lived for sixty years in Wednesbury, where her parents and grandparents spent all their lives, but now has a quiet little cottage in Shropshire where she can indulge her passion for storytelling. It is a passion that has reaped dividends, with her novels regularly appearing in bestseller lists.

Praise for Meg Hutchinson:

'Hutchinson knows how to spin a good yarn.' *Birmingham Evening Mail*

'The mistress of simmering sagas.' *Peterborough Evening Telegraph*

'Meg Hutchinson's storytelling skills are attracting a bigger and bigger audience.' *Newcastle Evening Chronicle*

MEG HUTCHINSON

For the Love of a Sister

HODDER

I

'I told you never to come to this house!' Myra Brent's eyes blazed with passion. 'I told you,' the words throbbed, 'never, never come here!'

'Myra, I . . .'

Quick and stinging, her reply a whiplash of words, Myra's mouth tightened.

'No excuses, I don't want to hear them. I told you to stay clear of this place, to stay away from me, I told you but you didn't listen. You never learn do you, Eden? But perhaps this will help you.'

The final word squeezing between clenched teeth, Myra Brent's hand struck hard.

Myra had never struck her before. Sitting now in the tiny house which had seen the growing of herself and her sister, Eden Brent seemed to feel again the sharp blow which had sent her reeling.

Why? She stared at the grate, dead and empty of fire for more than a week. Why had Myra's eyes blazed, why had her whole body shaken; why had she been so angry? It wasn't as if she had acted boldly; the very opposite was true. She had taken care to avoid the main approach to that house, coming to it by way of the surrounding fields and asking at the stables if one of the hands would let her sister know she was there.

Myra had run across that cobbled yard, the skirts of her dark blue dress flapping beneath the crisp starched cotton of her apron, her eyes throwing darts of fury. She had not even asked the reason of the visit.

Numbed as much by her sister's treatment of her as by the January frost, Eden made no move as the door to the scullery opened and a thin woman, shawl knotted tight beneath flat shapeless breasts, bustled into the darkened room.

'C'mon now, wench, it'll do no good yoh sitting there catchin' your own death o' cold. It be over and done, your grandmother be laid to 'er rest and though you mightn't think so this minute you 'ave to get on wi' life.'

'I tried to tell her . . .'

'Ar well, yoh done your best, can't nobody do more.'

Dora Benson drew the closed curtains a few inches apart following the custom of returning the household gradually to the full light of day after the burying of a family member.

'I would never have gone to that house . . . never gone against her word . . .'

'Like I says, wench, yoh tried, can't never be said as yoh didn't. But that sister o' your'n wanted no hearin' of what yoh went there to say, so that's it an' all about it. A man can lead a hoss to the brook but he can't push its head 'neath the water.'

'Gran would have liked her there.'

'I'll make no denial o' that,' Dora nodded, 'but it ain't always given that what a body would 'ave liked be what a body gets.'

'But why would Myra not listen?'

Fetching sticks and coal from the bucket beneath the shallow brownstone sink in the scullery, Dora set to laying a fire.

'The answer to that be knowed by none 'cept the wench 'erself and I 'ave no doubt you'll hear the tellin' o' it in time; 'til then you must carry on as your grand-mother trusted you would. Now, go fill the kettle from the pump while I gets this fire to lightin'.'

'*I told you to stay away from me . . .*'

Taking the kettle into the yard shared with three other households, the words her sister had hurled at her echoed in Eden's mind.

'*. . . you never learn do you?*'

Eyes brimming, she swallowed hard. That had been one lesson she would never forget.

'Who was the young woman paying you a visit, Myra?'

Ava Russell's sharp eyes stabbed at the chamber-maid she had summoned to her sitting-room.

'I . . . I've had no visitor, mum.'

Ava's smile was cold. 'But it was no servant of mine you spoke with yesterday out there beside the stables.'

How did she know? Which one of the staff had told of Eden's coming to Moorcroft House? Keeping her glance on the beautiful carpet, Myra hid the quick alarm triggering along her veins.

'It was not any staff of this house, was it?'

Could she go on denying the visit? Myra's brain sought for a way to do just that but her mistress's swift intervention gave her no time.

'I have the right to know the identity of any person calling at this house! You will furnish me with that knowledge or . . .'

The pause was deliberate, heavy in its meaning. Either Ava Russell got what she asked or a servant got the sack. Myra could not risk dismissal. She kept her glance on the carpet while her thoughts flew desperately in and out of her mind. Without her wage, Eden and their grandmother would be unable to manage, but to tell this woman of her sister . . .

'I'm waiting!'

Myra felt her insides twist. She could hear laughter in that voice, the taunt of malice. This woman knew her own power and revelled in it. With one word she could take away another's living, destroy a family dependent upon work as domestic servants. But there was something else, infinitely more cruel, of far more unmitigated evil, and that something must not touch Myra's family.

'I think p'raps you be referring to the gypsy woman, mum,' Myra answered with the only feasible thought she had, 'there was one called yesterday.'

Smoothing the skirts of her jade-coloured moiré taffeta gown, Ava Russell observed a few moments of silence, a silence she knew would tear at the nerves of the young woman standing before her, and enjoyed it to the full. The feeling of superiority, of dominance, the thrill of having another at her mercy never dissipated, never failed to set fire to her blood, and today she would feel that burning.

'A gypsy you say.' The gown smoothed of its non-existent crease, Ava's hand rested on her knee, the smile remaining on her lips, frigid and static as if held there by the grip of ice.

'Yes, mum, called at the house about three o' clock.'

Poor stupid fool! Ava's enjoyment heightened. Did the girl truly think she would be believed? Did she expect to fool Ava Russell with so lame an explanation? But what better could be expected of the lower classes? Really . . . Her inner smile as cold as that on her face, Ava chided herself . . . You should not have looked for a more intelligent lie – the girl just does not have the brain for it.

'A gypsy,' she repeated. 'And it was she who spoke with you before the stables?'

'Only for a minute or so, mum.' Relief at having her explanation accepted, Myra raised her glance to the woman regarding her with dark eyes. 'I told her she would have to leave, that the mistress didn't tolerate gypsies calling at the house.'

'I see.' Ava nodded, the light shooting blue darts from her elegantly coiffured raven-black hair. 'Then I must be mistaken, for the person I saw you with was dressed like no gypsy nor did she carry any basket of pegs or laces. In fact, she was dressed quite respectably as I recall, most neat and tidy in her maroon coat and bonnet. You are certain she was simply a gypsy, someone you had not met before that moment?'

She had seen! Myra's nerves jumped again. She had seen Eden, had watched them together in the yard. How else would she have known of the maroon-coloured coat and bonnet that were Eden's Sunday church clothes?

All of this reasoning showing clearly in her servant's blue eyes, Ava Russell's appetite for vindictiveness sharpened. But she must not satisfy that particular need too soon; she should exercise patience. Fruit savoured most was a fruit one had waited the tasting of. Tomorrow was another day and that would be followed by as many as Ava Russell chose. Lifting one well-manicured hand from her lap, she held it at chest level, each finger splayed in an affected gesture. Her tone conveying none of the satisfaction running inside, she addressed the servant.

'As you have said, Myra, I do not tolerate gypsies or vagrants. You did right in telling the woman to leave.'

She thought she had got away with it. Ava Russell's cold smile warmed to one of self-appreciation as she dismissed her maid. But that girl was merely on a leash, one which would be reeled in when the time was right!

The world was no different, the house was as she remembered it; her bedroom was the same small room with its chest of drawers, one plain wooden chair and her bed with a rag rug beside it; yet everything was different.

Unable to sleep, nerves quickening at every sound the night brought, Eden Brent stared at the darkness above her head. Somewhere up there should be a ceiling, to her left should be a door, yet all the knowledge of the past sixteen years of living in this house seemed to have evaporated, to have gone from her mind, leaving a blankness, an emptiness which held no marker, no indication of where she was or where she should go.

She had never thought she would feel like this, to feel so isolated from all she had known; now for the first time in her seventeen years she was afraid.

There had been no sign of her grandmother being ill. Vision lost in the black of moonless shadow the pictures in her mind showed vividly clear. The day had gone as so many before it, the cast iron range black-leaded to a silver sheen, the living-room polished and dusted, the quarry tiles of the scullery floor scrubbed, and the yard swilled down with buckets of water to which had been added the usual copious amount of 'Auntie Sally', the strong-smelling, dark, oily liquid bought weekly from the carter and used, Grandmother said, to keep down vermin.

As a child Eden had delighted in watching Grandmother add a little of the liquid to the water with which the floors of the living-room and bedrooms got their weekly scrubbing, laughing her pleasure when allowed to stir the bucket's contents with a wooden stick, asking, 'What makes it go all creamy?' and getting no answer other than a brusque 'Stop blethering, child, the water be gettin' cold.'

It had always been that way, Gran being abrupt and pretending to be too busy to answer. It had taken a long time to realise, a long time to acknowledge, that the woman who had been their mother, father and grand-mother was not an oracle, that she did not hold the answers to all things. It had come as a shock.

Surrounded by darkness, silence heavy in her ears, Eden remembered. The teacher had asked 'What are shooting stars?' The children had looked questioningly at each other, none daring to say aloud the thought in their minds. 'They be shootin' stars, just like yoh says.' The teacher had waited a few moments and, when no reply was forthcoming, had tutted her impatience and told them she would ask the same question the next day. Eden had released the breath caught anxiously in case she was ordered to stand up and give her own answer. Myra would know, her sister knew a lot of things because of being older; and if Myra didn't know, then Gran would because she was even older. But Myra had no explanation and Gran had grumbled of 'kids betherin' on when they could see a body were busy.' So she had gone to school the next day with no more knowledge of shooting stars but with an under-standing that to her child's mind was far more profound. Her grandmother had offered no solution, given no definition; she had not taken Eden on to her lap after supper and given a reason as to the why and wherefore of a thing which puzzled a young mind. Could it be that, contrary to her long-held belief, her grandmother was not all-knowing?

Somehow it had seemed like a betrayal. How could she think thus of her grandmother? It was a sin and she, Eden Brent, was the vilest of people.

But once she had not been so. The pictures in her mind changed, flashing from a thin, scraggy eight year old to a taller girl, her shape more defined, buds of breasts soft mounds beneath her cotton frock. Blue-green eyes clear and sparkling with interest in life, fair hair gleaming like a spring sun, thirteen-year-old Eden Brent was a pretty child.

The headmistress of twenty years had retired, her place taken by a middle-aged, gaunt, sharp-featured, razor-tongued woman whose every word conveyed her feeling that her new post was beneath her, that the running of a school whose pupils were the offspring of colliers, nailers and foundrymen was entirely unsuited to someone of her class. Miss Jones! Eden's eyes closed trying to erase the memory, but it remained, stubbornly imprinted on her inner vision.

Three years Eden's senior, Myra had already left the all-girls' church school and secured a post as house maid at Moorcroft House, home of one of the town's prosperous industrialists. Eden hoped the same might be given herself.

She had missed her sister terribly.

Eyes wide open now, Eden stared into darkness which had no power to hide the visions of her mind.

Myra's monthly afternoon visits home were something Gran and she awaited with pleasure, her own a tingling excitement that tickled all over. Gran had allowed her to stay off school, calling next morning to state the reason for her grand-daughter's absence in her flat 'don't you go arguin' o' me' tone. But on each occasion the headmistress had later summoned a frightened young girl to her private room plying her with questions. What had Myra talked of . . . ? Had she spoken of her mistress . . . ? What did the other servants gossip about? And all the time those keen ferret eyes had watched her face.

Why had she been interested in what Myra talked of? It hadn't been as though her sister were still a pupil. She had kept her answers brief, resenting what, to her young mind, seemed interference in something not the headmistress's business. She had said none of this to Gran, and the interrogations had gone on until one day she had been asked if she would like a position as a domestic servant.

This had been Eden's dream. Not that she wanted to leave Gran . . . but to have a smart uniform, to be able to bring money home as Myra did, that was all she wanted. Miss Jones had said that were she prepared to work hard, a post could most probably be procured for her. A week later she had been summoned again.

Eden shivered at the memory. Dressed in a thin cotton frock her grandmother washed at the end of every school day, drying it before the living-room fire and smoothing it with the heavy flat iron to ensure a neat clean appearance the next day, she had tapped at the door bearing the name 'Miss Jones' above the awesome title 'Headmistress'.

'You have a neat hand with the sewing needle, so I am informed.'

The girl had nodded, hands held behind her back, as school required, eyes nervously lowered to wooden floorboards that shone from nightly polishing by a caretaker and his wife, both of whom viewed the head-mistress with the same trepidation as did the students.

'That is a quality which will serve well in a position of ladies' maid.'

Ladies' maid. A jolt of pleasure had raced in her blood. Did this mean a post had been found for her?

'But a girl of your years, and with absolutely no ex-perience of the requirements of a finer way of life . . .'

Miss Jones had paused and the pleasure had dropped away from Eden like a stone.

'. . . however . . .'

Again that dreadful pause, animal-sharp eyes assessing the girl whose fingers twisted anxiously.

'. . . however,' the thinly marked lips compressed before her next words, 'if you are prepared to do as you are taught then it is possible to get you to that standard of requirement. Are you willing?'

She had been more than willing. She had danced all the way home in a dream of smart uniforms and deliciously frilled caps and aprons, bubbling her words until Gran had told her sharply to 'Stop your fidgetin', you be jumpin' like a flea on a dog's back.'

It had been agreed, Gran giving her blessing. But within a month the bubble had burst.

Turning her face into the pillow, Eden hid the trembling tears.

The bubble had burst, but the shards of it were still stuck in her heart.

2

'That be the lot, there be no more in the copper.'

Beads of perspiration glistened like diamonds in the light of several candles on the flushed face of the scullery maid. Her cheeks deepened to a further shade of red as she emptied a bucket of steaming water into the bath housed in an exotically appointed room adjacent to her mistress's dressing-room.

'It'll take time to boil another copper . . .'

'No need for that Letty.' Myra Brent glanced at the girl whose breath heaved noisily in her lungs. 'I will let you know when the bath is ready to be emptied.'

'Fill the bath, empty the bath, fill it, empty it! Be the same one day after t'other! Why for 'eaven's sake? Why do a woman need to wash all over every day? T'ain't natural . . .' Empty bucket in hand, Letty Holden grumbled her tiredness. '. . . t'ain't as though 'er does anything to soil even 'er 'ands; 'ain't never 'ad to do nothin' for 'erself, not in all 'er born days, 'er would even 'ave a body wipe 'er arse for 'er, supposin' any o' we was willin'.'

The door closed on the girl's ire. Myra Brent gazed into the whispering flames of a fire around which she had draped white fluffy towels.

'. . . 'er would even 'ave a body wipe 'er arse for 'er, supposin' any o' we was willin' . . .'

Letty Holden's words echoed in Myra's mind but immediately became swamped by her own, saying what they had so many times before: '*There are worse services than wiping another woman's backside.*'

Worse services! Myra's eyes screwed tight against the thought. Worse services! And she, Myra Brent, had to perform them.

'I think perhaps Desert Dreams – the perfume is so very sensuous.'

Myra's eyelids flew open. She had not heard the footfalls of the woman now standing behind her, a woman whom she knew watched her with spite-filled eyes. But spite was not all Ava Russell desired.

Hands shaking, Myra reached for a pink crystal flagon from the cabinet and emptied a little of the heavily scented contents into the bath.

'Yes, it was the right choice.' Ava Russell, the hem of her silk robe whispering against the floor, swayed across the room and halted before her maid. 'The perfume is so alluring, so heady . . . so full of promise.'

Returning the delicately wrought stopper to the flagon, Myra's nerves jerked. The pause between words had been fleeting, subtle, but the inference was heavy. Tonight was to be no different to so many others.

'The water is the correct temperature? You have tested it?'

The voice was soft, smooth as the silk its owner was

wearing, but each word rubbed like gravel against Myra's heightened nerves. Replacing the flagon among others equally pretty, struggling to control the quiver in her voice, Myra answered quietly. 'It is hand-warm, mum, just as you like it.'

Just as she liked it. Ava Russell's inward smile spread. But all of her life was just as she liked it . . . and it would never be otherwise. Allowing the robe to slip from her, she twisted and turned to admire her naked body reflected in mirrors draped about with vibrant silks. Yes, life would always be as Ava Russell wanted it.

Stepping into the bath, lowering luxuriously into the perfumed water, she watched the slim figure of her servant take the robe and drape it carefully across a blue velvet chaise-longue half-hidden by sweeping drapes echoing those partly concealing the mirrors. Then as the figure turned, she waved a hand languidly.

She glanced at the soap Myra had brought from the cabinet. 'Rose of Shalimar! A perfect accompaniment for Desert Dreams; they both have that captivating enchantment of the Eastern world. Together they breathe love and desire.'

Love . . . What did this woman know of love? Myra's glance rested on the palely tinted soap. Love meant caring for people around you, whether servant or kin, yet Ava Russell harboured such feelings for none other than herself. But desire . . . yes, her mistress knew that well enough: it ran as permanently in her as the blood in her veins, desire which had to be satisfied

in whatever manner she chose . . . but the desires of
Ava Russell were merely pacified, quieted for the
moment, never totally satiated.

'There will be no need for this.' A fingertip flicked
the pink face flannel Myra held with the soap. 'We will
use our hands, it is so much more enjoyable.'

Laying the flannel aside, Myra felt the breath bubble
in her chest. If only she could run from this house . . .
But she couldn't . . . she could not bring more hardship to her grandmother and sister. Bending to dip the
soap into the water, her teeth clenched as Ava's hand
rose once more.

'No, my dear . . .'

The affected sweetness of the tone brought a sickness to Myra's throat.

'. . . not like this, they get in the way. We enjoy our
bathtime much more without their hindrance, do you
not agree?'

How could she not agree? How could she tell this
woman of her true feelings, of the disgust, repugnance
and loathing that filled her each time she was made to
partake in Ava Russell's nauseating self-satisfying
pastimes.

Sickness solidified into a choking lump in her throat,
Myra looked down at the fingers touching the frilled
apron covering her dark blue dress. Like the claws of
a hunting hawk. And she was the prey. She shuddered.

She could not look into those taunting eyes, must not
look into them! Putting the soap into a dish shaped like
a wide-open lotus she forced her trembling fingers to

release the ties of her apron, then the buttons of her dress, removing each of her undergarments until she too was naked.

Eyes resting avidly on mirrors which portrayed every angle of Myra's slim body, Ava Russell breathed approval. She had done well in getting rid of her previous ladies' maid. This one was younger and prettier, altogether more to her taste . . . and when it palled? Then she would find another. Money was the key that opened any treasure box . . . or the legs of any poverty-stricken girl!

Relaxing her head on the towel placed for that purpose against the rim of the bath, she let her eyelids close slowly. Ignoring Myra's half-choked sob, smiling as she slid a little further beneath the water, she purred, 'Now we are both ready, my dear, let us begin.'

There was no way out. Myra touched the bar of soap to the scented water. Hadn't she tried, hadn't she applied for another position, any position that would take her away from this house? But without a reference no mistress would employ her, and Ava Russell would furnish no such paper; even dismissal from her service had never been tainted by that particular brand of spite, as others who had once laboured under this roof had testified. This woman kept folk beneath her thumb even though she had no further use for them; that was how it would be with Myra Brent. Yes, she could walk out, turn her back on this demeaning life . . . and take what? Perhaps she could accept abject poverty, even the workhouse . . . but Eden and their grandmother?

She could never inflict such terror on them. She must accept the horror, continue in this house and in the abomination of its mistress.

Tears sliding over her cheeks, teeth clenched against the repugnance of the ritual she had to undergo, she soaped her hands then, mouth trembling, passed them over the other woman's breasts, squeezing gently, playing over the erect nipples as she had been instructed.

Eyelids lifting, Ava Russell's dark animal eyes glinted a pleasure which spoke of more than physical satisfaction; they glowed with the deeper gratification of knowing the humiliation her maid was suffering.

'You have such soothing hands, their touch is so seductive, you give pleasure . . . a pleasure we both share, one we can share now . . . like this.'

Her glance riveted to the reflections of the many mirrors, Ava stretched a hand to the trembling girl. Cupping each of the tight breasts for a moment she trailed a finger over the taut stomach to nestle in the soft silky hair of the vee at its base, her free hand pulling that of Myra to touch between her own parted thighs.

One candle lit the room given as her own, its pallid glow flickering over a narrow bed while, beyond its reach, shadows enveloped a chest of drawers and a washstand. Myra Brent's eyes, drowned in tears, saw nothing of these, she saw only a naked girl, an older woman's hand caressing her slender body.

She had tried, as she did each time, tried to wash

away the touch of Ava Russell's hands, scrubbing at her breasts and between her legs, scrubbing until the bite of carbolic soap stung the lacerated skin; but the touch refused to wash away, the horror of it remained, a vileness which caused her flesh to creep.

Had it been like this with the girl who had previously filled the post she held now? Had some other maid been subjected to the same terrible degradation? None of the household staff had ever spoken of her. The few times she had enquired of the girl, mouths had firmly closed and backs had turned. It seemed as if no such person had existed, yet there had to have been someone, a woman like Ava Russell would not deny herself a ladies' maid. Then why dismiss her? Was it that she refused to take part in her mistress's games? Had she resigned rather than be abused as she herself was?

If only she could do the same. Trembling from the effects of the treatment she had been made to endure, her flesh crawling with the memory, Myra snatched up the candle, carrying it to the washstand where she began the scrubbing all over again. Doused in icy water, skin raw and bleeding from the harsh brush, she sank to the floor oblivious of everything save the tearing of her heart. Curled into herself, her face hidden between frozen fingers, she sobbed brokenly, 'Lord, please! I can't go on . . . I can't . . . I can't . . .'

But the words, whispered so desperately, were swallowed by the silence. There was no one to help her, no way to escape the evil of Ava Russell; Myra was trapped at Moorcroft House, trapped by the love of a grandmother and a sister.

The girl had visibly trembled on being informed her assistance would not be required with tonight's bathing. Shivers of relief? Ava Russell watched through her table mirror as her maid lifted a heavy satin gown from the wall-length cupboard of the dressing-room. Yes, the quick look darting over the girl's face had told beyond doubt the trembling was that of relief. But it had needed no shaking limbs, no quick look of thankfulness crossing that drawn face, to tell her that.

It had been amusing at first; the shyness, the blushes, the obvious sense of unease at what she was instructed to perform. It was that way with each girl at the beginning but they had all learned, learned that Ava Russell must be satisfied in all things . . . but satisfaction was waning!

Stepping into the gown, standing still whilst deft fingers fastened the back of the close-fitting bodice, fingers which no longer sent the swift arrows of desire shooting along her veins, Ava's lips tightened. Myra Brent had proved amenable and docile, but mere compliance was not enough.

Seating herself at the dressing-table, Ava looked at the young woman adding a spray of feathers to the coiffure she had painstakingly arranged. She was clever with the duties of ladies' maid, she took good care of gowns, saw to it that every aspect of her mistress's wellbeing was taken care of . . . But maids to do only that could be found anywhere; the maids she relished needed to have fire, needed to have desires that matched her own.

'Which necklace will you be wearing, mum?'

The question brought Ava's glance to the jewellery box held out to her and suddenly she wanted to chase away that expression of relief she had seen flash over the tired face, to see it replaced by uncertainty and . . . and yes, by fear. Touching a hand to Myra's she pressed gently her reply a whisper of soft intimacy.

'I will leave that to you, my dear . . . whichever you choose will please me, just as you please me in other things, as I know you will be eager to do again when I return this evening.'

The box had almost dropped from the girl's hand and the look as their eyes had met had been one of revulsion, and despair.

Seated in a box at Wolverhampton Theatre Grand, Ava smiled to herself. Maybe she should wait a while, keep Myra Brent a little longer; to act hastily, to dismiss the girl now, could have its disadvantages.

Raising her fan to her mouth, Ava hid the smile reaching her lips. A change of entertainment, a small *divertissement*, it had its attractions; after all, instilling fear could be as amusing as tipping the skirt.

'I agree entirely . . .'

The whisper behind its own covering fan brought a swift colour to Ava's cheeks. Had she spoken aloud? Had her thoughts somehow found their way to becoming words?

'. . . I too find this whole thing boring.'

She had not spoken aloud. Ava's startled nerves subsided as the second whisper emanated from behind the fan.

'I had hoped my feeling did not show, but now I feel so terribly guilty.'

'I know that feeling only too well.' The fan fluttered with the woman's reply. 'But we must all be seen to do our duty . . . unpalatable as it sometimes proves. But for myself, well let us say this is not to my taste; no, not my idea of a pleasurable evening.'

What *was* her idea of a pleasurable evening? Closing her own fan, Ava directed her glance to the stage on which three over-dressed and over-large women were singing the maids' chorus from the Gilbert and Sullivan operetta *The Mikado* but her attention was concentrated on the figure beside her.

Lenor Medwin was plain. Her skin faintly sallow, red-brown hair owing more than a little to the henna bottle, she tried to hide these obvious shortcomings beneath gowns of outlandish styles and a deluge of expensive jewellery, the result of a husband's manufacture of iron. They had met several times at dinner parties given by Wednesbury's industrial élite, and also at occasions such as this – charity evenings – the proceeds of which were given in aid of comforts for soldiers serving abroad.

With the curtain lowering for the interval, the house lights glittered on jewellery adorning every woman in the audience. Real or paste? Ava mused, her gaze wandering over the crowd. Whichever, they were worn as much to impress as to dazzle . . . each gleaming piece a testimonial to a man's wealth. Had those gems been earned by a wife's love shared in the marital bed or were they a salve to the conscience of a man indulging himself outside?

Fidelity! Ava's mouth twitched, holding back a laugh. It could be betrayed in so many ways . . . and not every one of them by the husband; a wife too could play that game of chance. But her own – which carried more risks than simply playing mistress to some man – that behaviour was frowned upon. Yet when it came to the push infidelity was somehow overlooked by society, the man being smiled upon as an 'old dog' while, at worst, the woman lost a few friends. What Ava Russell played at would not, if discovered, be overlooked; society would not turn a blind eye. Being mistress to a man was accepted, being lover to another woman was not.

How many of the folk in this theatre could possibly guess? How many could have the faintest idea of her particular proclivities? How many, looking around at the beautifully gowned and coiffured women, could have any notion she preferred sexual pleasures not with her husband, or any other man, but with a female? Lesbian! Her breath slid through nostrils flaring with the thrill of all that the word entailed. Woman in love with woman. But Ava Russell was never in love with her companions in fornication, she was in love only with the sensual pleasures they afforded.

A whore! The fan rose to hide a breaking smile. Yes, she supposed she was. A whore, whom if found out, would be hounded from the country, shunned by the so-called respectable; therein was the danger . . . but danger was the cream on the cake, adding flavour to an already enjoyable sweetmeat.

A whore! Ava applauded quietly as the curtain rose for the second half of the operetta. She was all of that . . . and she would enjoy the fruits of being so again tonight.

3

There was no more to be done. Eden Brent wandered through the empty rooms of the only home she could remember. Gran had brought her and Myra here after their parents' death. 'Who knows what took 'em?' her grandmother had said years later. 'Be God's will an' we must bide by it.' But the platonic words had hidden a heart broken by the loss of an only living child. Now grandmother as well as parents had been taken and her sister had chased her away.

She had hoped Myra would come home, be there to say goodbye to the woman who had loved them both, but Myra had not come . . . Why? There had to be a reason! But then there was a reason, her sister had not known . . . she had not waited to be told but merely shouted at her to go away. Now she was doing as Myra wanted; she was leaving Hobbins Street. Monway Colliery was taking the house. They had allowed Grandmother to remain there for her lifetime, Grandfather having been killed in an accident underground, but now that her lifetime was ended the house could be used for a working family.

There had been no use in contesting the decision.

The house, as all of those in Hobbins Street and the others surrounding it, was the property of the colliery. They had given Eden a week in which to vacate and now, with all of the bits and pieces gone, every floor-board shining from the scrubbing they had received, it was ready to be handed over.

Bits and pieces! Eden's eyes brimmed. With no place to go she had been unable to hold on to the few items of furniture so cherished by her grandmother. They had been bought for a few shillings by John Kilvert, the pawnbroker, and the gloat on his face as he drove his cart away said he had got the better of the bargain. But things might have been worse – John Kilvert could have refused to buy the furniture and that would have meant leaving it to the bailiffs who would have paid nothing.

Bits and pieces! Tears which had brimmed now spilled on to Eden's cheeks as she came to stand in the living-room. Bare and silent, cold biting up from the quarry-tiled floor which had lost the rugs she and her grandmother had pegged from worn-out clothes whenever they could afford to replace them with a twopenny skirt or a threepenny jacket bought from the second-hand stall in the market-place, the room seemed to wait.

For what? Eden pressed her hand hard against trembling lips. To swallow more lives and leave no trace? Where was the warmth, the love that had surrounded two small orphaned children, and the laughter they had shared? Where the gentle kisses which had soothed away tears, the delight of summer evenings with a grandfather naming flowers and insects between puffs of a clay pipe? Where the pleasures of making little men from pastry given by Grandmother, her head shaking with disapproval when two little girls ate the raisins meant for eyes and buttons so more had to be given from the crockery jar kept in the cupboard beside the fireplace.

Throat choked, Eden cast a slow look about the barren room. Nothing! *That* was what remained of the lives lived in this house, *nothing* to say they had ever lived.

'You be goin' then wench?'

Brushing away her tears, Eden turned towards the figure who had joined her in the cheerless room. They had been close in friendship, this woman and Grandmother, helping each other through thick and thin, through the joys and through the sorrows; but how many joys had her grandmother's life held? How many had any family of the men labouring in mines and foundry for hardly enough wage to feed them? Joy was a scarce commodity in Wednesbury.

'Yes,' she nodded, 'I'm going, Aunt Dora.'

'Where to, wench? You 'ave no kin 'cepting that sister over across to Moorcroft an' you says you won't be a'goin' o' that house.'

Eden reached for a woollen shawl from the line of pegs her grandfather had fixed on the back of the living-room door, the one item of her grandmother's she had refused to let go, and wrapped it about her shoulders, tying the corners around her slender form.

'I said you can stop along o' me.' Dora Benson's work-worried eyes played over the young face. 'Our Jack an' the other three can sleep afore the fire, it'll do 'em no 'urt and give you time to sort y'self.'

Sort herself! Cold fingers stumbled with the tying of the shawl. No home, no work, a sister who had rejected her, how did she sort that? Fear that had steadily grown over the days since her grandmother's death, the fear of facing the reality of her situation, surged in Eden's throat. She was alone!

'No, thank you, Aunt Dora, it is kind of you to offer but I think it best to leave now.'

Dora held the slight figure close, her voice trembling with emotion. 'Well, if you be sure . . . but should you find things be too much then you comes back to Dora Benson, we'll find room for you, wench, be no second thinkin' to that.'

A house filled to bursting with a family of her own, yet Dora had offered to take her in, to give her the room occupied by her own sons! Shawl drawn tight against the bite of a sharp wind, frost crunching beneath button-sided boots, Eden walked away from Hobbins Street, from the only life she had ever known. She could have accepted Dora Benson's offer, stayed a while longer, but what would have been the use of that; it would have served only to delay the inevitable.

'You should ought to wait a while,' Dora Benson had advised on hearing Eden's decision to leave. 'When Myra comes, you know 'er alliz comes once a month, what do I tell 'er? Where do I say to look for you?'

She had said that she would write to Myra once she was settled. The lie still sat inside her like a stone. Truth was, she would not write to Myra, she would not contact her in any way. Myra had chosen her life . . . a life she did not want saddled by a younger sister.

Reaching Union Street, the smell of hot food brought her to a standstill. Pangs of hunger pulling at her stomach, she touched the pocket of her skirt feeling the few coins nestled inside it. Most of what she had received from the sale of her grandmother's household furnishings and from the pawning of linen and personal clothing, including her own Sunday church suit, had gone to pay the undertaker for the coffin and the use of a horse-drawn hearse; 'a waste' some folk in Hobbins Street had called the use of that hearse and the coffin could ''ave been brought to the buryin' on a 'andcart same as it be by other folk'! Eden's fingers touched her pocket again. What had been muttered by neighbours, other than Dora Benson, was no doubt sensible – pennies saved were pennies that brought food to another day's table; but her grandmother had deserved better than being wheeled through the streets on a handcart.

The expense of a 'proper' funeral, a wreath bought from O'Connel's shop, the glass-panelled hearse drawn by two black horses, black feathers on their heads, and the payment for the services of the priest, had swallowed all but these last three shillings. It was all that stood between herself and the workhouse, three shillings to ward off an existence she had often heard people speak of as 'hell on earth'.

A picture of a low, forbidding building sprang to her mind, its heavy oak door crossed with iron hinges, tiny windows seeming to refuse the light of day. How many times had Grandmother hurried herself and Myra past that place in Meeting Street? How many times had she crossed herself and called on the mercy of God to keep them from being taken into it?

Three shillings! Eden's hand closed protectively around the coins. She must not waste a single farthing. But not to eat! How many days could she go without food?

Wrestling with her thoughts, Eden's mouth watered as she looked at the display of meat and sausages set in trays of steaming gravy in the window of the cookshop. She had to find work. That might involve many days of walking, days which, without nourishment, would sap her strength, and nobody would be fool enough to employ a girl half-dead from hunger.

Pork and two slices of bread – threepence.

Beef and two slices – threepence.

Sausage, egg and two slices – fourpence.

Eden read the words written with whitening, their letters beginning to trail pale tears down the steamy glass.

Piggy in a bed. That was what Grandmother had called a sausage sandwich. But for Eden Brent there could be no piggy in a bed today; fourpence for one meal was far beyond resources which had to last heaven knew how long. But for a penny . . . the shop sold a slice of bread dipped in gravy for a penny. It was common sense.

Slice of bread in hand, fighting the guilt of spending her money, Eden walked on to the Market Place, wiping her fingers on her handkerchief as she came to the stalls grouped closely together. Carters and wagoners shouted at people to move out of the path of their lumbering vehicles; harried women, babes in arms and toddlers hanging on to skirts, returned the same in like measure. It was a scene she had witnessed so many times when shopping alongside Grandmother, enjoying the bustle of it all, the jaunty comments of stallholders, Grandmother's swift repartee. But that had been when there was buying to be done. Would any stallholder be as friendly knowing there was no money to be spent?

It had not taken long to find the answer to that question. Hands tucked beneath the shawl seeking warmth her body did not have, Eden turned away. No one wanted an assistant. 'A body 'neath the feet, that be the last thing I be needin', be more nuisance than they be a blessin'!' That had been the reply given by most when she had asked for employment; others had proved not quite so polite.

What had happened to her world? The question that had grown so familiar over the days, flashed again in her mind. A few hours was all it had taken for that world to be stolen from her, to be shattered completely. First had been Grandmother, dying so unexpectedly, then Myra turning her away, and finally the loss of her home.

Tears glistening on her lashes, Eden lifted her glance

to the two church spires, one black, the other green, the landmarks of Wednesbury.

Like her grandmother and her sister they were part of a life, past and over; she would never see either of them again.

Next week she could go home. Myra Brent gathered the towels which Ava Russell's guest had used. She had thought the humiliation of being pawed by her mistress was the most degrading thing she would ever encounter . . . but that was not so. Last night's 'amusement' had been shared.

Putting the used towels aside for laundering she replaced them with fresh ones, her hands shaking; her mind tingled with the memory of those sickening hours.

Myra had been told to wear her best apron, the one with broderie anglaise inserts on the frilled bib and shoulder straps, to make certain her matching cap was spotless and her sleeve cuffs well starched while her dark dress was to be exchanged for the rarely used lighter blue bombazine.

Closing the door of the bathroom tidied to perfection, she stood with her back slumped against it, eyelids pressed tight, towels clutched tight. If she could shut out those pictures . . . just for a moment . . . but they stayed with her as they had stayed the whole night through, tormenting, plaguing, suffocating her beneath the nightmare of shame. And still they were with her . . . They would be with her to her grave!

Being told to wear her best uniform had meant only

one thing. Her mistress was to entertain a visitor she wished to impress. The visitor had been a woman, someone Ava Russell had met at the theatre.

A guest room had been especially prepared with fresh flowers, its linen scented with rose-water, a fire completing the air of welcome. She would help the guest freshen her toilette, Ava Russell had told her; she would take care to see to it that any request was dealt with immediately.

Any request! A sob rising in her chest, Myra's eyes opened. Forcing her legs to move, she walked through the dressing-room and bedroom, averting her glance from the bed her mistress had shared.

There had been no pretence, no effort made to hide the intention.

It had been an intimate supper, no other guest, the dining-room lit only by candles, and every dish chosen and prepared, as with the guest room, to impress.

'*I don't go askin' who 'er be, an' neither should you. Do as you be paid to do an' don't go askin' o' questions be the motto I lives by, an' I reckons it be safest!*'

The cook had been abrupt when asked if she knew the identity of the mistress's visitor. Her reply was short, her lips had clamped shut and that was how they had remained, at least until Myra had finished her own supper and returned to her duties.

Having deposited the towels in the laundry room, Myra stood staring out over the gardens at the rear of the house. Like Moorcroft itself, the grounds were immaculate but, unlike the house, they hid no evil; the men who worked in them were required to do no more than that, their duties were to please only by keeping the grounds . . . but hers, her 'duties' involved more, much, much more . . . and now those duties were to be extended.

A keen breeze caught at Myra's dress but the coldness of it was not the cause of her shudder. Long and hard, it rose from her very depths.

She had been helping the guest to retire for the night; as ladies' maid that was expected, but not what followed, no ladies' maid nor any servant should be called upon to . . . Myra shivered again but the pictures in her mind were relentless.

The woman was already dressed in her white satin nightgown, red hair loose and brushed ready to be braided for the night when Ava Russell had entered the bedroom.

Would her guest care to bathe before retiring? She herself always found a warm bath so relaxing, so conducive to a restful night's sleep.

There had been no demur on the part of the visitor and the expression in the mistress's flint-sharp glance had warned Myra: there would be no demur on the part of the maid!

'*Myra's hands are so gentle and relaxing,*' Ava Russell had cooed watching her guest lower herself into the jasmin-scented water. '*I must ask you to excuse my choice of word but really "seductive" is the only one that does justice to Myra's expertise; really my dear, you should let her wash you . . . I always do.*'

And so it had been, but only after Ava, giggling coyly, had suggested her friend be bathed in the manner she herself preferred . . . by a maid stripped bare of every stitch of clothing.

And the woman had enjoyed her bath, flattening her shoulders and lifting her breasts to the stroke of Myra's fingers, her breath quickening with every sliding movement over belly and legs, her eyes closing, a cry ripping from her as a final gasp left her quivering. But that was not the end; it was not all the hospitality her guest must be given, not while other entertainment was on hand. And so the process was repeated. A large bowl of freshly scented water at her feet, Ava had shed her own nightgown to stand naked on a large towel. Then, the other woman's eyes burning with the same desire as moments before had burned in her own body, she had cupped Myra's breast, licking a tongue over the nipple while her free hand had nestled between her legs. And her mistress had laughed as she invited her eager guest to do the same.

It had been a nightmare worse than any other. Tears clouded Myra's eyes but not the pictures they saw.

The touching of her body had gone on, first one mouth and then the other, hand following hand until her clenched lips had parted in a scream, a cry stopped by Ava Russell's sharp blow.

'*Appetite, Myra, is filled with craving . . . and we both know how strong is the passion such feelings arouse, do we not, my dear?*'

She had smiled when speaking, her dark eyes vibrant

with a meaning not lost on the woman whose rapid breathing and hot eyes revealed the ravening of her own appetite.

'*But we must not pamper our domestics. They must know what is and is not permitted, they must learn to be satisfied with what they are given.*'

The tone had hardened on the word 'permitted'. It had been a way of telling her maid that any dissent, any refusal to take part in these 'amusements', would result in dismissal . . . dismissal with no hope of further employment. But even seeing the tears squeeze beneath Myra's tightly closed eyes, Ava Russell had not hesitated to add to the embarrassment and shame she knew flowed in the girl she had caught in her web of immorality. Cupping one small breast, she had touched it with her lips before murmuring, '*Tomorrow . . . I promise tomorrow all of your longings, all of your cravings, the desires you so long to be quenched, will be utterly satisfied.*'

A vicious squeeze of the breast she had kissed bringing a gasp of pain, Ava had turned away, a lecherous, almost carnal, glow to her dark eyes, a smile still curving her mouth.

'*But now, my dear,*' the murmur had been soft, an invitation, couched in velvet promise as she had reached to take the hand of the woman already trembling with the strength of her own arousal, '*I think it is time for bed.*'

The bed prepared for Ava Russell's guest had not been slept in, the scented sheets smooth, the pillows showing no indentation. But her mistress's bed had displayed the ravages of frenzied activity.

An activity to be enjoyed again?

Hands covering her face, Myra gave way to the despair that grew with each new day.

Yes, the events of that night would be repeated and she, Myra Brent, would be forced to take part in them.

4

Ava had never asked if her ladies' maid visited her own home during the precious few hours of freedom which came only once in every month.

Dressed in the plain brown coat and bonnet allowed for 'visiting', side-buttoned boots polished to a high gleam, Myra almost ran from the precincts of the house she had grown to hate.

No, Ava Russell never enquired as to where she would spend her afternoon, but as to *how* it was spent she gave explicit instruction. She was to speak to no one of her duties at Moorcroft. She would tell no person anything of the mistress of that house, and always she finished with the same words: 'There are those in the town who would relish nothing more than to gossip about Ava Russell; be sure, be very sure, you do not provide them with the opportunity.'

Household staff *did* talk of their employers. Hadn't she often heard those from other houses chatter about a master or mistress when visiting Cook? Did Cook ever speak of her own mistress's likes and dislikes, of what happened during her bathing?

The shame that thought aroused brought a burning

to Myra's cheeks. She had long since stopped hoping others at Moorcroft did not guess what transpired, her own unhappiness must have been an indication, even supposing the previous maid had not divulged the awful truth before having left. Then they – cook, scullery maid and gardener – must all have asked why she, too, had not resigned, they must think . . .

The awfulness of the thought brought her to a standstill . . . they must think she liked what went on, that she, like Ava Russell, enjoyed those disgusting episodes!

'But it's not true, dear Lord, you know it's not true!'

Her cry rang across the frost-bound heath, bouncing off the outcrops of limestone that jutted from the ground, echoing and re-echoing on the cold, sunless afternoon.

'It's not true!' The cry dropping to a whisper, Myra's hands came together lifting to her lips. 'Help me,' she prayed to the silence. 'Show me the way, show me how I can leave that house without bringing suffering to Gran and to Eden . . . Help me, Lord . . .'

Words trailing away, hands falling to her sides, Myra felt the futility of her prayer weigh like a rock in her stomach. She had no right to ask that of God, no right to ask deliverance; what she did was wrong in the sight of heaven, it barred her for ever from the mercy of the Lord.

No forgiveness! No deliverance!

Four words. They chimed like a church bell in Myra's mind. Four words that said she was beyond redemption. Four words which spelled damnation!

★

'Grandmother is dead?'

Myra's brows drew together, her blue eyes widening in disbelief.

'Ar, wench, been dead this last week an' more.'

'But . . . but how, why? Gran was never ill.'

Thin to a point of disappearing, Dora Benson touched a hand to her face and brushed away a stray strand of hair turned prematurely grey by her hard life. Continuing to hammer and cut nails from a narrow strip of iron, she answered the girl.

'It don't be for folk to go questionin' the ways o' the Lord. 'E chose the time o' tekin' your grandmother, God rest 'er, an' though passin' of 'er brings grief to your 'eart, you should thank 'Im, 'E d'ain't see fit to 'ave 'er lie on a bed o' pain for months afore 'er goin'.'

Her grandmother had suffered no pain. That was a blessing she should give thanks for, but the pain in Myra's own heart drove away all thought save one: she had not been there, not been with the woman who had raised her, not been able to speak of the love she had for her; not been there to comfort Eden.

Shock of learning of her grandmother's death had driven all else from Myra's mind, it had kept her from realising her sister had not yet appeared. Now, glancing towards the kitchen, a few yards from the brewhouse which need had turned into a nail-making workshop, and asked if her sister was there.

Dora Benson's arm rose and fell, hammer striking

iron in a regular rhythm, an accompaniment to the words sounding between.

'No, wench, Eden don't be to the 'ouse, 'er don't be along o' we.'

'Not with you!' Disbelief which moments since had gleamed in Myra's eyes darkened to confusion. 'But she has to be . . . Grandmother's house is . . . is filled with strangers . . .'

Laying aside her hammer with a brief glance at her sons saying the work was to continue, Dora wiped her stained hands on the dark apron swamping her wasted body.

'C'mon, wench,' she said gently, 'come to the kitchen, a cup o' tea be what we both needs.'

'Aunt Dora, I don't understand, why was I not sent for, why was I not told . . . and where is Eden?'

Spooning tea into a teapot – its cream enamel pockmarked from years of wear – Dora scalded the leaves with water from the kettle hung constantly over the low fire before replying.

'You *was* sent for, though sent might not be the word in a true manner o' speakin', for it were all over afore anybody could be sent for . . . As for your sister, I can't be tellin' where 'er be. Listen,' Dora shook her head as Myra made to speak again, 'as you yourself said out there in the brewhouse, your grandmother never showed sign of no illness, was nobody guessed as there were aught amiss wi' 'er; not me, not your sister, not nobody in all of Hobbins Street. Kept things to 'erself did Rachel, least said soonest mended were 'er way, an' that way 'er held to the end. 'Eart, that were what the doctor said when 'e were called, a complaint of the 'eart, weren't nothin' as could 'ave been done about it so you needn't go frettin' yourself as to what you should or shouldn't 'ave done. You was workin' along of Moorcroft House, it were the money you earned kept a roof over your family's 'ead and 'elped put food in their stomach, so don't you go a finding of a rod to whip your own back. You've always been a credit, Rachel knowed that, 'er took a great pride in you and what you do over to Moorcroft.'

A great pride! Suddenly the tears welling inside were too strong for Myra to hold back, and they erupted in great heaving sobs. Grandmother had been proud . . . but she had not known the truth, had not known what her granddaughter was called upon to do for the money she brought home. Where would her pride have been had she found out? How much love then for the child of her own son . . . how much disgust?

'Cry it out, wench,' Dora's eyes, moist with sympathy, played over the sobbing girl. 'Tears be a way o' easin' away sorrows; though some teks more than others, they all gets less painful as times goes on: I telled the same to your sister when 'er cried over your not wantin' to be listenin' to what 'er come to tell.'

That day Eden had come to Moorcroft House, the day she had shouted . . . had slapped . . . Oh God! Breath caught in her throat, Myra recognised the reason for her sister going against the request she never come there. Eden had come to tell her of

Grandmother's dying, to bring her back to Hobbins Street so she might kiss that dear face one last time, to walk behind the coffin to the churchyard where together they would see it laid to rest in the same plot of ground that held their grandfather. But she had refused to listen, she had simply driven Eden away.

'I never thought . . . I never dreamed . . .'

'O' course you never,' Dora answered the murmur, ''ow could you 'ave, like I told Eden, you would 'ave come 'ad you knowed.'

'I would have if only I had given Eden the chance to speak, but I didn't!' Myra's head lifted sharply. 'I gave her no time to explain, I wanted her gone, wanted it so much I slapped her.'

That had been the most unbelievable part of what Dora had been told. She sipped the hot tea she had poured into a mug as chipped as the teapot, Myra's drink having been served in the one china cup used only for visitors. Myra had not taken time to hear what her sister had run all the way to tell, she had not wanted the bother. Dora sipped again, thoughts replacing each other rapidly in her mind. But if Myra Brent hadn't wanted the bother, why were she here now? And if, as Eden had sobbed, Myra had turned away, wanted no more of her family, why the tears? And they were real enough, there was no play-acting at back of them.

'I was so angry . . .'

Myra Brent spoke now only to herself; her words were not for ears other than her own, knowledge of that bringing her to her feet, Dora rose from the table to stand before the small cast iron fireplace, but the cramped space that was both kitchen and living-room was not enough to close off the half-sobbed murmurings.

'. . . I could only think of the danger to her, of what would follow her being seen . . . I couldn't risk that happening . . . of her being drawn into the same dreadful . . . I couldn't chance Eden being seen by . . .'

Replenishing the water in the kettle, Dora pretended she had not heard, but the ends of her nerves suddenly tingled. What was the danger the wench murmured on? Why was her afraid of her sister being seen along of that house? What was it had Rachel Brent's granddaughter trembling like a leaf in the breeze?

But all of this were the wench's business; to hear her when none of the telling was intended seemed to Dora to be sly and underhand. Uncomfortable with the feeling she rattled the lid of the kettle noisily into place, reminding Myra she was not alone.

'There,' she turned to face the girl at her table, 'that'll be nicely on the boil come supper. You be welcome to eat wi' us, my Jack will walk you back to Moorcroft.'

Fingers curling into her palms, Myra felt ripples of revulsion run along her spine. Return to Moorcroft . . . The very thought made her want to run and run and never stop. She prayed each night, even coming here to Hobbins Street this afternoon she had asked the Lord to show her a way of leaving that house for ever, she had begged . . . The thought broke and with its halting a great weight seemed suddenly to lift away from her shoulders: she had asked and she had been answered. Heaven had seen fit to take her grandmother but it had given a gift in return; the gift of freedom! The responsibility of keeping a roof over the heads of her family was gone, she could take Eden, they could leave Wednesbury, find a place where they could live together. She was no longer under any obligation, she need no longer suffer the obscenity, the debauchery, of Ava Russell's 'little entertainments'. From this moment she was free, no more would she place herself in the service of anyone . . . and neither would her sister. There was other work they could do, they were both good at sewing, Eden as well as herself had shown an aptitude for needlework.

A smile shining where tears had glinted, Myra glanced at the woman she had been taught to address as Aunt even though they shared no blood.

'I won't be troubling Jack to walk me to Moorcroft, Aunt Dora. You see, I am not going back there.'

'Not going back!' Faded eyes opening wide, Dora Benson stared at Myra. 'But you 'ave to, it be your livin'.'

Her smile travelling to her mouth, Myra shook her head. 'Not any more; if I can wait here for Eden to come back I intend we go find work elsewhere.'

'You can wait 'ere, that you knows without the askin', but Eden don't be comin' back. Her left after your grandmother's 'ouse were emptied of its bits o' furniture.'

Newly discovered delight and the elation of release

from the abuse of Ava Russell drained rapidly from Myra.

'I said as 'er weren't to this 'ouse.' Dora watched the colour drain from the face that for a minute had smiled. 'I did tell you, wench, I said as 'er don't be along o' we.'

Eden was not here? She was not living with Aunt Dora? But it was *obvious* she was here, of course she would be with the woman who had helped mother them both. Perhaps she had misunderstood . . . Yes, that was it, Aunt Dora could not mean Eden had left for good.

For one brief second, hope bloomed in Myra's heart but was as swiftly killed by the cold breath of reality. Dora Benson was too poor to waste anything, even words. What she said was what she meant. She had said that Eden had left after Grandmother's house was emptied of its contents . . . that had been days ago! So where was she? Who was she with?

A picture of herself standing naked beside the bath, Ava Russell's hands stroking her body, brought Myra to her feet, words trembling in her throat.

'Did . . . did Eden say where she was going . . . who . . . who she would be with?'

The answer had been no. Myra ran from street to street and shop to shop asking of her whereabouts. Eden had taken that slap as a complete rebuttal, she had seen it as repudiation. To her it had seemed that she, Myra, no longer wanted any connection with sister or grandmother, that her failure to attend the funeral had implied they were no longer family.

Effect of the thought sapping her strength, fingers pressed hard against a rising sickness, sobs the reflection of the pain slicing through her, Myra folded into herself, her cry a whisper in the growing darkness.

'What have I done? Oh dear God, what have I done!'

5

The night's lodging would have cost ninepence.

Eden clutched the pocket which held the remainder of her three shillings as she left the White Lion Inn. She had not thought to have to pay so much: ninepence would have kept Grandmother and herself for two or three days, yet the landlord of the inn had shrugged when she had questioned the cost. 'You takes it or you leaves it,' had been the terse reply and she had left it. Darkness had already set in. She felt it would be unsafe to traipse the streets enquiring for a cheaper lodging yet she could not afford a hotel or inn.

She must find some place less expensive for, as well as a bed, she must buy food. Admitted the landlord had offered a decent supper but, at ninepence a night, she could not stay there. Perhaps if she had asked for some employment . . . A place providing rooms and meals must surely have linen in need of repair, but the sideways glances of the man who had spoken to her had set her nerves quivering so she had thanked him and left; even so she had not breathed easily until she was once more out on the street.

Her shawl was scant protection against the biting

cold. She glanced the length of the road lined on both sides with shops selling a variety of wares, and once more her stomach churned with hunger.

She had lingered too long at the house, wandering from room to empty room, wanting to be gone yet somehow unable to leave, unable to break the ties of the heart. Even when she had closed the door for the last time, she had stayed awhile with Aunt Dora, afraid to part from the one person she felt had any love for her. If only Myra had come, if only she had listened, then she would have come and not returned to Moorcroft. They would have found a place to live together, sisters sharing as they had always shared before Myra had become a ladies' maid. How grand they had both thought that . . . a ladies' maid! Yes, it was grand for a girl from Hobbins Street, so grand it had turned her away from her family.

'You best move yourself if it be you don't 'ave a likin' for bein' knocked down. Wagoners hauling iron to the canal don't 'ave too much care of folk standing in their way.'

'What?' Eden blinked, feeling a tweak at her skirt.

'I was sayin', you best step outta the 'oss road if it be you still wants to be livin' termorrer.'

A hoarse curse and the crack of a whip recalling the last of her wandering senses, Eden felt herself pulled sharply backward.

The hand releasing her skirts balled into a fist

shaking at the rumbling wagon, a louder curse echoing after it.

'Told ya!'

A face sprinkled with freckles and topped by sand-coloured hair, grinned at Eden.

'. . . told ya them wagoners gives no mind to folk daft enough to go standin' in their way.'

'I see that.' Eden felt an immediate surge of liking for the boy grinning at her, brown eyes gleaming like polished mahogany. 'Thank you for pulling me from the path of that one.'

'Weren't nothin'.' The grin spread. 'Seth Butler be a mean bugger, don't give a sod who he runs down, but there be ways of dealing with him, like tekin' the peg from a cart wheel so it works its way off the shaft and the whole lot tips sideways, spillin' its load.'

That was a dangerous thing to do. Teeth clenched against the cold held back Eden's response. This boy had saved her from what might have been a serious injury; could he also cause one by doing what he spoke of?

'Joby Timmins done that . . .'

Eden's shiver hid the quick breath of relief. She did not know the boy smiling at her but she was glad he had not interfered with the wagoner's cart.

'. . . Joby pulled the peg from the wheel of Butler's wagon after his little wench were knocked down by it; nobody said as much but everybody knowed it were Joby done it, said as how it should 'ave broke Butler's neck same as that little un's leg were broke . . .'

A steam whistle shrieking in the distance made the boy turn in its direction.

'Wait,' Eden touched his sleeve, several inches shorter than the arm it covered, 'please, could you tell me where I can rent a room?'

'Tek it you don't mean one along of the White Lion or its likes?'

A shake of her head affirming his guess, the boy's mouth twisted thoughtfully.

'There be old mother Marsh . . . her has a room empty since her son were killed fightin' in the Crimea, but whether or not her'll tek you in I can't be sayin'.'

He had given her directions, his words tumbling over each other as the steam whistle screeched again.

Huddled into herself, nose and mouth covered by the shawl protecting her face from flurries of snow beginning to fall, half of Eden's mind tried to remember the way the boy had told her to follow, the other half praying the woman would rent her the room.

She had refused!

Beneath the covering shawl Eden's mouth had trembled.

'I can be tekin' no lodger!' The woman had snapped when asked. 'That there room be my lad's, he'll be a' wantin' of it when he comes from the war . . . that'll be soon now, he be on his way, he'll be 'ome soon.' She had closed the door then, words filtering faintly as she shuffled away.

Trying hard not to give way to tears that would

freeze on her lashes, Eden stumbled through the thickening snowstorm. The cottage had proved to be a fair distance from the town but she must go back or spend the night beneath a hedge, to do that would mean her likely freezing to death. Stumbling over a jutting stone the coins in her pocket jingled against each other. Two shillings and eleven pence . . . At ninepence for a bed and supper and food during the day it would cover less than three nights . . . and if no employment was given her in that time?

'*God in His mercy keep we from that place.*'

Her grandmother's heartfelt words seemed to cry on the wind. The workhouse. Snowflakes thick on her eyelashes, Eden struggled on. Two nights . . . and then she would have to apply to the workhouse!

Blinded by whirling snow, head bent against a driving wind, her limbs so numbed they no longer seemed part of her, Eden gasped for breath which brought no relief. If only she could rest, just for a little while, then she could go on. Rest . . . just for a minute . . . just for a minute . . .

'*You be tired, my little wench.*'

It was a voice she knew, a voice she loved.

'*Come set along of me, it be warm here against the fire.*'

The fire was so bright . . . the flames rising from its scarlet heart danced like tiny birds, exotic in their plumage of carmine tipped with blue and gold. So warm, so beautiful . . .

'*Rest you now.*'

At her side. the familiar voice was low and gentle.

'*You be safe here . . . you be safe along of me.*'

It was so warm, she could feel the heat of the fire on her face, feel the softness of a pegged rug beneath her feet.

'*Rest you now.*'

Soft and tender, benign with the love she had always known, the words brushed her ear.

'Gran?'

Seized in a flurry of wind-driven snow, the whisper was whirled away, but the answer, itself no more than a murmur, sounded clear in Eden's tired mind.

'*. . . Ar, my little wench . . . it be Gran . . . I be here along of you . . . rest, my little love, rest you beside me . . .*'

Sighing with contentment, Eden lay down, her eyes closing, her mouth curved in a smile beneath the huge, soft flakes laying a covering of white over her body.

'Where did Myra say she was going?'

'Her didn't, mum, her just said as her would be back same time as usual.'

But she had not returned at her usual time, she had not returned at all! Hiding her annoyance, Ava Russell glanced at the pretty ormolu clock set on the mantel above the glowing fire.

'I am becoming concerned,' she said, allowing a faint crease to settle between her brows. 'I wonder if we should send the stable hands to look for her, after all she might have tripped . . . she may be lying injured somewhere.'

This woman wouldn't worry if the wench were hurt,

not even were her dyin'; the only worry Ava Russell ever had were for her own comfort!

The cook hid her thoughts beneath a shake of her head. 'I reckons that be a waste of time, mum. It be snowing heavens hard out there.'

'That is my worry!' Ava cut in sharply. 'Myra could be lost in that storm.'

'If you'll forgive the saying, mum, that don't be my thinking. Seems to me to be more like her seen the extent of the storm and, guessing it could well be on for the whole night, decided to stay put where her be and come back here once it be mornin'.'

'I hope you are right . . . we must pray that you are right, that Myra is safe.'

Pray! Hands clasped across the front of a spotless, heavily starched apron, Polly Jupp concealed the disdain that remark brought. Ava Russell prayed for nobody other than Ava Russell, and any true concern her might be feeling would be for herself.

'Myra be a sensible wench,' she said, grey eyes displaying no sign of her inner feelings. 'Her won't have set off in no storm. No, mum, I thinks you should put your mind to restin' on that account.'

It was that very safety that was the cause of the disquiet niggling inside Ava. She glanced again at the clock. The girl had always returned on time, never more than a few minutes after six, and now it was nearing nine. Almost three hours, time enough to have reached the house regardless of the storm . . . But if she had decided not to return . . .

A flush of alarm tingling her nerves, Ava almost started to her feet but recovered herself. It would not do to allow even a hint of the trepidation beginning to form in her mind to display itself. Servants gossiped, and gossip spread, and if that happened some people were apt to ask why . . . Why was Ava Russell so concerned over a maid, when any of a dozen could be hired next day?

'Of course,' she nodded. 'Myra is far too sensible to set off in weather as bad as this. However, if she should have done so, if by some mischance she should not return in the morning, then we must know where to look for her. Are you quite certain she did not say where she was going?'

There was a bee in Ava's bloomers and it were about to sting her arse. The thought brought a degree of satisfaction to Polly. Holding it warm to herself, she replied, 'If her did, mum, then it were not to me. Should I ask the rest of the staff did her say it to one of them?'

'No!' The answer was quick, too quick! Seeing the glint in her servant's eyes, Ava realised her mistake covering it with a small shake of her head. 'No, there is no need, I am probably fretting over nothing.'

That were a lie an' all! Polly kept her own look inscrutable. Ava Russell were frettin' all right, but why, when her had never given a tinker's cuss about anybody who worked in this house? Hands still grasped across her middle, she glanced towards the clock and said briskly, 'You will be wanting your bath tub filled, mum; the water be hot, I'll have the girl bring it up?'

Once again Ava shook her head, a brief dismissive movement as she rose from her chair. 'I shall not be requiring the bath this evening nor will I take supper in the dining-room. You may have a tray sent to my room.'

'Very good, mum.' Bobbing the merest assent, Polly Jupp left the room. Why was Ava Russell not wanting of that hot water? The answer were 'cos that wench were not here. Rapid as raindrops in a thunderstorm, thoughts raced through her mind. Bathing every night . . . tcha! Her had never done that while the master were living, a sponge down each morning and a bath once a week had been her routine, but since her husband had died (of a broken neck following a fall from his horse) things in this house had taken a very different turn.

Reaching the half-moon-shaped hall, Polly's glance travelled around it. *This* was all as it had been before the master's death: the gleaming mahogany of coat cupboards; the wall tables each supporting marble statuettes of lovely women half-covered in floating draperies, the names of their creators too foreign for her tongue; paintings by artists the master had named as Stubbs, Landseer and Turner. Oh yes, all that was still here – the first glimpse of the interior of Moorcroft that was seen by visitors, meant to impress . . . and to deceive!

Not all of this house was as it had been left by Ava Russell's husband. It had not taken long . . . In the five years of widowhood she had disposed of much of the contents, leaving empty those rooms once used by guests staying for party weekends or longer summer-time visits; more than half of this once beautifully furnished home was now no more than a sham, a pretence . . . just as its owner was a sham.

Following along the short corridor which took her to the kitchen, Polly Jupp's mouth tightened. The mistress of Moorcroft led a life of deception. To the people beyond this house she might well appear the soul of propriety living the widow's role of a quiet, slightly withdrawn woman, reluctant to partake in society without the support of a husband. But nothing could be further from the truth.

Pouring herself a cup of tea, Polly sat at the table.

The love between a man and a woman, the love heaven had ordained, had found no place in this house; wherever Samuel Russell had found satisfaction it had not been in the bedroom of his wife. And only months after he had been buried, those carryin's on in that bathroom had started.

Staring into the fire burning in the well-polished range, Polly sipped her tea, only the pressure of her fingers around the large cup belying the acrimony of her thoughts.

Oh, the mistress believed none below stairs knowed of what went on, but Polly Jupp knowed. It were Polly Jupp had held a young wench sobbing of the terrible things Ava Russell had had her do, things never meant to be done woman to woman; a young wench who'd run away only to be found days later floating face-down in the canal. No, Myra Brent were not the first to be caught in the talons of that woman, not the first young wench to be sullied . . . and neither would her be the last.

'Brushing the muff' were what them carryin's on were called among Wednesbury folk and they gave short change to any woman thought to have a fancy for it; that much were known to her upstairs and that, like as not, were responsible for the death of that maid.

Death by misadventure! Polly's fingers tightened further pressure turning them white against her cup. That had been the verdict of the coroner but it weren't the verdict of Polly Jupp. To her way of thinking there had been no misadventure; the drowning of that young wench had been deliberate and the one behind the doing of it sat in this house. And unless Myra Brent returned tomorrow, then the canal would take another young life in its dark waters, for Ava Russell would suffer no risk of scandal.

Blue-tipped flames danced upward, drawn into the black void of the chimney. Gone as that young maid had gone. Lowering her cup, Polly heaved a long sigh. To tell what were held in her mind would do naught but bring a prison cell for herself. There were no proof Ava Russell's hand were at the back of that drowning. Likely her had paid well enough for a secret to be kept; but naught stayed hidden from the eyes of heaven, and one day it would take its reckoning.

6

Where could Eden have gone? From the window of the room she had rented Myra stared into darkness. Relentless, the storm raged, whirling great white flakes painting all that lay beneath. Was her sister out in this? Surely not. Eden would have found shelter somewhere. But Myra had not discovered where that somewhere was. She shivered against the chill which, despite the fire, pervaded the tiny room but she remained at the window, hoping even now that she might see the slight figure of her sister. She had enquired at every place she had passed but no one owned to having seen Eden. Then, as evening began to darken into night, she had been forced to find a place to stay.

She had seen the scrap of card. The proprietor of a small general shop had lit a lantern hanging over the goods displayed in the window and as its light caught the glass pane she had seen the advertisement. Scrawled in flimsy writing, it had proclaimed a house for rent.

'Ar, I knows the place . . .'

Blue-striped apron reaching from chest to feet, the

man behind a counter strewn with all manner of wares fingered a generous moustache.

'It be the first turning to the left, last 'ouse in the row, but there be nobody along of there, folk who lived there be gone to their daughter along of Dudley.'

'But the card . . .' She had looked with despair at the shopkeeper his face sallow in the sickly glow of that one lantern.

'Means what it says.' He had twiddled the moustache, enjoying the moment. 'Be for rent.'

He had said no more, but his eyes had run the length of her, taking in the drab coat and bonnet and, no doubt, the look of anxiety she knew etched her face and gleamed in the depths of her eyes. Had he thought her without the means to pay for a lodging? Or had he thought her a woman of the night, a prostitute looking for a dry place in which to ply her trade?

Despite the chill of the room, Myra's face flamed again in the sudden rush of heat which had suffused her in that shop. Indignation, offence and disgust obvious in her terse 'thank you', she had left.

Snow hurling itself at her in a wild frenzy, she had glanced towards the well-lit façade of the Talbot Hotel facing on to the market place. Maybe she could use a little of the money she had intended giving Grandmother, take a room in that hotel for just one night? But even as the thought took shape it was followed by another, one which warned against that or any other of the hotels Wednesbury boasted, for any one of them might have a guest who knew Ava Russell.

But would that guest recognise her ladies' maid? Common sense had argued against such a possibility but another, which her grandmother would have called a sixth sense, was stronger. Heeding the fears it kindled, she had trudged her way to the High Bullen. Only the length of Trouse Lane lay between this point and the heath. To be caught there, and in a snowstorm, was a hazard she must not put herself in. This time common sense had prevailed and she had entered the Grapes Inn.

'There be a room,' the landlord had said, running a quick look over the figure brushing snow from her eyelashes. 'But it be for one person only, so should you be thinkin' of entertainin' . . .'

'I require a room for myself only.' She had mustered every shred of dignity, her reply cuttingly sharp, but still the flood of heat had coloured her cheeks.

'So long as that be understood,' he had answered.

'Pay no mind to Jesse.' The landlord's wife had smiled apologetically, showing Myra upstairs. 'He tells the same to any wanting lodgin'; as he says, Jesse Newman runs a clean house, don't hold with no 'anky panky.'

The woman had put a match to the fire already laid in the tiny grate then, advising as to supper, had turned back to her duties in the kitchen.

Myra drew the curtains, shutting out sight of the snow-covered street; the mound that was Church Hill, robed now in pristine white; the dark shape of the spire of Saint Bartholomew's rising into a sky beginning to accept the silver touch of the moon. Myra crossed to the bed. Slipping between sheets smelling of soap, she closed her eyes, whispering the prayers her grandmother had taught in the firelight. But tonight another was added . . . a prayer that asked tomorrow she would find her sister.

'Be 'er goin' to be all right . . . ? 'Er don't be goin' to die, do 'er?'

'No, 'er don't be goin' to die, not if I can 'elp it, though it'll be no thanks to you. Of all the daft things to do sending 'er along of the Marsh cottage! You knows nicely the woman be a bit strange since the losin' of that lad of her'n.'

'I said as 'er mightn't tek a lodger.'

'You shouldn't ought to 'ave said anythin'. I've told you times afore about talking with strangers!'

'But . . .'

'This don't be the moment for buttin'!' Body as cold as her humour, Sara Melia snapped at the lad standing at her side. 'Help me get this poor soul along of the 'ouse.'

Risking his mother's ire no further the lad did as she bid, half-supporting the figure they had found lying almost hidden by snow. He had known of old mother Marsh's strangeness; all the lads at school had known and often gone to stand and shout at her gate, scampering like flies when she came from the cottage wielding a broom.

'That be a besom,' Cyril Hawkins had once said on

hearing what they had been up to. 'That be the true sign of a witch. Her flies on that at night to catch them who've annoyed her, an' her'll come for you when it be next full moon.'

'That one be soft as a brush and not near as useful!' his mother had said on finding why, at the very next full moon, he had been too afraid to go to bed alone. 'Frightenin' little 'uns be the only thing the noggin-'eaded lout be good for. I'll take a stick to his backside when I catches up to him, and I'll take it to your'n an' all for being daft enough to pay mind to 'im!'

But he *had* paid mind. For months the fear had remained with him, holding him rigid in his bed each time the moon reached its full. The thought of some avenging witch coming at him out of the darkness had never left him.

The weight of the burden slumped against him pressing his feet deep into the cloying snow, Davy Melia glanced at the great silent orb spreading the black sky with a silver radiance. It was with him now!

'Here, close against the fire.' Sara caught the expression on her son's face as the door of their home clicked shut behind them. At thirteen, he was street-grown, wise in the ways a boy without a father had needed to learn, but in others life had yet to oust the child in him.

'Take the bricks from the oven and put them to warming my bed, we'll put the wench in there. I can sleep afore the fire tonight.'

Gently easing the ends of a damp shawl from fingers

cold as those of a corpse, Sara did not catch the next look to pass across the boy's face, a look of fear at war with determination, but she heard the strength of the outcome in the reply.

'The bricks will be going into my bed. I'll be the one sleepin' afore the fire.'

The child was losing ground to the man. Sara felt the warm touch of pride. His father would have found no fault in their son.

'Be 'er going to be all right?'

Having helped his mother to carry the half-conscious figure to the bedroom, Davy voiced his question again.

A sharp retort rising to her lips, Sara checked it. She had tongue-lashed him for his thoughtlessness but, without his help, the girl would have been laying out in the open all night . . . maybe dying from cold, for the clothes she wore were no match for a winter's night. It had taken courage to tell of his encounter with a young woman, of sending her on what he had known to be a fool's errand, a brave step to confess in the face of a mother's anger . . . one more step of the man! A proud smile on her face she replied quietly.

'God 'as lent his hand to your'n, seems it be His will the wench will live. Now it be mine, you gets y'self from this room while I puts 'er to bed. You'll find broth simmering on the hob; bring me up a dish of it in five minutes.'

'I don't want to . . . I don't want to. . .'

Damp skirts gathered in her hands, Sara turned at

the muffled whisper. Beneath closed lids the eyes of the girl she and her son had brought in from the night moved restlessly.

'I don't want to . . . it don't be right . . . you shouldn't be asking that . . .'

Stepping closer to the bed, Sara watched shades of emotion flick across the pale face, the agitated turns of the head. Whatever was at the back of this girl's being away from her home were behind her still.

'. . . that isn't what I have to do . . .'

Caught by the intensity of the murmur, the sheer denial echoing in the words, Sara listened closely.

'. . . it can't be, Myra would have told me . . . my sister would never do what you ask . . .'

Seeming to watch moving pictures the closed eyes continued to move but Sara made no move to wake the girl who moaned softly.

'. . . Myra wouldn't do that and neither will I . . . you can't make me . . . I won't, I won't!'

What was it this girl had refused to do, what had given rise to such revulsion?

Disquieting questions, Sara thought, taking the bowl of broth her son had brought and handing him the wet clothing to be strung on the line tied above the fireplace. Disquieting enough in themselves but more disturbing yet was the one which followed; who was the cause of it?

'She has not come back?'

Lenor Medwin broke off as tea was brought by a

maid who bobbed a curtsy as she was waved impatiently away.

'No!' Ava Russell's reply was as tight as her mouth.

'But you said . . .'

'I know what I said . . . that she would return to Moorcroft.'

Hands shaking, Lenor poured tea into dainty china cups spilling as much again into the saucers. 'But she has to come back,' she whimpered, 'she must be made to return.'

Refusing the proffered cup, Ava Russell looked disdainfully at the woman seated opposite. Lenor Medwin liked the games but not the consequences, and there would be some painful ones should a whisper of what she indulged in reach the ears of her husband.

Keeping none of that disdain from her tone she answered. 'I am confident the girl can be persuaded to return!'

Lenor's plain face suffered under the worry of that reply. 'Persuaded!' she mewed. 'You mean she may not wish . . . she might no longer want her position!'

There was no 'want' about it, no maybe. Myra Brent had long desired to resign her post as ladies' maid. Only threats of what would happen to her sister and grandmother had kept her returning to Moorcroft. So why was it different this time? Ava tossed her head impatiently, keeping the question to herself.

'An unfortunate choice of word,' she said sharply. 'Of course the girl has no wish to leave her post.'

'Then why hasn't she come back?'

The intervention, quick and sharp, caught Ava off guard. She must speak and act with caution; Lenor Medwin's anxiety bordered on lack of control. Should it break it would mean more than her own fall from society . . . so it must not be allowed to break!

'I would have thought that to be obvious, my dear.' Adopting a softer tone, Ava's hard mouth relaxed to the hint of a smile. 'The girl's guardian is not a young woman, she has taken with some illness, the influenza so I am told. That is the reason Myra is not yet back at Moorcroft.'

'But could not someone else nurse the girl's guardian?'

Obviously unmollified, Lenor's anxious stare posed the unstated. What if the girl should inadvertently mention anything of those activities . . . those very private activities . . . shared with her mistress and the friend of her mistress?

Friend! Ava's own glance showed nothing of the acrimony that description aroused. Lenor Medwin was a tool, a means whereby amusement might be found, a plaything to be used then tossed aside without further thought . . . but a friend? Ava Russell wanted no friend!

'That is being taken care of.' She smiled more openly. 'I have arranged for that. I would have done so earlier but Myra asked to be given leave to stay home a few days longer.'

'Is that wise? I mean given what she knows . . . what she could reveal about us.'

About *you* . . . given what she knows about *you*, is what you really mean! Ava's glance rested momentarily on the hands twisting together in the other woman's lap. Lenor Medwin was concerned for Lenor Medwin and that concern was too near the surface. Drawing on her gloves Ava retained her composure.

'Myra is a sensible girl.' She rose from her chair. 'She knows that speaking of our little romps could bring dire results for herself. Think of it, my dear: a maid dismissed her position on being caught stealing, a girl attempting to revenge herself upon her mistress by making some preposterous allegation she had been subjected to indecent behaviour – what magistrate would believe that? Especially were an item of jewellery to be discovered beneath the mattress of her bed. You can put all fears from your mind, Myra Brent will not be disclosing any secrets.'

No, the girl would not be disclosing any secrets! Sitting in her carriage, Ava thought over what had passed between herself and Lenor Medwin. The talk of a guardian being ill of the influenza, of Myra being afforded a few days at home in order to nurse her had been lies; but not everything she had said had been lies. What she had said about there being no disclosure of secrets had been the truth, that she would make certain of . . . but not by accusing the girl of stealing jewellery.

Staring at the landscape yet seeing none of it, Ava's mind worked busily.

A girl in the magistrates' court, whether believed or not, the taint of it would settle. Ava Russell, though pronounced innocent of such wicked accusations, would nevertheless be whispered about behind women's fans, speculated about by men talking over cigars and brandy.

But that must not be allowed to happen. Lips compressing hard together, Ava's cold eyes gleamed.

It would *not* happen.

But, in order to ensure the girl's silence, the girl must first be found. That was no problem for she was not lost. She had told none of the staff at Moorcroft of her destination but where else would she go other than to see her family?

Was her ladies' maid so naïve? Did she really think the location of that home was secret? She had guarded it well enough, not speaking of it to anyone, but that did not mean Ava Russell did not know.

Poor Myra! In the privacy of her carriage Ava laughed softly. Had she forgotten the letter of recommendation she had brought with her on applying to Moorcroft for a position as domestic, a letter which spoke clearly of her background?

Hobbins Street. The name stood clearly in Ava's brain. She had read it only yesterday. Written in the neat hand of a teacher at Myra's school it was stated as the address of Rachel Brent, grandmother.

But had that grandmother changed her place of living? Had she, in the three years of Myra's being at Moorcroft, moved to some place else? Ava's hands tightened on her bag as a flicker of doubt edged her mind. If that was so, then where *had* Myra gone?

Dark ribbons of smoke-blackened houses stretched either side of the narrow streets through which the carriage passed, yet they remained invisible to Ava. Her eyes saw only one image: a young and pretty girl, a frilled apron tied over a dress the colour of her deep blue eyes, a starched lace-trimmed cap perched atop hair which shone like morning sun. She saw only Myra Brent.

Was she at Hobbins Street?

The time had come to find out.

7

'I didn't do it, Gran . . . I didn't do . . .'

A long sob bringing life to the words rushing through her sleeping mind, Eden woke.

'Gran,' she whispered, 'Gran . . .'

Teeth clamped hard on the tears trembling in her throat, Eden tried desperately to stem the truth, to keep reality from her mind, to hold the illusion, to believe the dream which said her grandmother was asleep in the next room, said Myra had not disowned them, said her life was as it had always been.

But the dream, the beautiful dream which gave her happiness, was a lie, a trap which closed about her each night, a safe, secure place hiding her from all that was truth. Yet every morning the pain of its falseness became an ever-sharpening knife twisting in her breast. Her life was not as it had always been. The love, the security, the joy of it was gone, shattered and broken beyond hope of repair.

'Gran . . .' Despite the pressure of tightly held lips the words fell into the silence of the dawn-filled room. 'Why . . . why did you leave me? Why does Myra no longer love me?'

Beyond the window, light spread across the sky as silent as the tears trickling down her cheeks, light which brought with it a new fear. Whose bed was this she lay in . . . who had placed her in it . . . and with what intent?

Her heart beating rapidly, a hand brushing away her tears, Eden threw back the covers with her grandmother's words speaking in her mind. *'This be no time for maudling, wallowing in pity for y'self; if somethin' be not suitable to you then you sets about puttin' it right.'*

And this was not suitable. She must dress and leave this place as quickly as she could.

'I sees you be awake, that's good.'

Her head twisted so rapidly on her neck she heard her bones creak a protest. Eden met the smile of a spare-framed woman, auburn hair faded and streaked with grey, her face touched by lines attesting to a life not filled with ease; but the eyes, the deep brown eyes held understanding, a look which stated she knew loneliness, heartache and fear, that they were companions which had travelled the years alongside her.

'I brought you up a sup of tea.' Sara Melia smiled. 'But you should get y'self back into bed for the day don't yet be aired.'

The day don't yet be aired. The same words her grandmother had used when two small girls had bounced on her bed eager to open a birthday present or to discover what delights lay in a grandfather's sock draped from the mantelshelf. Eden gulped the emotion of memory.

Though she had stepped no nearer the girl to whom

she had given shelter, Sara saw the nuance of unhappiness flit across the sad little face. The wench had
gone through the mill, life had dealt a blow her was not
yet recovered from; yet seemingly she had suffered no
thraipins, no bruises spoke of physical violence; and
the clothes her wore, though they were naught as 'adn't
seen the insides of a pawn shop, were clean, the
patches on petticoats neatly stitched and the gusset of
the bloomers carried no trace of a monthly cycle. Was
that the result of a good scrub and boil or of a babe in
the belly? Could that be the reason of this wench being
out on the 'eath? Had her been turned out . . . left to
cope with the fruits of her sin?

Sin! Placing the cup on a table barely big enough to
hold it, Sara felt resentment thicken in her throat. Who
gave folk the right to say what were right and what were
wrong? Who were it deemed a woman carrying a
bastard child were the only one treading the path of evil
while oft times the man responsible suffered no such
judgement?

The girl wore no ring, no golden band on her finger.
If it were her were carrying, there were no sign of its
legitimacy, no attestation of a father proud of a child
to come. More seemingly it was the leavin's of a fly-
by-night, a man who had taken his pleasure then run,
leaving behind a wench who would know a lifetime of
condemnation and a child forced to wear the same
badge, the stigma of being born a bastard, a child
whose every step through life would be taken beneath
the shadow of shame.

Was this wench no better than her should be? Sara looked at the girl she had dressed in one of her own cotton nightgowns, itself bought from the pawn shop. Denial born of instinct rose to answer Sara's thought. There was nothing of the whore in that face, drawn and frightened, yes, but given the trials of last night, lying out on the heath with no mortal soul for company and no shred of comfort, what young wench wouldn't look so? But there were no hardness of the mouth, no calculation in them eyes and, what of them cries made in her sleep? Did them be the cries of a prostitute? No! Sara reached her decision. Whatever had pushed this girl from her home, it couldn't be business of the night.

'I put a spoon o' honey in that there tea. You should drink it, whether or not you takes it sweet for honey gives a boost to the body.'

Again her grandmother's philosophy. Eden glanced longingly at the cup, steam spiralling from its contents.

'You be wonderin' where you be and how it be you come 'ere.' Sara saw the flash of anxiety cross Eden's face and nodded. 'Well, that don't be surprisin', but standin' in a chilled room wearin' naught save a nightgown don't be the best way to hear the tellin', and seems you have no likin' to put y'self back in that bed I best go fetch up your clothes and then we'll talk over a bite o' breakfast.'

She had left the house, said goodbye to Aunt Dora. Shivering, Eden dressed quickly, the clothes the woman had left with her still warm from the fire. She had walked away from Hobbins Street to go where?

Fastening the buttons of her skirt, she tried to halt the flow of memories, but one on the other they flowed in her brain like ripples on a stream.

Myra's slap . . . her failure to attend their grandmother's funeral . . . the house being taken back by Monway Colliery! But even had it not been repossessed she could not have stayed; the memories and the unhappiness of them would have weighed too heavily. Yet she had dawdled along the streets, looking in each and every shop window, using any excuse to step inside . . . for what?

Smoothing sheets and pillow case she tidied the bed, then folded the nightgown neatly. Standing with it in her arms, she stared at another, fresher picture in her mind; the picture of two little girls dressed alike in dresses of sky blue trimmed along the bodice with small pink bows, matching ribbons tied about long plaits of fair hair, heads bent over the serious business of making daisy crowns.

She had wasted time walking the streets of the town she was ready to leave for ever, dawdled with one hope in mind: to meet her sister. But there had been no Myra, no sight of the sister she loved.

Nightgown clutched to her, Eden blinked away the tears she felt resting on her lashes. Myra did not want her any more, that she would have to accept. The life they had lived and shared together was over, snatched from her in a single day, but nothing could rob her of what was in her heart, of the love she had, the love she would always have, for her sister.

★

'You'll do no such thing!' Sara Melia shook her head vigorously. 'Whoever 'eard the like, a day's work 'cos of bein' given a night's lodgin' . . . where be the charity in that!'

'The charity will lie in your allowing me to repay what I was given.'

Her outburst halted by the quiet dignity of the girl facing her, Sara Melia felt that same instinctive certainty she had felt the previous night; this wench were no trollop, her had been reared gentle and with the teachin's of good manners.

Faltering on how to answer, not wishing to tread on the girl's feelings, yet considering her own – feelings which said never to look for payment when doing a body a good deed – Sara took the neatly folded night-gown.

'That be all well and good,' she protested, 'but the giving of shelter shouldn't need no repayin'.'

'Kindness does,' Eden answered simply. 'I was taught always to repay . . .'

'And I was taught never to seek a shillin' after givin' a farthin'! I hears what you be sayin' but this be Sara Melia's 'ome and while her be mistress of it there'll be no askin' of payment for a kindness! Now get you to eatin' that porridge afore it be stone-cold.'

The woman had refused to give her some form of work which would pay for the night spent beneath her roof. Now she was offering breakfast! Eden glanced at the dish set on a table covered with a spotless cloth.

Porridge sweetened with honey and smothered in warm milk – it had ever been a favourite of hers and Myra's on cold winter mornings.

Defying any control the tears that memory brought rolled down Eden's cheeks. Returning from putting the nightgown with the rest of the weekly wash, Sara heard the deep sobs and stepped back into the scullery. Give the wench a minute or two, let her cry out her hurt for kept inside it never healed.

'Be it too forward of me to ask where you be goin'?' Minutes later, sitting together at the table, Eden's tears subsided, Sara posed the question that had been on her tongue the past hour.

'It isn't too forward at all, it . . . it's just I don't know.'

'You don't know!' Sara frowned. 'Then if you don't be knowing where it be you're goin' how will you know when it is you be there?'

She sounded so like Grandmother. Eden smiled inside. A great deal of logic but said in a roundabout fashion.

'Look, wench,' the reply she waited for not having come, Sara leaned across the table, touching her lined hand to one which showed no sign of nail-making nor chain-forging. 'If you be in trouble . . . if you be with child . . .'

'No!' Eden's blue-green eyes gleamed a truth Sara knew impossible to fake. 'I am not . . . I mean I never would . . .'

'Then that be one cause we can dismiss. But there be somethin' giving you heartache and if Sara Melia be good at nothin' else her be good at listenin' and holdin' locked away any confidence be her so asked.'

'It . . . it might all seem so silly, so childish.'

'Ar, it might.' Withdrawing her hand, Sara stood up. 'But what 'pears trivial to one be a matter of purpose to another. All I will say be this, a burden shared be only half as heavy as one carried alone.'

'It happened so suddenly . . . there was no warning.' Eden had not intended to speak but the first words breaching the barrier the rest followed, tumbling without pause until she had told it all.

Sara had not sat watching the girl tell her story; it would come easier were things carried on as normal. Pouring the tea she had freshly brewed in consequence of that line of thought, Sara placed a cup near to Eden.

'It be hard losin' loved ones,' she said, resuming her chair as the whispered explanation tailed away. 'But that be part of living. We can face it or turn from it but we don't 'ave the altering of it; death be the one fair thing given in this life, it be shared equal . . . whether pauper or king all gets the same. You says your grandmother loved you, that her cared for you from your being a babby. Now answer me this. Last night when you was caught in the storm, what made you lie down, what persuaded you to walk no further?'

'Nothing persuaded me, I . . . I suppose I was just too tired to walk any more.'

'But supposin' that were not the way of it?' Sara pressed quietly. 'Supposin' it were summat else halted your feet?'

You be tired, my little wench.

Startling in their clarity, the words returned.

Come set along of me, it be warm here against the fire.

Her face paling, Eden remembered.

'A voice,' she said, 'a voice, I heard it so distinctly, it . . . it said to rest, it said . . .'

She was suddenly back in the past. Her head bent against driving snow, her limbs numbed by the cold, she was alone in a world of darkness, but in that terrifying world a voice of comfort called.

I be here along of you . . . rest, my little love . . .

'Go on, wench,' Sara urged when it seemed Eden would say no more. 'Speak the rest . . . tell what it be your mind heard.'

'It . . . it . . .' Half in the past, half in the present, Eden stumbled. 'It said to rest, to sit beside the fire . . . that I would be safe.'

Sipping from her own cup Sara watched the nuances of emotion cross the pallid face. The wench were struggling with more than just words.

'What was said to you?'

'I was alone! There was no one with me to say anything!'

Halted by the confusion so obvious in the cry, Sara chose her answer carefully.

'The words you felt in your heart, those your mind spoke, they was gentle? They said no harm?'

'No.' Eden's frown quickened. 'They . . . they were only kind.'

'And the voice, though naught but the thinking of

your brain,' Sara was quick to reassure, ''ave you the remembering of it . . . of how it sounded?'

'Comforting . . . it sounded comforting.'

Returning the cup to the table, Sara stared at it for several moments. 'It told you to rest,' she said, looking up, 'it said you would be safe . . . but the voice which spoke them words, it be known to you.'

Startled, Eden met the woman's steady gaze. How could she know that which she had not admitted, even in her own heart?

'You knows, wench, tell y'self it be an untruth if the telling gives you ease, but Sara Melia sees it in your face, it be in your eyes; the voice that spoke from the darkness brought you no fear 'cos you had the recognisin' of it.'

. . . *Ar, my little wench . . . it be Gran . . . I be here along of you . . .*

Knuckles pressed against her mouth, Eden fought the rush of emotion, the rising need for what could not be, the need of her grandmother's loving arms.

'You 'ave to bring it out.' Sara spoke gently. 'Put words to what be inside.'

'It was imagination . . . only that, it could have been nothing more.'

'Imaginings be powerful things, they can soothe or they can worry, best way be to bring them into the open, 'appen they won't seem so frightenin'.'

Fingers gripping the cup she had been given, Eden stared at its contents trying to find the courage to answer.

'I thought . . .' She paused. The woman would think her mad, think her deranged.

'P'raps it be better should I tell it.' Sara's lined face smiled compassion. 'You thinks the voice speaking to you out of that storm were the voice of your grandmother.'

. . . Ar, my little wench . . . it be Gran. . .

Eden caught her breath. She *had* heard those words, she *had*!

'I sees by your look I be right.' Sara nodded. 'An' it be my guess I be right in saying you was told the very same.'

'How could it have been?' Eyes bright with tears clung to Eden's. 'My grandmother is dead.'

'But her spirit don't be.' Gentle as it was, the woman's quick response lost none of its emphasis. 'Her be with the Lord an' it be His mercy give leave for her spirit to walk beside you, to comfort and keep you from danger, the danger that waited not many yards from where you laid yourself down.'

'Danger?' Eden's frown returned.

'Ar, wench, you was in danger from more than the cold. A few more steps an' you would 'ave been among the gin pits, holes left from the diggin' of coal, shafts left open and without cover. Anybody not knowin' the whereabouts of such treads a dangerous path. Folk 'ave been lost in them more times than a few. That were what the spirit of your grandmother kept you from.'

The fingers gripping the cup were white with pressure, the lips trembling, the breath jerking from a throat held tight as Sara went on.

'Your grandmother cared for you, reared you tender as any mother could 'ave done, so think, wench, think on what you be about, what her would 'ave wanted you to do. Would her truly 'ave said to turn your back, to run from the first hurdle life has thrown at you, or would her 'ave told you to face up to them? Told you that only by facing trouble can it be overcome?'

Yes, Grandmother would have told her that. Tension breaking under a shudder that rippled the length of her, Eden's fingers released her cup.

But would she have told how to face the heartbreak of a sister's rejection?

Myra Brent was not at Hobbins Street! Her tightly corseted body ramrod-straight, Ava Russell sat in her elegantly furnished drawing-room, her features displaying none of the tension building inside her as she listened to her cook.

'Birks was sent, mum, as you instructed. Said as the woman at the next house told him the grandmother had passed away more'n a week since and that the house had been taken back by Monway Colliery, that another family entirely was living there.'

'And Myra?'

The cook's head shaking briefly gave the answer Ava dreaded, but she listened, her face displaying none of that inner worry bordering so closely upon anger.

'Myra d'aint never go to Hobbins Street, least that were what be told by Birks. He says the woman who were neighbour to the Brents from long afore them two granddaughters were brought to live at that house told him clear; Eden had gone to give the tidings of the grandmother's passing to her sister Myra who was in service along of Moorcroft, that when her returned her were in tears. Seems Myra had slapped her, saying her were never to come to that house again . . .'

The girl in the yard, the one Myra had professed to be a gypsy! Ava's fingers tightened in her lap. She had been no wayfarer and her neat clothing had shown her to be no vagabond.

'. . . well, Myra never showed to the funeral.' The cook's sharp eyes had caught the minute movement of Ava's tightening fingers but her mind, equally sharp had years before taught she remain blind and deaf to anything not specifically shown or instructed by the mistress of Moorcroft. '. . . and as for the younger wench, her were gone from Hobbins Street in less than a week . . .'

'To go where?' Incisive as a blade, Ava's snapped question cut across her cook's report.

'Nobody knowed, mum. Birks asked special like, says he put that self-same question, the answer being her were bent on leaving Wednesbury altogether, p'raps them two wenches met up and decided to go find a place together.'

Ava kept her expression even, though beneath the tight corset her stomach lurched. Of course they had gone off together, two sisters to plot and scheme, two sisters to threaten Ava Russell!

'Perhaps,' she answered levelly. 'In that event I cannot be of assistance though I would have preferred to help should it have been needed.'

It be y'self you would 'ave preferred to help! Dismissed from the drawing-room, Polly Jupp smiled knowingly. Ava Russell had got the wind up, her were nervous of what might come of Myra Brent's just up and leaving, not only this house but the town. The wench had slung her hook, not that Ava were piddlin' her bloomers over that; no, Ava were all of a cummujin due to something else entirely . . . and Polly Jupp knowed what that summat were!

Passing along the narrow corridor which led to the kitchen, Polly nodded to herself. Yes, her knowed what were bothering that woman upstairs; it was fear of who else might come to know of them capers in that bathroom. Who else, now Myra Brent were free of this house, might learn the secrets of Ava Russell!

8

'I don't be asking of it and I won't be taking of it.' Sara Melia pushed the silver coin back across the table.

'But, please,' Eden's distressed look lifted to a face whose work-worn lines were deepened by a frown, 'I have to repay the kindness you have shown me, you would not let me share in your work so . . .'

'So nothing!' Sara pushed the coin further, her tone adamant. 'I'll not take a shilling, I'll not take a farthing. After all, it were my lad with his thoughtless ways sent you off to old mother Marsh's place . . . eh, the daftness of him! Sometimes I wonder will he ever leave the way of childhood behind? But one thing I don't be wondering on is that his ears be stinging still with the boxing they got last night after I got you put to bed, though I must tell in his favour that, were it not for his guiding, you would surely have laid out there all night, or else staggered into one of them gin pits. Either way you wouldn't have lasted long.'

'I would like to thank him.' Eden glanced to a window through which the sky looked grey and leaden.

'He don't be here,' Sara followed the glance, 'he is always up at first light and off to help with the loading of carters' wagons or to stand the line in hopes of a day's labour. Usually comes home with coppers enough to see food on the table, but then that don't be until well after dark for he says carters pulling into the Turk's Head or Golden Cross taverns be willing to pay sixpence to have him take the horse and cart to the stabling yard, leaving them free to get to their night's comforts the sooner. And sometimes he is given the same by gentlemen arriving at the George Hotel or even the White Horse, but either way I don't see him back to this house until after nine at night.'

So late! Passing about her shoulders the shawl which had been her grandmother's, Eden caught the corners together in a knot beneath her breasts. She could not wait so long.

'I'm sorry there don't be a room here to offer you for good but we could manage for a day or two.'

'You have already been more than kind,' Eden's smile reflected her gratitude, 'and I thank you as I would like to thank your son. Please will you do it for me?'

Sara Melia's nod was gentle. 'I'll do that, wench, and the lad will be right glad to hear you bear him no ill will for sending you where he did.'

Picking up the coin, Sara followed Eden outside and pressed it into her hand. 'Take your money, for your need be greater than mine. The Lord walk with you.'

The last echoing in her ears, the shawl pulled close against the sudden shock of cold, Eden followed the way she had been directed. She had tried to repay as she had been taught. Maybe one day the chance would be given again.

Bell Street. Myra walked slowly through the rooms of the house she had rented. She had left the Grapes Inn and, on the advice of the landlord's wife, had hurried to the Market Place. 'You'll likely get a ride with one of the carters, many of them sets off from there, but you need hurry for once their wagons be loaded they don't waste time.'

She had hurried, her boots crunching the snow lying crisp and hard as she ran the length of Upper High Street, her lungs aching from the bite of frost-laden air as she raced, panting, into the yard of the Turk's Head, a prayer repeating over and over in her mind that a wagon would still be there.

She could ride with him and welcome. The one remaining carter had looked at her, his glance questioning beneath heavy caterpillar eyebrows. For a moment she had thought he would ask why she did not take a tram or even a train and her throat had tightened. Had she answered she could not risk being seen by anyone who might recognise her, that her best chance of leaving Wednesbury unnoticed was by way of a carter's wagon, the man might have thought her to be evading the law and refuse to take her.

But he had not asked. He had simply said he was travelling only as far as the next town, Darlaston, and if it were her destination also then she was welcome.

It was not only a way of protecting her face from the sharp sting of a dying winter that she had held her hands across her nose and mouth but a way of hiding her features from anyone disposed to glance at the figure huddled beside the driver of the heavily laden cart. Moorcroft was often visited by tradesmen making deliveries, and staff enjoyed a few minutes gossiping with them, a casual mention of a young woman dressed in brown coat and bonnet asking a lift of a carter . . . Ava Russell had sharp ears and long arms; it would not prove so difficult for her to trace where her maid had gone and bring her back!

The thought had sent a shiver through her body and beside her the man had felt it. Taking the thick woollen muffler from his neck, he had passed it to her, making no comment as she wound it about her head.

He was going to Darlaston but there were calls to be made first in Moxley. It would take a longer time so if she was in a hurry . . .

She had shaken her head at the implied suggestion, murmuring there was no rush for her to reach that place. But what was that town like? It could have been the moon for all she knew of it, but to ask him would have revealed she had never visited it and thus had neither friend nor relation among its people. That in itself would arouse suspicion, so fears of what she might or might not find had remained locked inside.

The journey had been slow. The ancient horse the carter called Solomon trod carefully on the ice-covered setts. Face covered by the muffler, Myra had watched buildings and streets familiar from childhood as the cart rumbled to the junction fondly called after the large cream-coloured stone built hotel, the White Horse. Either possessing the wisdom of his namesake or the knowledge gained from years of following the same route, the horse needed no touch of the rein to guide it to the right where they joined the Holyhead Road.

She had fought the impulse to look at the police station standing solidly opposite the imposing Wesleyan chapel. Had Ava Russell discovered she was not at the house in Hobbins Street? Had she reported her missing? Were the constables even now on the watch for her?

Biting deep into frost-crushed snow, the wheels of the cart had rumbled like thunder as they passed the gleaming red brick of the ornately façaded Town Hall. Grandmother had taken her to watch the opening celebration, a man among the crowds hoisting her on to his shoulders while Grandmother held Eden in her arms. Had it really been only seventeen years since that bright day in 1872? And was it really only three of those years since she had gone to Moorcroft? Years which had proved an eternity! A river of questions poured into her mind, each bringing the visions of memory. Like sitting in a quiet, sun-filled classroom of the school stood in a street to the left, her mind in another place, another age, as the teacher read aloud the deeds of Ivanhoe, or the adventures of King Arthur's Knights of the Round Table? Then the sympathy she had felt for the pigs she had known to be taken to Hollingsworth slaughterhouse at the corner of that same street. Pawn shop, grocer, draper, confectioner, the cart passed them by, memories following like spectres calling her not to leave. But she had to leave, not only to safeguard herself from Ava Russell but to find Eden, to find her and take her far from Wednesbury; to go somewhere they could live together in safety.

But was this town far enough away? The carter had asked nothing as he set her down at the Bull Stake, and she had told him nothing, not her name nor her reason for coming there for what he did not know he could not repeat. Nor had she asked any passer-by for assistance; she could see and she could read, she must find for herself what was needed.

The resolve in mind she had trudged several streets, her boots wet from snow turned to slush. She had found what she looked for at James Belcher, Estate Agent, in Pinfold Street.

'*A small property.*' A heavily whiskered man had smiled across a vast desk. '*But adequate for what you describe and not too far from the town centre, I think you will find it suits you very well.*'

She had refused the offer of being escorted, asking instead that the address be written for her. The less noticeable her arrival at Bell Street, the easier she would feel. Opening the scullery door she looked out over the communal yard. She would share one of two privies with two other families. Not so different from Hobbins Street. She closed the door turning back towards the room which, as in her grandmother's house, must serve as kitchen, dining-room and living-room. But it was all she needed.

Shivering against a cold dampness that drove into her bones, it took all of her strength not to give in to the misery inside her. But that she must not do, she must stay strong if she were to find Eden, and she would find her . . . Please God, she would find her.

'It is all taken care of, there is absolutely nothing to worry over.'

'Thank goodness for that!' Lenor Medwin's plain face relaxed visibly. 'I have been so . . . I dreaded every moment might bring an accusation, that Arthur may in some way have found out about . . . about . . .'

Ava smiled. An inner prayer thanked the Fates for freeing her from the ties of marriage and the subordination a wife was expected to show a husband. Widowhood suited her very well; being answerable to no one suited her even more.

'You can put it completely from your mind.' Across the comfortably appointed bedroom, Ava's smile was reassuring. 'Arthur will not find out . . . There is no one beside ourselves and Myra who knows anything.'

'But the girl is not here . . . She hasn't come back.'

'No.' In the light of gas lamps turned low in their ornamental brackets Ava's dark hair shimmered like blue diamonds at every shake of her head. 'I thought it kinder to let her remain a while longer with her grandmother.'

Lenor fiddled with the ribbons of her silk nightgown, its bright emerald colour serving only to highlight her sallow complexion and the falseness of her hennaed hair. She felt far from reassured. The wench could spill her secrets, tell them to God knows who. Money! Her fingers pulled hard tearing away the slender tie of silk. The girl had nothing . . . she was simply a maid but Ava had said she was sensible, intelligent even . . . The tie dropped from suddenly shaking fingers . . . Intelligent enough to realise the possibilities? The money she could demand for not relating what she knew to Arthur!

'I don't think it wise, I . . . I think she should be brought back . . . I mean we can't be certain she won't speak of . . .'

Lenor Medwin's anxiety had not abated. Ava felt a flutter of irritation. Despite the assurance that everything was as she would wish, that the girl would do or say nothing which could cast a slur, Lenor Medwin was still nervous. The smile remaining soft on her thin mouth, Ava crossed to her companion but, as she touched her lips to the pallid cheek, her mind closed like a vice about just one thought. Ava Russell did not tolerate threat, whoever it came from! That would be dealt with just as Myra Brent would be dealt with, but not yet; after all, where was the sense in disposing of something which was of use? Lenor Medwin might not give the same pleasure, her body not shapely and firm as a young woman's, her hands not building fires which scorched along every vein yet still she was of use.

Lenor Medwin provided some, if only a little, of the solace needed to ease that particular desire . . . to give the thrills which came from brushing the muff.

Calmly and gently, as if she were soothing a difficult child, all trace of irritability subdued behind the deceptive smile, Ava guided the fretful Lenor towards the wide bed.

'If you feel Myra should be brought back to Moorcroft then that is how it will be, I shall give instructions first thing in the morning; in the meantime let us not waste the few hours given to us, we have to wait so long for that which delights us both.'

It *did* delight; Lenor had never known such enjoyment, such gratification with Arthur. A small breath escaping her throat, she felt a swift liquorice rush, a quickening of the stomach, a tightness of chest and throat that held her breathless, gasping for the pleasures to come. Ava was right, they must not waste these precious hours. A soft moan was muffled by Ava's mouth on hers, her eyes closed on her silk robe rustling to the floor, Ava's lips transferring to her breast while her naked body was pressed slowly backward on to the bed.

She should have stayed. Sara Melia had offered to have her stay a while. Resting against the curved wall of a bridge, Eden stared into the waters of a canal. Grey and still as lead, they reflected a sky threatening yet another storm. Eden shivered, her teeth clenched against the cutting wind. Why had she refused? She could have slept on the floor beside the fire, there would have been no need for the boy to give up his bed. The boy, Sara's son . . . She stared at the dark sluggish water. She had not seen him since he gave her directions to the Marsh cottage, she had had no chance to thank him for bringing her in from the heath or for the use of his bed, but Sara would do so, she had promised as much.

Why had she not made that an excuse for remaining at that house? Why had she not said she wished to stay to thank the boy herself? It would have been logical.

It would 'ave been an untruth.

Clear and sharp as the frost rimming the heath, the words of her grandmother rang in her mind.

Comfort of the body be no comfort if bought by a lie, and the mind can never rest easy under an untruth.

Those words had admonished two small girls caught in some mischief or other and it seemed they admonished now.

Grandmother had been so wise, so practical. Gathering her skirts close about her, Eden slid to the ground, the body of the bridge a shelter against flurries of snow driven before the strengthening breeze. She would have known what to do, known where to go.

Head pressed to her drawn-up knees, Eden felt warm tears trace her cheeks. How would Grandmother have reacted to being rejected? How would she have dealt with being disowned by one she loved?

Not by running away! The voice in her head answered sharply.

Problems don't go away simply 'cos you refuses to face them, nor does turning your back mend a broken heart.

'Gran!' Beneath the shawl, it was a soft cry, 'Oh Gran, what can I do!'

'Well, you could stand on your feet . . . Unless of course you are trying for a bout of pneumonia.'

'I tried, Gran, I tried . . .'

'Then I suggest you try a little harder or the next person to come along will find you frozen to that bridge.' Even as she heard the words in her head, Eden's arm was grasped firmly and she was hauled upright.

'Don't you have more sense than to go sitting on ground solid with frost!'

That was not Grandmother's voice, nor was it her touch. Dazed by the sudden jerking to her feet, her mind not yet sorting the real from the imagined, Eden stared at the man still holding on to her.

'Lucky I came along.' He shook her roughly. 'Another hour and it could have been too late. Has no one ever warned you of the danger of sleeping in the snow . . . or could it be you just ignore advice!'

'I . . . I was not asleep.'

'I don't suppose you were sitting on the ground huddled against a canal bridge either!' Brittle as ice crunching beneath his feet, the reply cracked out.

Stung by the harshness, Eden's senses returned with a jolt, making her retaliation equally sharp. 'And I don't suppose you enjoy playing Sir Galahad!'

The hand dropped from her arm and a smile

appeared in dark eyes. 'You know me already, and there was I hoping my play-acting would go unnoticed! But I suggest we both move on before we freeze.'

Drawing the shawl close, seeking every atom of warmth it allowed, Eden met the smile with hostile eyes. 'Thank you, but your suggestions are not needed, I can manage quite well for myself.'

His smile dying as quickly as it had sprung to life, his hand moved like quicksilver to grab her in a grip of iron.

'Manage what!' Harsher even than before, the words grated from lips suddenly drawn tight. 'To throw yourself into the canal? To sit down until the cold sucks the life from you? Or to run a little farther away? That is what you are doing isn't it, running away? Well, I can't see that being of much help with your problems. Turning your back and refusing to face what life dishes up solves nothing and neither will it mend a heart you think to be broken.'

What did he know about her heart? What did he know about her feelings? Anger flaring, Eden tried to shake the hand from her arm but the grip remained firm.

'I see I have struck a nerve,' he said brusquely. 'At least that is a start.'

A flicker of apprehension, despite her efforts to hide it, gleamed beneath the anger in Eden' s eyes. 'A start of what!'

Had he heard that tremor of quandary in her voice? Did the sudden trepidation she was feeling show in her eyes? She was alone with a stranger, with a man whose grip on her arm told of strength her own would be no match for. Nerves dancing, Eden tried not to show the fear beginning in her stomach.

'A start of returning you to your senses.' The terse declaration was accompanied by a tug on her arm which snatched her free of the bridge. Her squeal of protest faded in her throat as she was dragged away.

9

He had not asked her name, he had not asked where she was from or where she hoped to go; in fact he had asked nothing.

Irascibility alive inside her, Eden watched the tall figure stride away.

He had not asked what brought her to that bridge, he had simply assumed . . . assumed she was running away!

But in that his thinking had been correct; she *was* running away.

The admission cooling her irate feelings she stared after his fast disappearing shape. There had been no asking would she accept his help, allow him to accompany her to a place more appropriate to her wellbeing than a canal bridge. Instead he had merely grabbed her arm and, despite her protests, had virtually dragged her along beside him. He had said nothing as they walked and, within a few yards, her own words had ceased, only small puffs of breath glistening white on the frosty air conveying her struggle to keep up with his long easy stride.

He must have known! Eden pulled tight the shawl

which had worked itself loose. He could not fail to have noticed her difficulty in matching his gait, must have felt her stumble over snow-hidden stones, yet he had not reduced his pace in the slightest.

Nor had he apologised for his handling of her. He had halted as they came in sight of a range of buildings rising stark against the wide, snow-covered emptiness. '*The Coppice*,' he had said. '*You will find somebody there who will give you directions to where you want to be . . . that is supposing you know yourself . . .*' With that he had left.

Drawing the shawl over her mouth and nose, she watched the figure now indistinct in the distance. He was gone and, strangely, so were her feelings of vexation; stranger still was the perplexity their fading left behind. Was it resentment tingling in the wake of anger . . . indignation at being treated as she had been? Or was it disappointment at his leaving?

But that was nonsense. She was cold and hungry and those were her only feelings!

Somebody there will give you directions . . .

The deep musical voice seemed to mock. Turning to the buildings, Eden hesitated. How did she ask the way when she didn't know where it was she wished to go? But she had to find a place somewhere and, as that stranger had said, to make that place a stone bridge would be to freeze to death in her sleep.

Renting a partly furnished house was an extravagance. Myra placed the coins she had counted several times into various small piles. There was so little left of the yearly salary she had been paid a month ago; salary she had intended for her grandmother. Looking at what remained of it, she wondered how two people had managed to live on such a sum. But they had and so must she.

Taking a house rather than a single room had accounted for a large slice of her twelve pounds. '*Thirty shillings a month,*' the bewhiskered estate agent had already dipped his pen into the glass inkwell given pride of place on a well-polished desk, '*but the property can only be let on a three-monthly basis. I trust that is acceptable to you, Miss Brent.*'

It hadn't been . . . Myra stared at the coins. Four pounds ten shillings to put a roof above her head. But she had needed privacy, somewhere she could come and go without question, without a landlady prying into her affairs. So she had signed the agreement and paid the three months' rent. Would that prove enough time in which to find her sister? But she could not allow that to become a question, it *had* to prove enough. Funds would not stretch to another three months even supposing she took employment. But there could be no supposition about that either; if she were to survive she must find work . . . but never again as a ladies' maid.

'I hopes you don't mind . . .'

Myra scooped the coins into her palm as a voice called from the scullery doorway.

'I've set a bucket of coal against you wanting a fire . . . there be a few sticks and some paper along of it.'

Going quickly to the scullery, Myra smiled at the woman standing in the yard.

'You can give it back when you gets your own,' the woman's glance ran over Myra, taking in the neat though drab-coloured coat, 'the jagger will be round in about an hour. He sells coal bought from pit bank wenches but don't pay near what it be worth, considerin' it can take close on a day to pick enough from them waste heaps to fill a sack. And mind . . .' halfway back to her own door, the woman turned, '. . . neither do you go payin' what old robber'll ask. It be well known that every sack he buys he splits to make two so you give no more than sixpence. Any arguin' and you give me a shout, he won't have no argy bargy with Ada Slater.'

The fire lit and the kettle hung from a bracket above it, Myra dried her hands. She had washed in water that had been covered by a thin film of ice. Privacy was one thing, an act of kindness another. She could not keep herself totally in isolation from her neighbours, for that in itself would arouse curiosity, but they would not be told all of her reasons for coming to live in Bell Street.

Pulling her chair close to the hearth, Myra went once more over her finances. She had bought sheets and blankets from a pawnbroker. She had almost walked past its sign of three brass balls, covered with snow, but then a bent figure carrying a cloth-wrapped parcel had alerted her to the business of the small, dingy shop.

'*Come from a clean house.*' The pawnbroker had opened a large parcel allowing her a glimpse of the bedlinen it comprised. '*An unredeemed pledge.*'

They had cost two pounds. Towels, tea cloths, two cotton tablecloths and cooking utensils had accounted for a further ten shillings, while the same amount had been asked for personal linen. Counting the rent she had paid, the cost of her night's lodging at the Grapes Inn, together with the food items she had bought and the coal she would be buying later today, her twelve pounds had already fallen to less than four.

In her rush to get away from Moorcroft she had given no thought to the expense it would involve. Food and clothing had been provided there and she had needed to spend none of her yearly twelve pounds. It had always seemed such a large amount when handed to her by Ava Russell; only now with three-quarters of it spent in a day did she realise the paucity of that sum.

She should have given thought! She should have had more sense! Remonstrance of the sort her grandmother would have given sounded loud in Myra's conscience. Would the estate agent perhaps release her from her contract? Would he return the money she had paid? And if his answer were no?

Caught in the dilemma brought on by her own thoughtlessness Myra dropped her head into her hands as another more worrying thought followed. What if Eden were not in Darlaston? What if she had left Wednesbury for a different location altogether?

'You'll find no charity here!'

He had stepped from the first of what had turned out to be three small houses, each a twin of the other. Eden stared, taken aback by his animosity. Old as Grandmother had been, hair more white than brown, his spare figure leaning heavily on a strong cane, a man glared back at her, eyes glinting like old copper.

'I said you will find no charity here!'

Loud on the crisp air, the repeated words cracked like pistol shots, clearing Eden's mind. Holding her stare, her tone as cold as the morning, she answered steadily. 'Thank you, but I was not aware I had asked for charity.'

'Just as well,' the reply whipped back, 'for there is naught of that in this place. Beggars find no welcome at The Coppice.'

So cold she could not prevent the shiver which made the whole of her body tremble, Eden made no effort to calm the storm suddenly stirring inside. Poor as they had always been, not once in her life had Grandmother stooped, or allowed her grandchildren to stoop, to begging; every crust they had eaten had been worked for, every farthing earned by the labour of their hands! Indignation flashed in her eyes, emphasis weighing icily on every word she spoke, slowly and clearly leaving no room for misunderstanding.

'You, sir, should recognise a beggar when you see one for it appears obvious you have driven many away, but I am no beggar, I ask for no charity.'

'Then you'll not be disappointed!' There was no hesitation in the answer. 'This be no almshouse and I be no philanthropist.'

For the briefest of moments Eden hesitated but that

moment was sufficient for the swords that flashed in her eyes to be sheathed and the ice which had weighted her voice to melt.

'No,' she said quietly, 'there is no charity here, and you, sir, are the poorer for it.'

Had it been a hiss of anger, the breath he had drawn so sharply, or had it been surprise? Shawl held protectively close, Eden walked on, the snow covered ground sucking at her feet as though reluctant to have her pass. First one man and then another! First the young and then the old! Both had spoken rudely, the younger assuming her on the verge of suicide, while the elder branded her a beggar. Neither had the solicitude or the compassion her grandmother had always shown towards those she thought in need; quite the opposite. They had each displayed a hardness of heart she found difficult to comprehend. 'A kind word lightens no pocket' was the maxim lived by in Hobbins Street, but here a different approach was made to strangers.

But then her own responses had hardly been of the kind that would have brought approval from her grandmother or from Myra; they would have thought her as ill-mannered as those men. And so she had been!

A tingle of reproof coursed along Eden's veins. Bad manners on the part of one person did not condone their use in reply. She had acted no better than those men.

Eden clutched the corners of her shawl. She was no longer in Hobbins Street! She no longer had the comfort of her grandmother or the love of her sister.

She was alone in the world and unwise to its ways, but she would learn . . . yes, she would learn.

Ava had lied to Lenor Medwin. What she had said about Myra Brent nursing her grandmother, that she would have the girl brought back to Moorcroft the very next morning, neither were the truth. But since when had telling the truth ever bothered Ava?

Sitting in the room her husband had used as a study and which she now used on those occasions when she wished to impress her authority upon those with whom she may have to do business, Ava Russell's fingernails tapped on the mahogany desk.

Never! The answer was never! Lying had been an ally in her life, a tool she always found useful and one she would not fail to employ whenever the doing suited her; and she was a master of the art!

Not that it had taken much proficiency to overcome Lenor Medwin's doubts. Ava's tight mouth thinned with contempt. One touch of her lips on Lenor's over-large breast, one flick of her tongue across the nipple, one stroke of those bare thighs, and all protest had faded. The woman's first shy acquiescence, the flush of colour to the cheeks as the clothes were gently eased from her body, the quick intake of breath that had become sighs of sensual pleasure, the soft hedonistic moans which had gradually turned to screams as hand or mouth had found the secret place between her legs, had at first provided . . . Ava's fingers stilled. What had Lenor Medwin's rapture provided for Ava Russell?

Delight? Only in the subduing. Satisfaction? Only in the domination. It was the power, the power she now held over the other woman, that was her own enjoyment.

Poor Lenor! The thin smile held no amusement and no pity. Lenor had run so willingly into the trap which caught and held, one which blinded the senses and prevented her from seeing the path she was following and the end to which it must lead. But Lenor Medwin was too lost to the pleasures of brushing the muff . . . and Ava Russell would not discourage the indulging of it. Let the woman have her pleasure . . . it would, after all, be paid for.

But on one thing Lenor made sense; Myra Brent must be brought back to Moorcroft.

'You asked Birks be sent along, mum.'

Bringing her hands to her lap Ava nodded, her glance travelling quickly over the man standing before the desk.

'You went to Hobbins Street some days ago. Tell me what occurred.'

The hard-faced bitch knew what had occurred! Polly Jupp would have given her word for word what had passed between him and the woman he had talked with . . . So why ask again?

'I told Polly . . .'

'Now you can tell me!'

The razor-sharp words snapped across the desk. Polly Jupp had said the mistress were edgy and that were no exaggeration, and lessen' he were mistook it had than somewhat more to do with that maid of her'n than just the wench's welfare.

'I went as you said,' he answered, his eyes alert to any reaction to his words. 'The house I were given to call at were lived in by others, they knowed nothing of a Myra Brent.'

'So you returned to Moorcroft.'

Her were trying to trick him, catch him out in a lie! The stablehand's fingers tightened on the cap they held. Her were checking what her had already been told, but for what reason?

Careful not to allow that curiosity to colour his answer, he shook his head. 'Not right away, mum, I thought p'raps the folk in the next house might be able to say where I could find Myra.'

'And did they?'

Catching the glint of anger in Ava's steel-hard eyes the stablehand smiled inwardly. He would act the dunderhead, let her think him a fool, make her ask for every item of information.

'No, mum.' He twisted the cap again, his glance falling as though he were afraid, but what he felt was not fear, not even curiosity, but a sense he could not yet define.

Exasperation pressing hard in her chest, Ava fought the impulse to sack him on the spot; but that could come later, when this dolt was of no more use. Control of her temper as tight as the corset laced about her body, her breathing deceptively even, she asked. 'Did they say anything at all?'

Holding to the charade, Alfred Birks glanced quickly at the mistress he pretended fear of, then just as quickly let the glance fall back to the cap clenched in his hands. 'Yes . . . yes, they said somethin' . . . well, the woman did, for it were a woman I talked with.'

The idiot had paused again! Hidden by the desk Ava's fingers twined painfully in her lap. Lord how long could she stand his stupidity!

'Her said as how Myra d'ain't never come to Hobbins Street.' Judging Ava to be near the end of tolerance and that by pushing her beyond that point would somehow be to his own detriment, he went on. 'Her said the younger wench, a sister by the name of Eden, had come to Moorcroft to tell Myra of their grandmother having died, but Myra sent her off with a slap to the face.'

'That was all the woman told you? There was nothing else?'

'No, mum, nothin' else . . . 'cept for . . .'

'Except for?' Ava's teeth gritted.

Feet shuffling, a slight choking of the throat adding to his air of nervousness, Alfred Birks hid his smile.

''Cept for sayin' Myra never was at the funeral and that the younger wench left from Hobbins Street less than a week after.'

'Did you by any chance enquire as to where the other girl had gone?'

This was no case of a mistress concerned for a maid. This probing were too deep for that . . . there was something more behind Ava Russell's questioning.

Pushing the thought to the back of his mind yet not entirely dismissing it, he answered, maintaining the illusion of a dull-witted brain, the smile he lifted to her deliberately inane. 'Oh, I done that, I asked special, I said where was her gone to? But the woman hadn't no knowing of that . . . said her d'ain't have that knowing at all.'

The story matched, though the delivery of its repeating had taxed her patience.

Alone once more, Ava's fingers untwined but her mouth held its tension.

So, Myra Brent had made no mention of any intended destination. That could point to only one conclusion. She hoped by leaving no track, by leaving no word of where she was headed, she could become lost to Ava Russell. But in that Myra was wrong . . . Myra was very wrong.

10

The man at the bridge had said there would be people here, someone from whom she might ask direction. But there was nobody.

Cold biting into every bone, Eden stared at the house the stranger had called The Coppice. Rising three storeys, the small glass panes of arch-shaped windows glittering in a struggling sun, it stood face on to a wide stretch of ground that reached to the group of buildings where that elderly man had spoken so rudely.

So much space, so different from Hobbins Street. Covered now by a sheet of snow it was beautiful, but in summer, with its bordering trees clothed in leaves, it must be a green paradise.

But why no people? The building showed no sign of disrepair, the windows, though shuttered, were intact. Could it be she had not been heard? Returning to the rear of the house she knocked again at the door she presumed was that of the kitchen, but as with that first time it brought no response.

Misery adding to the cold, Eden glanced across the spacious yard to where a line of low, wide-doored buildings edged yet wider grounds. Carriage houses and stables. Grandfather had told Eden and Myra stories of himself as a lad working as stableboy in a house big enough for a lord of the land to live in while its grounds would cover half of the town of Wednesbury. It had been like listening to wonderful tales of magic and fairy castles and she had never thought to ask why would he have left so beautiful a place to go and live in a tiny house in a town constantly overcast by the smoke of iron foundries and the dust of collieries. But then that house had never seemed tiny and the inside had held no trace of dust. For two young children it spoke only of love, of being cherished and cared for, and that aura had never changed.

But, memories drifting into her mind, Eden felt the hot sting of tears. The sense of being loved, of being part of a family, had suffered a dreadful blow with her grandmother's passing; then with Myra's slap it had died, leaving in its place a stifling emptiness. What had given rise to that slap? What could have been the cause of Myra's anger, of her rejection? Was it . . .

But she would not think of that, not now, not ever! Myra had chosen her own life, a life without the ties of love, and she must do the same.

'Been nobody lived there this twenty years. Place be empty all but one week each two month, that be when the house is cleaned and aired.'

Why couldn't he have said she would find no person in that house? Was there some sort of satisfaction in seeing her trudge all that way only to trudge back?

Repressing the comment rising bitterly to her tongue, Eden glanced back the way she had come. Standing at the head of what, during that long walk, had seemed an interminable distance, yet now she guessed was the drive up to the front of the building, the house stared back at her. It looked lost and lonely; abandoned by all it had known. A dart of sunlight played for an instant across a window and, to Eden, it seemed like a glittering tear and, despite herself, she felt a swift tug of sympathy. The house, beautiful and obviously cared for, was a place of unhappiness.

'The cleaning was finished a week gone, won't be folk there again until Lent be passed.' Several weeks! She could not wait that long. Conscious that the drawing closer of her shawl did not completely disguise the shiver she had not wanted seen, Eden turned her glance to the man who had stared at her as she drew level with his garden gate. Lips too stiff from cold to smile, her 'Good day' no more than a murmur, she made to continue but a movement of his cane had her pause. Maybe he relented his not speaking of that house being uninhabited, maybe . . . but her 'maybe' died as he spoke sharply.

'Be a fair walk to Tipton, should that be where you are headed, and some half mile the other way should it be Wednesbury you want; either will seem a lot further given the drag of snow 'neath the feet.'

What would her grandmother's attitude have been

towards someone so obviously cold and distressed? A
hot drink, a bowl of soup and, as welcome too, a kind
word! A hot drink . . . a bowl of soup! Eden's insides
quivered at thought of the comfort they would bring.
But to ask for charity *and* to have it grudgingly given,
would stick like a stone in her throat.

'Thank you.' She forced out words which did not
want to come. 'I am grateful for the directions you
point out. Please give my regards to your wife.'

She had looked openly at him while speaking, seen
the nuance of anguish flash across copper-coloured
eyes, the tight pain-filled clench of the mouth, a look
complete in its despair but which was gone as quickly
as it had come.

'I have no wife.'

He spoke calmly but the essence of pain seemed to
linger beneath the words. He too was lonely, as lost and
lonely as that beautiful house, as she was herself. She
had not seen that loneliness when they had talked
earlier; her only awareness had been of a brusqueness
she had read as rudeness.

'I live alone,' he was speaking again, 'I look to none
and I depend on none.' Did he think her about to ask
for a lodging here at this cottage? Did he perhaps
expect her to beg for his charity? Eden shuddered,
frozen to the marrow, more hungry than she had ever
been. A long walk either way was exhausting to think
about; but to ask anything from this man, so averse to
giving even a word of warning that she would find no
one at that house . . . the thought choked her.

'Like I said,' copper eyes as bright and sharp as a hedge-sparrow's held fast to Eden's, 'I give nothing. This cottage be no charitable institution.'

Sympathy which had welled only seconds before drained swift as water over a sluice. She had been right in her assessment of this man, there was not a charitable bone in his body.

Huddled into herself, muscles tensed and cramped against the cold, Eden winced with the ache of drawing her body to its full height.

'I observed that from speaking with you earlier.' She thrust one hand into the pocket of her skirt. 'I thank you for your advice regarding the distance to the nearest towns. That, I think, should pay for it.'

Withdrawing her hand, Eden placed two coins on the gatepost and, without another word, walked quickly away.

She had tried to make her questioning appear to hold no cause except for a mild curiosity as to the reason her maid had made no return to this house, but her efforts had failed.

Alfred Birks broke the thin film of ice on the surface of a trough adjacent to the stable of Moorcroft House, and filled a bucket from its contents.

If Ava Russell had thought to pull the wool over his eyes, then she had best think again. Alfred Birks were not the fool she might take him for. There was more to that business than that woman was willing to speak of;

business, if luck played on his side, he intended to make his own.

Carrying the bucket to the one stall still housing a horse he placed it in one corner. In the days of Samuel Russell every one of these eight stalls had held horses and the coach-house two carriages and a governess cart, but these, as with the rest of the stables staff, had long been got rid of and, according to the snippets Polly Jupp allowed to drip from her tongue, *he* might be in line for the next dismissal. But he would not go with nothing, and instinct said this affair of Myra Brent could go a long way in providing him with the financial rewards he deserved.

Forking hay into the feedbox he left the stall, slipping the bolt across the half-door before crossing the yard to the kitchen of the house.

'Asked had I been to Hobbins Street then had I talked with the folk in the next house, but her already knowed all of that for you told her, didn't you, Missis Jupp?'

Boots left outside the kitchen door, hands and arms scrubbed to the elbow, a piece of ragged cloth covering the seat of the hard wooden chair he sat on, Alfred Birks held the large mug of tea which accompanied his meal.

'I told her all, just as you said it to me.' Answering as she came from the larder Polly set a large fruit cake on the table. 'I said as how you had done all her had instructed.'

Alfred watched the knife slice cleanly through the cake. Did Polly Jupp know the reason of Ava Russell's wanting to see him? Had this woman told the mistress all he had said or had a bit been left out here and there? Saying nothing of the thoughts riding inside, he took the plate with its generous portion of cake.

'I don't know why it be her had to have the seeing of you herself for I'd already told all you said.' Seated now with her own piece of cake, Polly answered the unspoken question. 'But then her don't have to have no reason for anything her does, not since the master died; can do as her likes and answer to nobody.'

Swallowing a mouthful of tea, Alfred kept to the dull-witted way he adopted while at this house; a man they thought had only half his marbles was spoke more freely in front of than one with the whole of a brain.

'Must be wonderful to be servant to nobody,' he said, mouth full of cake. 'I wish I had money such as the mistress has got, and a house like as this to go along of it.'

'So do I, lad, but had I a house such as Moorcroft it wouldn't see the carryin's on this one . . .'

This one sees! Swallowing hard, the deliberately noisy appreciation of hot sweet tea covering the cook's slip, Alfred finished the sentence for himself. The carryings on . . . What exactly were they, and did they have anything to do with Myra Brent's leaving her post without notice? The more he thought of it the more likely it seemed. But he would ask no more questions of Polly Jupp though he would bet a year's wage her

could give answers to them all, were her so minded.
But a stablehand prying into matters not of his concern
would raise its own enquiry and that were the last thing
he wanted. He'd keep his mouth closed and his head
down . . . until he'd discovered what it were had Ava
Russell as nervous as a cat with its arse a'fire!

'This be the wrong direction to be walkin' in if it be
Wednesbury you wants.'

The wrong way! Eden's breath caught in her throat
and she knew that to release it would release the tears
surging behind it.

*Turning your back on a problem don't be the solving
of it.*

The words of her grandmother had flung themselves
at her as she had walked away from that old man and
with them had come others, those spoken by a much
younger yet equally acerbic man accusing her of
running away; an accusation which had caused her to
reconsider. She should not give in, leave the town of
her birth because of being alone. Other women left to
fend for themselves managed to live, to find a way of
earning their bread. She was no different. But the
pathways worn across the heath had been hidden by a
covering of snow and she had missed the way.

'This here be Gospel Oak. We be quite a step away
from Wednesbury and seems you've walked every one
of 'em.'

'Yes.' Eden nodded as the smith laid aside his
hammer.

'Well, you don't be in no state to walk 'em back, least not afore them bones o' yours be thawed out. Set you there alongside the forge while I pours you out a sup of tea.'

Too cold to refuse and too grateful to worry about charity, Eden took the chipped enamel mug, holding it between both hands as she sipped.

'I trusts you ain't come by way of the 'eath, that be a risk when the weather be fine, but the way it be to-day . . .' He paused, using the cloth tied about his neck to wipe the perspiration from his brow.

'I came by way of the towpath.' Tears warmed away by the hot sweet tea, Eden answered, 'that is I followed it after leaving a house called The Coppice.'

'Ah, then you turned left when it was to the right you should 'ave gone, but The Coppice . . . Were a time I got work aplenty from there but that be many years gone, The Coppice . . .' he mused, '. . . but ain't been a soul there for twenty year or more . . . I be surprised to hear it being lived in again.'

Relishing the warmth of the mug and the heat of the forge, Eden glanced at the well-muscled man replacing the strip of cloth about his neck.

'It isn't lived in,' she said, 'but I was not given that information, rather the opposite. I was told there would be someone there would give me directions.'

'Don't tek no guessing who that be – gettin' on in years, leans on a stick, spoke to you from a cottage at the end of a wide avenue leading to the big house?' Looking at her over a large enamelled jug as chipped as the mug he refilled, the blacksmith's eyes reflected the glow of the fire in the bed of the forge. 'Be that the one failed to tell you?'

Needing no answer, he filled a mug for himself, then set the jug on one side of the forge, placing a saucer over it to keep out the dust.

'I've heard folk talk of him afore this,' he said, using the anvil as a seat. 'Waspish be the kindest account given of that one, though I teks that on hearsay for I ain't never had the meeting of him for myself, nor can I say I have the missing o' that!'

Waspish – was that what the elderly man had been? But had she behaved any better?

'You'll have found no meal along of the towpath . . .'

Her thought interrupted, Eden glanced at the face streaked where the cloth had rubbed a line in the black dust of iron and soot.

'No.' She shook her head. 'I passed a small house some halfway between here and the path which led to The Coppice but it also was empty.'

'I knows the place and as you says that be empty, much to the dislike o' many a bargee hoping to buy his meal or pick up provision for his journey. Been sadly missed has old mother Shipton, 'specially so by the cut folk, her dying be a loss to many.'

'But why have her family left the house empty?'

'That be no riddle.' The smith laughed, his huge hand reaching for Eden's empty mug. 'It be 'cos of her 'aving no kin to live in it. Childless her were and no relative o' no sort with which to spend her days, not that her would have left the cottage her husband built and her were brought to on the day they were wed. That being the way it is, the place has remained empty since her being took from it.'

Loath to leave the warmth of the smithy yet reluctant to keep the man any longer from his work, Eden got to her feet one hand reaching into her pocket.

'You have been very kind,' she smiled, 'and the tea was most welcome.'

'Eh, wench!' His own smile fading, the man shook his head slowly. 'I don't have the knowing of ways o' Wednesbury folk, but them along o' Gospel Oak asks no reward of a kindness 'cept that the Lord alone can give.' Folding her fingers over the coins held on her palm, his smile returned. 'I sees you've been reared so as not to expect to be given free from other folk and that be fitting, but your sharing a minute with me be a kindness o' its own and I gives you the thanking of it.'

He had not taken offence at her offering to pay for the tea she drank, and his manner had been pleasant and friendly. The other side of the coin! Drawing her shawl about her, Eden glanced towards the village the blacksmith said lay a short distance away. Today had taught her the meaning of yet one more phrase used by her grandmother.

Ought she to have knocked on every door? Should she have asked at every single house?

Fatigue dragging at her, Myra sank on to a chair drawn against an unlit fire. Had she been misled in thinking that to be unnecessary, had it been a mistake? But the streets she had walked all day, the houses she had called at, had been so very like those of Wednesbury; cramped and small, many of them back to back, sharing a communal yard which housed privies and water pump, while others boasted a pig sty with its pig snuffling and grunting as it gorged some household scraps.

It had felt like she was coming to another world as she had sat on that carter's wagon, a place she would find strange and hostile. But the strangeness lay in its familiarity, its similarity with all she had known before entering into service at Moorcroft. The people of this town, those to whom she had spoken so far, were no different to those she had known during her years of growing. Their clothing was patched and the all-purpose living-rooms she was cordially invited to step into as sparsely furnished as Grandmother's had been and, like that house, they had shown no trace of the smoke which, like Wednesbury's, belched from the throats of factories or the dust of collieries which left the vomit of black soot across every building. All of it had been as she would have found in Hobbins Street and its surroundings, one household knowing all that went on in others the length of the street, one woman telling what every other would tell. It had seemed pointless to ask at every door. Yet it might have been the wiser thing to do. Maybe someone among those warren-like streets might have seen Eden, someone who had spoken with her and dismissed it as of no importance.

Rising to her feet, each movement agony in her aching limbs, she reached for the matches, the small box the only ornament on the mantelpiece above the cast iron firegrate.

She had been at fault presuming every woman would say what the previous one had said. She should have asked them all!

Tiredness quickening a sob in her chest, Myra sank to her knees, the matches dropping from fingers lifting to the tears she had not the strength to hold back.

She should have asked them all!

Despair folding her body into a tight ball, regret giving life to the cries choking from her lips, unhappiness rocking her back and forth, Myra heard only that sentence shout again and again in her head.

She should have asked them all!

★

She had walked to the cottage set back from the towpath. Mother Shipton's cottage, the blacksmith had named it.

Eden gazed at the smooth waters of the canal, a grey velvet ribbon stretching away on both sides.

She had stood staring at the small house. Shutters closed across the low windows, chimney devoid of smoke that gave it life it seemed . . . not dead . . . no, not dead . . . sleeping, waiting for someone to awaken it.

But she had not that right; the cottage was not her property. So why had she come? The words of that stranger at the bridge, the words her grandmother would also have said, '*You are running away*', had rung in her mind as she had walked away from that other small house set at the entrance to the long pathway which led to The Coppice, they had echoed sharp and accusing branding her mind. Yet still her steps had turned towards this cottage.

Drawing closer along the towpath she had felt it almost knew she was coming. Though the windows were shuttered it seemed as if eyes watched her every step. So strong had that feeling been she had wanted desperately to walk on, to leave the house far behind, yet, as she drew level with the tiny garden in which beneath the covering of snow might sleep the flowers of spring and summer, her feet refused to carry her farther.

It had been so strange. Eden's glance remained on the still waters of the canal. She had wanted to go on but a stronger force than her own had held her. Then had come the whisper. Faint at first, hiding in a corner of her mind, soft as a baby's breath, a murmur on a summer breeze. But as she stood, the murmur had grown, become a sigh, become a word . . . Welcome!

The cottage was unlived in, it had no owner. But it was *not* hers. The latter thought had held her beside the wooden gate, but stronger still came the repeated word . . . Welcome.

It was almost as if the house called to her, as if an essence of something cried out to her to enter.

Something . . . or someone?

Overhead the blanketing clouds parted, allowing a pale yellow promise of sun to dapple the grey water.

Had she unwittingly leaned against the gate or had it really been as it had felt? That gentle hands had closed warm and loving over her own cold ones, hands which drew her to a door which yet again seemed to need no help from herself before opening.

She should not have entered. It was trespassing, it could even be construed as burglary – a crime which could have her sentenced to prison should anyone claiming ownership discover her there. But, as the door had swung inward on its hinges, that one word beating in her brain had intensified until the very walls around her had seemed to echo with the same . . . Welcome!

She had opened the shutters and daylight had streamed in at the windows, filling the room, touching furniture, lamps, fireplace, as if with a blessing. For long moments she had stood listening to the intimate whispers seeming to emanate from every article, from each corner; rustles and sighs answering the gentle touch of light, whispers of a shared love.

How long had the blacksmith said the house had stood vacant? Recall had been vague, lost somehow in the shadows, as though its telling had been insignificant. Standing in the living-room, bathed in the welcome that felt tangible and real, she had whispered back and, to her heightened senses, it seemed the cottage took its first breath of a new life.

The house was vacant but it was not empty. The thought had brought no fear. The body was gone of the woman the blacksmith had named Mother Shipton, but her spirit remained. Bricks and mortar could not whisper, they could not account for the feeling, so real inside her, a feeling which said she was wanted here. So what else could it be but the quintessence of that woman's love, so strong as to remain part of the very walls themselves?

What had Sara Melia's answer been to her saying it could not have been her grandmother's voice seeming to speak from the heart of that storm . . . that her grandmother was dead . . .

'. . . *but her spirit don't be* . . .'

Clear as when they were first spoken, the words returned. '. . . *her be with the Lord an' it be His mercy give leave for her spirit to walk beside you, to comfort* . . .'

Could the same thing be happening again? Was the spirit of the woman who had lived so long in this small house, who had known happiness and tears here, somehow passing care of it to her? Was she somehow saying, Live here as I once did, love the cottage as I loved it?

Fantasy . . . a dream borne of the desire for warmth and shelter?

Eden turned to face the cottage.

Maybe it was all of that . . . but, as she had walked through the tiny rooms which, apart from a light film of dust, appeared as they must always have been, even to sticks and coal laid ready for a fire, the feeling that it waited for her became even more positive. So she had asked. Sinking to her knees beside the fireplace her words a whisper in the silence, she had spoken what was in her heart.

'If what I feel . . . what I sense . . . is wrong, that I am not wanted here then I ask God in His benevolence allow the presence in this house, the spirit I feel to be that of Mother Shipton, to impart that knowledge to me; to tell me so I might apologise and leave.'

She had not known what else to say but in that moment a stream of sunlight had smiled into the room and, from its golden heart had whispered the word . . . Welcome.

'Same way as them others, mum, you asks me they all be done by one man; stands to reason . . . I mean if one be exactly like the other . . . Lord what be the world coming to when a wench don't be safe!'

'We all ask ourselves that.' Ava Russell took the newspaper the cook had brought to her sitting-room.

'I asks meself somethin' beside! I asks when do them

there constables be goin' to catch whoever it is be doin'
them wenches in, be a disgrace that's what it be, folk
don't feel safe walking the streets.'

'I'm sure the man will be apprehended soon. In the
meantime . . .'

'In the meantime, how many more poor souls goin'
to be murdered?'

Aware her outburst had been uncalled for, Polly
Jupp followed it with a quick apology then, with a bob
of a curtsy, left the room with the same speed.

'*Ripper Strikes Again!*'

Bold black letters spread across the front page.

'Third woman found murdered.' Ava's eyes
followed the rest of the report. 'A young woman
thought to be of the age of twenty years has been found
dead in an alley connecting Great Western Street to
Potter's Lane. Police have as yet issued no formal
identification but a member of the public present at the
scene of the discovery said the woman was a prostitute
who plied her trade in the vicinity of the railway station
and the Great Western Hotel. It was also related the
body appeared to have been mutilated in a similar
fashion to two other women whose bodies were found
last year, each slashed with a knife. When asked for a
statement, Inspector Silas Perry refused to comment,
saying only he must await the coroner's report.'

Same way as them others . . .

Polly Jupp's remark returning to her mind, Ava laid
the newspaper aside.

No trace of the killer of those women had been

uncovered. Someone maybe coming into the town by train and leaving quickly by the same way. That had been the only conclusion the constabulary had drawn. But which train . . . from where . . . and did the killer return to the starting point? These questions had been posed by the newspapers and none had received a satisfactory explanation.

If only that dead woman were Myra Brent! If it were the corpse of her maid lying in the morgue, then a source of worry would be lifted from her shoulders, for the dead can make no accusation of the living.

But that was like wishing for the moon, a dream which could never know reality. She could not afford to dream.

Her mouth a grim line, Ava rose to her feet.

She must have the satisfaction of reality. Myra Brent must die!

Yes, Myra Brent must die, that was the only way her secret would be entirely safe.

In her bedroom Ava paced like a caged tigress, her mind seething. Every minute the girl remained alive was one more minute Ava Russell stood in danger of being exposed. What a field day a story like that would provide the newspapers with.

'*Wife of Samuel Russell, late proprietor of Russell Coach Axle and Spring Manufacturing, denounced*!'

Headlines bold and dark as those read minutes ago seemed to blaze before Ava's eyes.

'*Maid tells of abuse by mistress. Ava Russell and her lover Mrs Lenor Medwin . . .*'

'No!' Ava spat the word through teeth clenched hard. Should that ever happen there would be no life for Ava Russell in Wednesbury, no life worth the living anywhere in the country. A rake, a libertine or even a lecher, a man could be accused of any of these and the country turned a blind eye; but for one woman to make love with another, to 'brush the muff', that carried a social death sentence.

But those headlines would never grace any newspaper. The time of dreaming was over. Myra Brent had to be eliminated . . . but first she had to be found!

12

It had seemed the answer to her troubles. The cottage having no occupant, everything being left as it was before its owner died, it was the granting of a prayer. But though the house provided warmth and shelter it could not feed her. True, the garden, visible now the layer of frost and snow had melted, would no doubt have herbs and vegetables planted in the autumn already poking their heads above ground; it would be weeks yet before most were suitable for eating, but early spring cabbage and tall sticks of sprouts could be picked now.

But ought she to pick any of them? The woman the blacksmith had said was elderly, had she been able to plant them herself? The answer would most probably be no. But somebody had, and that somebody would come to reap them when time was right. Would that same somebody order her to leave? That was more than a possibility and it was one she must be ready to face.

Then where would she go? Eden blinked against the strand of hair the breeze blew across her eyes.

'You will see more clearly if you allow me to take those from you.'

Deep in her thoughts, Eden had heard no step. Startled now by words which seemed to come from nowhere she turned quickly.

'You need to see when walking in these parts, whether it is the towpath you are on now or the heath. Neither of them is to be treated indifferently.'

The man from the bridge! Eden blinked again, her arms tightening about the bundle he tried to take from her.

'I am not about to rob you!'

Even against the glare of the sunlight reflecting from the waters of the canal, Eden saw the strong jaw stiffen, and for a moment it seemed he would turn away, but then he spoke, mockingly quiet.

'Anything I might have wanted from you I could have taken at that bridge, but then, as now, my only interest is in saving you from a possible accident. My advice . . .'

'Your advice is not asked for! But tell me what pleasure do you get by creeping up on people?'

Inches from her face, his sable-dark eyes gleamed. 'None!' he returned coldly. 'Nor do I get any from speaking with a woman who doesn't recognise a kindness when it is offered her. But wanted or not I will give my advice. This towpath, or that of any other canal, is not for daydreamers. The heath is pock-marked with disused mining shafts and the paths between them are mostly overgrown. Take your mind from your feet if only for an instant and your next step could very easily be your last. Do I make myself clear? And one more piece of unwanted advice: get yourself a small cart in which to carry your shopping, that way you will have your hands free to brush the hair from your eyes.'

. . . a woman who does not recognise a kindness . . .

The shawl in which she had carried the goods she had purchased lowered thankfully on to the table, which almost filled the cottage's small living-room, Eden breathed a sigh of relief at being able to rest her aching arms, but it was a sigh mixed with a fair amount of irritation. That man had mocked her. What other connotation could she place on his tone, on his attitude? She was a daydreamer, a woman without sense enough to look out for herself, wasn't that what he had meant? Well, kindness or otherwise, she could do very well without advice from him!

But a polite thank you, that should not have been too much for her to give. A twinge of guilt plucked at Eden's mind as she stared disconsolately at the items she had bought from the village of Gospel Oak.

She was no better than the old man who lived in the grounds of that graceful house, and certainly she had not the warmth of spirit or the kind manner the blacksmith had displayed towards her that day she had rested beside his forge.

'. . . *your sharing a minute with me be a kindness o' its own and I gives you thankin' of it.*'

It had been said genuinely, and the smile accompanying it was just as honest. The twinge of guilt sharpened, colouring her cheeks with self-reproach. What had been offered to her on the towpath had been more than simply a word of advice, infinitely more; it had been an act of kindness . . . one she had snubbed.

Grandmother would have been ashamed of her. Putting the last of her meagre provisions into the food cupboard, Eden swallowed hard.

She was ashamed of herself.

'You are sure you are up to it?' Trim in pale blue cotton, piped at collar and cuffs with white, brown hair drawn back from a small harassed face, Miss Sophie Brooke, dressmaker at Bull Piece, looked keenly at the young woman asking for employment. 'I accept only the best stitching, my customers expect it and I pay for nothing less. The piece you show me, is it your own work?'

Weary from days of walking and of nights going hungry because money spent on food meant less for lodgings once the rental on the house in Bell Street expired, Myra Brent tried not to let her tiredness show as she nodded.

'And might I ask where you learned to sew like this?'

How many more questions before the woman decided to give her work or tell her to leave? Myra met the suspicious stare. 'I was taught needlecraft at school in Wednesbury, but more so by my grandmother. If you wish confirmation of that petticoat you hold having been stitched by myself then I would ask you to give me a piece to sew. Tomorrow I will return it and you can judge the work. If it does not answer to your satisfaction then I will pay the cost of the cloth.'

'You obviously have high regard for your handi-
work.'

'I have high regard for my grandmother's teaching,
she would accept no second best.'

'Mmm.' Sophie Brooke glanced again at the petticoat. Spotless, well-ironed, each stitch small and
perfect. If this was truly the work of this woman then
she had indeed been well taught, and her manner and
way of speech confirmed that that teaching carried
over into more than needlecraft.

Handing back the petticoat, she took a half-worked
blouse from a table and carefully wrapped it in tissue
paper.

'This is delicate work,' she said, 'the material is the
finest voile and the client it is for is particular in her
requirements. Can you have it finished by tomorrow?'

Hurrying through the streets still busy with black-
garbed women, small children holding to their skirts,
Myra clutched the parcel. How could she finish that
blouse and still search for Eden?

Reaching the house, smelling the musty dampness
which one small fire in the evening could not cure, the
hopelessness of Myra's life closed like a tomb about
her. Why did she go on, why try to find Eden? Her
sister would not want her, she had broken that relationship, ended the love that had been between them from
birth, ended it with a sharp slap to Eden's face. Letting
the parcel drop to the table, she stared at the dark hole
of the empty firegrate.

Why go on! A sob, deep and wracking, rose in her

chest. She crossed the tiny space to the shabby dresser. What if she *did* find Eden, what if she knew of those bathtimes at Moorcroft? Eden would not only reject her, she would despise her.

No sensation of wood beneath her fingers, mindless of everything but the desolation of that thought, she drew open a drawer.

Perhaps Eden had been told . . .

The blade of the large kitchen knife glittered like silver raindrops as tears blurred.

Perhaps Eden had been found by Ava Russell . . .

Myra's hand closed over the handle of the knife.

Perhaps her sister was already caught in that woman's vile web!

The knife slid easily from the drawer.

It was her fault . . . if she had gone with Eden when she had come to the house . . .

Held between her fingers the knife blade gleamed as it rose.

Eden had spent the last of her money. Rolling pastry on a board she had fetched from the scullery and scrubbed with boiling water, she calculated her resources.

The penny she had spent at the cookshop and the tuppence she had left on that gatepost had reduced her three shillings to two shillings and ninepence, and that had slowly dwindled as with each day she had been obliged to buy food. Now all that was left was the shilling she had put aside to pay to any relative of

Mother Shipton should they come; payment of rent could offset an accusation of using the cottage without permission. But how many more days would a shilling pay for?

You *will* find work, you *will* be able to add to the shilling in that pretty vase on the mantel. That had been the promise she made to herself every morning when she woke and the prayer she said every night before sleep. But the hope went unfulfilled. Each day she bought a few sausages or a cut of meat from a family who had slaughtered a sheep or a pig, a bag of flour and a halfpenny worth of yeast from the mill, and sometimes a few potatoes or a turnip from the farmer's wife who also sold her milk. Every day she spent more of her precious coins; now, but for that one shilling it was gone. And if that should not prove sufficient to appease the righteous anger of any owner of this house? Covering the dish of meat and potato with the pastry, Eden pressed the edges with her thumb . . . Then she would be sent to prison.

But maybe it would never happen, maybe chance would be given to add to the shilling . . . she could dream. But carrying the pie to the oven, Eden knew in her heart that dreams, so like many other things in life, were only for childhood.

And her childhood had been so sweetly filled with dreams. How could she ever have foreseen they would be broken, replaced by the heartache of her grandmother's death, by the misery of her sister's alienation? But they had, and all she had left were memories.

Adding chopped leeks to the suet and seasoned flour already in a heavy pottery bowl, Eden's mind repeated words her grandmother had spoken.

Dreams be all well and good, but they best be left on the pillow for, though they feeds the mind, they don't never feed the body. You can't live the dream.

The answer would have sufficed a few weeks ago but now it was replaced by a thought to which even her grandmother's down-to-earth reasoning might have provided no answer. What was life when dreams failed?

Adding water to the bowl she mixed the ingredients together then rolled the resulting dough into small balls between floured hands.

What was life when dreams failed? Had she not had a taste of that already? Spooning leek dumplings into a broth of barley and mutton bones which had simmered in the oven for the best part of the day, Eden held the sting of her own answer in her throat. She had been given a taste . . . What was yet in store?

It repeated again and again as she cleared the table, as she washed the implements used in her cooking, and asked yet again as she rinsed her hands and face then tidied her hair.

What could her future hold but more of the unhappiness she was experiencing now? Grandmother had been right; you could never live the dream.

Nor could she go on living in the comfort of this house. Knotting the corners of a cloth she had wrapped about a basin of broth, Eden cast a glance about the small room. This cottage had embraced her, the breath of it had whispered of friendliness but, though the reception it seemed to offer had nourished her spirit, it could not nourish her body. And now the last pennies she had allowed herself were already spent and, once the food it had bought was gone, what then?

It would not go so quickly if you did not give half of it away!

Remonstrance jabbed incisively as she picked up the basin holding it beneath her shawl.

That was a logic she could not argue with. Basin held against her midriff, Eden set off along the towpath. Her food would last twice as long if she kept it to herself, the worry of what to do when finally it ran out deferred for many days.

But the teachings of childhood were stronger than logic. A kindness done to a stranger . . . an act of charity when given from the heart counts more with heaven than all the wealth of kings – again her grandmother's words, words which smiled in her heart.

Reaching the track that led away from the towpath and across the heath, Eden kept strictly to its path, aware of the pitfalls the man from the bridge had warned of. Who *was* he? Where was it he went when he strode away from her . . . and why did he figure so often in her thoughts? Did her subconscious use him as a means of keeping other thoughts away? Did her brain substitute the misery of losing a sister with the anger of being accosted by a man?

That was a logic she had no wish to dwell on; she

would forget that man, forget his rudeness, forget she had ever met him!

Resolve quickening her step, holding at bay thoughts struggling for recognition, she drew level with the huddle of houses at the entrance to the drive of the graceful house she knew as The Coppice. Bathed now in the pearl-pink gleams of a sun that had banished the last traces of winter and now warmed the days of spring, it stood as if waiting, beautiful windows glittering as if with anguished tears. Its heart is broken. Try as she would, Eden could not push the thought away, she could only listen as it came again; its heart is broken . . . just like your own!

It was the same powerful feeling she had experienced on entering Mother Shipton's cottage, the feeling that it waited for the return of love. But *she* could not enter that house as she had the cottage, *she* could never be given care of it, but she shared its sadness.

Away in a copse of tall trees, sentinels to the silent building, a wood dove cooed and was answered by its mate, the gentleness of their call serving to add to the aura of melancholy. What had happened there? What could have caused so beautiful a house to be left abandoned? She would not know the answer, the same as she would not know why a sister had been abandoned!

'I tell you as I have afore, I've naught to pay with!'

Snatched from her reverie by the abrupt call, Eden walked the last few steps to the gate. Leaning heavily on his stick the man, who might well be caretaker of the larger property though he had not said he was, regarded her with a sharp almost accusing stare. She had met with that same unfriendly stare, the same flat antagonistic greeting each evening she came. At first he had banged his stick on the gate saying he wanted no charity. A smile hovered on her lips as Eden remembered her reply and how it had taken him aback. He had expected her to turn tail and run but instead she had met that fierce copper glare saying evenly, 'And I tell you as I have afore, I require no payment.' With that she had placed the meal of sausages bedded in mashed potato firmly on the square-topped gatepost and, wishing him good-night, had left without a further word.

There were so many queries to this place. She scooped up the dish she had left yesterday, washed clean as before, and walked swiftly back the way she had come. Not only did that elegant house emanate a sense of despair, of infinite loneliness, but so did this man. What had made him so bitter as to see the world through a mist of hatred? But no, not hatred! Eden checked the thought . . . it was pain; he saw the world darkly, saw it through the shadows of pain. What had hurt so much? What was behind the caustic manner, the harsh uncivil words? She would not ask, but they would not deter her from coming to his gate, from bringing him a share of her food as she had from the first she had cooked, as she would continue to do for as long as she remained in the cottage.

13

Ava Russell's concern were for somethin' other than a maid, they could be got anywhere in this town. Why then were Myra Brent so special, what were different to any other wench?

Alfred Birks' squinty eyes stared moodily into his half-filled tankard, the questions he had asked himself time and again since being called to that sitting-room revolving in his brain.

It weren't the safety of the wench had Ava Russell fretting, no, that cold-'earted bitch fretted over naught save the wellbeing of 'erself. The worryin' were for herself which meant the Brent girl must be holdin' somethin' over Russell's head.

That hadn't took a lot of figurin'. Alfred took a swallow of beer. He had worked that out at the start. What he couldn't work out were what it could be kept that wench away from Moorcroft. If her did have a cudgel to beat a mistress over the 'ead with wouldn't her be there at that house doin' it instead o' disappearin'?

That were another mystery . . . Why the moonlight flit? A shout of men's laughter drew his glance to the other side of the smoke-filled taproom of the beer house. He had asked around, asked if anyone might have come across her when looking for a doxy to spend sixpence on, but if Myra Brent had taken on business of the night then it seemed her had found her custom elsewhere than Wednesbury.

Emptying the tankard with one gulp, Alfred strode out into the street. There were money to be made from this, he could feel that in his bones, and it would be a sight more money than he would ever earn skivvying in a stable! But to eat the fruit you had to first find the tree.

Making his way along the Shambles he glanced at the near empty stalls besieged now by children begging for left-over meat.

He had done that, fought for scraps thrown like bones to dogs; ragged-arsed kids who, having grabbed a bit of scrag end or mebbe a couple of sausages, ran home faster than the Prince of Wales' best racehorse. But he would fight for no more leftovers and, once he found what it were had the mistress of Moorcroft piddlin' her fancy silk drawers, then Alfred Birks would live high on the hog.

'You give me an hour to slake my thirst then I'll be ready an' willin' to pay you sixpence.'

'Sixpence! You'll be lucky!'

'Ar, I will that . . . a lot luckier than you if your price be higher . . . I pays no trull more'n sixpence.'

'You'll get no woman open her legs for a tanner, nor play with your tool for that much neither.'

'Then I be sixpence better off.'

'Keep your tanner . . . and that you got in your trousers, stick it up your arse for a jug 'andle.'

The slanging match over, one which caught no heed other than his, Alfred watched the woman flounce away and her potential customer turn into the building stood on the corner. He had seen that man before, seen him in the Market Place with a wagon.

A sharp flick of the hand accompanying a snarled invective driving away a second woman bent on adding to her nightly earnings, Alfred entered the same building. He had talked with carters, shared ale with them in several of the town's hostelries but not here in the Green Dragon. If luck were with him then tonight he might find what he was looking for . . . and it wasn't any daughter of the night!

He had been no more friendly than on the other evenings she had walked to his cottage . . . but he had not forbidden her to come again. The dish which had held the previous evening's meal . . . had he washed it after eating the grey peas and bacon bits she had cooked or had he thrown them away? If the latter were true then why not tell her not to bring any more or was it a pleasure to him to have her walk to that cottage simply to throw away the meal she brought? Did bitterness spread so far?

The pottery dish clutched beneath her shawl, Eden followed the towpath, a narrow band of grey beside waters that glowed green-gold in the last of the setting sun.

But she did not share her meal with him for the reward of praise, she had no desire of payment, only a word of thank. '*The giving of charity be no gift when payment be looked for.*'

Grandmother's words to two young girls giving their precious halfpennies, saved for a visit to the fair, to a beggar at their gate spoke again in Eden's mind. Like the old man living at the entrance to The Coppice he had expressed no thanks yet grandmother had suffered no word to be said against him, adding only to her own.

'*A kindness gladly done brings a smile to the face of heaven, but if given only in exchange then the angels weep.*'

It had been a salve to their feelings, a calming of ruffled feathers, though not all the wisdom behind the words had been understood. But I understand them now, Gran, she smiled inside. Give willingly with no mind to what that giving brings you, or else do not give at all. Yes, she understood . . . and she would go on sharing with that sad, embittered old man until her last crumb was gone.

Which could not be many more days. She had used her money frugally, buying a handful of potatoes, the cheapest of meat, to which she had added sprouts and cabbage taken from the garden behind the cottage. Mother Shipton's vegetables or someone else's? Either way, her taking them was stealing. She was a thief! Shadow touching her as the sun slid away from the horizon, Eden shivered. Thieves paid a dreadful price. But it was done, those vegetables could not be replaced, but her taking them would always be a guilt in her heart.

'I told you to watch where you place your feet when walking these parts. The canal makes a cold lover and its arms rarely let go.'

Totally oblivious of being followed, Eden gasped, her fingers releasing the dish.

'A towpath is no place for dreaming just as a bridge is no place for sleeping.'

A flash of fear leaping to her eyes, Eden turned to stare into a pair which held no smile. Sable-dark, they glinted, catching the grey of a darkening sky.

'You!' She tried to make her tone one of anger but knew it echoed the relief flooding into her.

'As you say . . . me!' There was no softening of the voice which was as cold and angry as the eyes and seemed to cut into her.

Fear already dissipated, relief becoming the anger she had striven to achieve, Eden snapped. 'Have you no thought . . . creeping up behind . . .'

'Hardly creeping.' He glanced at his own sturdy boots then reclaimed her eyes. 'As for thought, it is obvious I have more than a young woman who walks the towpath alone ignoring any advice telling her that to do so could be courting danger.'

'Your advice,' Eden snapped again, 'is not welcome, neither is it necessary. I have walked this path for some time and not once have I been accosted . . . until now. It seems you feel you have some God-given right to interfere in my business but that is a delusion you should rid yourself of. I do not need your assistance . . . in *any* way.'

Bending easily, a movement as supple and feline as his walk, he gathered the pieces of broken pottery.

Standing erect once more, head and shoulders above her, his eyes glittered like black ice and when he spoke it was quiet thunder. 'Then I apologise . . . for this.'

Thrusting the remnants of the dish into her hands, he strode away, the shadows of the heath wrapping him until he might never have been real.

But he *was* real. The shards of what had moments before been a perfectly useful dish still held in her hands Eden resumed her way. He was so real, he plagued her mind; even when asleep, he was there in her dreams. But she did not want him there, and as for her being in any sort of danger . . . who but himself had ever voiced more than a 'good day' as she walked to and from Gospel Oak or followed the track to The Coppice? No one approached her, no one barred her path . . .

The thought freezing in her brain, Eden came to a halt. There, coming from the door of the cottage, a man . . . a man who watched her, who waited . . . and it was not the man whose advice she had chosen not to follow.

This time he had struck gold, gold that would soon be in his pocket. How much . . . how much should he ask, fifty . . . a hundred? A hundred pounds! Alfred Birks hugged the thought as he left the Green Dragon. What did it matter how much he asked? If Ava Russell wanted to find Myra Brent as badly as he felt she did then he would get his money; that or she could whistle for the information he had gleaned from that carter . . . and it would be a hell of a long tune.

It had taken two pint tankards of ale plus a shilling to wash the carter's memory clear, two pints Ava Russell would pay dearly for.

'A *wench*!' the man had answered, the look that came with it clearly expressing the calculation going on in his mind, one that said how much of a charge could his information bring . . . how much silver to his pocket?

'*My sister, her run away from home and our mother be taken ill of the worry of it. If you 'ave met with her I asks in God's name you tell me.*'

The lie had run easily from Birks' tongue, the forced tear he had scrubbed from his eye having the effect he had hoped for; yet it had taken that second tankard and a shilling to part the man from what he knew.

'*Was a wench such as you describes, picked her up a few weeks since.*' He had clutched the handle of the pewter tankard, guarding against the possibility of its being snatched away once his talking were done. Alfred Birks frowned. That was precisely what *he* would have done but the carter had proved too smart. '*It were down at the Turk's Head, I were finishing takin' on a load when her asks could her ride alongside.*'

'*What name did her give?*'

His answer had been ignored while the carter sank his nose into the tankard, then wiped a line of froth from his lips with the back of his free hand.

'*D'ain't give no name . . .*'

Walking quickly along Church Street, Alfred's frown returned, seeming to bring with it the taste of sourness of breath the carter's loud belch had blown into his face.

'*. . . her d'ain't say and I d'ain't ask.*'

Was he going to have to lure the man outside, draw him into the narrow confines of the Shambles and kick the rest out of him? Irritation combining with the rancid taste of the man's breath curdled to a ball in his throat Alfred had gripped his own tankard with both hands, wishing it was the throat of the carter.

'*Seemed her were upset by summat,*' the man had resumed after another swallow of ale. '*But if as you claims her were runnin' from home then that don't be startlin'.*'

No, it wasn't! What had been startling was managing to hold back the urge to choke the man! Having reached the point where the road became the beginnings of the rise that was Church Hill, Alfred slipped through a low wooden gate set in the high walls surrounding Moorcroft House.

'*Said 'ardly a word the 'ole of the journey.*' Slurred by the rapid downing of ale, the carter's words had come thickly. '*I told her where it would be I was goin' and that it would take time for I was goin' by way of Moxley.*'

Going where? He had wanted to hurl the question, to follow it with a fist, then shake the rest of it loose of that froth-lined mouth. Patience was no virtue of Alfred Birks and it had stretched about as far as it would go.

'*Darlaston don't be the other side of the world,*' the carter had continued in the nick of time. '*But it be far enough for my old hoss, and far enough for that wench so it seemed for that were the place I left 'er.*'

Darlaston! Crossing the spacious ground which skirted the once immaculate gardens of the brick house, Alfred stood a moment staring at its silhouette dark against the moonlight. He had kept his patience with that carter and it had paid off. Tomorrow he would be paid again . . . but not with words. Tomorrow he would be the man with information to sell, and it would be more than two tankards of ale and a shilling would see the buying of it.

Satisfied with his night's work, Alfred Birks crossed to a minute building set a little way from the stables, and slipped inside. Once an extra feed store, now the one tiny room was his home.

One room! He stared around him. One room in which to eat, sleep, to live his life! But not for much longer. Alfred Birks was going places, he was going to have a better life, a very much better life . . . and Ava Russell would pay the cost.

What would it take to get some sense into that girl's head?

Andrew Denby angrily pulled the shirt from his back.

Was it obstinacy that made her disregard his warnings or was it sheer stupidity? Stripping away the rest of his clothes, he climbed into the tub. Relaxed by the warm water, he closed his eyes and mulled over the confrontation that had taken place on the towpath. Lord, he could have picked the girl up and thrown her into the damned canal! Maybe he ought to have done, perhaps that would have cured her obstinacy, for it was that and not stupidity that lay behind her reactions.

She had answered him tit for tat, countered his words with her own, the edge of them as sharp as his own. Some might construe that as stupidity: a young woman alone, daring to invoke a man's anger . . . or something infinitely more hazardous to herself. But she had dared and, were he to admit it, he admired her for doing so.

Warm water soothing tiredness from his bones, he let his thoughts run. Settled herself in the old Shipton place, that much he had heard gossiped between bargees pulling into the basin and the men who unloaded and re-loaded their narrowboats with cargo. That in itself was a source for concern; he would place his life against any of the men he knew bothering that young woman . . . but he did not know every man who passed this way. Try telling her that, try explaining the risk she might be taking? Andrew Denby smiled. It would be like spitting in the wind. So he must do what his own father would have counselled: 'Act on advice, don't just talk about it.'

Stepping from the tub he rubbed his body with a large towel. Taking the decision and augmenting it had presented no difficulty . . . but should she find out! But then he must make quite certain she did not.

Dressed in a dark suit, a pearl-coloured silk cravat at

his throat, he reached for matching gloves. Glancing at his reflection in the mahogany-framed cheval mirror his mouth firmed. His appearance was orderly enough . . . pity his damned mind was not!

What was it with that girl? Worn boots, patched skirt, a shawl over her head . . . the towns were filled with such women. Lord, he had seen hundreds . . . yet he had not seen one like her. There was something about her, something that shabby clothes could not hide, something he could not define, yet it was under his skin, in his mind. Whoever that girl was she had made an impression on him he was finding difficulty forgetting.

And what of those visits to that cottage in the grounds of The Coppice? Why did she go there each evening? Perhaps more of a question was why did *he*? Impatient with the answer, which like other thoughts of that girl plagued him.

Dismissing his coachman he took the reins of the light chaise. Guiding the horse between the tall, stone-built gateposts of Woden Place his mind immediately slipped to that other house, those other gateposts.

The first time he had seen that girl go there and watched her speak for a few moments with the old man, he had smiled to himself. The lady's intentions would bring her no reward there! That man's sharp tongue could make bitter aloe seem sweet; she would pay no second visit. Yet she had, and to his chagrin so had he.

Allowing the horse to find its own pace along Ethelfleda Terrace and on into Church Street, he gave his mind the same freedom. He had watched her come to the gate of the cottage, seen the walking-stick lift ominously; but she had not flinched, nor drawn back from the threat: quite the opposite, she had stepped forward, placed a cloth-wrapped bundle on the flat-topped post then left . . . she had simply turned and walked away.

That first evening had been a coincidence. He had spotted the slight, shawl-wrapped figure while returning from Lower Wood Colliery. Had it been curiosity that caused him to follow her? Refusing to admit to a stronger drive, Andrew pushed the thought aside. What he had seen had left him wondering. It was obvious the man had nothing to give apart from harsh words; she would learn that and not go there again.

Yet she *had* gone again . . . and so had he. But it was the errands of business had him pass that spot each evening.

Bringing the carriage to a halt outside the George Hotel, he nodded to the polite greeting of an ostler running to take the vehicle and walked into the chandelier-lit lobby.

He had been returning each evening from business which had him pass The Coppice. This was what he told himself. The only problem with that was he knew it to be a lie.

14

The doctor had diagnosed Lenor with an illness of the heart.

Returned from visiting her friend, Ava Russell paced her own private sitting-room.

'There must be no stress, no worries of any kind.'

Stress! Worries! Ava's fingers clutched each other in the anger she could not show whilst at the Medwins' house. What did Lenor Medwin know of either? Wasn't Arthur Medwin well placed, was not his business one of the most lucrative in the town? Yet something was pulling at the over-dressed Lenor. The saffron gown had been the usual expensive creation, its abundance of frills and bows serving only to highlight a figure of equal excess, and the jewellery, the rings on every finger, the pearls surrounding the fat throat all had confirmed that any worry Lenor Medwin may possibly experience could not come from a financial source. So why had Lenor stressed the doctor's words?

Ava's fingers pressed tighter, driving her fingernails into her palms but the pain went unnoticed beneath her agitation. She had asked the question and had known the reply before it was spoken. Lenor Medwin was afraid of her husband finding out . . . afraid he would get to know of her extra bedroom predilection.

But how could he? Neither of them was foolish enough to let slip any clue and only they knew of those delights shared at Moorcroft and in Lenor's own bedroom.

'*No, Ava, we are not the only ones who know.*'

The alarm which had come with that answer had struck like a physical blow blocking the breath to Ava's lungs, cutting off the flow of blood along her veins until her brain swam.

But it was not swimming now.

Lowering herself into a chair, whalebone corset holding her ramrod straight, Ava stared at the window overlooking the rear gardens of Moorcroft. But she saw only a sallow-complexioned face, eyes alight with alarm, full lips trembling. Lenor Medwin's face!

The woman had gabbled, dismay raising her voice until Ava's own, sharp and dominant, had quieted the flow.

What caused her to believe them discovered? What proof was there?

She had expected more of the fear-driven rambling which had stampeded from the terrified Lenor, but the plump figure had withdrawn a single sheet of paper from the bodice of her gown.

'*This.*'

It had been one simple word but the trembling of the hand passing it spoke vividly of the anxiety coursing through that plump body.

Ava's thin lips clamped hard, short breaths of temper snatching into her nostrils.

The note written in script had carried two sentences.

'*Two hundred pounds or your husband knows of your brushing the muff. Leave the money in the third pew of the parish church nine o'clock Saturday evening.*'

She didn't have any money, Lenor had wailed. Arthur said she had no need of it, seeing everything was paid by himself.

Jewellery . . . sell some of your jewellery. Ava's face darkened remembering the reply that suggestion had brought. Arthur Medwin had long since sold any jewellery of worth using the proceeds to bolster a failing business. Every piece adorning his buxom wife was fake as no doubt were many of the paintings and statuary in the house.

Asking Arthur was out of the question. Lenor had collapsed at the suggestion. Yet the money must be paid or . . . but there could be no 'or'; the scandal would destroy them both . . . not that the fate of Lenor Medwin worried her in the slightest.

But her own fate, her own standing in society . . . that was a different matter.

Behind thinned lips, Ava's teeth ground her fury. Paying some filthy blackmailer was galling no matter whose the coin, but when it was Ava Russell's then it became unthinkable. Yet she had been forced to think. If her own reputation was to remain stainless, then the money had to be paid and, without help from Lenor, it was Ava Russell must do the paying.

There was only one way of raising so much. Her glance passed to a document lying on a small elegant Sheraton table.

'You be certain her don't know it be yourself has shopped her, it don't be you that's given the game away?'

The voice had not been loud but the words had carried on the somnolence of the spring afternoon.

Returning to her carriage Ava had halted, the arch that gave on to the steps of the Medwin house shielding her from view of the speaker.

'Course I be sure.' The reply had been softer, feminine. 'I told you didn't I . . . I were passing the bedroom when I heard it, the mistress agasping and agroaning somethin' awful. Well, knowing as the doctor had said her heart were not strong as it might be I was set to go in, but then I heard the other one, I heard Ava Russell warning her not to make so much noise . . . but noise about what? Not bein' able to think what it might be had the mistress going on like her was, I peeped through the keyhole . . . that were when I seen what I seen.'

'And that be goin' to make our fortune. I asked for two 'undred pounds.'

'Two 'undred!'

Ava heard the gasp . . . She also heard the answer.

'Two 'undred, an' that be only the start.'

They had jumped apart as they caught sight of her coming down those steps, Lenor's personal maid and her avaricious accomplice, the girl darting away on the errand she had been sent to carry out, her glance at her man friend asking had they been overheard. But Ava had climbed into the carriage without looking at either of them. So far as they could be aware, Ava Russell had heard nothing.

Nor could they know what she had left behind!

Her mind had worked quickly in that bedroom. Lenor's dread of having Arthur discover her affair was fast becoming panic and that could not be allowed to develop into confession.

She had spoken softly to the overwrought Lenor, as a mother might speak to a frightened child. But Lenor Medwin was no child, and no mother would do what she did next.

She had led her friend to the velvet day-bed telling her she must rest. Rest! Ava's clenched teeth released their pressure and her tight mouth eased. Lenor must not become overwrought, her heart must not be subjected to any kind of pressure, Ava would see the money was paid. They would not meet again except in the presence of others.

In the privacy of her sitting-room Ava smiled. That had been her moment of triumph, the moment her quickly conceived plan had begun to bear fruit.

'*This would be the last time we can touch each other so tenderly, the last time our lips can meet in a kiss,*' she had whispered, brushing one hand over the befrilled bosom. '*We can never share our love again.*' It had been the perfect *coup de grâce*, the blow under which Lenor had crumpled. She enjoyed brushing the muff, the thrills she never got from Arthur's love-making, and the thought of it being snatched away for ever had had her weeping.

The memory of what happened next made Ava's smile broaden, displaying the contempt inside her.

Lenor had lifted her face to look into eyes she thought sensitive with the emotions she herself was feeling. Stupid fool of a woman; the only emotion coursing through Ava Russell's veins had been that of cold hard anger. But it was an anger she had kept hidden. Allowing a sham of a sob to escape, she had pressed her mouth over Lenor's. A moment later she had whispered, '*Once more . . . one last time let us hold each other.*' The hand resting on the plump bosom had tightened as their mouths touched again, the shudder rippling through Lenor one of longing for the rest of that delight.

And she had not disappointed her friend. Still holding the other woman' s mouth, she had released the fastenings of dress and bodice laying bare the full breasts. Then as her mouth transferred its caress to Lenor's hard nipples, Ava's hands had lifted skirts and pulled silk drawers free of a body pushing itself to meet the fulfilment of passion.

It had been passion kept long from satisfaction. Ava's entwined fingers laced more tightly. The movement had been one of satisfaction.

Lenor had cried her need, whimpered her desire for that all-encompassing, heart-stopping thrill, but the wonderful agony of suspense was made to play on.

Fingers tracing past the knees and up over quivering thighs, the caressing of that moist vee at the base of the plump stomach had brought cries of pleasure each held by kisses. All the time Lenor's body had squirmed and lifted, seeking that ultimate fulfilment, that uncontrollable flare which swamped the mind, ripped away the last vestige of control before at last allowing final gratification. And, as intended, it had proved Lenor Medwin's final gratification. Her desire had been slaked . . . and her life extinguished.

It would all appear as the doctor had feared. Lenor's heart had stopped . . . but the reason why would not be discovered.

Going over her subsequent actions, Ava checked each detail as carefully as she had before leaving Lenor's bedroom. Her clothing had been replaced, the gown decorously covering her feet, her bodice securely fastened. Ava's own handkerchief, sprinkled with eau-de-cologne, had patted the tiny beads of moisture from the dead face. Her friend having expressed a tiredness she, Ava Russell, had left. That would be her reply should any question be asked.

It had worked perfectly. Lenor had suffered a heart attack and died in her sleep . . . and no one had questioned the cause.

Rising to her feet, crossing to the tall sunlit window, Ava stared out over the expanse of grounds of the house deeded to her by her dead husband's will. One source who could expose her own sexual proclivities had been removed, but another still remained. She had brought the letter home with her, had torn it into a thousand pieces then burned them. But that was no safeguard. That pair knew the name of the other woman involved, they knew Lenor's lover and they would not forego the benefits that knowing could bring them. The maid and her greedy friend would not let such an opportunity slip easily from their grasp. The next demand for money would be sent to Ava Russell and it was certain it would not be long in the coming. Ava's mouth resumed its tightness.

When it did she would be ready!

He had stood beside the door of the cottage. Pausing in the peeling of the last potatoes purchased from Gospel Oak village, Eden glanced at the window beyond which the canal lay as smooth as green velvet.

She had not noticed the stocky figure until he was almost at the gate then her mind had rocked beneath a barrage of questions. Who was he . . . why was he here . . . had someone sent him to evict her . . . was it his house? All and more had raced in her brain until one more question had drowned the rest, had stilled the mêlée in her mind but left her body trembling: Was the purpose of his visit darker than any of those reasons? Was his quarry not the house, but herself?

The thought and the horror beneath it had her rooted to the spot. Transfixed by her own fear she could only stare. Then he had moved, come to stand on the towpath only yards from her . . . yet still her legs had been like stone.

'I seen the smoke risin' from the chimney . . .'

At last he had spoken but her own tongue was cleaved to the roof of her mouth.

'. . . the place . . . it bein' empty since Mother Shipton's passin' . . .'

He had paused then, snatching the worn cap from his tousled head, holding it folded between hands stained with the labour of years.

'. . . if it were kin to you the old woman were then I asks pardon for callin' her as I did, but everybody on the cut knowed her as Mother Shipton.'

He had received no answer but, as he made to move towards her, the pieces of broken dish had dropped from her hands. Recognising the fear pulsing through her, he had halted saying quickly.

'I means you no 'urt. Like I says, I seen the smoke from the chimney and wanted to be sure there were no mischief afoot, ain't a bargee plying the cut would turn a blind eye to that. They all 'ave reason to thank that woman for one thing or another and never once were one turned from her door. Boatmen be grateful of a kindness and don't ever go forgettin' of it. None would see this house ill treated; t'were to mek sure it hadn't been taken by vagabonds that I took the liberty I 'ave. I knows now that don't be so in which case I will be takin' leave of you.'

'Wait!'

There had been something about the man made her call to him. A quietness of speech? The candid look in the eyes which did not leave her own? Even now, more than a day later she could not decide; she only knew that in that one moment she had felt all fear evaporate and in its place a warm trust.

'Wait!' she had cried as he turned back to her. 'I am not kin to the woman who lived here.'

'Don't make no odds.' He had returned a strangely penetrating glance. 'You be welcomed by that house and by them as travels the canal. You'll come to no harm while you bides here.'

He had gone then, but today others had called, among them wives of the narrowboatmen and all had endorsed the sentiments of that first man. They were happy she was in the Shipton place and, unless she had objection, the practice of mooring one or two narrow-boats alongside for the night would begin again.

She had no objection. She had caught the friendly smiles of those hard-working people. She had not been seriously afraid alone in this cottage but, with the comfort of folk so near at hand, she could know the pleasures of leaving open the shutters of her bedroom, to watch the moon, as she had loved doing from childhood, paint shadows on the wall.

But moon shadows were not the only ones that had danced, others less fleeting now played in her mind. Her food could not last much longer unless . . . but she would not do that . . . she would not spend the shilling she had set aside to pay a claimant to this cottage.

So what would she do once that tiny larder was totally without food? There was only one thing she could do . . . leave or starve.

Resuming her task, the potatoes washed, sliced and layered over scraps of beef scraped from bones given her from the abattoir close by the village and which she had slowly cooked with onion and barley, she covered the dish with its lid and carried it to the side oven of the fireplace. It would continue to cook slowly while she was making her regular journey to that other small house set beside the driveway of The Coppice. Maybe this evening, the old man who had not offered his name, had never passed a truly civil word with her, might greet her with a smile.

There had been no smile!

Last evening's dish, wrapped in the cloth she had carried it in, tucked beneath her shawl, Eden walked the mostly overgrown track which led to the towpath.

There had been no civil word nor had any name been spoken. He had stood as on each previous evening, leaning heavily on a cane, mouth firm and eyes piercingly sharp.

She in turn had smiled, placed the dish which held a portion of boney pie on the gatepost then, wishing him 'goodnight' had left.

It took only a matter of moments yet in that time, as every other time she had visited, she sensed the old man's loneliness. But she could not push a friendship he obviously did not want. He may not eat the food she brought but that would not prevent her bringing it but, at the same time, she would respect his wish; she would not infringe further upon his privacy, but do only as she had before: place the dish at his gate and leave.

The crack of a dead twig breaking her thoughts, Eden's quietness of mind changed swiftly. The man from the bridge, the one who had accosted her a second time on the towpath . . . He was once again behind her . . . following her!

Vexation lighting her eyes she wheeled about. A man was indeed standing behind her . . . but it was not the man from the bridge.

15

The sewing she had been given to do had been accepted, the dressmaker nodding approval of the fine stitching before giving her a delicate lawn petticoat to be sewn for the day after next. But the money she had been paid for her labour was paltry. Tears of weariness pressing against drooping eyelids, Myra rested the cloth on her lap.

Was it lack of sleep that made her vision blur? Or was it the poor light of the lamp by which she sewed that was affecting her sight?

She could not spend more money on lamp oil. She needed every penny if she were to pay the rental on this house. But she would not be able to pay it! She had gone without food, without fire to cook by or to warm herself, all in order to save the amount necessary, but to no avail. Starving herself of food, saving every copper she earned . . . still she had not the money it would require to stay on in this house.

The folk in Bell Street were amiable whenever she met them, but they, like herself, were struggling to make a living so her limited socialising only when in a shop or in the street was not viewed unfriendly.

Shivering from cold she glanced at the cheap tin clock set above the empty grate. Almost two o'clock. In four hours she would be out and about the streets, scanning the faces of women scurrying to take the hand-made nails and home-forged bolts to a nail-master or those returning with a fresh load of iron rod. The women of Darlaston, like their counterparts in Wednesbury, had hard lives; and what of *her* life? True, it wasn't spent bending over a hot forge or hammering endlessly on an anvil, yet what did it hold but hunger and emptiness? Was what she was living now punishment for the way she had lived at Moorcroft? Was heaven punishing her for the wicked things she had done with Ava Russell and Lenor Medwin?

Tears which had pressed all day for release spilled down pale, drawn cheeks. Blinking against their persistent flow she laid the needlework aside and carried the lamp upstairs.

The bedroom felt colder than the living-room. With hands almost numb Myra struggled free of her clothes, and slipped a cotton nightgown over her head. She gasped at the cold touch of it against her body. She would say her prayers in bed . . . Grandmother had never allowed that! Trembling, she paused.

'*Honour the Lord by kneeling when you prays, an' thank Him you 'ave strength of body to do it.*'

Her grandmother's words seemed to whisper from the night shadows. Myra's heart twisted. What would her grandmother have said had she known of her granddaughter's duties in that fine house? Of the demands of its haughty mistress?

Sinking to her knees beside the bed, fingers pressed hard against a trembling mouth, holding thoughts in silence her own words formed.

I did it for you, Gran . . . for you and for Eden.

It was not the man from the bridge. A sudden fear paralysing her limbs, Eden clutched the empty dish more tightly beneath the shawl. She had not seen anyone on this track before, yet surely men coming and going from the collieries or the iron foundries must use it? Eden's brain searched for a reason why the man was watching her but returned only a question: if that were so, why did he not continue on his way? Why just stand there?

'Now, there be a sight does a man's 'eart good.'

Followed by a leer that had Eden's heart lurch sickeningly he took a step forward. The tip of a tongue licking along his lips, his speech thickening he spoke again, the leer now an evident threat.

'But it don't only be the 'eart a man likes gladdened, it be other parts, an' you be just what parts of me be a needin' of.'

Speed denying the stockiness of his build, he covered the remaining space separating them, the force of him bearing her heavily to the ground.

Breath knocked from her, the blow of the hard ground to her head knocking her nearly unconscious, she could offer no opposition to the man intent on ripping away her clothing.

'That be the way I likes it: no backchat; and tits be what I likes to play with while I takes me a ride.'

Blouse torn open, chemise pulled away, the man laughed, the sound low and feral like the growl of an animal.

'There'll be no ride for you!'

Astride Eden, the man turned, a cry of anger issuing from his throat as he was snatched away.

'. . . and no walking either!' A closed fist smashed heavily into the surprised face. '. . . there'll be nothing for you but broken bones!'

The speed which had brought down his victim, the strength which had borne her to the ground, proved of little use against the hand which held him. A cry coming from a mouth spurting blood, the stocky figure tried desperately to squirm free but the grip in which he was caught held like steel.

'Thought to have yourself a good time, did you!'

Every word accompanied by a blow, Eden's attacker jerked like a puppet on a string. 'Well, I hope you are enjoying what you are getting now!'

A final blow sending him stumbling, the man was off across the heath.

'You think to have got away with what you were about,' Eden's rescuer murmured as he watched the fleeing figure, 'but that notion is as doomed to failure as your attempt to rape an innocent girl. The morning will see you in a police cell.'

Thank God he had called at that cottage, thank God even more that he had been in time.

Drawing the shawl from beneath the still-dazed Eden, Andrew Denby covered her with it then, as a moan indicated her senses were returning, he turned his back and walked off to stand a few yards away.

Anger against the man who had been set on raping Eden swung rapidly into another channel and, as he heard the sounds of her rising to her feet, it spilled over.

'When in God's name are you going to take notice of what you are told!'

The voice vibrated with wrath but to Eden it held the reassurance of safety. The man from the bridge . . . it was the man from the bridge. Hands trembling, hindering the fastening of the few buttons left to her blouse, she drew the shawl tight about her shoulders, tying the corners in a knot beneath her breasts. It was not this man had sought to harm her and something seemed to tell her he never would . . . not in the way that other one had tried . . . but the anger in his eyes! Blinking through tears, Eden saw his blaze as dark and fierce as burning coals. He would not rape her, but the fury of him . . . what form would that take?

'You damn little fool!'

She did not have to wait long for the answer to her question for, with that expletive, he closed the gap between them and shook her hard.

'When the hell are you going to learn!'

Released from his grip, confused by the effect of sudden heart-stopping fear, followed rapidly by the

swift, breath-snatching surge of relief at hearing his
voice, of an inner confidence that her ordeal was over,
suddenly gave way to resentment. Her own eyes
blazing through the filmy veil of tears, Eden threw
words at him.

'Whatever I need to learn I do not need you to teach
it!'

Vexation rasping on his tongue, Andrew Denby
hurled back. 'Somebody has to, if you haven't the sense
to listen to others!'

'To yourself you mean!'

The snapped intervention was no longer hardened
by anger. Andrew held back the irritation ready to
colour his own reply. The words had broken on a sob
and the hands clutching the shawl were shaking.
Reaction to what had happened, to the fear she had
undergone, was turning to shock; she needed to be got
back to the Shipton place. There would be time for
argument in the days ahead. But of one thing there
would be no argument; she would visit that old man
only if she was accompanied there and back, and in
that the feisty miss would have no say!

He had said no more, the man from the bridge.

The hot drink given her by the wife of a narrowboatman he had called to assist her, the knowledge the
woman had promised she and one of her sons would
stay the night in the cottage living-room, should have
soothed the tension which had built out of that awful
happening on the track leading from The Coppice. But,

lying in the bed that sympathetic woman had helped her into, Eden's eyes were wide and her mind restless.

He had not spoken a word from her hurling the accusation she would not listen to him, not even to say his name or ask her own; but his anger had seemed to throb, to emanate from him in ice-cold waves. But why had he felt so strongly? Was it masculine pride, had his authority been flouted? But he had no authority over her . . . she did not have to abide by anything he said.

'You can't make me do it!' Eyes wide moments before began to droop, a restless mind wandering towards the edge of sleep.

'I won't do it . . . you can't make me!'

Soft, trembling with emotion, the murmurs hovered on the edge of silence.

'Gran doesn't make me . . .'

Claimed by sleep, the dream which had plagued so often in the years from her leaving school returned in vivid detail.

'*You are learning very well.*' Hands folded across a pencil-straight body, sharp features seemingly drawn tighter by snatched-back hair, eyes small and ferret-bright looked at a girl not yet clear of childhood. '*But becoming a ladies' personal maid involves more than the learning how to set a breakfast tray or the correct mode of speech. To better serve a mistress we must be certain our own personal hygiene is of the very best. In order to ascertain that yours is you must remove your clothes.*'

'*They are clean, Gran had me change every stitch before I came.*'

'*Your clothing always appears clean.*'

'*Then why must I remove them?*'

The drawn face seemed to close, the voice became clipped.

'*That is one more thing you have yet to learn, a ladies' maid never queries her mistress! Now, stop being foolish, child, and remove your clothing.*'

Held in the chains of sleep, Eden watched the fair-haired girl hesitate then, as the headmistress tutted her irritation, slowly began to unfasten her dress.

Hands caught together across a corseted stomach clenched more tightly together, animal eyes glinting while the woman's tongue touched across tight lips as the dress and petticoat were laid carefully aside.

'*And the rest!*'

Eyes though closed seemed to see the young face lift to the older woman, perplexity drawing a line between finely marked brows.

'*Come along, child!*' the imperious voice commanded. '*Do as you are told. I cannot put my name to a reference without ensuring you carry no sign of illness.*'

'*I'm not ill, you can see.*' The young girl held out both arms.

'*Not all disease shows only on the face and arms. There are those which affect the private parts of the body. A mistress will expect a reference stating you are in* total *health and the only way I can attest to that is to examine you myself. Really, Eden, there is no need for shyness, we are both of the same gender.*' A forced smile hovering about taut lips, but eyes still holding their animalistic gleam, the woman's voice became breathy and rasping. *'Come, my dear, I only wish to help you attain a post as ladies' maid . . . to do so I have to see all your body. Now, remove your bodice and drawers like a sensible child.'*

'No!' The word cried loud in her dream whispered on Eden's lips as long, pencil-like fingers reached for her. The refusal hurled again, Eden jerked into wakefulness.

Rigid from tension that nightmare always left behind, her bones aching from the effects of the attack in which she had been knocked to the ground, Eden lay absolutely still, only her mind racing from question to answer.

Could what her teacher had said be true? No. If it were, Myra would have told her of it! Did a prospective mistress demand such an intimate examination of a girl? Of course not; Myra was a ladies' personal maid, and she would never have agreed to such treatment! It had to have been lies, all lies . . . but told for what reason?

Moonbeams gliding through unshuttered windows danced to silent music but Eden saw and heard only what was in her mind.

She had grabbed her dress and petticoat, struggling into them as she ran from the house. The voice of the headmistress had called to her but she had not stopped running, not until she was back at home, safe in her grandmother's arms.

Lies! Eden's eyelids lowered, the silent reprimand sending a tingle of guilt along her spine. The woman she had run from was not the only person not speaking truthfully that night . . . she too had lied.

'*I don't want to be a ladies' maid,*' she had answered her grandmother's concern, her demand to know the reason for tear-streaked cheeks. '*I thought I did but it was no more than a frilled apron and a lace cap I really thought about. The other things are so silly. Why is it important for the handles of cups to each face the same way, why towards the teapot and not away from it . . . and why be it so positive a hairbrush be laid before a comb on the dressing-table? Petticoats and drawers to . . . to be folded one way and not another?*'

Her voice had faltered on the words 'petticoats' and 'drawers'; that had been when Grandmother had held her at arms' length, the sudden stricture of her mouth speaking its own suspicion.

'*Tell me the all.*' She had spoken in that particular tone which warned she would stand no nonsense. '*I wants the full reason of your changing your mind!*'

But how could she say she had defied the head-mistress? What if what had been asked was a normal requisite of obtaining a position of ladies' maid? Wouldn't Gran be angry with her . . . make her carry on with a training which now distressed and disgusted her? There had been only one way, lies! And she had told them.

She did not want a life of pandering to one woman, of being at her beck and call all hours of the day and night, of regarding petty little things such as forgetting to scent her mistress's pillow before helping her to bed as an absolute unforgettable essential; she wanted to do the things she had been taught to do, to cook and sew . . . but most of all she wanted to be here at home with her grandmother.

The last had been indisputably true . . . but the rest! Whether believed or not, she had been put to bed. But next morning Grandmother had accompanied her to school.

'*Don't come no truck wi' me!*' Grandmother had said, facing the headmistress' autocratic stare. '*I hears what my granddaughter telled as to her reasons for wanting no more of becoming a ladies' maid same as I have my own reasons of doubtin' the truth of it; so there'll be no more of her visiting of your house!*'

A look of alarm had flashed across those ferret eyes but the answer given was cold and haughty.

'*Then that is unfortunate for Eden, for without training she will not attain anything like the position of ladies' maid, in fact . . .*' cold and venomous the eyes had flicked to Eden '*. . . she will never amount to anything other than she is now, she will never do any good!*'

Had the headmistress thought that reply to cow Grandmother . . . to have her behave in the submissive manner she was accustomed to receiving from those she thought of a lesser station than herself?

Watching the pictures in her mind, Eden saw the very opposite happen. Her grandmother's back, always as straight as a beanpole, had stiffened, her stare becoming colder than winter ice. '*Doin' any good, or amountin' to nothin' be yet to be seen, but this much be already certain,*' Grandmother' s voice had risen then, carrying clearly through glass partitions to classrooms where teachers tried in vain to pretend it could not be heard. '*Rachel Brent don't be so gullible as to believe all a frightened young wench be tellin', neither does many another woman in this town; they 'ave their own surmising and like my own it tells them all don't be as it should in this school. Since your comin', young wenches 'ave avoided meetin' their mothers' eyes and many be cryin' in their sleep. You 'ave had your say as to my granddaughter's future, now you harken to my prediction of your own. Should that which be niggling the back of my own mind — and doubtless that of many another — ever come to be spoke by a child brought to tears at treatment meted by your hands, then you'll find yourself lyin' at the bottom of a pit shaft with a rope tied fast about your neck!*'

She had never entered that school again. The pictures fading from her mind, Eden's eyelids lifted. Grandmother had not questioned the truth of what she had been told . . . but had doubt been there all the time? Had she thought her granddaughter to do something of which she was ashamed?

'But I didn't, Gran!' In the quiet solitude of her bedroom, the words whispered out as they had so very many times before. 'I didn't do it, Gran . . . I didn't do it!'

16

Lenor Medwin was buried. The service had been lavish, the floral tributes opulent, the mourners expressing their sympathy to the widower. But was that sympathy misplaced?

Ava laid aside the newspaper in which the whole episode was reported. She had watched Arthur Medwin closely from behind her fine chiffon mourning veil. True, there had been no smile, no indication of anything but sadness at the loss of his wife . . . yet, regardless of the outer display, she had sensed a relief, a liberation. Lenor had said she had enjoyed little satisfaction from her husband, that he did not give the delectation or the gratification she enjoyed from brushing the muff . . . Could it be Arthur Medwin also had a penchant for playing the other end of the field? Were his own preferences those of homosexuality . . . did Arthur Medwin's choice of a lover take the form of a man?

'Excuse me, mum, young Alfred be asking could he 'ave a word with you.'

She had known this would come. Alfred Birks and that personal maid of Lenor's had lost the chance of getting money from that quarter, but they still had another. They knew the identity of Lenor's female lover, knew she would not chance their speaking out; they realised the fruits of blackmail were theirs for the taking and they meant to reap the harvest sooner rather than later.

Her expression showing none of this, Ava nodded.

Reaching again for the newspaper, she made a pretence of reading it when, moments later, Alfred Birks was shown into the room with a warning 'not to go tekin' too much of the mistress's time'.

'There be no need.' The answer followed the closing of the sitting-room door behind the departing cook.

'What I 'ave to say will tek no more than a couple of minutes.'

'Then you had best say it,' Ava replied coolly.

'Ar, I will.' Alfred Birks smirked. 'An' it be this. I knows the things you an' Lenor Medwin got up to in this house and hers, I knows all about the filthy games you played an', lessen you wants the whole town to hear of them you'll pay me to 'old my tongue.'

Folding the newspaper with slow deliberate movements before laying it again beside her on the silk covered couch, Ava looked up. 'I see, and what is your "holding your tongue" going to cost?'

The savour of victory already sweet in his throat, Alfred spoke quickly. 'Five 'undred . . . five 'undred pounds an' that be it, you won't never hear from me no more.'

'Five hundred!' The gasp also was pretence. She

had known he would come and she had known what he would demand and she had also guessed the price would cover the loss of money he had hoped to come from Lenor.

'Be little enough for a lifetime of silence.'

Silence! Ava's thoughts were acid. A silence which would last only as long as the money did and then he would be back for more. Aloud she said, 'I do not keep such sums in the house, I shall need time to get it.'

'Third pew of the parish church, nine o'clock Saturday evening or else I tells what I knows!'

That, too, she had expected, a repetition of what had been written in the note she herself had destroyed, except that the ransom of silence had increased.

At her nod he turned, then paused as she spoke again, her voice cold and ice-bound as her eyes.

'Mister Birks . . . as from this moment you are no longer in my employ. You will be gone from Moorcroft in one hour.'

Gone . . . yes, he would be gone, but not far. Ava stared at the door which had closed behind the departing Birks. He would not forego what he must clearly see as a life which held no more need of labour . . . He would return . . . and so would his demand for money.

'You be sure you be up to bein' left?'

The woman who had slept the night in the cottage looked keenly at Eden, at the shadows below the eyes

which said the girl had slept badly. Living alone was
not good for a wench of such tender years but, judging
by the look on the face of the man who had brought
her here last evening, there was no need of her being
alone.

'I am quite sure, thank you, and thank you for
staying here.'

'I'd stay longer were the choice my own, but if the
cargo don't reach where it should when it should then
my man loses the boat . . . and that means no 'ome;
gaffers don't give no mind to whys nor wherefores,
their only thought be the money in their pocket and a
late delivery can 'ave that lessen. That be more'n
reason to take a man's living from him.'

'Of course you must go on. As for my being left
here, that will be only long enough to put everything
as I found it.'

'You don't be stoppin'?'

'No.' Eden met the surprised glance. She could tell
the woman the reason she must leave, that every
penny except for the shilling set aside in payment for
using this house, was gone. She must move on or
starve.

'That be a pity. Word was the Shipton place was
same as it 'ad been, an' there be more'n a few boat
families glad to 'ave the hearin'.'

'They thought its owner was returned?'

Glancing to where a man whistled from the narrowboat the woman called her answer as she walked
towards it.

'Weren't that. They knowed it were not Mother Shipton, but they 'oped it were a body would carry on the same and this cottage be again a place where a meal could be bought. A boat with no woman aboard counts that a blessing, while others be glad of the chance to buy supplies. But then you knows your own way best . . . though I still thinks your leavin' be a pity!'

Lifting a hand in answer to a wave from two children, Eden watched the horse-drawn boat glide slowly away. Turning, she let her gaze drift over the small house. Spring flowers studded the tiny patch of garden gleaming like jewels in the morning sun while windows, freed of their shutters, seemed to smile at their reflection shining on water that lay like a ribbon of satin. This house had welcomed her, she had felt the warmth of it seep into her . . . it would break her heart to leave.

'*A place where a meal could be bought . . .*'

The words echoed like the house itself shouted them.

'*Counts that a blessing.*'

Was this her own blessing? Was she being given a second chance? Perhaps . . . but could she accept it?

Indoors once more, Eden asked herself the question again. Could she remain here on the chance of the boat people buying her cooking?

'Me father says to ask will you put a meal for two in this along wi' a loaf of bread? 'E says do this be enough to pay forrit?'

Standing in the open doorway of the cottage,

sunshine a nimbus at his back, a lad clutched a cap in one hand while the other held a coin which glinted on his coal-blackened palm.

A smile welling deep inside, Eden took the metal billy can and filled it with broth.

Her question had been answered.

'You are the young man whose mother brought me in from the snowstorm.' He was also the same one who had sent her on what he had known would be a wild goose chase!

Leaning nonchalantly against the gate of Shipton cottage, a sandy-haired lad smiled. 'The same, but afore you rips me off for what I done that day let me say I'm sorry, it won't never 'appen again.'

Maybe not, but only if she did not give him the chance. Eden remained wary.

Recognising the distrust made plain in the giving of no reply, the lad's smile broke afresh. 'That be the honest truth. I 'ave more sense than go against word given to Mister Denby.'

'Mister Denby? Who is he and what does he have to do with your being here?'

'You knows 'im, he be the same as walked you from The Coppice an evenin' back. Said he wanted somebody he could trust . . . an' that somebody be me.'

He straightened as he said it, a tug at his jacket an indication of pride. He was taller than she remembered, stronger looking, the glint of pride adding tangibly to his stature.

The stranger on the bridge, a man she had met several times since, but who had not given his name . . . why would he send a lad here?

'I don't understand.' Eden's brow creased. 'Why should this . . . this Mister Denby send you here?'

'To walk you to and from that house along of The Coppice. Says to be here at this time every evenin' and not to leave your side 'til you be back safe in your 'ome.'

How dare he! How dare that man presume! Vexation rising hotly, the crease on Eden's brow deepened. Words rattling like hailstones, she returned, 'I have no need of an escort! You will kindly go back to your Mister Denby and tell him so!'

'I'll do that, miss, tell him what you says, but not 'til I've done what were told me to do.'

'But I don't want you to walk with me!'

'So I understands, but then I don't relish goin' against anythin' Andrew Denby tells to do, nor would anybody else if they knows what be good for 'em.'

Was that a warning for herself? Irritation a flare in her eyes, Eden made to answer but the lad's words came before she could.

'I'll be no trouble to you. I won't even speak unless you asks it, that be a promise, only don't refuse . . . for Mister Denby . . . well, he be payin' good. It be more'n I can earn in a whole day along of Wednesbury. Them there carters pays no more'n a copper or two, no matter the load to be shifted.'

Wednesbury! In an instant Eden was in the market

place, a small child holding her grandmother's skirts while she haggled the price of an already worn-through coat, small feet tapping the setts as she followed to The Shambles where the bargaining was repeated, Grandmother complaining a breast of lamb or a knuckle end of pork be far too costly, standing resolutely until it was reduced to suit her purse. Memory a living ache, a pain that tore her heart, Eden's irritation died.

Wednesbury held no easy living for folk of her walk in life, nor would it for this lad and his mother; they would earn their bread like the people she had lived among from childhood, the families herded together in so many tiny houses, so many narrow streets, each man and woman, so many sons and daughters, all labouring dawn to dusk in order to live.

'I be sorry for misleadin' you the way I did, truly I be. Please miss, say you'll let me walk along of you, the money will be of great help to me mother.'

Drawn from the tide of memory threatening to swamp her, Eden caught the look in those brown eyes. No longer the brightness of mischief, the twinkle of roguishness; what they held now was a plea, the hope behind it burning like a flame . . . a hope she could not deny. She had once thought opportunity might come by which she could repay the kindness of Sara Melia; this, it seemed, could be that opportunity.

'Five 'undred pounds!' Alfred Birks caught his accomplice in his arms. 'Five 'undred and not even the makings of a protest. That were something I 'adn't expected. To agree to pay what were asked an' no bones made!'

'Ava Russell said her would pay?' The late Lenor Medwin's maid freed herself from the hug.

'Couldn't say otherwise.' Shifty eyes gleamed. 'Her knowed I holds the upper hand, that should I speak of her carryin's on, then her would be finished, not only in Wednesbury but everywhere's else; brushin' the muff don't go down well with any sort 'cept them as plays it! 'ere! Does you dip your fingers?'

Laughing at her outraged gasp, Alfred caught the girl to him, his hands clasping her buttocks.

'But you don't needs to, you gets plenty of the other. Alfred Birks be generous with what nature give 'im.'

'Just so long as he be generous with me and no other girl.'

'You don't share with anybody.' Alfred kissed the panting lips. 'What be in my trousers be for you . . . in fact I be goin' to give you a little bit of it right now.'

'No!' The girl giggled as he caught her hand. 'I can't, I'm supposed to be sortin' the mistress's things.'

'You'll like sortin' this better.' Pressing the hand he held in his close up against his crotch, he laughed again, a thick throaty sound that stayed in the mouth.

The girl beneath him in the stable loft, her breasts bare and her legs spread wide, Alfred felt his hard flesh jerk. His generous endowment was all hers . . . until inclination proved otherwise!

She was a fool! Lust satisfied, Alfred watched the

girl skip across the large cobbled yard then disappear into the kitchen of the imposing house. She was a fool to believe herself the only wench to savour the delights of Alfred Birks, and she was an even bigger fool to believe he would share any part of that five hundred pounds with her. True, he had enjoyed what she had given so often, enjoyed the feel of her body beneath his; but five hundred pounds would buy him many more . . . and not one to hold a threat over his head.

Slipping from the stable, checking there was no one around to see him leave, he ran for the cover of a nearby copse. Resting a moment among the trees he breathed hard. He had thought long on that problem. It was the one flaw, the one crack which could have the whole plan collapse. He had tried telling himself it would not happen, that she would be too afraid to disclose the part she had played in blackmailing Ava Russell, but something at the back of his mind had warned him otherwise, something he had heard but could not quite remember . . . something about 'a woman scorned'.

Leaving the shelter of the trees, his breathing level and even, he crossed the wide expanse of ground lying to the rear of the Medwin house. Going by way of the front approach was too risky, there were still visitors coming to give their condolences to the distraught widower, visitors who might just wonder what an all too obvious servant was doing walking along the main drive.

Distraught widower! He snorted softly as he came

on to Hall End following the road to where it joined Ethelfleda Terrace. If that maid were to be believed, and there were no reason of her not being, then Arthur Medwin were no more distraught than Alfred Birks would be when his present titillating partner was removed. And she would have to be.

Away to his left the clock of the parish church of Saint Bartholomew rang nine times. Glancing at the spire, no blacker against the night sky than it was in the light of day, Alfred smiled. It would be there in the place he had specified. Ava Russell would not chance the world learning of her dirty game; it would be there, all five hundred, and soon it would be in his pocket.

'Give an old soldier tuppence for a bite o' bread . . .'

From a narrow alley a cracked voice called from darkness the moon did not penetrate. That way lay Trouse Lane and a few yards from where he stood now those few stone steps locally called the Church Steps.

A beggar! Alfred made to go on his way, then paused. In less than two minutes he would be a rich man, he would be well able to toss tuppence to an old man . . . In fact he would be well able to afford a lot more.

'Wait you there, old 'un.' He grinned in the direction of a bent figure hobbling from the gloom, a stick tap-tapping on the ground. 'Wait you against the Church Steps. I'll be passing that way in a minute or so an' I promises you'll 'ave more than enough to buy yourself a bite. You will 'ave enough for a whole bloody meal with money left over to buy the same for a couple of weeks.'

The beggar's grin expanded by the murmured, 'God bless you sir, God bless you,' Alfred glanced once more along the rise of the hill to the spire rising against the sky.

17

The shilling the boatman had paid for the broth she had ladled into that billy can (together with a loaf of bread and several slices of beef cheek she had pressed the day before) had bought enough ingredients to make more broth, and some faggots that she could team with the quart of blue peas.

Blue peas! Eden mused over the term. She had often asked why they were called blue when in fact they were a greyish green, and always Grandmother had clucked sharply, ''cos that be what folks calls 'em, an' that be all about it!'

Myra and she had shared knowing looks when answered in that testy 'don't bother me now, child' fashion; yet they had not dared to voice the suspicion each guessed niggled in the mind of the other, the incredibly wicked supposition that Gran was not the holder of all knowledge. It had been one of childhood's fantasies that Grandmother was the very font of wisdom, one she and Myra had not held quite so true once they had left those childhood years behind; yet even so they both held that recognition to themselves.

'Following your usual occupation, I see.'

Startled by the quietly spoken interruption, Eden clutched the provisions she had parcelled into her shawl.

'Daydreaming. You really ought not to indulge whilst walking alongside a canal.'

'So you have said ... several times!' The first element of surprise faded, Eden snapped tartly.

'So why is it you continue to do it?'

The groceries seeming suddenly to weigh more heavily in her arms, Eden felt herself flush beneath a startlingly clear gaze. How did this man always manage to come upon her when her mind was a thousand miles away? Holding tight to it now, refusing to let it wander an inch, she answered in that same acid tone.

'Because it pleases me to do so, almost as much as it would please me not to have you continue to give what I have previously pointed out to be most unwanted advice. In short I wish you to ... to ...'

'Keep my nose out of your business! Is that the phrase you were looking for?'

'Exactly!' Eden hitched the parcel-filled shawl higher in her arms.

Inches above her head, sable eyes echoed the smile curving a sensuous mouth. 'I don't think I can do that ... at least, not before I am absolutely sure you have learned those lessons needed to be learned by all folk living on or beside the canals.'

'Or those walking the path to The Coppice!' Eden hitched the shawl again. 'Tell me ... what is it has you thinking I am not capable of seeing to my own safety?'

As if wiped by an unseen hand the smile vanished leaving eyes and mouth chiselled granite. 'Haven't you had proof of that already? Is it going to take yet another attack . . . yet another man's lust to convince you? We are not living in Paradise! The quicker you get that into your head the better!'

The flush which, until that moment, had tinged her cheeks pink, now flamed scarlet. She shrivelled inside with each memory of that attack, memory which always left the questions: Did her rescuer think she was a willing partner in the scene he had come across? Did he think her guilty of such obscene behaviour?

'Give me that before you drop it!'

Hands brusque as the voice took the bundle from her, holding it easily in one arm whilst the other propelled her forward.

Inside the cottage Eden had made her home, the bundle of provisions lowered to the table, his eyes locked once more with hers.

'I advise . . . no, I *suggest* you remain more aware when out walking . . . leave your dreaming until you are in your bed.'

Colour gone now from her face, Eden held the tenebrous stare. Growing up in Hobbins Street, among the rough and tumble of neighbours' children who, from the earliest age, were taught to stand on their own feet had taught her the same. Now the defiance she had so often shown to those boys who thought to play the bully stirred in her as she replied quietly.

'Thank you, Mister Denby . . . it is Mister Denby, is it not? Thank you for your suggestion; now, *I* suggest . . . no, I *require* you no longer send the Melia boy to walk with me to The Coppice.'

Would he argue with her, raise a threatening hand as those childhood adversaries had done? Eden dismissed the thought with speed. They were not children to squabble and fight, but the slight tightening of the mouth said plainly that the man watching her was not one to negotiate terms.

'Forgive me, Miss Brent . . .'

Eden's senses quickened. How did he know her name?

'. . . Davy Melia furnished me with your name, as no doubt he gave mine to you . . .' he paused, a hint of amusement rising behind his dark stare, '. . . the lad is quite communicative; however, to your requirement . . . I regret I cannot agree to it.'

'Then I will pay him myself.'

The intimated smile died instantly, leaving a stone-hard glare matching the hardness of his voice. 'Davy Melia, as is his mother, is in my employ. Whilst that situation remains, he will do as I instruct. However, should you prefer the services of both be terminated then that is something I can agree upon.'

It was a threat, much more refined than those made by childhood protagonists but, nevertheless, a threat. There was no question he was well aware her circumstances were not such she could reimburse the Melias' loss of income. Andrew Denby was not so different after all; he was determined on his way every bit as much as the Hobbins Street boys had been.

'Well!'

It was a strident, unequivocal demand. To refuse would bring hardship to a woman who had helped her; that was something she could not do. Using every reserve of dignity, though the spark of rebellion still flared, Eden nodded acceptance.

'Eh, mum, it be a terrible shock an' no denyin'.'

Ava Russell reached for the newspaper held out by a weeping cook. 'I couldn't help seeing,' the woman raised a corner of a spotless apron to dab red eyes, 'I couldn't help but see, what with it bein' right on the front page. Oh, it be terrible! Who could 'ave done such a wicked thing, who? I mean he were a good lad. Why it be our Alfred, Alfred Birks?' Behind the apron, buxom breasts heaved again.

'So what has he been up to should cause so much grief?'

The apron lowered with a swish. 'T'ain't so much what he's been up to as what somebody else been up to.'

'Then what is it someone else has been up to?'

'Murder!' The word hiccuped behind a fresh torrent of tears. 'Murder be what's been up to. Found with his chest stabbed and throat cut across, poor little bugger; wouldn't harm a fly, wouldn't Alfred Birks, nor never do nobody a bad turn.'

Not unless it resulted in doing himself a good one!

Ava left the newspaper folded on her knee, the glance she now gave her cook that of disbelief. 'That is absurd! You have made some mistake . . . no one would want to murder Alfred Birks!'

'Want to or no, that be what somebody been gone and done . . . ain't no mistake, as you'll see yourself when you reads the paper. It be young Alfred Birks, an' him with his throat an' chest cut through. Be like them murders along o' London, p'raps it be the same killer come to our streets.'

'Now, that is enough of such talk,' Ava said as the apron flapped up again. 'For all we know the newspaper could be quite wrong in its report . . . it certainly would not be the first time.'

'But, mum . . .'

'No!' Ava's customary snap served to halt her cook's sniffled reply.

'If it should be as you fear, then no doubt we will be informed by the constabulary; until then, I expect you to attend to your duties as normal.'

Alfred Birks dead! But had the victim, a man killed by foul means, been positively identified as Birks? Polly Jupp seemed convinced; but then her cook was hardly someone to seek fact over gossip. Taking up the newspaper, Ava glanced at the heavier black heading of a column halfway down the front page.

'*Body Found Slashed*!'

Polly Jupp was right so far, how much more of the woman's snivelled story would prove the same? If it *all* did, if it *was* Birks who had been found dead, then two obstacles to her continued social standing had been removed; first Lenor Medwin and now Alfred Birks . . . both a threat . . . both gone. Drawing a deep breath, she took up the newspaper.

'. . . *the body found beside a small flight of steps midway between Trouse Lane and Church Street was identified as being that of a Mister Alfred Birks* . . .'

Ava's pent-up breath escaped slowly. Birks was dead. She was free of him and of his blackmail. Fate had favoured Ava Russell. Now, if only it would reveal to her where Myra Brent was to be found.

Myra Brent! She thrust the newspaper aside. That fool Birks! She had sent him to the grandmother's house; she had phrased her own conversation with him in such a vein that he would think her concerned for the wellbeing of the girl; surely he would have enquired of his acquaintances! But if he had, he had said nothing of it to her and, if he had brought word to Polly Jupp, then the woman would have said so.

Two people who could betray her no longer lived. Ava's fingers curled into her palms. But another most probably was alive, and that probability spelled danger. She was not completely rid of the threat of exposure. What benefit was there in two sources of jeopardy being removed while one even greater hazard remained!

Rising to her feet and walking to the window, Ava glanced to where a corner of the stable block showed above the screening tiles.

Birks! Her brain spat the name acidly. The dung the

man shovelled from the stables had been of more use! He had failed to find Myra Brent but the hunt would not end with his death. It would go on. Her missing maid would be found and, when she was, then the threat to her mistress's secret would indeed be over!

She had agreed. It had been achieved only under pressure . . . his pressure.

Andrew Denby's long strides carried him swiftly past workmen hammering and sawing, men who worked for him every one of whom had a word of greeting.

'There be a request for carriage of a shipment from the Moxley Iron Works up to the India docks along of London.' A heavily starched winged collar seeming to support a whiskered face, the clerk of Denby Boat Builders handed a sheet of paper to his employer.

'Will you be requiring me to write that we can't oblige?' The clerk fingered the pencil permanently lodged behind his right ear.

'Turning custom away does not make good business.' Andrew glanced at the clerk. 'Are you absolutely sure we can't handle the Moxley freight?'

Removing the pencil and running the tip over a list of names written neatly in a black-bound ledger, the whiskered man took a moment to answer. 'There be no boat standin' in the basin, and them as makes the London run don't be due back afore Wednesday next.'

'Isn't *Midland Queen* due in today?'

It was a question that had not needed to be answered.

Andrew Denby knew the times of arrival and departure of every one of the boats he owned as well as the weight and content of cargo, but dutifully the man again touched pencil to ledger.

'Ar,' he nodded, still with his eyes on the page, 'the *Midland Queen*, her be due t'other side o'midday.'

'She will be here an hour before that. I passed her as I came along the towpath. Her skipper is a good boatman and not unfamiliar with the London run, he did it many times for my father. Ask would he take the Moxley iron . . .' he smiled as the clerk looked up, 'be sure to tell him it is a request.'

'He'll know that for 'imself, all the bargemen as works for you knows they don't never be ordered.'

'Then assure him also my request does not come without a token of gratitude . . . the pay for that run will be doubled.'

Yes, the cut folk in Andrew Denby's employ knew their master for his fairness in his dealings with them. They also knew he had taken more often to walking to the boatyard or the basin, and that had them asking why? The question in his own mind, the clerk returned to the outer office unaware the same question played in the mind of his employer.

He had used the threat of withdrawing employment from young Davy Melia and from his mother, used it as a means of extracting an agreement from a young woman he scarcely knew and with whom the few dozen words exchanged had been less than friendly. His head resting against the high-backed leather chair,

Andrew Denby ran a hand through thick dark hair. Why had he engaged in such tactics, why use other people in order to get one young woman to agree to his proposals? It was a practice entirely foreign to him . . . but then so was wrestling to keep thoughts of her from creeping into his mind during waking hours as well as before falling asleep at night.

She had been caught in that last vicious swipe of winter, had lain down during that snowstorm then found and given shelter by the Melias. Apart from her name that was all he knew with any certainty. He had guessed she was running from something . . . maybe someone, but that was only a guess.

Fingers resting on his head, he stared at the picture forming across his vision: the picture of a shawl-wrapped figure huddled against the wall of bridge spanning the waters of the canal. She had seemed so fragile beneath that shawl, so vulnerable, half-frozen and blue with cold, yet she had found enough inner fire to argue with him . . . and resolve to make her own way. Staying alone in that canalside cottage proved the courage of that; not many young women he knew would be prepared to live that way.

But she was like no other woman of his acquaintance. There was no air of affectation about her, no coy smiles or exaggerated helplessness, no feminine wiles; so what attracted him so that he often walked between his business at Willingsworth and that at Gospel Oak . . . and why come by way of the towpath or past the grounds of The Coppice? Lowering his hand, he breathed out slowly. Why ask questions he already knew the answer to!

'*Ar, Mister Denby, I knows Shipton Cottage.*'

Davy Melia was young, but life had equipped him with a sharp brain and a nose which could smell a sixpence were it buried in a midden. He had carried out the task assigned him and reported.

'*. . . it be the same wench took up livin' in old mother Shipton's place, the one Mother and me found lyin' out on the 'eath. Near enough froze her were. Her name be Eden Brent, but that be all Mother told.*'

Pictures fading, Andrew Denby reached for the pen set on a brass inkstand but still his brain would not free him.

'*That be all Mother told . . .*'

The phrase had played many times since his first hearing it and it repeated now. Could it be that the lad's mother knew more? Did she perhaps know where the girl in the snow had come from, what she was running from? He could ask, he could even order Sara Melia to divulge any other item of information she might have gleaned regarding Eden Brent, even threaten . . . but no more of threats! Mind snapping shut at the thought, he dipped pen nib into the ink.

Whatever he may learn of that girl it would not be at the expense of anyone's peace of mind.

18

The fry – liver, heart and kidney – she had purchased from the abattoir that morning was almost cooked. Bringing it from the oven, setting the hot dish on a cloth protecting the table she scrubbed twice every day, Eden strained the diced meat. Setting the gravy aside she mixed freshly boiled onion with a slice of bread broken into small pieces. What more had her grandmother added when cooking faggots? Touching her hot cheek with the back of her hand, she glanced beyond the unshuttered window to where a narrow-boat was mooring. Shipton Cottage was becoming a regular stopover for ever more barge people and the food they bought there received high praise, especially the dish she was preparing now.

'*That always be supposin' it ever does get done!*'

The admonition given two little girls 'helping' with grandmother's preparing of a meal sounding in her mind, Eden returned her attention to the table.

She added a sprinkling of sage and a couple of bay leaves taken from the tiny rear garden to the bread and onion and seasoned the whole with salt and pepper. Then, adding the meat, minced the whole together before fashioning it into palm-sized balls. Now came the part Grandmother forbade tiny hands from touching. She and Myra had stood, noses almost touching the table, fascinated as the kell, the delicate lace-like lining of a pig's stomach bought with the fry, was wrapped around the balls of meat. Smiling to herself, Eden carried out the procedure allowed her in later years then, faggots set in neat rows in the large roasting pan, placed them in the oven.

Straightening, Eden glanced about the room. In reality it wasn't so very different to the house in Hobbins Street, a living-room that must also serve as kitchen, a scullery leading to an outhouse and privy while upstairs held two bedrooms. But outside could be a world far removed from that she had known, that world of narrow streets their houses cheek by jowl with foundries . . . those endless foundries and workshops that belched their black streams of smoke over Wednesbury. Surrounded by open heath, the canal a silent highway, Shipton Cottage was a haven of quiet peace.

If only Myra were with her. Unbidden, the thought slipped into Eden's mind and, for a moment, she allowed it to play freely. They would have shared the work of cooking, enjoyed the pleasant moments of conversation with passing boat people . . . But she must not dwell on what might have been, those were dreams she should not harbour. Myra had left the life they had once shared, she had chosen a home very different to the one given by their grandmother, chosen a new life with new friends. It was what she so obviously wanted; freedom from the drudgery of Hobbins Street, from that tiny house . . . But, freedom from her sister? Yes, that slap had said as much.

A tap at the door recalling her attention, she opened it to a smiling Davy Melia.

'Eh, that smell be a banquet on its own, it be waftin' all along the towpath, fair makes the mouth water. Be faggots or my name don't be Davy Melia.'

A smile touching her own mouth Eden nodded. 'You have the nose of a gourmet.'

A hand brushing vigorously over his face, the lad looked crestfallen. 'I . . . I washed afore I come, me mother says to always wash afore comin'.'

Now *she* was embarrassed; he thought the words she had used meant he had a dirty face. Apology bright in her eyes as it was quick to her tongue, she explained the term she had used.

'I ain't never 'eard no such word, but if it means as you says it do, that I be an excellent judge of food, then I reckons I be a . . . a . . . a what you said.'

'Then I think we should put you to the test.' Reaching a plate from the dresser, Eden spooned a faggot from a batch taken earlier from the oven. Covering it with rich gravy she handed it to the watching Davy.

'I thought never to taste cooking the equal to me mother's,' he said, a forkful of the savoury meat already in his mouth, 'but yours be; no wonder the cut folk be talkin' of it the way they do.'

'Well you had best stop talking until your mouth is empty. Your mother will be asking where it is you learned such a habit.'

A grin his answer, the lad gave all his concentration to his plate.

She had grown very fond of Davy Melia. His company, and his flow of gossip picked up in the town, were like sunshine after rain; they refreshed and warmed her mind. Washing the utensils of her cooking, she nodded as he brought his empty plate then asked could he dry for her. This was how she thought Myra. . .

Refusing to let the thought linger, she removed her apron as they both returned to the living-room.

'I takes it you be goin' along of The Coppice.' He watched her wrap a dish in a clean white cloth. 'Why is it you goes there every evenin'? T'ain't as though that old man be pleased of seein' you . . . leastways he don't show it. Be he some relation?'

'No.' Eden shook her head. 'He is no relation.'

'Then why . . . I means, why bother? He be a grumpy old bug . . .'

'That is one more thing you are going to have to watch! Let your mother hear that kind of language and she will . . .'

'Tan me hide!'

'Until your backside bears a very good imitation of leather.'

Her reply bringing a grin as wide as his face, he took the dish she had wrapped. Leading the way from the house, he waited while she placed a broom diagonally across the doorway indicating temporary absence, then fell into step beside her.

Easy in her company, he walked a while in silence but his mind continued to question. If the old man were no relative then why these visits? Why take him food that were never paid for, not even with a smile or a thank you? Words bubbled from brain to tongue and slipped from his lips.

'Payment is not important.' Eden answered the impromptu question. 'A smile or a word would be nice, I admit, but it is not necessary. I will go to that gate so long as I live in Shipton Cottage, and I will continue to offer food. He may not eat it, but that also is of no consequence.'

'The man might be old . . . and mean-tempered he certainly is . . . but I reckons him not fool enough to be throwin' away what you brings.'

'Perhaps.'

Flicking a pebble with the side of his boot, Davy watched it curve out over the water then drop, spreading widening circles on its smooth surface. 'Ain't no p'raps about it, but what do you mean when you says his lack of thanks be not necessary, and not eatin' what you brings of no consequence?'

Were the questions put by the man paying this lad to walk at her side would she answer so readily? Knowing she would not, Eden nevertheless replied. 'I do what I do because I feel the man is lonely . . . that it is a broken heart responsible for what some see as churlish behaviour. He is full of sadness. The beautiful house he may watch over has an air of that same unhappiness, of despair. I think he may have suffered a loss great as my . . .'

Was she about to say a loss great as her own? Glancing sideways, Davy saw the quiver of Eden's mouth, her fingers draw the shawl closer as if shutting out some unwanted intrusion. Each evening of walking with her he had wanted to ask what had brought her to live by herself. What was it caused the look he some-times caught on her face? A look which said she had lost her world.

The words formed in his brain but, as on every other evening, that was where they remained. 'Ask naught that be no concern of your'n,' was his mother's counsel. 'Ask no question and you'll be told no lie.'

Glancing again at a face he thought prettier than that of any wench he saw in Wednesbury, Davy Melia's lips closed.

He would ask no question . . . but that was not from thinking Eden Brent would lie; it was because . . . because of what?

Colour rising in his cheeks, he turned his gaze to the placid waters of the canal.

The problem of Alfred Birks was removed, there would be no more ransom of silence . . . not unless that maid of Lenor's . . . but she would not dare!

Secure in the thought, Ava Russell allowed herself a smile then dismissed it as a tap to the sitting-room door heralded her cook. It had been several days since the finding of Birks' dead body and still she snivelled. Not on account of sorrow! Ava's lips firmed. The woman was not the heartbroken friend she pretended; she was simply enjoying the drama.

'Be a police hinspector asking of seeing you, mum.' It was followed by the loud sniff Ava had expected. 'Will I tell you be home?'

The police! Ava's brows drew together. Why would a policeman call at this hour?

'I will try to be brief as I can, ma'am, but questions must be asked . . . you understand.'

Polite, but by no means servile! This man would not be dismissed as would any servant. Ava glanced at the accompanying uniformed constable standing just within the door, a pencil poised over a notebook.

Ava indicated a chair and, when the inspector was seated, asked, 'Questions . . . to what purpose?'

'The death of a Mister Alfred Birks. I trust you have heard of it.'

'Of little else from my cook these few days. She has been quite upset by it all.'

'Understandable, ma'am, understandable.'

'Quite.' Ava nodded. 'But your coming to this house is not, so why are you here?'

'Corroboration, ma'am, corroboration. We has to be certain facts, as we have them, be correct. Your cook tells me the deceased worked here as groom and coachman for a number of years.'

'Six,' Ava answered. 'He was hired by my late

husband. His service and manner were always commendable.'

'Tell me if you will, ma'am, the evening of his death . . . had you given permission for him to be free of duty?'

Behind the inspector, the constable touched the tip of the pencil to his tongue. Why all these questions . . . did these people think she had murdered Birks! Keeping the fire of irritation doused beneath a frigid tone, Ava replied evenly.

'As a widow I rarely have need of my carriage in the evenings, Inspector; an annual charity event, midnight mass on Christmas Eve, but very rarely more so, unless directed otherwise, my groom had permission to spend his evenings as he would.'

'My thanks, ma'am.' The inspector rose. 'That be all I needs to ask. I hope it hasn' t been too painful. You won't be troubled again.'

She would not be troubled again! The policemen departed, Ava smiled, the pleasure inside her warm and voluptuous. That inspector could not know how true his words were; she would not be troubled again, her dirty little blackmailer was gone.

'It be the same one, I be certain of it, the newspaper said he were groom along of Moorcroft an' that be the name of the 'ouse he said were his place of service.'

'I don't care to know his place of service, same as I don't want you to speak of what you 'eard being talked of. You keep your mouth closed, Davy Melia, the dead be dead an' they be best left to lie in peace.'

'But . . .'

'But nothing!' Sara Melia's lined face showed a new source of worry as she rounded sharply on her son. 'You don't be a babby no more, you knows well the consequence of owning to knowin' or even hearing of a man killed in the street. It would have them constables afetching you to the station for to answer questions and only the Lord hisself knowing how long that would take or the results of it. Some things have a funny way of turning out. What be thought of as helping has a way of bouncing so it hits you on the head. You owns to knowing anything and it could be *you* gets the blame . . . you be the one landed in court on a charge of murder.'

'That couldn't never 'appen, the police . . .'

'The police needs to be seen to 'ave done what they gets paid to do!' Sara cut short her son's response. 'They needs to reassure folk they be safe and there be no more danger lurking the streets, that the killer be caught . . . and if they can't do it one way then chance be they'll do it another. That be one chance I won't have you take . . . you hear me, Davy, I won't have you take no chance!'

He had promised. Heaving the last of six dozen crates of soap and candles on to a wagon, Davy stood to catch his breath. His mother was mistaken in her claims but, even so, he had promised to say nothing of what he had heard that evening of a man asking questions regarding a woman. The Green Dragon was not a place his mother would approve of but the landlord allowed him to stand inside the taproom while nights were cold, and it had been chilly that night.

'*My sister, her run away from home . . .*'

The words had caught his ear and he had looked to where a younger man sat talking with another he had recognised as a carter who sometimes gave him work. Hoping that might have been the case that night, he had edged closer. The carter had given a ride to a woman, but she had given no name.

The younger man had seemed riled by the answer . . . a young man whose description seemed to match that given in the newspaper. But wenches often run away and it were natural a brother should be seeking her . . . so why was it the more he thought about what he had seen and heard the less natural the younger man's behaviour had appeared?

'Be you finished, young 'un?'

The shout bringing his mind to the present, Davy jumped from the cart, surprise having him almost miss his footing as he landed. The owner of the wagon and the carter in the Green Dragon were one and the same.

'Bit of a to-do along of Church Street the other night, so I hears.' The man wiped the remains of his breakfast from his whiskers with a brightly spotted cloth. 'Fella done in wi'a knife . . . what be the world comin' to?'

His mother had voiced the same. Davy watched the wagon's owner bring several coins from a pocket, fingering through them and selecting two.

'There ya go, young 'un,' he flipped the coins,

'reckon that bloke were done in for his money for talk hereabout. Reckons there were none in his pockets when he were found . . . but then what some don't know for sure they invents. As for meself I be certain he had a bob or two more'n he paid for ale.'

'You knowed him then!'

'Not personal.' The man heaved himself to the driving seat, gathering the reins in weathered hands. 'But I seen his picture in the paper, it were a face I'd seen afore . . . that I would stake a sovereign on! Asked me right there,' he tipped his head towards the tall cream-coloured building, one wall emblazoned with the name, Green Dragon, 'asked 'ad I given a ride to a young wench some time back, seemed 'er were runnin' from 'ome. I told him I 'ad . . . but it cost him two tankards of ale and a shillin' beside.'

A young wench . . . runnin' from 'ome.

The coins he had caught dug into Davy's palms as his hands closed tight. Eden Brent had been running from something, could she have been fleeing from home? Was the man found with his chest and throat slit Eden Brent's brother!

19

There was no place left to enquire. Myra eased off her boots, grimacing with pain. The soles were almost non-existent, worn away by the hours of tramping the streets asking if anyone had seen Eden. She could well have been asking had they seen the Queen, for their answer would have been the same.

She had hoped this town might hold her sister, that if she searched hard enough she would find her. But all of the searching, all of the praying, had been to no avail. Eden was not in Darlaston, she couldn't be; otherwise someone somewhere would have known of it, told where she could be located. But there had been nothing, not one single word of hope.

Boots laid aside, she glanced at the grate set with coal and sticks, at the kettle hung on a bracket. She could light the fire, make herself a hot drink . . . but the time spent on doing was time she could not spare. Forcing herself to her feet, wincing at the sting shooting through them, she went into the scullery. It was already dark, the sun having gone down well before her return to Bell Street, but she ignored the candle. Rinsing her hands in cold water she returned to the living-room, the dampness of its walls thick in her nostrils.

Lighting the lamp, she placed a clean cloth across her knees to ensure the pale lemon silk for a blouse did not become marked, she threaded a needle. The lease she had taken on this house was up. She had tried to save enough money to renew it but had failed. Tomorrow she would return the key to the estate agent and take her finished needlework to the dressmaker. The money earned would feed her for a few days, a few days more of searching.

But in which town? She held the delicate cloth closer to the lamp, blinking as her tired vision blurred needle and stitches. Where could Eden have gone? The answer was anywhere . . . Her sister could have gone to any town. She would have had money with which to purchase a tram ticket, the selling of Grandmother's belongings would have given her that.

A train ticket! The cloth she was working fell from her cold fingers. Trains travelled the length and breadth of the country and Eden could have taken any one of them!

It had been only weeks . . . just weeks since another woman's hands had fondled these breasts, since soft lips had closed over nipples teased to hard points, weeks since gentle fingers had played between wide-spread legs . . . yet it seemed years.

Standing naked before the long mirror of her dressing-room, Ava Russell stroked slowly along her hips and across her stomach, breathing deeply as she cupped each breast.

She had denied herself the pleasure of a lover for what reason . . . respect for Lenor? Hardly that! The thought that Myra Brent would return? But she had known deep down that would not happen.

Releasing her breasts, trailing her hands slowly, voluptuously, over her waist and stomach, breath catching in her throat as her fingers touched the silken bush of pubic hair, Ava smiled at her reflection. The days of denial were ended!

Reaching for clothing laid ready, she dressed languidly, holding drawers several moments below the vee of her legs before drawing them slowly over it. That was the way they would be removed, a woman's lips following their long slow withdrawal.

She could buy a woman of the street; half a crown would have any one of them do what was asked. But women of that calling might be as liberal with their tongues as with the selling of their bodies. She could go to a place where men indulged their sexual excesses whilst believing their wives to know nothing of their fornications; a brothel would doubtless cater for all tastes while being less forthcoming with gossip – the continuance of their business depended upon discretion.

Fastening the buttons of a dove-grey suit, Ava toyed with the idea of visiting such a house of pleasure. She could go to Wolverhampton, Birmingham, any town where she would not be recognised . . . but what would she return with? Prostitutes were not exactly sisters of the church, their faith was not as pure nor their habits as clean, and she was not in the market for a dose of the clap!

Securing a band of black velvet about her left arm, she took up a bonnet circled about with ostrich feathers, then discarded it. Bright colours and feathers would draw attention. Selecting instead a hat of the same grey as her suit, its low crown allowing a fine black silk chenille veil to fall to her chest, she picked up black gloves and bag and took a final look at the result in the mirror.

It would look well her being present at the funeral of Alfred Birks; a caring employer paying respects to a trusted servant. Ava glanced again in the mirror, the veil was an excellent touch . . . it would hide her smiles; and when that delight was over she would go shopping. But the goods she purchased would have no disease, they would not be procured at any street corner or bawdy-house, nor from the school which had furnished her with Myra Brent. Why pay that head-mistress when she could obtain the same merchandise for nothing? The workhouses were full of young girls, any one of whom would gladly exchange that life for one as ladies' maid.

Ashes to ashes . . .

Beside the open grave, a priest, in white lace-trimmed cassock over dark robe, raised a hand in final blessing. Standing a few yards away, Ava silently intoned the irreverent accompaniment heard muttered once in childhood.

. . . *The Lord won't fetch you*
So the Devil must.

'It was good of you to come, ma'am, I know Alfred would have appreciated it.'

Already walking away from the graveside, Ava paused as Lenor's maid caught up with her.

'Who'd have thought,' the girl sniffed, 'who'd have thought such a thing could happen?'

Who indeed? Ava watched the lace-trimmed hand-kerchief lift to dab tear-stained cheeks. No doubt it had belonged to Lenor as had the coat the girl was wearing. But the killing of that man was a blessing for Ava Russell!

'We . . . we was going to wed. Alfred had asked would I wed with him.'

'And what will you do now?' Ava kept her tone sympathetic.

'That be it, ma'am,' the girl sniffed again, 'with the mistress having passed away I no longer be required as ladies' maid so I thought to wed right off, but now with Alfred gone then that be gone with him.'

'Was there no other position for you at the Medwin house?'

'None were vacant, ma'am, 'sides which, the rest of the staff will be finished soon for the master be selling up . . . going to live abroad if what I hears be true. . .'

Arthur Medwin selling up . . . going to live abroad! Ava's interest kindled. Now why was that, do you think? And would the handsome young buck so often seen in his company be going with him?

'. . . the house is almost ready for closing . . . The master couldn't live there with his grief . . . but we will all be living in grief supposing we can't find other employment.'

'You should encounter no difficulty. Your mistress spoke well of you.' Ava watched the priest, the only other attendant at the funeral, walk quickly towards the church.

'That were kind of her, God rest her soul.' The girl crossed herself piously. 'But with her passing quick like her did I be left without statement, and no mistress be like to employ a maid who don't have such; they asks proof of standards.'

The priest had disappeared into the confines of the large soot-covered church. Ava glanced about the enclosed graveyard. Except for herself and the girl it was deserted.

'I see your difficulty,' she answered, her glance returning to the face being dabbed yet again with the lacy handkerchief. 'Without reference a post will be unobtainable. However, I am myself without a personal maid and knowing your late mistress's regard of you I am inclined to offer that position to you, to become permanent only, if after a period of six months, you prove to be satisfactory.'

Cutting off the profuse thanks with a wave of the hand and instructions to come to Moorcroft House the next evening at eight, Ava walked away.

Watching the figure pass beneath the lych-gate the tear-stained face broke into a smile. So, that haughty bitch had seen her difficulty; well, she would soon be seeing her own. She thought the claim made by Alfred Birks had died with him. Walking slowly towards the ancient gate through which so many mourners had passed, the girl's lips moved in a whisper: 'That is where you are wrong, Missis Ava Russell, that is where you are so wrong.'

'I still can't fathom why you bothers wi' the old bug . . .' Davy Melia caught back the word but not the grin, 't'ain't as he appreciates it.'

'We have been over that before and I gave my reasons then.'

'But not to speak a word don't seem natural.'

'*We* speak.' Eden smiled at the strapping lad walking easily beside her. 'We both speak to him, Davy.'

'Good evenin'! Two words! Don't see how you can call that talkin'.'

'It's enough. He knows we go there in friendship and nothing more.'

'Wouldn't get nothin' more of that miserable sod!' Davy Melia's sunny face hardened. 'Mother offered to clean forrim once and he waved his stick at her like her were a burglar. Drove her off with words so harsh her were in tears. I wanted to go break his bloody neck, and I would 'ave had Mother begged me not to. So I made her promise in return, promise that when the cleanin' along of that big house were done her wouldn't call at that cottage nor speak to the man should her see him.'

Surprise overriding a reprimand for his swearing, Eden asked. 'Your mother cleans at The Coppice?'

The dish the old man had placed ready for collection tucked in one arm, Davy reached with the other to pluck a leaf from an overhanging branch.

'Goes in there every few weeks. No real cleanin' . . . I mean scrubbing or the like, ain't nobody to leave footmarks or muck things up . . . Her just has to air the rooms and dust what don't be covered wi' sheets. I went along wi' her once, but not no more . . . It be a miserable place, just like him who thinks he be its guardian!'

'The house is not miserable, it is sad; sad and lonely as the old man, sad as we all become when we are no longer loved—' She broke off abruptly. She had not meant to speak that way, to intimate her own lack of love.

Folding the leaf nimbly between the fingers of his free hand, Davy bit a tiny piece from the central crease then, holding the leaf to his lips, proceeded to blow into it. She hadn't needed to say her were lonely, livin' as her did spoke for itself . . . but her had said 'we' . . . 'we are no longer loved'. That included herself. The rasping whistle of air passing through the tiny hole in the leaf grating on the balmy softness of the evening, Davy let his thoughts run.

Had somebody stopped loving her, was that what she had meant? Was that somebody a man, a boyfriend? A brother! The whistling died suddenly, the broken leaf falling from his fingers. Eden Brent had run from something, that much he was certain of, and the young man he had overheard talking with the carter in the Green Dragon had been asking of a runaway sister. But the newspaper had named the man Birks . . . while Eden . . . but wouldn't using her real name lead to her being found, didn't it make sense to give another?

Walking now in silence, he went over each thought again, his mind searching for points he may have missed yet, as before, it returned to the same final question. Was that murdered man brother to Eden Brent? If so, her had made no mourn of what had happened to him! The thought gripped, holding his brain for several seconds before releasing it to another equally disturbing. Did love between kin die so easily? Did lack of mourning mean Eden no longer held feeling for a brother? He couldn't, he *wouldn't* believe that of her. Davy's defences rose, protecting the girl he had come to like so much. So why had he seen no trace of tears? Unless, of course, Eden did not know of that death? That were the more believable. He had seen no newspaper when calling to walk with her to The Coppice and there were no other way news could travel out to Shipton Cottage . . . but that were wrong! Davy's brain hurled the next thought like a stone . . . that were reckoning without the cut folk!

'You are very quiet, Davy.' Eden broke the silence, glancing at him as she spoke. 'Did I offend you when I spoke of the house being lonely and not miserable? If I did, I'm sorry.'

Sandy hair caught the scarlet rays of a setting sun and gleamed like fire as he shook his head. 'You give no offence.'

'Then you think me silly saying a house can be lonely.'

'I don't think no such thing.'

The answer did not come with his usual laugh. Eden felt the abruptness of it and the fact he did not follow with his usual banter added to a sense of something troubling him. Though what it could be eluded her. About to ask a reason she was prevented by his own question.

Coming to a halt, his face lit by those same scarlet rays, he asked, 'Eden, can I ask somethin'? But afore you answers I 'ave to tell you, there'll be no 'ard feeling on my part should you tell me to stop pokin' me nose . . . That be what Mother would say were her standin' along of us now . . . and like to catch me round the ear to go with it.'

'Well, I will not catch you around the ear,' Eden smiled, 'I don't want another dish dropped – I have broken enough already – so ask what it is you wish to know.'

'I were wonderin' . . .' The words reluctant on his tongue, it seemed he would say no more, then in a torrent they rushed out. 'I 'eard two men talkin', one middle age, the other younger, it were the youngest, he were askin' of a wench run from home, said he were seekin' after her . . . that he were brother to her an' . . . an' I knows you 'ad run from somethin', be it that man? Be he your brother?'

Was that the reason for such unaccustomed silence, the unusual reticence? Eden caught the laugh before it reached her lips but the smile of it remained evident in her reply. 'Davy, I have no brother.'

'Then it don't matter none.'

The words had come with more than a light breath of relief and the grin spreading its width across his pleasant face echoed what she heard. Davy had thought some man to be her brother . . . but why the swift return of spirits on finding he was not? Falling into step beside him as he walked on, Eden waited for some explanation of what it was he had dismissed as of no consequence then, when he reached again for a leaf, folding it as before, she put the question quietly.

'Don't matter none,' he repeated, blowing into the folded leaf. 'Seein' Alfred Birks don't be brother to you, then there be no reason of your mournin' 'im bein' dead.'

Eden jerked to a standstill, her eyes wide as she stared uncomprehending at the lad snipping at the centre of a leaf. 'Alfred? No . . .'

A frown of confusion drawing lines across his brow, Davy watched the inconceivable become the impossible, the nuances of those emotions shadowing that pale face.

'No!' Eden's words were a whisper. 'It can't be true, there has to be some mistake . . . a terrible mistake. Alfred can't be dead!'

Reaching Shipton Cottage Davy settled the shaking Eden into the chair he drew closer to the fire.

The man were not her brother.

Swinging the bracket with its kettle over the glowing coals he set to making a pot of tea.

'*I have no brother* . . .'

They had been her very words; yet, being told of that man's death had her trembling. A task he had performed many times before, brewing tea needed no concentration, so Davy's thoughts were free to play on.

Not her brother . . .

But a sweetheart? Nothing had been said in that regard. So was that what Alfred Birks had been to her? Was he the man responsible for her having left her home? Had he been at the root of those words, 'sad as we all become when we are no longer loved'?

Taking the cup from him, Eden met the boy's troubled eyes and it seemed she read the questions behind them.

'Alfred Birks was not well known to me.' She rested the cup on her knee. 'He came a few times to my grand-mother's house in Hobbins Street. He came to walk Myra back to Moorcroft House those evenings it was too dark for her to return there alone.'

'Myra?' Davy stirred sugar into a second cup, sitting with it on the opposite side of the fireplace.

'My sister.' Eden swallowed the lump rising in her throat. Even now it was painful to speak of Myra. 'She was ladies' maid at Moorcroft and Alfred was the groom. It . . . it was knowing him as Myra's friend . . . It came as a shock hearing he had died . . . But how did you hear of it?'

One upset was enough. Davy's mind reacted swiftly. He would not tell her the manner of the man's dying. A slight shrug and a brief shake of the head adding to the innocence he trusted was in his look, he answered. 'Read it in a newspaper . . . it said only he had *passed away*, d'ain't give no cause.'

The newspaper had given no cause, was that not unusual?

Troubled by thoughts which had persisted since Davy's leaving, Eden climbed the narrow stairs to her bedroom.

Alfred Birks had been a groom, no one of importance to other than family, so why had a report of his death been printed in a newspaper?

Full and brilliantly golden the moon bathed the small room in light. Turning out the lamp she had carried with her, she crossed to the window. Below, the canal glittered, a sparkling band winding across a shadowed somnolent heath, a barge moored almost at her door dark and comforting.

It was all so beautiful, so different from anything she had known in Hobbins Street, the scenes she and Myra had seen when peeping from the window of the room they shared. And what of Myra now? The views from the windows of Moorcroft would be gentler than the roofs of houses, the forest of tall, smoke-blackened chimneys of iron foundries and the winding wheels of collieries seen from Grandmother's house. Even so, they could be no more peacefully serene than the view from this tiny cottage.

Reluctantly leaving the window, Eden prepared for bed. Her prayers said, she added a further one for the soul of Alfred Birks. God would not mind her asking he be given eternal rest even though a relative stranger asked.

Lying in bed, she watched the ballet of shadows dance to soundless music, her mind restless as the moon glided shapes.

What had caused the death of Alfred Birks? Why did no mention of that appear in the newspaper report?

Beyond the window an owl hooted, joining song to the rhythm of the night, but Eden did not hear.

Had there been an accident? Had he died of an illness? Fingers tightening on the sheet, Eden's mind asked a more terrible question still. Was that illness one Grandmother had a fear of? Could it be that the cholera or maybe the smallpox that had ravaged the town many years ago had returned? A chill, sudden and frightening, ran along every vein.

What of Myra . . . could she be infected? Was her sister fighting death!

20

Eight o'clock in the evening was not a time she would have expected to be told to present herself for an interview, but then the only master at Moorcroft House was its mistress and she could suit herself in all things.

The late Lenor Medwin's personal maid lifted a deep blue coat from a cupboard in her own room. Arthur Medwin had been dismissive of his wife's clothing. Her maid could keep anything she might wish to have; as for the rest they could go to charity.

Charity! She smiled. For Dilly Madely, charity began at home, *her* home, and that was were it would stay. Those of the dresses, suits and coats she had no liking for would be sold, and the money they fetched would lie beneath her mattress.

Glancing again at the coat she had altered to fit her, Dilly replaced it in the cupboard. It might not be wise to go asking for the post of ladies' maid looking as well-dressed as the lady herself . . . and certainly it wouldn't be wise so long as it were that stuck-up Ava Russell was being asked.

Dressing quickly in the featureless fawn that was the walking-out suit she regularly wore, the same plain brown bonnet and cotton gloves teamed with it, the girl glanced at her reflection in the cheap mirror hung on her bedroom wall. Perhaps for the moment it was better to look drab as always; that way would draw no comment from the other staff she would pass leaving the house. Picking up her bag, she passed the cord of it over her wrist. She had told no one of Ava Russell's offer, that way no one would have the delight of sniggering if she wasn't given the post; but soon, post or no post, nobody would snigger. Dilly Madely would wear every one of that cupboard's fine clothes and more besides; the money keeping Ava Russell's secret would pay . . . it would pay for a very long time.

Could that woman possibly know of her walking out with Alfred Birks, that it was Lenor's own maid had told him of the doings in that bedroom? So what if her did! Dilly tossed aside the slight fear that edged along her nerves. There were nothing her could do! A jaunt in her step, she walked quickly through the kitchen returning comments with saucy answers and, once outside, allowed a smile to spread greedily across her mouth. No, there were nothing Ava Russell could do . . . except to pay.

Hidden beneath the drab fawn skirt of Dilly's costume, the pretty green leather shoes taken from Lenor's wardrobe tapped the footpath. Whoever had killed Alfred had taken the money from his pocket. Of course, no mention had been made of *that* in the newspaper, no report of robbery. But then nobody would suspect a man of Birks' class to have such an amount, and Ava Russell would not admit to paying him a farthing more than his yearly wage.

It must have puzzled that woman as much as it had puzzled herself. Dilly's thoughts were brisk as her steps. Had he talked to someone of going to collect the money from the church, bragged to them of how smart he was? But he was not that much of a fool. He would have known the dangers of that, known words said were words repeated if the listener were not given coin enough to hold the tongue still . . . and Alfred Birks were not a man given to sharing. But now he would not have to . . . and neither would she!

Coming to Ethelfleda Terrace, she paused. Maybe she should walk by way of Trouse Lane. There would be folk about, the road would still be busy with men leaving their place of work or going to the ale houses; and women . . . there would be those also, children clinging to their skirts while they haggled for the cheapest cut of meat or the last few chops before the butchers closed their stalls in the Shambles; then there would be the others, those women of the night waiting for any man who would pay sixpence to take their pleasure, and maybe not just men! Dilly smirked remembering her late mistress . . . maybe women were also willing to buy their pleasure.

Trouse Lane! She could go by way of Wellcroft Street and join it there. But that was a long way around whereas the Terrace . . . indecision chafing, she stood a moment. It was half the distance!

Overhead, the moon sailed from a sea of cloud, its brilliance bringing back the day, while atop the hill the clock of Saint Bartholomew's church rang out.

A quarter of an hour, that was time enough to go by way of the longer route . . . but Lenor's shoes pinched, the woman had been stout but her feet had been small. Trying to ease her toes, Dilly grimaced. The less walking she did the better . . . but going by way of Ethelfleda Terrace meant passing the alley where Alfred had been . . .

Toes pinched together throbbed painfully. Bloody shoes! She glanced at her feet and then again at the sky. The moon was brilliant, it had the whole length of the road lit up . . . She could be at the other end in a few minutes . . . besides nobody would hang around the place where they had killed a man . . .

A sharp sting lancing both feet, Dilly's mind was made up. Footsteps echoing in the silence, she began to walk.

'Spare an old man tuppence for a bite o' supper.'

A cry of fright rising to her lips, Dilly whirled to meet the voice, then gasped her relief at the sight of a figure bent low over a walking stick, feet shuffling in steps more painful than her own.

'Lord, but you give me a scare!' It was a half-laugh, one of solace on realising the speaker was old . . . so old a stick was needed for support. For a moment she had known real fear . . . but an old man could do her no harm.

'Tuppence would buy a supper . . . I ain't 'ad a

decent meal for I don't know 'ow long . . . nobody cares about the old.'

Alleviation of that sudden fear, consolation of its being unfounded, of hearing the weak, cracked old voice, wakened a streak of pity in Dilly. Tuppence wouldn't empty her purse . . . and with the bounty soon to be hers she could afford to buy an old beggar a supper.

Turning to where the bent figure dragged itself towards her, she took the bag from her wrist, opened it and took out the small purse. There were two pennies among the coins it held; he could have them.

'You be welcome . . .'

The words stilled on her tongue, the real fear of moments ago becoming a terror she could taste in her mouth, an abject horror which had her rooted to the spot and filled her wide-stretched eyes with an unspeakable truth. A scream passing no further than her throat, she stared at other eyes . . . eyes glittering like a serpent's from the shrouded face, watched the bent figure move, watching as, soundless in the silence, shining silver in the moonlight, a blade rose . . . and plunged!

'A young woman should have called here last evening.' Ava Russell looked up from the household accounts book as her cook entered the study.

'D'ain't nobody come 'ere last night, mum, least not afore I went to me bed an' that were not a minute afore I should ought to 'ave done.'

'She should have called at eight o' clock.'

The older woman's head shook briefly. ''Ad her 'ave called, mum, I would 'ave knowed for I sat in the kitchen same as I always does . . . sat 'til goin' to my bed.'

'The young woman who should have called.' Ava closed the book decisively. 'She is probably known to you, Dilly Madely by name, she was the late Mrs Medwin's personal maid.'

'Young Dilly . . . yes I know 'er, mum, bright young wench wi' a sensible 'ead on her shoulders.'

Sitting at the heavy desk which had been her husband's, Ava's mouth tightened visibly, her face displaying a displeasure not lost on her cook. 'I had arranged with her to call in respect of obtaining a position here.'

And I bets I know what position that be? The thought kept suitably inside, the woman's head shook again. 'I can't go thinkin' why it is her d'ain't show up, not after you was kind enough to think of her regarding employment; it don't be like Dilly Madely to turn her back, there must be a reason at back of it, mum, that be all I can say.'

'But that is not all I can say!' Each word cracking like breaking ice, Ava slipped the closed book into a drawer. 'Should the girl call, you are to tell her the offer of possible employment is withdrawn, that her services will not, after all, be required. Failing to keep an appointment, especially one that is no less than an act of charity than dropping coins into a beggar's hand, shows an acute lack of manners. Maybe it bodes well she did not keep that appointment for rudeness is something I can tolerate in no one, and much less so in a paid servant.'

'Charity!' Returning to the kitchen the cook mumbled to herself. 'Ava Russell don't know the meanin' o' that word . . . and, as for manners, they should apply no matter your station in life; but does the high an' mighty Ava Russell practise as her preaches? That one sees rudeness in others while thinkin' herself pure as a lily!'

Reaching the kitchen she slammed the door behind her. Young Dilly Madely had done the wise thing in not coming to Moorcroft, and her would be wiser yet to get as far from it as possible.

Alone in the study, Ava withdrew the accounts book from the drawer. Opening it she ran a glance over figures already cemented in her brain. Even with only a cook left as permanent staff the drain on finances showed little relief. Could she dispose of the help brought in once a week? But laundry was something that had to be done. The gardens then? The fellow who came a couple of days a week, his wage could prove a saving; but what would that tell the outside world?

Why were the proceeds from the axle works falling every month? Didn't she run them as her husband had run them . . . didn't she call to account every penny laid out in the buying in of raw materials as well as the paying of wages . . . and had she not reduced those wages not once, but twice?

Would Samuel Russell have done that? No, he would have been too weak, he would have worried for men having too little to support their families; and when the colliery had finally given the last of its coal would he have done as she had? Would he have left those miners to their fate? No, he would have paid them until he himself became a pauper. But not so Ava Russell; she would become no pauper nor would her house show sign of lack of money, the grounds would continue to be cared for . . . As for the inside, only those rooms used to receive visitors need show affluence.

But there was no real affluence left at Moorcroft! She glanced again at the truth displayed in columns of figures. What wealth Moorcroft had once contained was long gone, and profit from the iron works was almost non-existent. How much longer could she maintain this house?

Returning the book to the drawer her eye fell on a folded parchment. How long could she expect to live in a house no longer hers? That paper lying in the drawer was one she had signed; a paper giving ownership to the bank of Moorcroft and all it held if the mortgage was not repaid in the time specified.

Five hundred pounds! One finger touching the folded sheet, Ava breathed deeply. She had raised that money in the only way possible . . . money she had needed to pay a blackmailer. But Alfred Birks was dead and with him his hopes of a comfortable life lived at her expense . . . And his lady love, the maid of Lenor Medwin? She would not dare attempt the same.

The threat had been removed from her life. The book returned to the drawer and the key turned in the lock, Ava rose to her feet.

The threat of Birks was no more, but that of Myra Brent . . . that as yet was not!

She had spoken to the people of Bell Street, those who had shown her friendship in the few minutes they could snatch from lives centred on making a living. She had said goodbye to them, now the key to that drab damp house was returned to the estate agent. Tiny pieces of stone broken and partly crushed by the constant movement of wagon wheels bit painfully through the worn-out soles of Myra's boots. All that remained was to take the blouse to the dressmaker and she could leave Darlaston.

Three shillings. The cloth-wrapped parcel held against her chest, she crossed the busy Bull Stake, oblivious of the threatening hiss of a steam-driven trolleybus and the shout of an angry carter, the wheels of whose vehicle barely missed the thin, hurrying figure. The dressmaker had promised three shillings for the stitching of that delicate blouse. She had sat the entire night fighting the blindness of eyes longing for sleep, hunching over the candle in order to see, each minute stitch an agony of worry that it might be placed wrongly or else be a fraction too large and, as a result, her work being pronounced unsatisfactory therefore bringing no payment.

Too weary almost to walk, she caught her foot

against the kerb, stumbling against a woman who pushed her away, muttering loudly of the evils of drink and the hell Myra could look to when death came for her. But what hell could be worse than the one she endured now, what death worse than the life she was living?

Her murmured apology ignored, Myra rested a moment beside the window of a small shop. Should her fear be realised, should that three shillings not be paid . . . Myra's free hand touched the two pennies pushed deep into a pocket. How long would that save her from the workhouse!

The thought trembling on her lips, she forced herself to walk on.

'I am with a client.'

The dressmaker's pert mouth firmed as she saw who it was had entered her establishment, her nose wrinkling at the sight of the tired clothes and pale, almost deathlike, quality of the face that looked back at her. She had a client, a very important client who might well take her custom elsewhere should she catch sight of the woman standing there, holding a parcel. It would be realised no person so obviously poor would be purchasing an *à la mode* garment . . . and a woman as wealthy as the client now in the private fitting-room would not frequent the same premises. That would be loss of a valuable source of business. This uppermost in her shrewd calculating brain, Sophie glanced towards the door at her back at the same time reaching for that which gave on to the street.

'As I said, I have a client,' she said, her tone hushed, 'you can wait outside.'

'But I have brought . . .'

'I said you can wait outside!' Sharp as the snap of a vixen's jaws the dressmaker's lips clamped together, a quick push sending Myra stumbling out through the door.

It would have taken no more than minutes to have looked at her work. Myra felt a wave of tiredness sweep the length of her. A few minutes to inspect the stitching then to pay the shillings; but they were minutes the like of herself could not be given when a client was present, and those shillings . . . What did the paying of those matter when attending a customer who might well be spending many sovereigns.

'The blouse I ordered . . .'

Imperiously loud, the words reached to where Myra waited.

'. . . it is ready, I trust.'

The dressmaker's reply was indistinct but the halting prevarication of it was quite clear.

'I said I would want it when next I called.' The voice reaching Myra brimmed with arrogance. 'If it is not finished then the order is withdrawn.'

'It is finished, ma'am . . .'

Obsequious in its apology the quieter voice floated to the pavement as the shop door was thrown open and the parcel snatched from Myra's hand.

'. . . I asked it be kept back until you had finished dressing.'

The door had closed again. Myra shifted her position but her aching body gained no solace from the movement. Please, she whispered in her mind, please let the blouse be acceptable, let me be given the price promised.

'. . . if you wish it, ma'am.'

The end of a sentence reaching her as the door opened yet again, Myra looked into the harassed face of the dressmaker signalling she enter the shop.

'The client is trying the garment.' It was a murmur, her glance going quickly to the closed-off fitting room. 'She asked to see the woman who had brought it . . . though for the life of me I can't think why. She may not speak to you but should she do so then you curtsy and address her as ma'am.'

Her clothes were not those of the wealthy and her appearance not at all that might be desired but they in no way affected the manners she had been taught from childhood to observe. Too weary to put the same into words, Myra simply nodded.

'Wait here,' the dressmaker hissed as her client called. 'And remember, you curtsy and call her ma'am.'

Why would that customer want to see the person who had stitched her blouse? What did it matter who had had the sewing of it? Myra stared at shelves filled with rolls of pretty fabrics, cases holding ribbons of silk and velvet. If it suited, then the woman would take it and if it did not meet with her approval she would refuse it; either way it could not be affected by who had made it.

'Of course, ma'am, it will be delivered this evening.'

Emerging from the fitting-room, the dressmaker laid the blouse on a highly polished counter, her fingers fluttering like anxious moths as they reached for several sheets of deep violet-coloured tissue.

'One moment.'

It was no request. Haughty, imperious as before, the voice brought a halt to the fluttering fingers.

'I shall not be purchasing this garment . . .'

A small gasp broke from the dressmaker but its distress made no impact on the client who had stepped into the body of the tiny shop, a client who looked with cold eyes.

'. . . I find the work most unsatisfactory. I suggest you follow my example, Miss Brooke. I suggest you refuse to pay whoever is responsible for such shoddy work.'

'Shoddy.' Myra looked up, her exclamation falling away as she looked into the face of Ava Russell.

21

'*The work is of a poor standard . . . were I you I would not accept it . . .*'

Ava Russell's eyes had stared into hers, the message they conveyed easy to read: you will pay one way or the other!

Walking away from the town Myra felt a bitterness such as never before.

'*Do you not wish to hear of your sister? The girl whose face you slapped the day she came to Moorcroft?*'

Ava had followed her from the shop calling quietly but the words had sounded loud as church bells beating in Myra's brain as they beat now. She had swung around to meet the cold sadistic stare of the woman who had been her mistress.

'*What do you know of my sister?*' She had thought the question loud but it had whispered from a throat dry with fear.

'*A more fitting question would be what do I not know of her . . . She is young, pretty as you once were, and she shows every potential of becoming a most satisfactory ladies' maid . . .*'

'*No!*'

'*Oh, but yes.*' The reply had come with the smile of evil. Tears clouding her eyes, Myra stumbled on.

'*You chose to leave my service.*' Satisfaction had throbbed in every syllable, dark eyes gloating. '*I, therefore, was put to employing a new personal maid. I was happy to give the position to your sister, and I must add that so far she has proved a very amiable choice. She is settling to her duties, and I expect that quite soon now she will carry out those more delicate ones, the services you yourself performed so "pleasurably".*'

'*There was never pleasure for me . . .*'

Ava Russell's hard laugh had cut away the rest. Coming a step closer she had hissed. '*You! But who is speaking of pleasure for you? What you did or did not feel was of no consequence, just as it will be of no consequence what your sister will or will not feel.*'

'*No . . . please, you can't . . .*'

'*Can't! Remember who is mistress of Moorcroft! No stricture governs what I wish to do within its walls, or with whom I share my pleasures.*'

'*Not Eden! She is . . .*'

'*If you were about to say your sister is not yet fully out of girlhood then your experience should have taught you, Myra. The young learn more quickly . . . and Eden is a most adept pupil. She will suit my requirements . . . every aspect of my requirements . . . But of course should you wish to return to Moorcroft, to resume your duties there, then I might have to reconsider your sister's employment.*'

The implication had been plain, the threat of it stark. She could go back to the hell she had left or Eden would be subjected to that same horror. There had been no pity in that hard face, no softening of those sharp tight features, only a glitter in the eyes that watched her, a glitter of triumph.

Women passing glanced curiously at the thin hunched figure, sobbing as it walked, but paid little attention to a spectacle they had witnessed so many times before; life was hard for the folk of Darlaston. If a pit disaster or a foundry accident didn't claim a loved one, then poverty or disease waited with impatient hands.

But none of those things was responsible for the tears Myra shed now; it was fear for a sister . . . fear of the evil that hovered over Eden, an evil that would suck her into a hell of depravity, a hell which would only be banished if she, Myra, returned to it.

And she *would*, return to it. Beneath the moisture clouding her eyes, Myra seemed to see the face of a girl several years her junior. Fair hair framed a small heart-shaped face, eyes fresh and green as a spring meadow, a skin so clear it might have been translucent, no mark of the smallpox which had killed her parents. Eden was touched with a beauty which even in childhood had set her a little apart; but it was not looks alone that created the difference between Eden Brent and her sister. Eden was a dreamer . . . she lived inside herself.

That was the reason of her own returning to Moorcroft. Myra blinked, her vision clear. Eden would have no defence against the wiles of Ava Russell. She was still that innocent of childhood, a young girl who knew nothing of a world beyond Hobbins Street. And she must never know!

A cough bubbling in her chest, Myra rested against a wall. Grandmother had always said they must care for each other. That was what she had been doing when she slapped Eden. Only the shock of the blow could prevent her visiting that house again . . . and now she must show that care again. She must return to Moorcroft; only that way could she keep her sister safe.

Pushing away from the wall, Myra's fingers brushed the pocket of her skirt, feeling the coins nestling inside it.

A ragged breath brought the cough rising in her throat. It had troubled her more and more in the weeks of living in that damp house, sapping her strength. Tuppence! The coins were hard beneath her fingers. The dressmaker had taken her cue from Ava Russell, she had needed no further urging to withhold payment for the work of that blouse, work they had both known was of perfectly acceptable quality.

But what did that matter now? Myra coughed again. She could walk back to Wednesbury. The tuppence in her pocket . . . She glanced to where she had rested against a wall, the wall of a shop, its bullseye windows almost concealing the wares displayed there . . . tuppence would be enough . . . Please Lord, let it be enough!

'I tells you, mum, it fair has me feared to step into the streets! A body don't feel safe no more, don't know should it be you will be the next one to be done in.'

'Done in?' Irritation at being disturbed laced Ava Russell's reply. Returning a folded sheet of parchment to a drawer of the desk, she looked at the woman worriedly twisting a corner of her starched apron.

'That be what I said, mum, done in . . . another poor soul found dead . . . I tells you, I be feared to sleep nights.'

Fingers resting against the closed drawer, Ava looked at her cook. 'Are you saying someone has been found dead?'

'That be eggsactly what I be sayin' . . .' The cook's bosom heaved. 'Found just as poor Alfred were found.'

Pressing her apron to her wet eyes delayed the woman's telling for several seconds, the interval filled with a moan and the shaking of shoulders. Then, the apron lowered, she began again. 'Killed.' Polly Jupp sniffed. 'Killed as were poor Alfred Birks, an' for what reason? The wench could 'ave had naught worth the stealin' of, same as that lad 'ad naught the worth of killin' for.'

Another murder! Upright in her chair, Ava regarded her cook with fresh interest.

'The town be full of it, they be talkin' of nothin' else.'

That was something she could well believe. Ava's fingers dropped to her lap. Gossip flew on rapid wings and none flapped harder than those which flew over Wednesbury.

'You should know better than to listen to rumours.' She spoke sharply. 'It will probably turn out to be no more than that, a silly tale told to scare people all over again.'

'Oh Lord, I does hope so.' The sniff sounded loud as before. 'I hopes it don't be as folk were sayin', that some poor wench be lying with her throat slashed.'

That was the second time of using the word 'wench' . . . the supposed victim of a murderer was a woman! Ava kept her silence.

'Be a terrible thing for folk to lie about.' Taking her mistress's silence as an invitation to continue with her news the cook went on. 'But it be even more terrible, supposin' what they be saying be the truth.'

'So, just what are they saying?'

Lifting the apron again, holding it beneath trembling lips, Ava's cook drew a long breath. 'They be saying . . .' the cloth pressed against her mouth, the woman paused, '. . . they be saying a wench were found this mornin', found by a man on his way to his work. They reckons he thought it were a drunk lying by the roadside but when he looked . . . Oh God, mum, if it be as folk says it must have shocked him summat awful.'

Ava's fingers folded together, a brace for the irritation rising in her. Why didn't the woman come right out with it, say what she had heard in the market place?

'Can you think, mum . . .' half-hidden by the apron the woman's mouth contorted, 'can you imagine what it must have been for to find what he did? Be a wonder if the poor soul ever knows a peaceful night's sleep again! I only knows if what has been said turns out to be truth then I won't never rest easy, not no more I won't.'

'You say this . . . this woman was discovered this morning?' Ava watched her cook nod assent. 'Then there has been no official report. So, until there is, until confirmation of what is no more than gossip is given then I suggest you forget what you have heard. There are people who enjoy nothing so much as putting fear into others and this story you have heard will no doubt prove to be just that, a scaremongering that has absolutely no foundation.'

'Please God you be right, mum . . . May the Almighty grant it be no more than that.'

She had not visited Moorcroft.

Lifting the cast iron pot from the bracket on which it had hung almost all day, Eden carried it to the table setting it on a cloth spread to prevent marking.

She had wanted to so badly, fears of Myra being taken with some illness plaguing her every moment.

Removing the beef cheek from stock she would later use for the making of gravy, Eden stripped the layer of skin from the interior of the mouth setting the meat aside to cool.

But if Myra had not been ill . . . she would have been so angry at having the demand for her sister stay away ignored. The thought had stayed, but the desire to see Myra, to know whether or not she was well, had remained.

Reaching for the parsley and chives she had washed

and set to dry beside an open window, she chopped them, the fragrance releasing a mouth-watering aroma to blend with the meat.

She had known she could not call at that house, yet the worry of what it could be holding had not left her for a moment. It had plagued her so much she had at last asked Davy Melia to enquire in the town. Had anyone fallen ill, had either of the diseases her grandmother had so feared returned again to Wednesbury?

Tender from its slow stewing, the meat chopped easily into tiny pieces. Adding them to the fresh herbs, seasoning with salt and pepper, Eden spooned the mixture into a variety of small pots, pressing it with the back of a spoon before covering the surface with melted butter.

There had been no report of any such illness. Eden felt that same relief she had felt on hearing Davy say so. But relief, sweet and welcome as it had been, did not remove the ache always in her heart, the questions which had never entirely left her mind. What was it had made Myra turn from her and from their grandmother? What was so unacceptable it had even kept her from seeing that same beloved grandmother to her grave?

Ought she have gone back to Moorcroft, ought she to have defied Myra, demanded to tell her of their grandmother's death?

'But I didn't, Gran,' she murmured, covering the pots with greased paper, 'I didn't do it.'

A key opening a locked door the whisper brought

memories flooding in. A girl running from the house of a headmistress who had demanded she remove every stitch of clothing, of that same haughty face, that autocratic denouncing that the girl 'would never do any good, she would never amount to anything'.

Turning her attention to the making of a kidney pudding which could be left atop the fire to steam for an hour, she added two cups of breadcrumbs to parsley, a grating of nutmeg followed, with a small amount of suet together with the sheep's kidneys she had prepared earlier. But the preparing of food did nothing to chase the spectres in her mind.

The prophecy had proved correct.

Binding the whole of the ingredients of the bowl with an egg whisked into a cupful of milk, Eden's thoughts travelled their own path.

The words spoken so savagely by that headmistress had been an ordination of truth. Her life had followed what had been predicted.

Placing the mixture into a fresh basin Eden covered it with a cloth. Tying the four corners into a knot she set it in a pan of water then hung the whole above the fire.

She would never forget the words across the chasm of years.

'*She will never do any good . . . she will never amount to anything.*'

And so it would be. She had done nothing except work alongside her grandmother, naught other than scrub and clean, learn the preparing of food. It was true she had not amounted to anything, not even the position of the lowliest scullery maid. A lump hard in her throat, she stared at the dull red coals of the fire. She had not given her grandmother the pride Myra had afforded, she had not attained the grand post of ladies' maid, one which had written pleasure across that loved face; and now she never would. Her grandmother would never have that same gratification from her youngest grandchild.

'Eh up, wench, that smell promises a meal the angels would 'ave the leavin' of heaven for.'

Turning quickly, Eden brushed a hand across eyes moist with the threat of tears, then touched her brow with the hem of the large apron which must once have belonged to Mother Shipton.

'Ar, wench, it be warm . . .' The bargee smiled at the gesture he presumed caused by the heat of the small room, '. . . but the heat of the devil's own furnace wouldn't keep me from the eatin' of a dish of what it be you 'ave cookin' atop that fire.'

'That will not be ready for eating for an hour or more.' Eden returned the smile. 'But there is boney pie ready for lifting from the oven, should you wish a hot meal, or fresh baked bread and newly pressed beef cheek should a sandwich be all you prefer.'

'I'll take the pie.' Handing her an enamelled plate the man counted out several coins while Eden cut a generous portion of pie setting it alongside a helping of potatoes and cabbage.

'Add to that a pot of that pressed chawl I 'ave the

smellin' of and a loaf of bread. That will mek a supper fit for any king, ar, or that little lady a' sittin' on England's throne; give 'er a taste of that and I reckons her'll be wantin' no more of what them there palace cook a'serves her up. But then the cut folk be 'oping that there queen don't go gettin' no tasting of what you provides, for that would mean our 'aving the losin' of you.'

Taking his plate, a pot of pressed meat and a small loaf balanced precariously in his hands, he grinned widely. 'There be them wouldn't tek no crown in exchange for what you cooks, t'were a blessin' for the cut folk the day you come to this cottage.'

A blessing! From the window Eden watched the man jump lightly aboard a laden narrowboat. She would not begrudge anyone that . . . but why could heaven not have bestowed its grace upon her? Why had she not been able to bring a pride to her grand-mother's heart? Now she never would; the most she would ever be, the most she could hope for, was to be what she was now: a nobody, an interloper who had taken another woman's home.

22

'Mother be along of The Coppice. If you don't mind, I can fetch her 'ome from there.'

Davy Melia looked at the young woman walking beside him. She had hardly put two words together since they had left Shipton Cottage.

'Won't tek no more'n a minute to run up the drive an' if old misery guts thinks to stop me then he's got another think comin'.'

The remark had brought no defence of the old man. Davy frowned, the freckles on his forehead falling together. Eden always stuck up for that old 'un, had a word to say as to the reason of his forever 'aving the bear on his back, so why not this time? Could it be her were also gettin' fed up of his never 'aving a good word? That don't be likely. Davy answered his own question. Were that the case, then her would hardly like to be bringin' him a supper. Then what were it had her behavin' different?

'Mother was sayin' just this mornin' . . .' Davy tried again, '. . . her were sayin' same as meself, why bother with him as lives beside the big house when he don't never 'ave a decent word to say to you. T'ain't as though it would tek a penny from his pocket, or d'ain't he ever learn civility costs naught?'

'I . . . I'm sorry Davy, what did you say?'

Even her voice didn't sound the same. Wanting to ask, yet somehow not wanting to know, he let the moment pass, saying instead, 'I were remarkin' on him you brings a meal to every evenin' and on his never speakin' a kind word for the trouble of it.'

'It's no trouble.'

'Nor ain't it no trouble to speak a thank you!' Where Eden's reply had been lifeless, Davy's was full of fire. 'Good manners don't cost not a brass farthing yet the way he refuses to use 'em they might as well cost a thousand pounds a word. He be a mardy old bug . . . Well, that's what he be!'

The essence of a smile rose to Eden's lips. 'The man is not bad-tempered, Davy, but he has been unhappy for such a long time it seems to have driven away every other feeling he might have had.'

'We don't know he be unhappy, and even if he is, then himself like be the cause of it. Probably drove folk from him with them sour ways of his'n.'

No, they could not be certain of what lay behind the man's churlishness, yet something inside Eden told it was an all-encompassing sadness, a sadness arising from something he blamed only himself for. Was it the sourness Davy had spoken of? Her glance travelling along the track, she saw the now familiar figure standing beside the gate, a bent figure that leaned heavily on a cane. Was it simply an irascible temper had made this man cut himself off from society, or was it something deeper, something which cast a long black shadow?

'The house be open, I suppose you will be wanting to take a look inside.'

Eden looked at the man regarding her above the gatepost. The face was drawn, the cheeks hollow, and dark circles ringed the eyes, but they were eyes that probed, sharp and keen as a knife.

'No . . .' She shook her head. 'I would not intrude.'

'Intrude!' He snapped at her. 'How can you intrude when there be none there to intrude upon! If it is the cleaning woman you are averse to disturbing, then there is no need. She will welcome another person with whom to speak.'

'And be civil in the doin' of it unlike some as be needin' no mention.' Davy's clouded features spoke all of the resentment inside him. 'Some folk don't 'ave the knowin' of a kindness when it be hitting 'em in the face! Come you on, Eden, come along wi' me to fetch me mother.'

The dish of kidney pudding and potato set on the gatepost, Davy turned to Eden but she shook her head in refusal.

'The lad be protective of his mother, that is good, it is what a son should always be.'

There had been a softness in the usually hard voice, a gap in the wall of bitterness with which he had surrounded himself, but in an instant it was closed. The cane rising, he growled, 'Fetch your mother, lad, and then be off before you come to regret giving freedom to that tongue of yours . . . And you . . .' the cane swung in Eden's direction, the tip hovering a yard from her chest, '. . . you go along of him. Do what you have a desire to do, go walk through the rooms of that house.'

Aware of the cane that could so easily strike, Eden glanced coolly at the lad beside her, his fists doubled, his features mutinous.

'Go on, Davy,' she said calmly, 'go bring your mother. I will wait further along the track.'

'I said for you to have the seeing of the inside of that house.'

Watching Davy sprint along the wide tree-lined avenue, Eden answered quietly. 'And I said I would not intrude.'

'Pah!' The cane struck the stone of the gatepost, setting the lid of the dish rattling. 'I tell you there be none there save that lad's mother!'

Already a few steps along the track, Eden turned. The pale essence of a smile that had hovered on her mouth when answering Davy touched her lips again. Her glance resting on the drawn face, she swung her head briefly. 'We both know that is not so.'

'Not so? I tell you that house be empty. I be . . .'

Again the chink in that self-built barrier! Eden watched the mouth clam, cutting off the rest, the veil that dropped over those sharp eyes.

'But not of love.' She spoke softly. 'I have not been inside, yet I feel that love. It reaches out, it calls for its

voice to be heard. There may be no living being within
its rooms yet they are filled with a presence, a sorrow
which it cannot banish. There may be no physical
evidence, no figure or body which can be seen, yet my
whole heart told me, told me that one time I stood
looking up at its windows and tells me again now: there
is a love in that house, a yearning to find what once was
but became lost. I think you feel that way also . . . I
think you have suffered that same deprivation, that you
also yearn for what is lost, but to find it you have to
face your heart.'

He might have answered, he might have spoken of
what her words triggered, of the cause of the emotion
his face could not disguise or his copper-bright eyes
keep hidden. But he had not, he had simply picked up
the meal she had brought him and walked away.

Looking at the door he had closed firmly behind
him, Eden felt a wave of pity. He could shut out the
world, close himself away behind locked doors, but
that would not heal the hurt or mend the heart her own
told her was broken. It seemed that for that elderly
man, love, as with herself, was set too deep; maybe, as
Myra had done, someone had withdrawn, taken that
love from him, snatched it away for some reason he
might not understand. But, though he had been
devastated by such cruelty, love still lived in his heart
as in hers; as it lived yet within that silent house.

Three days. Ava Russell gloated quietly as she walked
into her dressing-room. Three days and then . . . Her

glance rested on the bath tub . . . and then her pleasure would begin again. That was how many days until Myra Brent returned to Moorcroft. There were things she had to do; that was what she had said; to disappear from the place she lived in without speaking of leaving to those who were neighbour and friend would arouse suspicion.

And what of her leaving this house whilst telling nobody of her intention? What did she think that to have aroused! But nobody in Ava Russell's employ would dare to speak of any business of her house. The thought calmed the spurt of anger ready to rise. Yes, that toad Birks had tried his hand, had threatened her with extortion, but the fruits of that blackmail, the harvest reaped, had not been the one expected. Yet Birks had been correct in one assertion, false though she had felt it to be. She would not hear from him again . . . and neither would anyone else!

A thorn which had threatened to prick . . . a thorn which had been cut away. Satisfaction spread its trail over a thin mouth. The man's death had erased the spectre come to rest on her shoulders, lifted the threat he had placed there. And as for his little flight of fancy, that maid of Lenor's, she would pose no problem, the assurance of any accusation she might make resulting in twenty years of penal servitude in a house of correction for herself . . . The smile of satisfaction deepened . . . there would be no accusation.

No, it would not come to that! Removing the gown

she had unbuttoned she stepped in front of the long mirror. Once again fortune had smiled on Ava Russell leading her to find Myra Brent. The girl had not known the dressmaker her mistress visited, no one had. She had guarded that secret as she guarded that other; so far as was allowed to be known, the gowns Ava Russell wore were created in an exclusive London salon, the railway train she professed to taking her there being in fact a train taking her to Darlaston.

Myra! Chemise loosened, Ava spread her hands over her breasts. The girl had realised her little fight for freedom was ended. Oh, it had been a lie she had heard, there had been no truth in the telling her sister was in service at Moorcroft, but what did a lie matter.

Fingers squeezing the soft mounds Ava felt her pulses quicken. Service! Yes, that girl would be returned soon, returned to the task that brought her mistress so much pleasure. But that would not be all she would bring. True, that younger sister was not here, but time would rectify that for, where one was, the other would call, and when she did . . .

Trailing her hands voluptuously along her waist, pushing away silk drawers, the thin mouth opened in a gasp, every nerve becoming a pinprick of fire, a flaming that enveloped in a seething ferment of passion, a craving desire as her fingers played in the moist vee between her legs.

When that sister called, then Ava Russell would have two personal maids . . . two young women to serve her.

*

She had bought herself a woman. Ava scrubbed at her body with the soap and hot water it had taken another shilling to have brought to this tastefully furnished room.

Her own hands, her own fingers, they had set light to her senses but when that light had faded the fire was not extinguished. It had smouldered, simmered and flared until she could think of nothing but the ecstasy of another woman's body, another woman's hands. So, for a second time she had come to this house, a place she had heard whisper of one evening she had visited the theatre. The two women had not been aware of her secreted in that tiny cubicle, but she had been aware of *them*, listening with attentive ears as they talked of Church House. '*It is no distance from this very theatre,*' one woman had murmured to the other, '*I am told it is a few yards from Mount Pleasant in the direction of Willenhall Road.*'

It had been more than gossip, more than an item of titillating chatter; it had been a passing on of information, and it had passed to ears other than those for which it had been intended. But, having a maid to attend to her special needs, having a woman friend eager to participate in those bathtime games, Ava had not needed to visit the place those two had spoken of; but with Lenor Medwin dead and Myra Brent no longer at Moorcroft, desire had proved too much. She had taken a train to Bilston and a hackney to Church House and today had repeated the journey.

Church House! It was a name that deceived, one which hid from society those practices society would not accept.

'Are you sure you have to leave?' A young, full-breasted woman pressed her own naked body against that of Ava. 'There is so much yet we can do together . . . so much more pleasure to be had.'

Lips closing over her breast, the tip of a tongue teasing the nipple, Ava's senses lurched and for a brief wonderful moment she opened her legs to the fingers exploring the soft intimate cavern. But then she had thrust the girl away, a girl who laughed with quiet exultation.

'You'll be back . . . you like brushing the muff too much to stay away.'

Yes, she liked it, but, no, she would not be taking the journey to Bilston again. From now on the pleasures paid for so expensively at Church House would be hers for no more than it took to pay a ladies' maid . . . And for the sister of that maid? One wage would suffice for both!

'Eh, mum, did you hear while you been out?'

'Hear . . . hear what?' She did not want to listen to the woman's drivel. Ava brushed past the fluttering cook.

'About the killin', mum, that I spoke of only this mornin', have you heard of it?'

'Only what you yourself told, and I want to hear no more.'

'But, mum . . .'

'No!' Ava's eyes warned of her irritation. 'I will hear no more tales of the market place. Silly, irresponsible gossip is all it is. You should have more sense than listen and much more than to pay heed to it!'

In her own room, coat and gown removed, Ava stripped away underclothes, tossing them aside for laundering, then walked into the bathroom where she poured water from a tall rose-painted jug into a matching bowl. She had scrubbed herself with the soap supplied by that house but she would not feel truly clean until she washed again here in her own room.

She had thought not to have frequented Church House after that first time but temptation had proved too strong. Demands of the flesh! She touched a towel to the body still crying out to taste again what she had left behind. Needs of the body that men thought a woman never felt! But they *were* felt, the necessity for fulfilment was as strong in female as in male; but where men could satisfy that passion with wife, mistress or street whore, the same was denied a woman. She must never own to a husband's attention leaving her wanting, never speak of the desire left unsatisfied, and certainly not seek that sweet delectation with another woman.

The towel falling from her fingers, Ava cupped her breasts, throbbing with the memory of a moist tongue, while her gaze ran over a stomach aching still for the gratification of a touch other than her own. But all of that would come again soon. Tomorrow Myra Brent would be back in this house.

The thought did not alleviate the pincers of desire squeezing every nerve but only added to its heat. But the normal practice of the day had to be observed. Dressing quickly, she went downstairs seating herself only minutes before tea was brought to her.

Setting the tray on to a Georgian cabriole-legged tea-table, one of the few items of any real value still gracing Moorcroft, Polly Jupp sniffed. This perfume were not that as had drifted into this house with Ava Russell's returning, that had been washed away an' replaced by another . . . It needed no guessing to tell the kind of establishment the first had been acquired in, whore houses catered not only for men, there were those where brushin' the muff were also to be had for a price. That bathroom 'ad seen no frolickin' since the passing of Lenor Medwin, an' Ava Russell were no woman to deny 'erself them pleasures for long . . . No, it needed no guessin' as to where the mistress 'ad spent her afternoon.

'T'weren't no gossip.' Standing straight, her hands together across an ample middle, Polly faced the woman only a salary had caused to be treated with pretended respect. 'That which I tried to tell you of this mornin', t'were no tale bandied about the market place, seems it be no tittle-tattle after all.'

Not lifting her glance from the tea she was pouring, Ava toyed with the idea of dismissing the woman without answer then changed her mind, asking instead, 'What chit-chat would that be?'

Not the sort you been listenin' to, none of the drivel

I'd bet a pound to a penny been a' pourin' into your ears the whole of the afternoon! Repugnance held behind tight lips, Polly Jupp sniffed again.

'Ain't just chit-chat neither,' she answered firmly. 'That which you called market-place tales were no less than the truth.'

There was a difference in the woman's attitude. Ava stirred sugar and milk into her tea. There was none of the deference, none of the respect she was usually so careful to show. Lifting the porcelain cup, Ava sipped twice. What was it? What was this truth the woman so obviously wanted her to hear?

'So.' She lowered the cup. 'What is this terrible truth?'

'It be terrible all right . . .'

The cup replaced in its saucer, Ava noted the lack of the word 'mum', the ignoring of that essential protocol.

'. . . be what I told afore, there were a wench found in the town, a wench wi' her throat slashed an' her chest ripped open, an' that not a dozen yards from where the body of young Alfred Birks were found an' him ripped in that self-same way.'

'A second killing!' Ava set her tea aside, her attention now given fully to the woman standing before her.

'That be right, an' what with them as 'appened last year that meks four, four people murdered right here in this very town. I tells you, it be the work of that Ripper that were doin' all of them murders along of London, the constables d'ain't never catch him along of Whitechapel an' nor they won't, 'cos he don't be

there no more, he be here in Wednesbury a satisfyin'
of his evil lusts on folk the like of Alfred an' that young
woman who were maid along of the Medwin house.'

'The Medwin household?' Ava frowned.

'That be what I heard.' Polly Jupp's head bobbed.
'The wench they found dead along of the Church
Steps be the same as you said to be expectin' to call
here at Moorcroft. It be young Dilly Madely.'

'Dilly . . . Dilly Madely is dead!'

'As a doornail. I spoke with a woman as lives next to
her poor mother . . . God help her . . . was fetched by
the constable to identify the body . . . to have to look
upon a daughter cut to ribbons by a maniac. Dear God
what be this world comin' to!'

'There can be no mistake?'

'None.' Polly's head swung decisively. 'Same as can
be none as to the sort that killer be lookin' to find,
though heaven alone be privy as to the why of that.'

'I don't understand. Surely a murderer would not
specify a particular kind of victim?'

'Wouldn't he though . . . wouldn't he!' Hands which
until now had remained still, twined with anxiety.
'Then why pick on two who it were obvious had no
wealth behind them, who it could be seen were
working-class? And them whor— them women of the
streets slashed to death in London, they had nothing
save what the sellin' of their bodies brought and that
would be nobbut a shillin' or two. No, I says this killer,
whoever he be, be looking to the serving class, the only
difference atwixt what he done in London to what he

be about here being he don't strike only at wenches, he will strike men an' all. But man and woman, they were both servants same as me, though that be ended here an' now. I'll be taking what be due to me an' leaving right now. Polly Jupp ain't going to hang around waiting for no knife to slit her throat. My bags be packed so I'll be asking for the money I've earned be paid now; and if you teks my advice you'll get yourself away from this town 'til such times as that murderer be safe behind bars.'

23

He had forced himself to stay away from Shipton Cottage. Setting young Davy Melia the task of walking the girl to and from The Coppice, hearing reports from him every day, there had been little need for him to see her himself and certainly no cause to visit that house beside the canal.

No need! Andrew Denby smiled grimly to himself. Why then was he here? This was not the route he took to the wood mill at Willingsworth or the coach and axle works along at Monway Field. Answering the polite greeting of men passing on narrowboats, he knew they also would be asking themselves the same question: why was the owner of Denby Boat Builders walking the towpath?

Reaching the cottage, he glanced at the heath running on all sides wild and empty of any other building. She should not live here alone. Even having arranged for a boat to moor here every evening and for that lad to walk with her to and from The Coppice he still worried for her . . . But why did he? That was yet one more question Andrew Denby was loath to answer.

'Mornin' Mister Denby, sir.'

From a little way ahead a man leading a large shire horse touched his cap, then grinned as the horse came to a halt.

'Old Pharaoh 'ere won't budge another step afore he gets his titbit from the little miss living along of that there cottage . . . I don't never have no argying with him no other place, stops and starts meek as a lamb, but when it be the Shipton house he be nearing, there he stands his ground as you might say . . . refuses to budge, does Pharaoh 'til he gets what it is he's set his mind to havin'.'

'Like his namesakes of old, they knew what they wanted and made sure they got it.'

'Don't know nothing of that,' the man smiled as Andrew rubbed the horse's nose, 'but if they were sensible as that hoss then I reckons they got what it were they set their mind on. Mind, it ain't just Pharaoh looks forward to reaching 'ere. The wench be a fair hand with a cooking pot and her charges be the same; if'n you ain't had a mornin' meal, Mister Denby . . . or even if you 'ave . . . you couldn't do better than purchase a bite from this 'ere cottage.'

'Something to eat would be very acceptable . . . but perhaps only narrowboat folk are welcome here.'

'Only people who lack good manners find no welcome at this door.'

One hand still on the animal's nose, Andrew Denby turned to see a young woman, her fair hair gold-spun in the clear sunlight, coming down the short garden path, her heart-shaped face wearing no smile. She was no more pleased to see him than on those other days, days when she had literally told him to mind his own business.

'Then I shall make sure mine give no offence. Maybe then I, like Pharaoh here, might be allowed a titbit.'

'He knows when we be comin' this way, knows a mile off, does Pharaoh, I swears he quickens his step no sooner we be turnin' off the main Navigation and following along the cut from Wiggins Pool.'

'Well, folk do talk of horse sense,' Andrew answered, stepping away as the horse swung its head expectantly, 'and it is quite obvious Pharaoh has an ample amount. A man can do no better than to follow his lead, always supposing I am allowed. May I, Miss Brent . . . may I purchase a meal from you?'

Acutely aware of the tall figure stooping to enter the cottage, feeling those sable-dark eyes on her, Eden filled the basin the other man carried then, wrapping a fresh loaf in the bandana he passed to her, accepted the coins he held out.

'Is that sensible?' The bargee having left, Andrew frowned, watching her count a number of coins into a box she lifted from a drawer, then put several in a pretty vase on the mantel.

'I beg your pardon!' Eden's own frown held more annoyance than question.

This was a good start! Andrew Denby held the mutinous stare. The girl looked more ready to throw him out than ask him to sit and eat. But she had proved on several occasions to act without thinking; this it seemed was one more of those times.

'I asked, Is that sensible, keeping a money box where it can so easily be found? And a jar is not exactly a safe.'

'It is safe enough, Mister Denby, or so it has been up to now!'

Tart as a sour apple. But this girl was not the picture she painted. She was sweeter, more tender beneath the façade of cold indifference; that he had learned from the praises Davy and so many others sang of her. Sweet maybe, gentle perhaps, but mindful of her own safety . . . definitely not!

'Up to *now*.' He emphasised the word. 'But people pass this spot every day and while I would not count the majority of folk dishonest there are exceptions.'

'Exceptions occur in many aspects of people's behaviour, Mister Denby. Some may take money which does not belong to them, while some take the liberty of making the business of others their own. Both are a grievance.'

As he had thought. Andrew Denby hid the smile threatening to curve his strong mouth. Tart, and certainly not easily cowed; nevertheless her idea of safeguarding the proceeds of her labours was as sensible as sitting against a stone wall on a freezingly cold day.

'Grievance or not,' he glanced to where the window was opened to the air, 'it has to be said, a box in a drawer and a pot on a mantel are hardly the most secure of hiding places.'

A kettle which had started to sing taking her attention, Eden swung it away from the fire. She should show this man the hospitality her grandmother had taught be observed no matter the caller: 'Rich as a Lord or poor as a beggar they deserve no less than a sup of tea.' Never before had she wished to ignore those words of her grandmother, but with this man . . .

Sensing her hesitation, he turned back to the door. She had never displayed any pleasure in his company, it would be unfair of him to impose it on her any further.

'Miss Brent.' He paused, swinging his head to look at her. 'Unacceptable as it is, I offer my advice yet again. Do not leave your money where it can be so easily found.'

'But that is the precise reason of my placing it where it is,' she replied quickly, 'at least that is the reason of the coins being placed in the jar. You see, Mister Denby, I do not know who it is owns this house, neither do I know the sum which might be required as rent. I have asked among the people of Gospel Oak but it seems they also do not know the present owner, they only know it belonged to an elderly woman they called Mother Shipton. But, being unaware of the owner of a house does not mean a person may live in it and pay no rent at all; it is for that reason I place a share of all that I myself am paid into that jar. If the owner of Shipton Cottage does not call before my leaving then the jar and its contents will remain where it can be found . . . and hopefully what it holds will prove sufficient.'

. . . before my leaving . . .

The words rang in Andrew Denby's mind as he strode across the heath towards Willingsworth wood mill. Of all the times he had thought of that girl he had not once thought of her leaving that cottage. But *why* leave . . . and to go where? If she had had somewhere to go, why was it he had found her huddled against a bridge? And, if there were some other place waiting for her, why stay all these weeks in that cottage?

But she had said, '*before my leaving*'. Why say it if she did not intend to go? And why had her words resulted in this feeling, this sudden sense of his world falling apart?

He had not asked for food. He had not once smiled or even wished her the time of day before leaving. Walking beside Davy, who whistled happily through a leaf, Eden let her thoughts dwell as they had all day on a tall figure whose sable eyes had held hers before he had stooped through the doorway and strode away. It had been abrupt, his leaving; he had looked for a brief moment as if he might say something but he had simply walked away.

It should not have bothered her; she should have welcomed his going but, instead, she had stared at the empty doorway, and somehow the day had lost its glow. That had been absurd, she had told herself, returning to the process of preparing another batch of the faggots so favoured by the bargemen with no wives to cook for them. But, work as she had, the day had retained a shadow, a gloom which even now lay over her like a cloud. Why had he come to Shipton Cottage? The question had plagued her all day but, as with so many others Andrew Denby aroused in her, she could find no satisfactory answer.

'He don't be there!'

The sharp note of surprise piercing her thoughts, Eden looked towards where Davy pointed.

'That old 'un,' he said again, 'he don't be there. Now that be a turn-up an' no coddin'.'

Like Davy had said, it was no lie. There was no figure at the gate, no man waiting for his meal.

'But he is always there.' Eden peered against the shadows daringly attacking the sky as the sun lost its hold on the evening, shadows strengthening and made bolder by trees and bushes lining each side of the narrow track.

'Well, this is one time he don't be.' Davy threw away the leaf.

Alarm replacing the torpor that had lain over her, Eden hurried forward. Maybe the old man was ill, maybe . . .

'The empty dish be there, washed as usual.' Davy had easily kept pace with the running Eden.

The dish she had given him the night before was indeed placed on the lintel of the gatepost, but the man himself . . . Eden cast a quick glance at the surrounds of the small house . . . where was he?

'Don't be usual, don't be usual at all.'

Davy voicing what was in her mind, she glanced at

the windows. No face looked back from any one of them, neither did the door open. Had their conversation of the previous evening annoyed him so much he had taken exception? Did he no longer want what flimsy relationship he had allowed to develop between them to continue? She ought not to have spoken as she had. Eden stared again at windows that showed no light of a lamp. Gran had often said her tongue ran away, leaving her brain to follow on behind. That was what she had done last evening, let her tongue run on without thinking.

'Might as well go back.' Davy, too, glanced over the silent house. 'He don't be goin' to come out, that be easy to see.'

For all her surmising of the reasons the man was not at his gate, Eden felt uneasy. Perhaps he was turning his back, saying without words that she was no longer to come here. There had never been any smile in those copper-hued eyes, no hint of any welcome on that drawn face, nothing to say he found pleasure in her brief visits, yet she felt a sharp dejection in his not appearing. Even his words of anger, or his cane rising to drive her away, would have been infinitely better than the feeling she had now, the feeling that once again something precious had been snatched from her.

Turning away, leaving her to pick up the empty dish while he carried the full one, Davy was already some way along the track when Eden's sharp cry brought him racing back, his brown eyes gleaming concern.

'Be somethin' wrong?'

'No . . . I mean yes. There is something not right about all this.'

'You mean the old 'un not showing here at the gate? But that be the way of 'im. I said he were a surly bug . . . Well, I said as he 'adn't a civil bone in his body and tonight I be proved right; can't even be bothered to come outside and say he don't be wanting no supper! I says to leave 'im to it, let 'im stew in his own juice for a while, mebbes he'll come out of it a mite tenderer than when he went in!'

'But how can we be sure his not being here at the gate is simply the result of ill humour? How can we be certain it is not something more than that?''

'More?' Davy frowned, then drew a short breath as the meaning behind Eden's reluctance to leave became clear.

'You means p'raps he be sick or . . . or worse?'

'We ought not to leave before finding out.'

In the last of the light Eden saw the look which crossed the lad's face. It was apprehension. But of what? Was Davy afraid of the man who lived in this house, or was he afraid of what he might find inside it?

'We can't do that wi'out going in, and that be one thing me mother don't have the tolerating of. If I goes into that place without the inviting her will have the hide off me.'

Lost among the swift-growing darkness, Eden's smile remained unseen. It was neither of the fears she had thought made Davy Melia reluctant to step into that cottage. It was a fear of his mother's anger and,

knowing his mother as she had come to do, Eden
owned it was not something anyone should take lightly.

'There is no need for you to go in,' she said pushing
open the gate, 'I will do it.'

'And 'ave me mother wallop me for lettin' you!
Seems I be in for a clout about the ears either way, so
I might as well be the one to look inside.'

Where was the moon? Alone beside the gate, Eden
probed the shadows with anxious eyes. It was so dark
she could see nothing but the black outline of walls and
roof. Please, the thought rippled on the silence of a
mind only too aware of a cane wielded by an irate hand,
please don't let Davy be harmed.

Dilly Madely would not be calling at Moorcroft, not
for interview for the post of ladies' maid, and not to try
her hand at the same stupid game her erstwhile lover
had tried to play.

Ava Russell extracted two five pound notes from a
box, locked it and deposited it in a bureau in her
bedroom.

First Birks and now Dilly Madely. Fortune was
certainly playing in her favour. Only Myra Brent
remained and now that she had been found she would
prove no threat. For, with the belief that that sister of
hers was here in this house, she would return as
arranged. Of course, as her mistress, Ava could have
demanded the girl return with her, travel with her from
Darlaston, but she preferred it this way.

Ava's feral smile touched the edges of her thin

mouth, making it even more hard and unattractive. Yes, she preferred it this way, somehow it added spice to the game. What was the childhood rhyme? She laughed quietly. 'Will you walk into my parlour said the spider to the fly'. Myra Brent would certainly do that, and so would Myra Brent's sister.

'I am sorry you feel you have to leave.' Returning to the sitting-room, all trace of the smile banished, Ava held out the banknotes. 'Ten pounds is the wage due. You did not complete a twelve-month.'

Miserly old cow! Polly Jupp's thought reflected her look. After fifteen years of dancing to this woman's tune her couldn't make a gift of the other two pounds! But nothing given meant nothing the needing of thanks, and Ava Russell would get none of those from her. Taking the money, she pushed it low into the bag hanging from her wrist.

'There be a hansom callin' for me in five minutes.' Polly looked at the woman whose house she had virtually run for so many years. 'Seeing you'll be by yourself after that time, I would advise you lock the doors. Like I says, nobody be safe in this town no more.'

'. . . *you'll be by yourself . . .*'

Her clothes removed, Ava looked again at her body reflected in her dressing-room mirror.

Yes, she was alone in this house, but not for many more hours; tomorrow Myra Brent would be back, the two of them together.

Hands sliding voluptuously over her stomach, Ava let the feline smile return.

The two of them together, two naked bodies, two sets of touching, caressing hands, a moist tongue to tease a nipple, a mouth to kiss, and most of all fingers playing in that warm vee bringing each to a gasping explosion of passion. Oh, yes. She gazed at the reflection watching from the mirror. Myra Brent would learn to play the whole of the game, she would learn all of the delights brushing the muff could bring . . .

Lips parted, eyes closing, fingertips stroking a soft slippery mound, Ava drew a breath of pure satisfaction.

Yes, Myra Brent would learn . . . and so would her sister.

24

Myra Brent was returning today. She would see to the managing of these two women who came daily to help with the general cleaning of those rooms still in use, and deal with the laundrywoman and the gardener and, of course, the tradesmen. Myra was a competent girl, well able to add the duties of housekeeper to those more entertaining tasks.

Standing in the kitchen, a part of the house into which she had rarely ventured, Ava looked with distaste at the reedy woman and equally unattractive girl. Mother and daughter, no doubt, and both nervous their employment was about to be terminated.

'There will be a new housekeeper arriving later today. In the meantime you will continue with your usual tasks.' Hearing the release of breath, knowing the reason for it, Ava smiled to herself, then continued. 'I shall inspect the kitchen and other rooms after you have left, rooms I expect to be thoroughly cleaned.'

'They . . . they will be, mum.' The older of the two twittered like a nervous bird. 'As . . . as to the midday meal, Missis Jupp give us both a dish of summat or other. Be . . . be we still to be given. . .'

'There is food in the larder, you may make a meal of that.'

Turning on her heel, taffeta skirt swishing, Ava swept imperiously away. She did not know what was or was not in that larder and she cared even less; food was not her main interest, right now there were other more important things on her mind like the letter received that morning.

The study door closed carefully, she crossed to the desk. Sitting in the chair that had once been her husband's, she allowed her gaze to pass around the room. She had not once entered here in the years of their marriage; it had been Samuel's inner sanctum, his place of privacy. From here he had dealt with all but the running of the household, that having been left to her. *'Business is not for a woman, she is not strong enough for the burden of that.'* Remembering, Ava's thin lips curled with contempt. Who, if not Samuel Russell's wife, had kept that business going since his departing the world? And the forging of iron had not been the only business he had relieved her from; that of the marriage bed had followed quickly. Samuel liked a woman beneath him while his wife had made quite clear she did not care to be that woman. The ensuing arrangement had suited them both: she would see to the comforts of his home whilst a mistress, or several mistresses, saw to the comforts of his body. But with Samuel's death she had become not only mistress of Moorcroft but of Moorcroft Ironworks, but they were failing.

Taking a key from her pocket she unlocked a drawer of the heavy desk and drew out a ledger. Opening it, she ran a glance over neatly recorded numbers. The requests for iron had begun to fall within two years of her becoming the foundry's owner. Because of her being a woman . . . because it was thought she had not wits enough to run an iron foundry? She had believed that, and why not? Didn't every man think the same of any woman? But it proved not only Moorcroft iron was failing . . . every manufacturer of that metal had seen their orders reduced. Arthur Medwin had sold up and so had many others, taking what they could salvage before every last penny followed the rest down the drain.

But she had not sold. Ava's glance followed the columns of numbers. She had held to the belief the setback was temporary, an overstock of iron which, when used, would see those orders flocking back. That had not happened. Metal was still wanted, huge amounts of it, but the metal required was not iron but steel; steel was the new god, only steel would do for bridges, for girders, for the making of axles, wheels and boilers, for more and more railway trains: steel! She slammed the ledger shut, she should have changed over to its making . . . now the money needed to pay for that change, to bring in new furnaces, rolling beds and all the other equipment necessary, was no longer in the bank.

In fact there was no money there at all, hence the letter. '*Repayments due on the mortgage taken on the*

*property known as Moorcroft House have not been forth-
coming . . . the bank strongly advises . . .'*

The bank strongly advises . . . Ava leaned her head
against the back of the chair, her eyes closing.

Returning that five hundred pounds was one more
thing she ought to have done . . . it was one more thing
she had not! Now most of it was gone. Settlements of
accounts to suppliers of iron ore, of coal needed for the
smelting of that ore and the paying of wages, though that
bill had become less as men had been dismissed from
their jobs. The drain on those five hundred pounds had
not ceased there . . . household suppliers had also threatened action should their dues not be settled.

Scandal! Ava's eyes opened. That was a slur she
would not tolerate! Scandal of any kind would not be
allowed to touch the name of Ava Russell. To avoid it
she had put the foundry up for sale. How much would
that realise? Would the proceeds settle the amount
loaned by the bank?

And if it did not? Locking the ledger away, Ava
walked slowly upstairs. But it would . . . it had to!
Maybe had she not spent so much on gowns. Cheap
as that dressmaker was in comparison to those salons
she had patronised during Samuel's lifetime, they still
were responsible for more than she should have spent,
but appearance mattered and hers mattered a great
deal. She would not be seen to appear reduced in
circumstances, it would appear as it always had. The
times she visited the theatre, charity events or even
Sunday morning service in church, her clothing would

be of the finest materials and the latest fashions.

And that other expenditure?

Taking the small box from the bureau she opened it. The expense of that visit to Bilston. It had been more than she could afford, she had not guessed a service bought in that establishment would cost what it had.

But it was a payment she would not need to pay again. The services of Church House would not be necessary any longer.

'Told to me while we was lying over at Monway Basin tekin' on a load of iron. The only time a body gets to speak with another is when you be picking up or setting down of a cargo, that or waiting to be passed through a lock, either way it be no more than a few minutes can be given . . . I'll tek a couple of pots of that pressed chawl, be right tasty does that, my man and lads reckon it be the best anywhere on the cut . . .'

Standing at the doorway of Shipton Cottage, a woman took coins from a pocket. She was dressed in faded blue cotton poke bonnet and equally faded cotton blouse, her dark skirt bearing marks of helping to load the boat that was of necessity home to her family, while the ankle-length apron covering it was of a whiteness that bore witness to the woman's efforts at keeping that family clean.

'. . . I tells you, wench, it must be fair worryin' to the mothers of young folk living in that town. Two dead within no time of one another. Has me glad me and mine lives on the cut.'

Another person dead! It could not be the result of some dreadful contagion . . . but any other cause of death would not have news of its happening passing mouth to mouth, so why this one?

Taking coins from the woman, handing her two pots of pressed meat, Eden felt the question press on her mind, only to be intensified by the woman's next words.

'The whole town be buzzing with it, first a man and now a young woman . . . both found with their throats cut across and their chests slashed. Lord, it fair meks the blood run cold a' thinking on it. Reckon it must be some lunatic broke from an asylum . . . stands to reason nobody in their right mind would go doing what be done to them poor young souls. Will be a blessing when he be caught, for folk can hardly rest easy knowing there be a killer on the loose.'

Stunned by what was said, Eden could only stand staring as the woman ran back to the narrowboat moving slowly along the canal.

A killer . . . two young people . . . a man and a woman . . . both found with throat . . .

The horror of it only now registering in her brain, Eden caught her breath. Davy had talked of a death, Alfred Birks' death, but Davy had not spoken of the cause, only that no awful disease had come to the town. But this woman had spoken of murder . . . and not of only one, but two.

'. . . *first a man and now a young woman . . .*'

Had Davy Melia known the man he spoke of had

been the victim of murder? Had he known, yet decided not to tell her, for fear of frightening her?

'. . . *a young woman* . . .'

The words seemed to scream at her, to pound in her brain as if they carried some warning.

'Myra!' It broke in a gasp, riding the crest of a fear, rising stark and terrifying, holding her breath, stifling her throat. Myra was in that town, Myra was a young woman!

No . . . no, please no! Fear now a riot gripping her mind, she snatched the shawl that had been her grandmother's and ran with it across the heath.

'There don't be nobody of that name 'ere.'

'But there has to be.' Holding one hand to the spot aching beneath her ribs, Eden half-sobbed. 'Myra Brent, she is ladies' maid to Missis Russell."

Wiping her hands on a dark apron, a needle-thin woman looked, with lacklustre eyes, at the girl leaning for support against Moorcroft's kitchen door.

'Was a wench 'ere, looked a lot like y'self; I seen her sometime when her were sent on an errand for the mistress, her would pass by the scullery or the washhouse just so as to speak to folk, nice young thing her was . . .'

'Please,' Eden interrupted desperately. 'Please, when will she be back?'

Hands rough and red contrasted against the dark cloth of the apron the woman smoothed into place. 'I don't be knowing this as fact but it might be as her won't be comin' back at all.'

'. . . *first a man and now a young woman.*'

Words which had drummed with every footstep as she had run across the heath became a harsh, jarring screech, a cacophony from which three words stabbed again and again.

'. . . *a young woman . . . a young woman . . .*'

The screech laughing into a thunderous roar, Eden slid into blackness.

'Eh wench, but you caused a body a right turn, faintin' away like that!'

Anxious but gentle, a voice lifting her to the light, Eden opened her eyes. 'Gran . . . Gran, I . . .'

'Don't be your gran, wench.'

Senses not yet returned, Eden glanced about the large room. A huge dresser filled with dishes each of a match, pans shining like dull suns hung in a row against one wall, a gleaming black range ambled along another. This was not home! This was not . . . 'Gran!'

'No, wench, I don't be your gran . . . but there be no need of alarm, you just had a faintin' turn, no doubt be 'cos you was out of breath, seemed you had been runnin'.'

Everything rushing back at once, Eden rose shakily from the chair she had been helped to. 'You . . . you said Myra . . .'

'You shouldn't go moving just yet.' The worn-out face took on a worried look. 'The mistress don't be 'ome but should her be, then it's certain her would say for you to sit awhile and tek a cup of tea.'

It weren't certain at all, the cleaning woman admitted to herself, relieved when Eden refused. Ava Russell were not a woman noted for the giving of anything to them thought beneath her.

' . . . *a young woman* . . .'

Eden drew a deep breath. It had to be asked. Holding the air a moment in her lungs, a moment keeping at bay an answer she dreaded, she clutched the shawl the woman had thoughtfully draped about her shoulders.

'I . . . I heard in the town, a young woman had . . . had been . . .'

'Killed. That be true. A young wench, seems her were maid along of the Medwin place, name of Dilly Madely if what folk tell be right.'

It was not Myra! Her sister was not dead! It sang in her like a hymn, a glorious song of thankfulness. Her sister was not dead!

'But that were not the name you spoke, not the wench you first asked after.'

Eden shook her head confirming the woman's words. 'It was Myra Brent, she is my sister.'

'And you thought . . . well, seems it be a different wench . . . God give peace to her soul and torment to the one who killed her . . .' the woman crossed herself piously, '. . . as for the one you speaks of, her that were ladies' maid here at this 'ouse; well, like I told it could be as her won't be back at all.'

'But I don't understand, Myra has been here for several years . . . has she been dismissed . . . has she done something wrong?'

Untying the straps of her apron, the woman handed it to the younger, equally tired-looking replica of herself. 'Can't be answerin' as to what that wench might or might not have done 'cept to say the rest of them as worked in this place must have done similar, for the all of them be gone along of her, including her as was cook for fifteen years. Be nobody left save for me and my own wench. We comes a few hours a day as does the old man come to see to the 'orse and do a bit to the garden.'

Breaking off, the woman listened to the chimes of a clock reaching from the hall.

'Be time for we to finish.' She glanced at her younger counterpart appearing from the scullery a shawl already drawn over her head and held beneath non-existent breasts with one hand, while the other passed a second shawl to her mother. 'I 'pologises for hurryin' off but it don't do to be out after dark, not with that killer stalkin' . . . You teks my advice and get y'self 'ome, same as we be doin'.'

'But the mistress, I have to speak with her, ask her about my sister.'

Enveloped in the shawl despite the warmth of summer, the woman answered quickly, her desire to be gone plain in its brevity. 'Then you'll have to wait in the yard. Don't be for me to say wait you in the 'ouse.'

They had left without another word, scurrying like two frightened mice, disappearing quickly from sight among the trees and bushes that bordered the grounds of Moorcroft House.

From the tower of Saint Bartholomew's church, a single bell rang the hour. Eight o'clock. She had stood in the yard for two hours. The breeze rustling through the trees had her glance nervously into reaches of the garden swathed now in the ink-like darkness of a moonless night.

'. . . *don't do to be out after dark . . . a killer stalkin'* . . .'

The woman's words twanged against nerves already taut as a bowstring.

'. . . *get y'self 'ome* . . .'

Somewhere in the shadowed depths a sound deeper than the rustling of leaves reached to where she stood. Fingers twisting the corners of her shawl, Eden stared, her own anxiety as evident as that of those cleaning women.

Myra was not in this house, she was not expected to return . . . And her mistress, what was to say she, too, might not return, that she was not gone to stay a while at some other place? She had not been told so, but then neither had she been told otherwise.

The sound, one she could not identify, came again. Anxiety turning to fear, she stared into that threatening blackness, stared at a darker shape emerging from the bushes.

25

'She was not at the cottage?'

Andrew Denby put down the pen he was holding, his gaze on the lad twisting a cloth cap between his hands.

Davy Melia saw the frown nestle between dark brows and answered quickly. 'No, Mister Denby sir, there were no broom across the door to say Eden were out so I called and when there were no answer I went in; the door it were open and . . . and Eden has said for me not to stand at the gate when I calls to walk her to The Coppice . . . but her were not nowheres in the place.'

'Did you check the garden?'

Davy Melia's head bobbed rapidly. 'I done that but her weren't there neither.'

Had she been taken ill? Not allowing the concern that thought aroused to show in his voice, Andrew Denby's next question was falsely calm. 'Did you go upstairs? Did you look for Eden in her room?'

He were allowed use of her name! Davy was also cautious, allowing none of the surprise it engendered to colour his reply.

'I thought of that . . . thought her might 'ave been tekin' a bit of a rest.'

'But did you go upstairs?'

This man could be sharp with words . . . and even sharper with action. Hearing the astringency contained in the tone of that demand, the cap twisted again.

'I . . . I thought mebbe her were sleepin'. I hollered Mister Denby, I hollered real loud . . . me mother says that betimes I shouts fit to waken the dead . . .'

The apprehensiveness of an answer filled with unspoken apology telling of the boy's own discomfort, Andrew Denby curbed the disquiet once more rising inside him. 'Davy,' he said calmly, 'tell me, please, did you look for Eden in her bedroom?'

Deep colour staining his face, Davy nodded. 'I did 'oller, be God's truth I did, then gettin' no answer I got feared Eden might be teken poorly so . . . so I went . . .' he swallowed hard, his fingers torturing the cloth cap, '. . . I swears on the Bible, I swears I knocked on both them doors, I banged 'em 'til my knuckles was sore but weren't no answer so I peeped in . . . honest to God, Mister Denby, it were fear for Eden had me look in them rooms . . .'

'I believe you, Davy, and it was the right thing to do. But did you not wonder had she gone to the village?'

'I did wonder, so I went there, but folk along of Gospel Oak said as her had been there that morning but not after that, nor had the cut folk seen her for I asked every one as passed but they all said the same thing; they'd called at Shipton Cottage but Eden weren't there.'

What time had it been when she was last seen? To ask the lad that question might serve to make him even more jumpy.

'I went from Gospel Oak straight back to the cottage in case Eden were back from wherever it were she was at, but the place were still empty. That were when it come to me her might already be gone along to The Coppice and that her were talkin' to the old sod . . . the man who lives nearby. Eden tries speakin' with 'im though he be so surly I wouldn't spare 'im the time of day. But her weren't there neither, and the man were missing an' all. Same as the evening afore. That were when I went 'ome but Mother said I should ought to come tell you, seeing as how you pays me to walk along of Eden. Her said I were not to tek money when it were not earned.'

It sounded exactly like Sara Melia. Andrew nodded, but his thoughts sped like windblown leaves. Eden Brent had said the money placed in the pot on the mantel was put there against her leaving. Was that what she had done? Had she gone as quietly as she had come . . . was she still running away . . . or had the fear she was running from caught up with her, had it come to Shipton Cottage? But what use were questions no one could answer!

His voice calmer than his mind, he closed the book he had been writing in when the lad was shown into the room that was the office of the boatmaking yard. Thank Heaven he had worked later than intended . . . Had he left sooner . . . !

Pushing away the thought of what could have been, he looked again at the sturdy figure waiting before him. 'Davy, you and Eden, you get along well?'

What did that mean? Davy Melia's hands became suddenly still, his pleasant mouth tightening. Did Andrew Denby think him responsible for the wench not being where it were thought her should be?

'Eden and me was friends . . . I would walk along of her without pay from you and I would kill anybody as dared lay a finger on 'er!'

The shoulders had squared, the polite deference to station had gone, the lad had made way for the man.

'So would I, Davy . . . so would I.' More of himself in the words than he should have shown, Andrew went on quickly. 'The evenings you walked with her to that house below The Coppice, did she perhaps speak of where she had lived before coming to the Shipton place? Did she say anything which might provide the answer to where she is now?'

'Like I says, I'll kill any man bringin' harm to her.'

There had been moments of waiting for him to answer, moments when he had seen conflict in those brown eyes, now he saw promise, and more . . . he saw threat. Where Eden Brent was concerned, this young man would acknowledge no master. His reply no longer that of a lad, Andrew Denby met the threat.

'I understand the feeling you have for Eden,' he said, 'but believe me when I say mine are a thousand times stronger.'

'You . . . you and Eden!'

Dark head shaking briefly, Andrew Denby smiled. 'No, not Eden, only myself. I cannot claim the friendship you enjoy with her. I fear she feels nothing other than animosity towards me, and most certainly not what I feel for her.'

'You have feelings for Eden?'

Again the man! Andrew smiled to himself, then at the figure whose hands no longer mangled the cloth cap. 'Yes, Davy, I have feelings for Eden.'

Had he expected the threat in those honest eyes to deepen, to become a challenge? Did young feelings run as hot and burning as his own? Relaxing into a grin, Andrew felt relief. His confessed feelings had not placed a wedge between himself and a lad he admired.

'That be wonderful! Eden . . .'

'Eden does not know of my feelings and you must not speak to her of them!' Rising to his feet as he spoke, Andrew watched the wide grin become a frown of puzzlement. 'I would have your word, Davy.'

No trace now of the boy who had been shown into the office, though not all confusion had gone from his brow, Davy nodded. 'You 'as it.'

Thanking him as he rounded the desk, Andrew asked again: Had Eden spoke of her life before coming to Shipton Cottage?

'Her never said much, and Mother . . . well, you knows Mother, Mister Denby.'

The respect was back. Striding across the cobbled yard, Davy keeping easy pace alongside him, Andrew Denby recognised a respect shown one man by another; like a chrysalis the shell of boyhood had broken and the man had emerged. Sara Melia sent a youth to Denby Boat Builders but she would receive back an adult!

Returning the respect, he answered, 'Yes, David, I know your mother, her tenet is: Ask no question.'

A flush of pleasure brought on by the use of his given name, the freckled face found yet another grin. 'Ar, them be her words and they were followed by me. I asked nothing and nothing were told me, not until . . .'

'Until?' A hand on the saddle of the horse brought to him by the watchman, Andrew turned a sharp look to the figure half-swallowed by shadow now encompassing the yard.

'It were when I spoke of a man being killed along of the town . . .'

Waiting until there was no more to tell, Andrew Denby swung into the saddle. 'She said her sister was maid at Moorcroft but her grandmother's house was in Hobbins Street?'

'That be what her told. I be going to both them places now . . .'

'No.' Andrew's sharp tone made the horse prance. A soothing hand stroking the arched neck, his words came more softly. 'No, David. It is best you return home. With talk of murder your mother will no doubt be uneasy; she will be happier having you there to take care of her.'

It had not been meant condescendingly. This young man had a strong arm and the courage to use it. It would be a brave man or a fool who threatened Sara Melia.

Cloaked by night gloom, Davy pulled a wry mouth. Eden Brent were a friend, and young women needed tekin' care of same as his mother . . . but to leave one for the other . . . !

'I understand your difficulty. You want to be with your mother yet feel an obligation to search for Eden.' Andrew recognised the cause behind the failure to answer.

'That be it, but . . .'

'You can't be in two places at the same time, no man can. Do as I ask, return to your mother and I promise I will go look for Eden.'

He had meant what he had said. Andrew Denby drove the carriage he had hurriedly collected from his own home. Dark and squat, huddled like so many frightened sheep, the houses of Lea Brook Square seemed to seek the shelter of the pottery kiln rising tall above them while on the opposite side of the road the lone black shape of a chapel seemed to shrink into the darkness. But though concern for Sara Melia had been genuine, it had not been all of his reason for sending her son home.

Then what had? Was it that he also felt an obligation to search for the girl he wished he could call friend?

Guiding the carriage along a still busy Dudley Street, his inward smile was grim.

He was not searching for a girl he would have as a friend. He was searching for the girl he loved.

★

'I waited at Moorcroft. A cleaning woman there told me Myra had not been at that house for some time but that I could wait in the yard against the mistress's return: I wanted to ask if it was that Myra was no longer employed in service there then could she perhaps tell me where I might find her. I waited so long but then, then I thought maybe the mistress was gone away and might not be returning for some time . . . but I had to try to find where Myra was, I had to, so I came here, I came to ask you, Aunt Dora.'

There were more than thought of the mistress of Moorcroft not returning had this wench afeared. Was it the same thing had filled them other two young 'uns with fear? Had this one had a brush with that killer? Dora Benson watched the girl gulping in air. No, it were not Ava Russell had the face of this wench pale with fright.

'You did right to come. Don't do to be on the streets by yourself, not these nights it don't.'

'I heard about Alfred Birks . . .'

'A bad business . . . he were a decent lad, so your grandmother told, always polite an' respectful.'

'It was a dreadful shock to hear, I thought it might have been some illness . . .'

Turned to the kettle simmering over the fire, Dora Benson felt her blood chill. The wench didn't know!

'. . . then today I learned it was not . . .' Dora's breath eased, '. . . today a woman told me a young man had been murdered. That was dreadful enough, but when she said a young woman had suffered the same it fair stopped my heart. All I could think of was Myra, could it be Myra had been killed!'

'Weren't Myra.' Dora turned from the fire, leaving the kettle on its bracket. 'Weren't your sister that maniac done for.'

Relief which had sung on hearing that same news from the woman in the kitchen of Moorcroft became tinged with guilt. It was not Myra's life had been taken, but did that give right to her own feeling, her own joy!

But she could not help feeling the wonderful comfort those words had given; she could not prevent the consolation of knowing the sister she loved was safe and well. Surely heaven would not blame her for that?

'I was so happy when I heard that woman say the name . . .' Eden's quiet confession was almost lost beneath the clang of hammers coming from the tiny workshop where the others of Dora's family worked at the nailing long into the night. 'Is that so wrong, Aunt Dora? I don't mean to be unkind.'

'Nor you ain't, wench, nor you ain't.' Eyes filled with sympathy rested again on the kettle, sympathy which turned to dread with the next quiet words.

'The woman could not tell me had Myra been dismissed her position. She said only that she had not see her at Moorcroft for some time. I thought you would know, Aunt Dora, I thought Myra would have come to you, maybe . . . Maybe left some word for me or . . . or perhaps said where she could be found.'

There was a mountain of grief in Eden Brent . . .

Dora swung the kettle from the heat of the fire . . . but the wench had higher mountains yet to climb.

'Did she, did she come here?'

At Dora's back the question was soft in its pleading but each syllable pricked her heart. She had seen this wench brought to Hobbins Street when nobbut a babe in arms, watched her grow, shared the caring of her and yes . . . felt the loving of her, like she were a daughter born of her own body. How then . . . how to tell a wench you loved as your own . . . how to break her heart? But seemed that were a burden placed on Dora Benson by the Lord hisself . . . who but Him? Drawing a long breath she turned to face the girl sitting beside her at the table. Who but the Lord . . . may He grant her strength!

A lull in the medley of hammering brought a moment's blessing of silence but Dora's ears were filled with the beat of her pulses. She had known that one day this might happen but had prayed that day be far in the future, that Eden Brent would have a man beside her, a man to hold her when night forced open the gate of tears, to comfort sorrow the slow passage of years could ease, yet could not erase. But Eden Brent was here now, and so was the time of truth. It would be a savage truth, cruel and heartless, one against which no barrier could be forged, no wall built high enough to close out the horror, to shield against the nightmare . . . It would be a gospel of truth, a gospel of pain!

The hammers resumed their clanging but to Dora,

caught by love for the girl watching her and the despair the telling of that truth would bring, it seemed each blow was a laugh of the devil.

But the devil's work had been done out there along of the Church Steps! No, this was not his ordaining; this was the moment chosen of the Lord, the moment of His bidding, and she must keep faith with it. Though the bitterness of that would be aloe on her tongue, she must tell all, there could be naught held back, naught left to question that would grow and fester in the darkness of doubt. But not to say what was known only to her, to keep secret what would always lie like a sword in her own heart, would that protect Eden Brent for ever . . . or would the ransom of silence be paid in vain?

'Yes, her come here.' Despite the clamour of the workshop the reply was quiet, each word showing pain on Dora Benson's thin, lined face. 'T'were a while since. Come to ask did I know of your whereabouts, where it were you might 'ave gone on leaving of your grandmother's house; but I could give no answer savin' the telling of your intent to leave Wednesbury altogether.'

'But where?'

'No, wench!' Dora lifted a hand against the interruption, 'Bide you quiet 'til the telling be done. Myra were all but spent when her reached this house. The walk from Darlaston had her exhausted, least so I thought. But it were not a fault of tiredness; that I realised next day when her couldn't rise from the bed I had laid her in, but the result of a sickness. The parish doctor were called for; we 'adn't the money to pay another. All credit to him, he examined her thorough. Myra had a sickness of the lungs, he said when that examinin' were over. It were one had been hurried in its path by lack of food and warmth, the neglect had been such that there were no escapin' of its result . . . Myra was dying. Cold had eaten into her, becomin' the pneumonia. That, together with the infection of the lungs, meant there could be no more'n a two day afore the end would come. Doctor said he would arrange for her to be taken into the infirmary along of the poorhouse . . .'

Eden's agonised sob brought Dora to her side. Holding her, feeling the emotions trembling wave upon wave, Dora's own mouth trembled. She had known the heartbreak her story would bring, she also knew she must give all of its telling.

'. . . I . . . I told him . . .' her voice cracking, she went on, '. . . I told him Myra Brent would lie in no poorhouse, that her would stay in this house with folk as loved her. I sat with her the rest of that day and though I begged her stay quiet, so her strength would last, her would 'ave none of it. Every word were pain to her, the coughing takin' her breath so it were longer and longer afore her could go on, but the look in her eyes, it were a look that pleaded time in which to tell. The all of what I could do for her was to listen and that I did though it had me pray the powers of heaven strike vengeance on the mistress of Moorcroft.'

Arms tight about the sobbing girl, Dora told the rest of her story. Of Myra's reason for the slap she had given, of her not knowing of her grandmother's dying, the abuse she had suffered only so there would be enough money to help her family and the futile search for her sister, one which ended when she had met Ava Russell in a dressmaker's shop.

'That woman vowed you was at Moorcroft, that should Myra not return to service there, then you would be made to practise all the vileness, perform them acts of wickedness herself had been forced into. That were summat Myra couldn't live with, nor turn her back on. Her would return to that house of hell but first her would come to one who might understand, one who in time could explain should her sister ever enquire why it was that slap were given and why it was the position at Moorcroft had been snatched from her. It was done of love.' Dora touched a hand to the head pressed to her chest. 'It were done to protect you. You asked did her leave some word for you? The answer be yes; her used her last pennies to buy pencil an' paper to write a letter, but there were no address on the envelope I found among her things so I kept it, kept it against the chance of meetin' with you.'

The envelope a blur amid tears, Eden lifted her glance. 'Myra, where . . . where . . . ?'

Her own throat so thick she could scarce answer, Dora dabbed her own tears with a corner of her apron. 'Her be alongside o' your grandmother. The folk of Hobbins Street, they all given of their ha'pennies and pennies. Together we scraped the cost of a box, plain though it were; and the little 'uns, them still at school, lads an' wenches both, they gathered the flowers that grows wild in the fields, bunched an' dressed them with leaf an' with ribbon took from Sunday frocks until every inch of that box were lost beneath the blossom: then the priest along of the church, him an' old Tom Higgins who digs the graves, they asked no payment. It be no consoling of the hurt the knowing of that will give now; the hurt you feels inside will go on for many a year, but this might, with the Lord's mercy, bring a comfort. Your sister were given a Christian burial, maybe not of the sort afforded your grandmother, for money d'ain't stretch to a stone to mark her, but the love that went along of Myra Brent, the respect with which her were laid to her rest can have no surpassing.'

Love and respect. Eden's eyes closed against the pain. Myra had been shown love and respect . . . but neither had been paid by her sister.

26

Moorcroft had been in darkness. No butler had answered his hand on the door and no scullery maid had answered at the kitchen. Where else was Eden likely to have gone? His fingers taut on the reins with anxiety, Andrew Denby's glance raked the street each side of the carriage. The one leading into the town from Lea Brook had been busy, as expected, but here in the heart of Wednesbury the difference was glaring.

The butchers' stalls in the Shambles were empty, no women hoping for a cheap cut of meat and no straw-hatted butcher tempting customers with calls of an extra couple of sausages with every pound bought. The narrow street was deserted as was the market square, its stalls lines of black-boned skeletons etched against the gloom of shadows retreating from the lantern lights of hotel and tavern, leaving darkness to gather over the empty square.

The town was afraid. What he had been told by David Melia, what he had heard from others when going about his business, the brutal murders of two young people had the whole of Wednesbury in fear.

Two killings . . . and the second victim had been a

young woman! Andrew Denby's blood chilled. Eden
Brent was a young woman . . . and she was here in this
town!

The hiss of steam from a train beginning its journey
from the market place had the horse buck nervously;
the jolt of the carriage jerked at Andrew's attention. He
must not give way to the alarm lurking on the perimeter
of his mind; he must stay alert if he hoped to find Eden.

Moorcroft was the house where her sister was
employed. Murmuring softly to the still fractious
animal, Andrew forced his brain to think calmly. That
girl had obtained the position of ladies' maid whilst her
sister had remained at home with their grandmother.
Home! A frown of concentration heavy on his brow he
strove to remember. Lord, why had he not paid more
attention to what the lad had said. He had been eager to
be gone, avid to begin the search for the girl who more
and more claimed his thoughts . . . But rashness, as often
he had found during boyhood, resulted in cold comfort.

Think! Fingers tight about the leather reins, he willed
his mind to the conversation he had held with the Melia
lad.

'. . . *Eden had remained with their grandmother* . . .'

Carts rumbling past, their drivers shouting their
disapproval of 'folk daft enough to 'ave a carriage stood
in the middle o' the road a' blockin' of folks' path',
made no impression on Andrew.

'. . . *remained with their grandmother* . . . *lived at* . . .'

Lord, where was it David said she had lived?

Owen Street? A mental shake of the head rejected

the name. Think, man, think! What name did the lad say? Breathing deeply, Andrew pushed back the dread, once more sending cold fingers probing along his veins. It was 'O' something or other. The lad had been so anxious his words had fallen over one another. Oldbury Street . . . Ogden Street . . . No, it had been neither of those!

''Ow long yoh o'bin a' goin' to keep that there carriage a' blockin' o' the street!'

That was it! Relief sweeping through him, Andrew called an apology to an irate carter complaining loudly at his path being obstructed. Like his contemporaries, this man failed to give the beginning and ending requisite letter to many of their words.

''Ow long yoh o'bin!'

Tautness released from his fingers, he flicked the reins putting the horse to a trot.

'O'bin.'

He breathed a smile. The name he had tried to remember . . . it was Hobbins . . . Eden's grandmother had lived in Hobbins Street.

Too many days had passed. Ava Russell's mind swirled, a pool of acid. The agreement had been for one day . . . one day and then Myra Brent would be returned to Moorcroft. But that day had passed into two, then three, then . . .

But counting, like the waiting, would not bring that girl back . . . She would have to be brought, and she would!

Reaching for the bell pull beside the ornate fireplace, Ava felt the bile of anger surge fiercer. It was no use ringing for a cook who was no longer here, and that cleaning woman . . . She did not want the like coming to this sitting-room; the smell of carbolic soap, the patched clothing and dreary face were too distasteful. She could go herself to the yard and tell the gardener to harness the pony cart. Yes, it was a task she could perform, had not her husband had the teaching . . . But since when did Ava Russell keep a dog and bark herself! Besides . . . eyes glinting like ice-covered rock despite the heat burning inside, it did not do to let all and sundry know her skills.

Would it be more propitious to wait until those two cleaning women had finished for the day, until they had left the house? But that would be evening, dusk would already be falling; by the time she reached Darlaston night would have the streets dark. She could hardly look for Myra Brent at night.

A hesitant tap supplementing her irascibility Ava glared at the door. What could the fool of a woman be wanting? Had the orders given her not been explicit . . . even an idiot could have understood!

Timorous as the step of a church mouse during mass, the tap brushed the door a second time, bringing a sullen snap from Ava.

'Beggin' pardon, mum . . .' The speaker did not enter and Ava did not invite. '. . . be a young woman askin' for to see you.'

'I will see no one.'

'Yes, mum, but her asked to tell you . . .'

Was the woman a complete imbecile! Ava's nostrils flared her impatience. How long could she go on without a housekeeper, without a personal maid? The cleaning woman hadn't the brain of a flea!

'. . . her asked to say her called last evenin'.'

Mouth open to order the woman back to her duties, Ava closed it slowly. A young woman . . . called last evening . . .

Irritation becoming the dull glow of satisfaction, tight mouth curving, Ava stared at the partly open door.

Myra Brent had returned! Ava drew a long breath, feeling it carry the savour of satisfaction deep inside. Myra Brent had returned! Once more the fates had favoured Ava Russell.

Going to stand at the window, staring out towards the trees and bushes bordering the grounds, she smiled, a vindictive, vengeful movement of the mouth. Myra Brent had returned . . . she would be sorry she had ever left!

'Why did my sister leave this house?'

Flung with the force of stones the words hit, spinning Ava about. This was not the woman she had followed from the dressmaker's shop! The hair, the bone structure of the face, the way of holding the head all were the same; only the eyes were different, Myra Brent had blue eyes where as this girl . . . her eyes were blue-green, a beautiful turquoise. But there was one more difference: Myra's eyes had lost their fire while the ones that stared at her now spat repugnance, spewed loathing as a volcano spewed lava. But if this was who she was certain it must be then that repellence would add pleasure to pleasure. She would enjoy breaking this girl as she had enjoyed breaking her sister . . . and in the process enjoy more . . . Yes, she would enjoy *much* more.

Hiding this behind an affected glance of bewilderment, she gave a slight shake of the head. 'Forgive me . . . your name?'

'I think you know that already!'

The girl had fire. Ava nodded to herself. But there were many ways of dousing fires . . . and she would use them all.

'. . . but I will tell you. My name is Eden Brent. Myra was my sister.'

Was? Ava's pulse tripped on the word. Had this girl made a slip of the tongue, used the wrong tense . . . said 'was' in place of 'is'?

'I will ask again,' Eden's voice throbbed, 'why did my sister leave this house?'

Was that cleaning woman still standing beyond that half-open door, her ears flapping to catch every word? Words that would find their way into half the houses in Wednesbury.

'A moment!' Ava lifted a hand. 'I think you would not want every person in this household hearing what it is you may wish to speak of.'

Skirts whispering over thick turkey carpet, she crossed the room, then standing in front of the door she closed, faced a girl whose every fibre spoke hatred.

The pulse that had tripped a moment before took on a drumbeat. What did this girl know? Had Myra gone to see her? Was that the reason of delay in her returning? Had the fool of a girl told of . . .

'I have no objection to anyone hearing what it is I have come here to discuss,' Eden was speaking again, 'in fact I intend it become public knowledge!'

She must go carefully . . . find out exactly what had Myra's sister so incensed.

'My dear,' she said quietly, 'surely you must know your sister is with your grandmother? She is not in this house simply because she is on annual leave.'

Bitterness of a strength she had never known before, lanced the reply from Eden's taut lips. 'Myra is with our grandmother but she is not on annual leave . . . Myra is dead!'

Dead! Like choral music the word swelled in Ava's mind. Myra Brent was dead! The last threat to the safety of Ava Russell, to the keeping of her secret, was removed! But she must not allow the jubilation of that to show. That same affectation of a moment before creasing her brow, she gasped. 'Myra dead! But . . . but how . . . when?'

Eden's stare blazed pure fire. 'You might do better to ask the cause, but then you know that . . . and so do I.'

There was more than resentment burning in this girl, more than fury had her trembling; there was passion, the passion of hate. Ava felt the cold of warning touch her spine. She must go carefully indeed.

'I know the cause?'

'Yes!' Eden hurled the word. 'Yes, you know, for it was you, you and your vile practices. That was the reason for Myra's leaving, she could stand no more of your abuse!'

So Myra Brent had told of those little pleasures! But it would have been told only to this girl . . . Myra would have been too ashamed to divulge it to anyone else.

The lies of a chit of a girl against a woman of property! She must be made to realise the harm that could bring upon herself. But not only upon herself. The drumbeat continued in Ava's veins. Mud could stick as easily to silk as to cotton, as easily to the wealthy as to the poor.

All pretence sliding from her like a cloak, Ava's eyes were black ice. 'Take care, Miss Brent. Justice wields a heavy hand and accusation not justified has it strike hard.'

'Then you should be prepared for the blow. My sister is dead!'

A laugh of pure venom cut Eden's words, Ava's own spitting like a cobra ready to strike. 'Your sister is dead . . . Am I supposed to show sorrow?'

The sheer indifference, the total lack of compassion, caught in Eden's chest, squeezing away any trace of excuse she might have found for this woman's behaviour.

'No.' There was no exoneration, no pardon. Cold and implacable, Eden's response came quietly. 'No, you should not show sorrow, that would be only one more deception. But you will show fear, and believe me that will be no falsehood.'

'Fear!' Ava's laugh slid deprecatingly. 'Fear of you!'

Her glance steady, though the intensity of it blazed, Eden gave a brief shake of her head. 'No, not of me but of what I will bring to light. Your fear should be of the proof I have, the letter my sister left showing you for the creature you are – a vile parasite feeding on the needs of others, a viper whose poison is injected into any who come in contact with you. You carry the cancer of evil, the abscess of corruption. It is a canker of the soul, lust which knows no cure, no satisfaction except that of abusing an innocent girl, of using her poverty to lure her into carrying out your unspeakable demands and, once trapped, there was no escape . . . none but death.'

As will be your own only escape! Ice-cold, the thought sat in Ava's mind though her face showed no sign of its residence. Instead she answered calmly.

'I advise you take care not to let your words be heard beyond this room. Meantime, perhaps you would take with you the things your sister left behind. Please wait here and I will bring them to you.'

Fate had smiled, but the god of fortune laughed. Upstairs in her room Ava flung open the door leading to her dressing-room.

First Birks had met his death, then Dilly Madely had felt the embrace and now Myra Brent. All were dead, all threat they had held eliminated. But now that of Eden Brent hovered. Did she truly have a letter written by her sister?

Reaching inside a tall mahogany wardrobe, Ava found what she was looking for.

The god of fortune was laughing now . . . but the one who laughed last tasted success!

Halfway back to the head of the staircase, she paused. That cleaning woman! How dare she speak with a visitor to this house, even one as insignificant as the Brent girl. Mouth hardening, feet silent on the thick carpet, Ava walked several steps then halted. The voice . . . it was no longer that of the cleaning woman . . . It was not a woman at all. Body tense, every nerve alert, she listened to the words carrying indistinctly.

'Davy . . . he said you would not . . .'

'I had to . . . I could not go on . . .'

'Then you should have asked . . .'

That last was louder, deeper. The voice of a man! But what man? Husband of the girl or . . . Ava's hands tightened on the petticoat and drawers taken from the wardrobe . . . a member of the constabulary? Had Eden Brent spoken with the police?

She had said she had a letter . . . If that were true . . . if she had shown it to the magistrate! But doing so, would bring disrepute upon her own sister, have her name despised and herself shunned by everyone she knew. The girl was no idiot; she would have reckoned with the results of speaking with the police.

A breath calming her turbulence, Ava laid aside the underwear, one free hand smoothing the bodice of her gown. Whoever was the man with Eden Brent, he was no representative of the law.

'What could Myra have left in this house?' Closer to the head of the stairs, Ava heard the words clearly.

'. . . she would not have wished to keep anything that reminded her of this house.'

Deep and pleasant-sounding, despite the edge of anger, the man's response was equally audible.

'Then there is no reason to remain. I will tell that serving woman to inform her mistress we do not wish to wait.'

We! Ava glanced towards the sitting-room. Not a brother, Myra had no brother, nor had there been mention of a marriage within her family . . . but then Myra Brent had made very little mention of her circumstances.

'There is no need for you to stay. I can return to Gospel Oak by myself. I will be at Shipton Cottage when Davy calls.'

'You will not return alone. However, I respect your need to speak privately with the mistress of this house. I shall wait for you in the carriage.'

Not a brother . . . and, if not a husband, then who?

Ava remained perfectly still as the door opened, her eyes following the tall figure striding across the hall.

Andrew Denby! Ava's teeth clenched. He had been to this house before. Samuel had often done business with him, saying afterward he was a young man it would not do to trifle with. But why would he come traipsing after the Brent girl . . . was it simply the dog following the bitch?

Waiting until he was gone from the hall, she returned to the sitting-room.

'I'm sorry.' She faced the slight figure which had not moved. 'I am unable to find the things left in Myra's room. It seems my housekeeper has stored them away. If you will say where you are living I will have them sent on to you.'

Tense as her slight body, Eden's reply twanged the quiet of the once-elegant house. 'There is nothing here that I would want. I have not called for what I might take but for what I could give.'

'Give!' Ava's laughed return was scathing. 'What could a poverty-stricken slut give me . . . apart from lice!'

She had not been able to fully comprehend what she had read in Myra's letter. Part of her had not understood . . . not quite accepted the awfulness written there. Now, looking at the sneering face of the woman who had been her sister's employer, Eden felt the truth rise solidly in her throat. Ava Russell was all Myra had claimed. Malignity and malice gleamed in those stone-hard eyes, rank bitterness twisted a line of naked savagery about the mouth painting the face with a look of cold, heartless cruelty.

The cruelty she had shown Myra? Watching the thin lips compress in a vicious line, the eyes become hooded with threat, Eden owned to what sounded in her mind. Ava Russell was a woman of evil!

Eden's fingers curled tightly into her grandmother's shawl at the horror of what she now acknowledged. In that moment it seemed that beloved voice spoke.

'*Don't go lettin' her see you be feared, stand your ground, me little wench . . . show her the love of a sister.*'

Her head lifted with courage drawn from those inner words, and Eden's reply was steady.

'I can give you more than lice. I can give you that which will bite harder and be much more difficult to rid yourself of. I tell you, the time will come when you will regret the degradation you brought upon Myra, you will regret the vile acts you forced her to perform.'

Loud and snatched, a breath hissed between Ava's clamped lips. 'Are you threatening me?'

Tightness still holding her body, Eden looked into glittering serpent-like eyes and, for a brief moment, it seemed the evil of the woman reached out for her. Then, like a hand taking hers, the strength of her grandmother flowed warm along her veins.

'Not my threat but that of heaven. What you have done is judged by that power and it will not go unpunished. Retribution will be taken and from this day my every prayer will be that the Lord make me His instrument of revenge.'

27

'I thought he were goin' to strike me, I seen his hands curl into fists and I thought he were about to give me a beltin'.'

Walking beside Eden, a cloth-wrapped dish in his hands, Davy Melia related that morning's meeting with Andrew Denby.

'I told 'im, I said as I couldn't be at your side every minute, I couldn't go sleepin' at Shipton Cottage like I was your brother . . . but that d'ain't have the curbing of his anger. I swears I ain't seen him go up like that afore. Oh 'e has a temper, that's been shown more'n once along of the boatyard, but this were summat different. Mister Denby were not just angry he . . . he seemed frightened like. Why do you reckon that be? Unless he were feared of that killer that still don't be catched . . . reckon that be it. Mister Denby were worried for that man, couldn't rightly be no more'n that.'

No, it was no more than that, Andrew Denby had no more reason to be anxious for her than any decent man was for a woman's safety at this time. All of Wednesbury was anxious for their safety. But why come to Moorcroft himself? Why not send Davy to bring her home to Shipton Cottage?

'I said as I would go find you but he hadn't the listenin' of that, he were off outta that boatyard like the devil held a firebrand to his tail. I hopes this don't mean I won't get to walk with you no more.'

Her mind on words other than those now being spoken, Eden made no answer but, in the silence that followed, she heard other words echo clearly in her mind.

'*What did you think to gain in coming to that house!*' Andrew Denby had been silent until they had left the town centre and were on the way to the cottage, but then the anger held inside him had breached. '*Have you no sense . . . crossing the heath alone . . . For God's sake, girl, if you have no thought of yourself, at least have some for others! Consider their feelings instead of just your own!*'

That had been the torch which had put flame to the feelings churning inside her. She had wanted to avenge her sister, to tell Ava Russell she had come to Moorcroft to do just that. But that had been a siren song, a lure calling its promise . . . but that promise had proved false. Ava Russell had simply laughed her contempt and she . . . Eden remembered her helplessness . . . She could no nothing. Then, with Andrew Denby's accusation, the dam holding those feelings of inadequacy burst, letting free the torrent that swept away all of her grandmother's teaching regarding politeness to other people.

'*Feelings!*' It had snapped from her, a verbal onslaught, sharp and bitter. '*Just whose feelings would that be? Missis Ava Russell's, the woman who drove a young woman to her death? Or perhaps you mean those of an elderly man, one who cannot bring himself to speak a pleasant word? Or are the feelings you refer to those of a younger man whom it seems cannot keep from interfering in the life of another person, one who not only does not wish his attention but positively resents it! Allow me to tell you, Mister Denby, I find no reason or excuse for behaviour towards affairs that have no business with you. Your attentions are uncalled for and are most definitely unwanted!*'

'Be you angry with me, Eden?'

'What?' Drawn sharply from her thoughts by a tug at her arm, Eden glanced at the freckled face, its usual sunny look displaced by one of apprehension.

'I asked . . . be you angry with me?'

A quick smile meant to reassure having no effect upon the dismay evident in his eyes, Eden asked gently, 'Why would I be angry with you, Davy?'

'For going to the boatyard . . . For tellin' Andrew Denby you wasn't home in the cottage an' that I couldn't be finding you nowheres I looked, and for . . .'

'For what?' Eden prompted as the confession tailed away. 'We are friends, Davy, and true friends need have no fear of speaking of what they did to help the other.'

'That be what I thought I were doin', honest Eden. I were thinkin' only to 'elp, otherwise I wouldn't never 'ave told 'im . . . we be friends, you an' me, but you won't want that no longer . . . Not once you find I d'ain't hold to a confidence.'

A confidence! What could he be referring to? Seeing the slight tremor of a mouth he was trying so hard to hold firm, Eden hid her question behind a smile.

'Davy, whenever we have talked together have I once asked you never to repeat what I have said?'

'No . . . not so I recalls.'

'And you don't recall because such was never spoken, so how can you have broken a secret you were not asked to keep?'

'That be right, you d'ain't ask such . . .' the smile chasing the tremor from the boy's mouth faded as quickly as it came, '. . . but me mother, her won't judge what I said not near so gentle as you . . . It'll be a cuff around the ear an' no mistake, her says as I talk afore I think, an' it be right, I does . . . but I were feared for you, Eden . . . so feared that when Mister Denby asked 'ad you made mention of your life afore comin' to Gospel Oak I . . . I told 'im everythin'.'

That was how he had known to come to Moorcroft! He had followed her there not to interfere in her affairs but to calm a young lad's fears, to assure Davy she had come to no harm crossing the heath.

'. . . *I find no reason or excuse*. . .' That was what she had said of his behaviour.

Eden felt the sudden warmth of shame.

What would Andrew Denby think of her!

★

She had had the audacity to come here to this house . . . to threaten!

Her cleaning women gone for the night, Ava Russell stormed through the silent rooms of Moorcroft House.

A letter, she had said, a letter written by her sister. That, supposing any such letter existed, was the only real threat. Eden Brent was penniless, as her sister had been, a pauper who could only dream . . . but was that all she was? True, *she* may have no money but the man who had followed her . . .

A niggle of alarm brought Ava to a halt.

Andrew Denby was no pauper, neither was he without respect and influence . . . influence that would go a long way in this town, influence which, if brought to bear, could well have the mistress of Moorcroft standing in a court of law!

Damn the girl! Caught with a vicious kick, a delicate *guéridon* toppled, snapping a slender fluted leg against the wall. Glancing at the broken stand, its circular glass top shattered as was the Leroy et Cie clock it held, Ava swore again. That was one more of Samuel's treasures she had intended to sell; that, more than anything left in these near empty rooms, would have realised a decent price . . . something she expected from the sale of the foundry but as yet there had been no offers!

Why was it taking so long? Because it was a woman who was selling! Did they think her so gullible that should they hold out long enough that she would part with the business for little or nothing? They would roast in hell before that happened!

Roast in hell! Was that not the verdict of the pious given to those who 'brushed the muff', given by the oh-so-puritanical-holier-than-the-saints-of-heaven women, many of whom no doubt practised the same even as they whispered against it behind their hands? And was it not the condemnation meted out by those charlatans, men who took their pleasures with others of the same gender! Roast in hell. Ava laughed contemptuously. Hell would be pretty overcrowded!

But not all of that region's torments were experienced only after death; there were some that were visited upon the living, some like that which burned in her now, the desire screaming to be satisfied.

Having reached her bedroom, Ava stared at the door which led into her bathroom. She had dismissed all intentions of visiting the workhouse, of taking another girl to train to her requirements. With Myra's return and her sister to join her, the two of them living at Moorcroft, two to satisfy the need which pulled and twisted, to slake the ravening which flicked and whipped between the legs until she must try to appease the longing for herself. But the sedative of her own fingers, the remission they brought from that ferment of longing was fleeting; it did not impart that heady, exotic, breathtaking emotion, that wonderful sweep through the whole of the body which brought cries to the throat, cries which begged for more.

But Myra Brent was dead!

Going into her dressing-room Ava flung open the door of a large wardrobe.

Myra was lost and the sister also. There would be no chance now of having *her* come to Moorcroft as ladies' maid, not with Andrew Denby in the background. That would be taking too great a risk; as Samuel had once remarked, '*He was a man who did not happily concede what he felt to be his*'.

And he must feel that of Eden Brent. He must have some claim or else why follow her here?

The dog and the bitch! Ava's stomach jolted with the eroticism the thought aroused. She must find her own bitch.

She ought not to have spoken the way she had. Grating the lump of suet she had obtained fresh that morning, Eden's thoughts were on the events of the previous day.

Rudeness had never been allowed whilst her grandmother lived and all of her own and Myra's lifetime the lesson had been taught: 'Good manners cost naught.' But it was a lesson she had forgotten.

Reaching for the stale bread left to soak in water until it was soft, she squeezed each piece until the residue of moisture was removed, then broke it further with a fork.

She had snapped angrily at Andrew Denby, thrown her accusations like missiles. She had felt him stiffen beside her as he drove the carriage, but he had made no reply to her volleys. He had remained silent the whole of the way to the cottage then driven away, still without speaking a word.

She added the grated suet to the bread, folding the whole with sugar, mixed spice and sultanas, then stirring in a beaten egg.

She had been too angry, too absorbed in her own frustration, to care about the things she had said but that indifference had lasted only a short while. Now she found herself remembering the tightness of that face, the straight line of the mouth, but, especially, it was the look in those dark eyes as he had helped her from the carriage. He had hesitated before releasing her hand and, for a brief moment, his penetrating stare seemed to reach her very soul and in that stare had been . . .

Spooning the mixture into a well-greased roasting pan, then sprinkling the surface with sugar, she placed it in the oven.

. . . in it had been . . .

Straightening, she stared into the fire.

What had she seen in those eyes? She asked herself now as she had asked long into the sleepless hours of the night.

It had not been anger nor irascibility, it had seemed to be none of the feelings consuming her as she met that stare, there had been no irritability or waspish contention but only . . .

Eyes closing, a long breath drawn against what the silence of dawn had finally forced her to accept, Eden twisted the cloth held in tightening fingers.

. . . those eyes had held the look of a man filled with distaste and, as in those long wakeful hours, the realisation added to the sorrow in her own.

She opened her eyes, breathed out and returned to the task of preparing food.

She regretted her outburst, felt humiliated by the remembering of her bitterness, but one thought overrode all of that, one thought which had her heart twist: Andrew Denby despised her.

She had tried to dismiss the hurt of that, a hurt which matched that of knowing she could do nothing to repay Ava Russell's cruelty to Myra.

Long accustomed to the task of cooking her hands worked quickly, leaving Eden's mind to the misery of her thoughts.

'. . . *her every touch, the feel of her body beneath my hand burned inside like acid . . .*'

The words written in Myra's letter had branded themselves on Eden's soul.

'. . . *believe me, my dearest sister, I stayed at Moorcroft only so you and our grandmother be kept well and safe. What I did whilst under that roof can never be forgiven of heaven, nor of you. But I do ask, dearest Eden, that you believe me when I say, I did it for you, and for Grandmother, I did it out of the love I have for you both.*'

'I do believe you, Myra.' Eden whispered against the tears thickening her throat. 'I believe you and I forgive you as I know God also will forgive.'

But how to forgive herself? How to live with the

knowledge she could not avenge the wrongs done to her sister?

'Help me, Gran,' she whispered again, 'help me punish that woman for what she did to Myra.'

Tying a cloth about the basin holding the kidney pudding she placed it in the pan of water bubbling gently over the fire.

Her grandmother could not help. Nobody could!

I'm sorry, Myra. Her heart cried out as she washed the utensils used in preparing her dishes, the pain of her failure biting deep while she tidied the small room.

She could only speak those words to a memory, apologise to the sister she carried in her heart . . . but there was an apology she could speak aloud, speak it to a living man, and it must be made now.

Quickly ensuring all would be well with her cooking until her return, she placed the broom diagonally across the cottage door, her steps rapid as she ran along the towpath.

'Be a woman out in the yard.'

Andrew Denby looked at the boatyard overseer who had come into his office. 'A woman?'

The man nodded. 'It don't be nobody I knows from the boats, I ain't never seen her here afore.'

Pen resting between his fingers Andrew allowed the ghost of a smile. His overseer knew every wife, daughter, sister and granddaughter who helped man the narrowboats yet this one had him puzzled.

'What does she want?'

'Be a bloody cheek her askin' . . . no, her tellin' of what it be her wants.'

'Which is?' Andrew's tongue remained firmly in cheek.

'Her said her be here to speak with yourself and that her wouldn't be takin' her leave until her had done just that.'

An ultimatum . . . and to his yard overseer! There were not many *men* with nerve enough for that. The hovering smiled reach Andrew Denby's eyes. How would his reputation sit with the others of the yard hearing the demand of a woman! Keeping the thought to himself he asked, 'A name . . . did the woman give her name?'

'Ar, Mister Denby, sir,' the overseer nodded again, 'her said her name be Eden Brent.'

Eden Brent! Andrew's fingers whitened with the force suddenly gripping the pen. What had brought her here? Had she been . . . the man who had attacked her that evening along of the path leading from The Coppice, had he returned . . . found her alone at Shipton Cottage . . . had he . . . ?

'Will I tell her you be too busy to go speakin' with her?'

'No.' Snapping off the thought that made the blood run cold in his veins, he coughed to disguise the tremble of the reply. 'Tell . . . tell Miss Brent I will see her. Have her come in.'

Miss Brent! Returning to the yard, the overseer pursed his lips. He had not used the title 'Miss' even

though it had not gone unnoticed the girl wore no ring
on her finger, yet Andrew Denby had used it. Now,
how come he knew her were no man's wife? And why
the tremor in his voice when he had answered? The
wench come to the boatyard might be unknown to
some but her were certainly knowed by Andrew
Denby.

28

What had she expected to find at that boatyard? The last of the day's chores completed and the next day's planned and catered for, Eden climbed the stairs to her room.

Her mind had been filled with the memory of the look she had seen in Andrew Denby's eyes and the nearer she got to his place of business the more she wanted to turn and run. But she had not turned, she had gone on, though it had taken every last ounce of determination to actually step into that yard and ask to see the owner.

The man she had asked that of had stared. In amazement that a young woman should demand he do as she requested? Or was it simply surprise that demand was to speak not with him, and not even through him, but to address herself directly to a man so obviously above her own station?

But, reluctant as he had been, the man had carried her request to his employer and, on his return to where she waited, he had touched a finger to his dust-laden cap before conducting her to that small room he said was 'the gaffer's office'.

She had never been in an office before.

Removing her clothes, laying them neatly over a chair, she sponged herself all over with water poured from a large jug liberally painted with pink briar roses.

She had lived almost every day of her life in Wednesbury, a town of a thousand workshops, metal foundries and coal mines. Yet, apart from Aunt Dora's brewhouse which served as a nail-making shop, she had never set foot in any one of them. Yet she had gone to that boat-building yard.

Fair hair, lightened by summer sun to pale gold and now released from restraining pins, shone in the light of the lamp placed beside the bed.

Her nerves had been stretched so much she had almost felt them twang.

She drew the hairbrush in steady rhythmic strokes through long silken strands.

The yard had been noisy with the sounds of saws and hammers, filling the air with the medley of sounds she had heard a distance away. One by one the sounds had ceased and the eyes of several dozen workmen had fastened on the figure of the young woman come to stand on their ground. Then, the one so obviously in charge had walked towards her and, in that moment, she had been terrified.

Eden set down the hairbrush, both hands pressing down on it to still the trembling that came with the recall of those few moments.

She had watched the figure approach, but it had not been the workman she had seen. Eden swallowed, the restriction building even now in her throat. The yard around her had faded, its place taken by a room with cotton lace curtains closed across its windows, a dark heavy sofa and, in one corner, glass-fronted cages of stuffed birds that added to the overall gloom. But it was not the room with its tiny dead birds that had her trembling; it was a woman . . . a gaunt sharp-featured woman, cold eyes gleaming, voice harsh and breathy as she reached for a young girl, a girl she ordered sharply to '*Remove your bodice and drawers . . .*'

Deep breaths stilling the shake of her hands, chasing the ogres of childhood, Eden stared about her own small room, resting a glance on chair, washstand, bedside table, each object giving reassurance that this, and not those pictures in her mind, was real.

Had she been trembling when that workman had reached her, when he had asked what was her business there at the yard? Perhaps not visibly, but it had to have been that old fear, a fear she had thought buried so deep inside of her that it would not rise again, that had made her answer as she had.

Grandmother would not have approved. Going to kneel beside her bed, Eden's smile was faint but her heart beat strong with love as she whispered, 'I apologised to that workman, Gran, I said I was sorry to have been so rude.'

And she had also apologised to Andrew Denby.

Her prayers said, Eden turned out the lamp, then crossed to the window, drawing open the shutters to a gentler, almost silver, light.

He had risen from behind a wide desk as she had entered that office. Broad and tall, it was he, not the wooden cupboards set along the walls, seemed to dominate the room and again she had felt the urge to turn away, to run back to the familiar surroundings of Shipton Cottage.

She might even have done that except he was around the desk and helping her to a chair before her feet would move.

Was something wrong? Had she been hurt in any way? Had someone come to the cottage?

Eden stared down at the silvered ribbon of water winding into the mystery of the darkened heath, but the mystery that held her was not that of night-shrouded land but of the look she had seen in Andrew Denby's eyes as he touched her. It had not been the stare of distaste; she had been wrong. He did not despise her.

A small cloud skipped across the huge silver orb sending shadows skimming across the water.

Shadows, too, had skimmed across those dark eyes. Shadows that had disappeared quickly, but not before she had seen what they held. It was not the look she thought she had seen the day he fetched her from Moorcroft. Today she had caught a glimpse of something far removed from that. Concern? Disquiet? No, his look had held . . .

Forehead touching the cool glass of the window-pane, Eden felt the rush of warmth to her cheeks.

It had held what her grandmother's look had held

when comforting a grazed knee or a cut finger . . .
Those eyes had gleamed not with reproach but with
affection.

But that was as much of a fantasy as dragons under
the bed had been to a child, and it must be banished as
she had banished other imaginings!

Moving from the window, Eden climbed into bed.

The man had been concerned to know her reason for
going to the boatyard and on hearing it had accepted
her apology with polite words.

But they were not the words of his eyes.

Heat flooding again into her veins, Eden turned her
face towards the glittering window.

No, they were not the words of his eyes!

'I tells you, wench, them there faggots and that pressed
chawl be a meal folk on the cut be happy to pay for.
Ar, and many the folk as don't work the cut would be
just as glad of the chance of buyin' or I be a Dutchman
. . . and I ain't that.'

Handing his coins to Eden, then taking up his
plate of faggots, the boatman breathed the delicious
aroma of the steaming meat.

'I don't be coddin' when I says what I just told,' he
smiled back from the sun-filled doorway. 'There be
many a folk be glad of the chance to buy theirselves a
meal the like of this. You just tek a few to market and
see if I don't be right.'

He was not pretending. Eden watched the lithe
figure leap aboard a narrowboat. Her food would find

ready sale. That was no more than the word of a
hungry man! But there were other hungry mouths . . .

'Help me . . . show me the way.'

Whispers so often spoken in her prayers returned
vividly. Was that prayer being answered? Was she
being shown the way? But even should it be as that
boatman had said, should her food sell, how could
that help avenge the wrongs done a sister? How could it
help show Ava Russell for the evil woman she was, help
prevent the horror Myra had lived with being visited
upon some other unwitting young girl?

'You said I might call when passing this way.'

Immersed in her thoughts, Eden had not heard the
light tap on the door.

'I hope you meant it.'

Flustered by the appearance of the figure which had
troubled her sleep, Eden stumbled a reply. 'Of . . . of
course . . . Would you care for some tea?'

It was all that would come to her tongue and she took
refuge in it, turning to lift the kettle and scald the tea
leaves placed ready in the little brown teapot.

'That would be most welcome, especially were it
accompanied by a piece of that bread pudding David
Melia sings the praises of.'

Those smoke-dark eyes . . . had they held that look
. . . could it have been . . . ? Stop that! Censuring herself
sharply and silently. Eden clattered cup against saucer.
Fetching milk from the coolness of the scullery, the
self-reproof continued to ring in her head. She must
not allow that thought ever . . . she must wipe it from

her mind . . . she was not a child and she could not harbour silly childish thoughts! Andrew Denby had looked at her with concern, nothing more than that . . . nothing!

'David was not exaggerating.' The tip of a finger rescuing a sultana threatening to fall, Andrew Denby smiled, pushing it into his mouth. 'This is truly delicious. Might I buy some to take with me? There are those at the yard who would really enjoy a piece with their mug of afternoon tea.'

' . . . *there be many a folk be glad of the chance to buy . . .*'

'But that is presumptuous of me.' Andrew caught the essence of a frown.

'No,' Eden answered quickly. 'It . . . it is just so strange.'

'Strange?' He laughed. 'What is so strange about men enjoying a delightful snack?'

'Nothing.'

Taking the tea she had poured, Andrew's smile gave way to a frown.

'I thought we had agreed upon no more misunderstandings between us.'

'It was a narrowboatman.' Eden knew a logical reply was called for. 'He called a while ago to buy faggots . . . they are something of a favourite with the canal people . . . He said there could be a market for some of the dishes I make and . . . well, it seemed something of a coincidence when you also asked could you buy some.'

'Boat people are well known for their common sense. If they say a thing is good, then you can rely on the fact that it is and, in the case of your bread pudding, I agree with the man. You should take his advice.' Andrew's smile returned. 'Take some of what you make, offer it to a wider market. You never know what can be achieved unless you try.'

They could almost have been a match for her grandmother's words; she had always said, 'A body don't have the knowing of what they can do if they don't never try.'

Wrapping a dozen slices of the fruity pudding in a fresh white cloth, Eden placed it in a basket alongside two trays of faggots and several pots of pressed chawl.

She had thought a long time on the words of the narrowboatman and of Andrew Denby. She had also thought on her own grief at Myra's suffering and her overwhelming need to ensure it happened to no other girl. Was this that way?

She had asked herself that same question, her mind repeating it again and again in the quiet hours of the afternoon until at last she had admitted the answer. Only heaven can tell.

The market place was as she remembered it. Eden's throat tightened as she looked at stalls familiar from her earliest days. She knew many of the women by name and, as she passed, they called their pleasure at her return and Eden smiled her own. Even if not one ounce of what she set out now on an empty stall should sell, her journey would have been worthwhile.

But it had sold. Every last crumb, every last scraping

of potted chawl, and many of the customers had asked would she be here again tomorrow?

Empty dishes placed in her basket, the cloth folded neatly on top, she called her goodnights.

'You tek care now, wench,' an elderly woman called as she packed her goods on to a small handcart. 'You get yourself straight 'ome and don't go dawdlin' . . . You don't want to be found as another young wench were found last night . . . found with her throat slit and her poor body laid open from stomach to chest . . . Rumour has it an old man usin' a walkin' stick were seen near where her lay . . . But an old man needing a stick to help him walk wouldn't 'ave the strength to go attackin' no young woman, now would he?'

Another murder! Eden felt her stomach contract. The day was already turning to evening. The streets were filling with shadows . . . and somewhere among them a killer watched and waited.

She had promised Davy she would always wait at Shipton Cottage, that she would not make that evening walk along the towpath unless he were with her. The basket clutched tight to her middle, Eden walked as quickly as she could. It had not been evening when she set out, the sky had not been filling with shadows, but she should have taken account of the time it would take walking to and from Wednesbury market place.

'. . . *When are you going to think of other people's feelings and not just your own?*'

She could imagine Andrew Denby hurling those words at her, but what words would he hurl at Davy?

Would he accuse him, say he was not doing that which he was supposed to do? But it was not Davy's suggestion she had followed, not his recommendation she take some of her cooking to sell in the market . . . but then neither had Andrew Denby advised she do so that very afternoon!

It had felt good having him sit at her table, having him smile at her instead of frowning, of seeming to enjoy their new-found cordiality . . . but how much of that would be left tomorrow? How would that fragile friendship stand when again he found her to be the same thoughtless, self-centred person he had found huddled against a canal bridge?

An ache pulling beneath her ribs, Eden slowed her steps to a steadier walk but her thoughts raced on.

What did it matter how Andrew Denby thought of her? She did not rely upon him for her living whereas part of Davy's and his mother's income did; should that be taken from them . . . should she be the cause . . . !

Halting abruptly, Eden was elbowed aside by a hurrying woman, several small children holding to her skirts, her voice echoing a trace of fear as she mumbled 'Some folk don't have common sense enough to get themselves 'ome nights!'

She had not used common sense. She had given no thought to not being back at Shipton Cottage by the time Davy called . . . of the consequences. Would Andrew Denby take away the Melias' living?

The grind of a steam train halting alongside, the call of its conductor to several alighting passengers to 'be safe 'ome', settled any argument her mind might have given. She would not allow the Melias to suffer on her account. Glancing only once the way she must take, she turned off Lea Brook Road to run quickly along the track that would lead across the heath, past the sad and beautiful house that was The Coppice and on towards the towpath.

She had hoped to run all of the way. The ache she had thought to be easing pulled more savagely, allowing each breath to be only short and shallow. A moment . . . a hand pressed to the pain throbbing beneath her ribs . . . a moment to catch her breath . . .

But in that moment, breath locked in her throat.

There along the track a few yards ahead of her, stepping free from a bank of grey shadow . . . an old man leaning on a walking stick.

She could go back . . . she could turn around and go back to Lea Brook Road. Transfixed by the sudden freezing of her limbs, Eden's stare remained on the figure slowly closing the gap between them.

'. . . *An old man needing a walking stick* . . .'

Fear transforming the words to ice blocks in her chest, Eden fought for breath that would not come.

'. . . *old man* . . . *walking stick* . . . *old man* . . .'

Like a hammer on an anvil it clanged in her brain, screamed in her mind and beneath it all was the urge to run.

He was coming closer. She could see him clearly now. Lungs tight and burning for breath she could not take, mesmerised by fright, she watched the slow approach. Etched against the fading light, the colour of clothes was indistinguishable, the face drooped to the chest invisible, but the stick . . . the stick moved in determined rhythm . . . in rhythm . . . but the sound!

Like a pencilled sketch, the shadowed scene she looked at became a night-veiled garden, a garden of trees and bushes black silhouettes against a charcoal sky, and the sound reaching her became the sound she had heard the night she had waited in that garden, waited for Ava Russell to return to Moorcroft, sounds that had helped send her hurrying away. She could hear them again now; a step, then silence . . . a step, then silence . . . The step was an old man's foot crunching on the pathway . . . the silence the result of his stick falling on grass!

'. . . *an old man needing a walking stick . . .*'

Breath returning on a cry, Eden saw the head lift, watched the stick rise, but the blackness that swallowed her closed the face away.

29

'Eh, you 'ad me all of a sweat . . .'

Davy Melia looked at the girl he had half-carried to Shipton Cottage.

'. . . I seen you lyin' all of a heap and I thought for sure I would need be callin' Webbs.'

'No.' Eden managed a pale smile. 'No, Davy, I wasn't needing the attentions of the undertaker.'

'So I found when I reached you, but Lord, you give me a turn. How come you was there . . . an' after promisin' never to tek that grumpy old bug . . . that old man a meal lessen I walked you there.'

There was reproach in the tone but Eden recognised the underlying concern.

'I was not taking a meal to him.' Accepting the tea in which he had stirred a spoonful of honey, she told of the narrowboatman, Andrew Denby's visit, of her subsequent journey to the market at Wednesbury and of her wanting to be home when he, Davy, came to walk her to the old man's gate.

'That be all well an' good,' he answered as she finished speaking, 'but bein' here the time I come for you shouldn't 'ave had you tekin' the way across the heath. Did nobody tell you. . .'

What had he been about to say? Eden accepted a second cup of honeyed tea. Had nobody told her she should have sense enough to stay off the heath with the approach of evening? Or that a killer had once again struck in Wednesbury?

'Still, you be safe 'ome now, so that's it and all about it.'

'No, Davy, that is not all that need be said.' Eden lifted a glance to the young face she had seen bending over her on that darkened pathway. 'As usual, I acted without thinking. It was foolish, I know that now, and, believe me, I am sorry I caused you concern; as for Andrew . . . Mister Denby, I will explain. I will tell him of my not being in the house, I'm sure he will not take employment from you and your mother.'

If only himself were as sure. Davy hid the thought behind the sipping of hot tea. That look on the man's face when told Eden could not be found . . . the way he had ridden from the boatyard as if all the devils of hell were at his back . . . it proved that, where Eden Brent were concerned, Andrew Denby were capable of more than giving two people their tin.

'You needn't add worry of that to your fears,' he said, putting his cup aside. 'Mister Denby be sharp at times but he don't be a man to let spite rule his head; but summat ruled your'n to 'ave you faintin' as you did. Was it summat you seen?'

He had not seen the figure on that path? He had not

seen an old man raise a walking stick? But he was there
. . . the man was there, Davy *must* have seen! But Davy
had made no mention of seeing anyone, not spoken of
a bent figure walking with a stick! Eden's brow creased
in a frown. Davy had said nothing of seeing anything
or anyone except herself. That meant the whole thing
had been a figment of her own imagination, an illusion
built out of fear; unreal, a figure formed of shadows . . .
but shadows made no sound as they moved!

'No . . . no it was nothing I saw. I was running . . . I
caught my foot against a stone and tripped.'

It was a lie. Had she told it for Davy's benefit or her
own? Told it to allay his fears or hers?

'Reckon you don't feel you wants to walk along of
that house tonight. That old man can go without a meal
. . . he don't deserve it anyway.'

She did not want to walk that dark path, to watch the
shadows loom and merge, their black arms reaching for
her. But not to go might arouse Davy's suspicion that
it had not been a trip over a stone that made her fall
senseless to the ground.

'You have reckoned wrongly, Mister Davy Melia.'
Forcing a smile, she took a freshly laundered cloth from
a line strung above the fireplace. 'It is a little later than
usual so I would rather you went home, I don't wish to
have your mother worry.'

'It be me needs worry should I let you go along of that
house by yourself; I wouldn't get to sit down for a week
after the tanning my backside would get.'

Not to mention the tongue lashing he would get from

Andrew Denby! Keeping the thought to himself he took the dish of faggots from Eden. Laying it in the centre of the cloth he gathered the four corners together and tied them into a knot.

'I thinks it be a waste o' time goin' to that place.' He glanced to where Eden was ensuring the fire was safe to leave. 'That old man, he were not to the house when we called last night so what's to say he won't be there again tonight.'

. . . He were not to the house . . .

. . . A young wench with her throat slit . . .

Poker in hand, Eden stared into the heart of the glowing fire.

. . . an old man . . . a walking stick . . .

Pulses pounding, fingers gripping the poker, Eden felt fear prick like broken glass against her throat.

. . . an old man . . . a young wench . . . last night.

Words shouted in her mind.

A figure in the shadows.

Shadows made no sound!

'Will I do that, Eden? Will I go take this on my own?'

Dragged from her thoughts by Davy's words, she replaced the poker with trembling fingers, rattling it against the grate.

'. . . it might be best I should. Seems to me you don't be up to trekkin' along of that house tonight.'

Either Davy had not noticed her trembling or he was tactfully overlooking it. Swallowing the razor sharpness in her throat, a breath steadying her shaking nerves, she turned.

'A walk in the fresh air is just what I need; it will blow the cobwebs away.'

'You be sure you be up to it?'

His look could not be mistaken for dislike. Eden smiled into clear brown eyes. It was open and honest, it spoke words of the heart, words which said he felt true concern.

Her own look gentle with gratitude, Eden nodded.

'Quite sure, Davy.'

It was a denial of what churned inside. Walking beside him along the towpath, she took no comfort from the light of a high moon, no reassurance from the black hulks of moored narrowboats.

She had not wanted to take that meal. Turning off the towpath, Eden felt cold fear against her spine. Trees she had taken no notice of before seemed to lean their branches over her head, twining them together until she was enclosed in a whispering tunnel of darkness.

A figure in the shadows.

Stifling a sob of fright, she drew closer to the lad walking beside her.

'T'were a shock to me, an' no mistake. For a minute my brain wouldn't have the tellin' of who it were stood in that kitchen, an' then I realised. It were him from the cottage along at the entrance to the drive.'

'The elderly man?'

'I felt like that when I turned to see who stood behind me.' Sara Melia answered the surprise in Eden's question. 'I tell you, I couldn't 'ave been more taken aback were I sittin' in the Queen's chair being crowned with gold. I hadn't been cleaning no more than an hour when he come.' Breaking the explanation only long enough to observe the ritual of drinking tea, brought from home, she went on. 'D'ain't give no reason of asking and I called for none. All he said were would I come to Shipton Cottage and ask would you walk along back with me and this were given along of the request.' Digging into a pocket of her dark skirt, Sara held out an open palm displaying a half sovereign. 'Reckon he must want to meet with you summat serious to pay such a sum. But that don't go meaning you 'ave to go along there should you not feel you wants to . . .'

A figure in the shadows.

A frisson of alarm settled along Eden's spine.

'He be there still; I felt I shouldn't ought to have left him sit a' waiting in the kitchen, not with me being entrusted to see the contents of that house come to no harm, but then a man of his years can't be like to do damage.'

A figure raising a walking stick . . .

Alarm became trepidation, bringing a tremble Eden tried to hide.

A shadow whose footsteps carried sound!

Davy might not have seen. Anxious in his searching for her, he could easily have missed a figure in the shadows . . . But she had not missed it . . . she had not missed seeing a figure raising a walking stick . . . the figure of the man who lived below that large house.

'You don't needs to go.' Sara caught the shudder. 'I'll just tell him as you be busy along of your cookin' . . . A wench can't be expected to leave off doing what brings her living just 'cos he asks it. Whatever he might want the sayin' of can have no spoiling by the waiting for evening . . . No doubt yourself and my lad will be walking there with a dish of summat though were it me in your place I wouldn't give the surly old soul the time o' day much less a meal.'

Those few moments enough for her to banish the thoughts bringing a shiver to her spine, Eden pretended a frown. 'Now, why is it I do not believe that?'

Her cup emptied, Sara Melia carried it into the scullery, long years of tidying after husband and son having her wash and dry them despite Eden's protest.

'It were a welcome sup.' The older woman smiled. 'I don't go making myself tea while I be to that house. I don't feel it to be my place and as for using that there crockery . . . Lord, I be terrified even to look, let alone touch! I swears it be finer than a moth's wing. But standin' here gossipin' won't buy the babby a new hat, as my mother used to say, so I'll be off back to my cleaning and this . . .' she took the coin from her pocket, the gleam of it glowing against her palm, '. . . well, he can have this back. Reckon that man thought the giving of such a sum would have me coax you against your will. But the old bugger can give 'imself a headache with the thinking, for coaxing a wench to do aught her has no will for doing don't be Sara Melia's nature.'

'I know that well enough,' Eden answered, as they

returned to the living-room. 'I will come with you, it should only take a few minutes.'

'But your cookin'?'

Had Sara seen her fear? Was the woman offering her a way of refusing to go meet with that man? But a half sovereign was more money than Sara might see for weeks of cleaning . . . and saying she would return it was no lie. The Melias were poor as herself but they had that same pride, pride which said 'Take only what has been earned'; and Sara had earned it by doing as she had been bidden. But this woman's mind worked, much the same way as Grandmother's. She, too, would have thought by returning alone the man might suspect her of simply finding a spot to sit ten minutes then returning with a reason to say why the girl had not come . . . and Grandmother's self-respect, like that of Davy's mother, would have her refuse to accept any payment overshadowed with suspicion.

All of this fleeting through her mind, Eden covered a large shallow roasting pan with a clean white cloth. 'This will keep until I get back and the faggots have only just gone into the oven so they will take no harm.'

'Bread pudding.' Sara nodded towards the covered pan. 'Now, there be a favourite of my lad . . . Has a sweet tooth same as did his father . . . God rest him . . . They would both eat a pan to theirself hadn't I been there to whip it from their hands, but I don't be sayin' nothing you don't know already for I hears every night of some titbit or other he be given along of your kitchen. I tells him it don't be polite to take without giving but I swears a brick wall has sharper ears than that one when he don't want to hear.'

'The pleasure of Davy's company is all the giving necessary. Please don't forbid him accepting those titbits.'

'Fat lot of good the trying would do.' Sara waited until the broom was placed across the door. 'That rogue would just get himself along to Denby's boatyard to be given a piece of pudding from there.'

Sara knew of the tray of bread pudding which went every day to that boatyard. Eden's cheeks coloured. Did she also know it was Andrew Denby himself who fetched it, that each time of calling he seemed less inclined to leave . . . and could he ever guess she wanted his visit to go on, wanted him to stay? But, of course he could not, nor must he! They had become friends, she would not have that friendship embarrassed by showing what daily was growing inside her . . . her love for Andrew Denby.

'That is offensive!'

Ava Russell's gloved fingers tightened, clutching the bag resting on her knee.

'Am I supposed to find it amusing? Was the offer supposed to have me smile? I assure you I find it quite the reverse and you may tell the bidder so.'

'I will, of course, do as you say, but might I suggest you give some thought . . .'

'Give some thought!' Resounding from the walls of the quiet room, the explosive response had the solicitor's clerk look up from his own desk beyond the glass partition. 'Give some thought to that? The offer is preposterous!'

Stubby fingers touching in a pointed arch, a plump bland face rested a chin on their tips, but the eyes regarding Ava held no such aspect. Sharp, acute, with an intelligence not detected by a first glance at the neatly whiskered face, they watched the annoyance play over the angry face. Ava Russell was a woman heavily in debt, a mortgage loan of five hundred pounds, not a penny of which had as yet been paid . . . and there was as much chance of seeing pigs fly as seeing that happen!

Expression bland as before, the solicitor lowered his hands. 'Of course, that is how this must appear to you.' He touched the paper Ava had flung back across the desk. 'But I would remind you it is the only offer to have been made.'

'So far! The only one so far!'

'The only offer made so far.' An inclination of his balding head acknowledged the outburst. 'That, if I might say so, speaks for itself. The property you have placed on the market has attracted one enquiry, the one which has resulted in the offer made here.' He tapped the paper with a forefinger. 'That would indicate what I have suspected for some time.'

'And what might that be?'

'The market for iron has declined. The demand now is for steel. To adapt the foundry to the making of that commodity would require a large amount of outlay. Should you envisage the making of steel tubes, for example, you would need to install one of the new Bessemer furnaces, draw bench, screw press and dies, plus various other tools. I advise you weigh the cost involved against the competition of existing steel works, of which the town has several.'

There was no money for the alterations he outlined. Teeth clenched almost painfully together, Ava was silent. The loan made by the bank was all but spent and it was a certain fact they would loan her no more.

'Do you wish me to instruct this offer be unacceptable?'

Watching the stubby fingers take up the paper, Ava's brain flipped through the possibilities open to her. She could hold on to the foundry, wait for the market in iron to revive; she could try raising funds elsewhere, but those were dead-end ideas. Iron smelting might never revive and, as for raising funds elsewhere, she would need collateral . . . But the house was already mortgaged and there was nothing else on which she could raise money. But money was what she needed; funds enough to take her from Wednesbury . . . from England . . . a house in Italy, no scandal of unpaid debts would follow her there.

'Will I write the offer is rejected?' The paper held at an enquiring angle the solicitor's razor-keen glance watched the hard face of the woman who had squandered Samuel Russell's wealth and brought his business to ruin. She had consistently refused to listen to advice, now she was about to pay the price.

'No . . .'

The expected answer, long drawn out as if it had required much thought, found no sympathy with its listener. The wife of Samuel Russell deserved none.

'No,' Ava said again, 'you will draw up a contract of sale. I wish to be rid of that property.'

The buyer had wanted only the land. Outside in the street she stood a moment breathing against the bile of anger and the cold bitterness of disappointment and frustration. The sum agreed was paltry and that solicitor had known, as he had known she would not refuse to accept it. Only the land! She all but spat the words. How much truth was there in such a claim and how much would prove to be a lie? But, truth or lie, that offer had been the only one made and, galling as it was, she had known she must accept or have a dead foundry hang indefinitely about her neck.

Time . . . that was a luxury she could not afford, time would make public the straits in which she now found herself, could eventually show the level to which she had fallen . . . time could destroy her!

But not if she moved quickly, and money from sale of the foundry would ensure accomplishment of that. She would tell no one her plans, not even the few servants remaining at Moorcroft. And the remainder of debt outstanding? A smile cold inside, she proceeded to walk along Lower High Street towards the town centre. Debt outstanding . . . that too would be left behind!

30

She and Davy had come here last evening, brought a meal to the man's gate. Beneath Sara Melia's conversation Eden's thoughts ran wild. It had appeared that, yet again, he was not home. The thought had brought respite from the fear which had nagged at her, eased the urge to grab Davy and run; but the lapse had been short lived. With their coming to the gatepost, the exchange of one dish for the other not quite completed, had come the sound which brought back all the dread, all the terror which had swept away her senses a short time before . . . Crunch and silence, crunch and silence . . . the sound of a step on hard ground . . . the silence of a walking stick on grass!

Even now, in broad daylight, Eden felt the same shiver she had felt then, the dryness which had grabbed her throat as a figure stepped from the shadows surrounding the small house.

It was the figure she had seen on the path . . . the same figure which had raised a stick! Fear had leapt in every nerve, fear which had shown as she had met that old man's eyes, seen the look which had said he had known her thoughts, said yes, he was the figure she had met on that path, fear that had verged on panic as for almost the first time he had spoken. Quiet and soft the words had followed as she turned away. 'We will meet again . . . soon.'

Davy had made no comment and she had been thankful for that but, once he was gone and she was alone in Shipton Cottage, the words had preyed on her mind. Had his words been a threat, were they saying the attack foiled by Davy's arrival would be repeated? But why attack her, what had she done to deserve such?

But what had Alfred Birks done? What had the two young women who had suffered the same fate been guilty of?

'. . . *an old man needing a stick to walk with* . . .'

The stallholder telling of a third killing had said an elderly man using a walking stick had been seen in the area of the murder.

. . . *an old man needing a stick.*

It rang in Eden's brain as it had rung last night. The man living below The Coppice used a walking stick . . . and on the evening of that murder he had been absent from his home!

'He don't be there . . .'

Sara turned to where Eden's steps had automatically come to a halt.

'. . . least that don't be where I left him. He were up there.' She flicked her head in the direction of the house at the end of the wide tree-lined drive.

Pulled so quickly from thoughts tumbling frighteningly in her mind, Eden's brows drew together.

'I know, wench.' Sara Melia smiled, mistaking fear for confusion. 'Set me to wonderin' same as yourself. Come to that house bold as brass and nothin' to show permission forrit he did . . . Lord, I should 'ave had more sense than leave him sit there . . . and stands to reason that be where he is still or else he would be here a' waiting at his own gate . . . which my own two eyes tells me he ain't.'

Was he truly in that house . . . or was he here in this small cottage? Was he watching unseen from one of its windows, waiting until she returned to pass this cottage alone? And what then . . . would he attack her as he had attempted to do yesterday, was that to be the fulfilment of the threat behind his quiet 'We will meet again . . . soon?'

Would Eden Brent become the fourth victim of a killer?

He had apologised immediately for not staying beside her on that path. He had seen her approaching, had waved his stick to draw her attention; he must have startled her for she had missed her footing and pitched forward. She had been unconscious and, knowing he could not carry her, he had made for the canal basin. There would be men there to bring her home and the wife of a boatman to care for her, but by the time they returned she was gone. He had intended walking to Shipton Cottage to enquire as to her wellbeing and offering his apology there, then moments later she and Davy had come as usual.

So why had he not given his apology then? Her brain had asked but her tongue had remained silent while his explanation went on.

'An old man is not as agile as he would wish. By the time I came from the rear of the house to the gate you were already left. I needed to tell you all of this, that is the reason for my asking you to come to The Coppice.' But had that truly been his reason . . . or behind the apology was there another?

Questions had torn at her, their answers whispering in her mind, answers which now brought the mark of shame to her cheeks. Climbing into bed, Eden's eyelids closed hard on the memory.

Fear! She had given in to fear, allowed the nightmare of it to override all common sense. She had mentally accused an elderly man, one about whom she knew virtually nothing, had convinced herself he had been about to attack her . . . depicted him in her own thoughts as a vicious, mindless killer.

The shame of that still weighed heavily. What would Grandmother have made of her stupidity . . . and would she have termed what had happened in that beautiful house called The Coppice even more stupidity?

Eyelids lifting, Eden stared into darkness concentrated by lack of moon.

He had been where Sara Melia had said she had left him. The same man who had accepted gifts of food without a single word of gratitude but, as he had risen to his feet on her entering the huge kitchen, Eden had become aware all was not the same. Lines about the eyes and greying hair and drawn cheeks depicted the years but, though he still held the walking stick, his body was somehow straighter, the droop gone from his shoulders; but it was the smile had struck her most . . . it had been a smile of happiness. Where she had convinced herself waited threat had waited welcome.

Deep in the well of darkness that was her bedroom it seemed the smile shone out at her again.

He had thanked her for giving of her time, for pandering to an old man's request. His voice had held no gruffness, none of the surliness Davy had often complained of, but a gentle pleasant tone as he also thanked Sara for her errand, though it became firm when refusing to take back the proffered half sovereign.

'Do you recall?' He had turned to her but had not asked Sara to leave, '. . . once telling me that in order to find that which was lost I must need face my heart?'

She had used those words, words which in turn she had spoken to herself. To find the cause of the love she had lost, a sister's love, she must have the courage to face her own heart, the courage which had taken her to Moorcroft.

Not quite fully recovered from the fright of going to that house, she had answered with a nod and he continued.

'That is what I have done. Though it took many weeks I did at last come here to this house.'

'This house?'

'Yes, to this house.' He answered Sara's quiet gasp,

smiling at Eden's own look of perplexed expression. 'It was you who said it, you, my dear, who said you felt a love reaching out, a love which called for its voice to be heard. It was that love I yearned for yet that same love kept me away. The sorrow was too strong . . . the love had been too deep . . . and so I lived with my pain, nurtured my wounds, allowed them to fester until they were beyond healing. But though heaven be sometimes slow in executing its designs, its pity is boundless, and in that pity it sent you. You were the balm, the antidote to the canker of poison I had allowed to grow deep within myself, you who showed the way to recovery. For a long time I fought against heaven's compassion, I did not want that healing. But day and night the words a stranger had spoken refused to be banished from my mind, words which said I must face my heart.'

They had glanced at each other, she and Sara Melia, both looks asking the same question: 'Why tell it in this house and not his own?'

Had he interpreted that shared glance? The half-smile which had touched his mouth traced a reflection of itself on Eden's.

'I am not as used as I once was to the company of ladies,' he had gone on, 'I ask pardon of you both for my lack of manners. My name is Tobias Jevons and The Coppice is my house.'

'Your house!'

Sara's surprise had echoed in the large kitchen, Eden's had shown only in her eyes.

'Mine,' he had answered. 'But my explanation will

perhaps be too long . . . I have taken a deal of your time already, Miss . . . ?'

Half of her mind had wanted to believe what it was hearing but the other half was warning this was a false friendship, a lure to bring her from the safety of Shipton Cottage. Pulled both ways, she had murmured, 'Eden . . . Eden Brent.'

He had taken her hand, his copper-coloured eyes seeming to see more than her face as he smiled. Had she felt uncomfortable? Eden stared at the face she seemed to see in the shadows, a face which had looked so different to the hollow-cheeked, gaunt one she had become used to.

No. Silent now as when it first came, the answer repeated in her mind. No, she had not felt uncomfortable with that penetrating gaze; she had been . . . happy? Lying there in the darkness, she mused over the feeling . . . Yes, she had been happy he had overcome the anger which had seemed always to be with him, happy his sorrow would fade, the healing would begin.

'We have met many times, Miss Brent, but not until now have I allowed myself the joy of speaking pleasantly to you. I ask your forgiveness for my surly behaviour; and you Missis Melia.' He had smiled at Sara with that same bright glance. 'I also ask your pardon.'

'Me? You 'ave no cause to go asking no pardon of me,' said Sara.

'But I have, my. . .' he had swallowed as if on a half-sob, '. . . my dear wife would have been unhappy at my lack of courtesy in thanking you for the way you have kept this house . . . the house where we were both so happy.'

Colour rising to her cheeks, Sara had reached for the apron left folded on a corner of a long high dresser, saying the job she was paid to do would never get done if she stood talking all day.

'Missis Melia,' he had said as she caught up a duster, 'would this old house of mine have the makings of a cup of tea?'

'Ain't no such. But I brings myself a bottle of it for a drink should I feel the need. You be welcome to a sup of that supposing you'll 'ave the accepting of it.'

'I think we would each find it acceptable. I trust there is still china somewhere about.'

'. . . *Finer than a moth's wing* . . .'

Sara's hesitation had spoken of her reluctance to handle delicate tableware but the man who claimed ownership of the house swept open a cupboard and reached down three white china cups and saucers, self-embossed with a design of oak leaves and acorns.

'There,' he had smiled, 'now we will share your tea, Missis Melia.'

Sara's fingers had trembled slightly as she had wiped the china on a cloth taken from a drawer of that long dresser. Kitchenware it may have been to staff who had once taken meals in this spacious room, but to Sara it still seemed fragile.

She should have helped! In the silence of

approaching dawn, Eden reprimanded herself. It should have been she who had wiped those cups, poured tea and handed it to the others, she should have relieved Sara of the fear of dropping one of those pretty pieces; she was no more used to handling delicate china than was Davy's mother but if any of it had been damaged blame would have been hers and not Sara's.

But it had not been broken, and while they had shared the still warm tea, Tobias Jevons had continued to speak.

'It was thirty years ago I brought Miriam to this house as my bride. She was not yet twenty and was as beautiful as a summer morning. We thought ours a happiness even heaven could not improve upon but when we learned we were to have a child we knew we had been wrong, for the happiness we felt was increased a hundredfold.

'Increased a hundredfold.'

Tears had thickened the softly repeated words and the bright copper eyes had glistened with moisture, but hard as it must have been for him he had continued.

'They were the most wonderful months. We pondered over the names we might give our child, Miriam's laugh one of amusement whenever I would tease that perhaps Obadiah, Peregrine or Zachariah would be appropriate for a boy. . .'

He had paused, taking a moment to clear the emotion memory brought to this throat.

'. . . but always she would declare our son would be named for his father and grandfathers and should our child prove to be a daughter then she would be given the names of both grandmothers. Heaven did grant us a son . . .'

He had paused again, fingers tightening where they held the walking stick.

'. . . but the gift was taken back. In less than an hour my son was gone from me and heaven also took his mother. My dearest wife was dead and to all intent and purpose so was I . . . the life I was left with had no meaning. I left this house when she did; on her burying day. I could not bear to enter it again, to walk through rooms which once had held so much happiness and now were cold and empty; but the pain of leaving, the feeling of somehow breaking faith with Miriam . . . so I closed this house and took over the gatekeeper's cottage. My heart told me I could never find my Miriam, yet something deep within my soul held me to this place . . . and now I know why.'

Beyond the window of her bedroom the night sky was paling to grey but Eden saw only a kitchen with a man sitting at its table.

'As you said, my dear,' the voice spoke on in her mind, 'there are things we maybe cannot see nor touch, but on coming here that first evening I sensed a presence so tender and compassionate, a love reaching out to me, and it was then that I knew the reason I had never sold The Coppice. It is here my darling waited, here I would find the comfort of that love I thought lost for ever, here my broken heart might at last be eased.'

He had asked then would she walk with him through

those rooms he had once walked through with his wife. All the fright he had roused in her that previous evening now gone without trace, she had accepted.

The house was as beautiful as she had imagined that day she had stared at it. Room upon room filled with furniture such as she could never have dreamed of, carpet so deep it felt she walked in grass-filled meadows, while paintings glowed on silk-covered walls. Only one room did he not open to her, one she guessed had been the room he had shared with his wife.

'I returned to the house on several evenings,' he had said when they stood together in an exquisite sitting-room. 'With the light of a candle I sat in this room . . . too long I am afraid, for the meal left on my gatepost told of your visit . . . Again, Miss Brent, I must apologise.'

The times she and Davy had brought food . . . the times he had not been standing beside his gate . . . she had thought perhaps . . . but he had been in the house of his memories, of his love!

Beneath the covers, Eden felt her body glow from the swift rush of shame.

How could she have allowed such thoughts to enter her mind? How could she have entertained the notion of his being a murderer!

'Now I know where it is my remaining years must be spent.' He had smiled as she had brushed away the apology. 'To that end I shall re-open this house, engage the staff necessary to maintain it. But there is one I would have live here not as a servant.'

He had asked that she take a seat. Eden stared to where dawn shone pale and opalescent behind a muslin veil of transparent cloud. It was well she had accepted for what had followed had her shaken to the core.

'I watched you closely.' A smile had held the same confession of regret as had his words of a moment since. 'My rudeness the first time of our meeting was, I fear, spontaneous; it was the way I had come to dealing with anyone approaching The Coppice. But as time went on and still you came, bringing food, never asking anything, always polite despite the incivility and disrespect you were given in return, I began to see you for what you are and not what I had thought you to be. I came to admire a courage I myself did not have, to appreciate the way you tackled adversity. You did not give in to self-pity as I had, you did not turn your back on life as I had done but grasped it by the wrist and forced it to walk beside you at your own pace. You have a tenacity and strength I would ask you to share with me. The footsteps of servants, the sound of their voices as they go about the duties, will give life back to this house but you could give back its smile, the joy I stole from it, return it from the exile I forced it into. Miss Brent . . . Eden . . . I am asking will you share The Coppice with me?'

31

The amount paid in exchange for the iron foundry had been far less than she had expected. The tools, furnace, the crucibles, nothing it contained had been wanted by the purchaser. The building itself was small, too cramped for the process of steel manufacture . . . it would need to be knocked down.

Lies! The hairbrush Ava Russell had been holding flew across the bedroom.

The buyer would not pay for what he could not use, it was simply the land he wished to purchase.

Lies! Ava's mouth clamped against the rage churning inside her. She knew it was lies and so had that damned solicitor! Most likely the two had been in collusion, a nice little payment for that solicitor should he get her signature on a deed of sale which brought the other a foundry for two hundred pounds.

Two hundred pounds! Bristling with temper she swept a hand across the dressing-table. Silver-rimmed crystal pots of creams and elegant vials of expensive perfumes spilled across the floor. She snatched up the cheque she had been given no choice but to accept.

What sort of house would *this* provide? What style of living, whichever part of the Continent she chose to settle? Not the style she wanted!

Forcing the storm in her mind to quieten, she took mental stock of items remaining in the house which might be sold. There were precious few and what there was must be sold without the bank's knowledge. But nothing was impossible until proved so!

First, the Meissen Samuel had given her for her birthday. Determination adding to the tight line of her mouth, she took the delicate porcelain figurines she had preferred to keep in her own room and wrapped them in a silk shawl.

Downstairs, the hall cupboard, a carpet bag . . . swiftly her mind moved. The cleaning woman . . . if she saw? But what if she did? She would not possibly know what was carried inside it!

But the woman had not been in the hall nor had she come into the drawing-room to see the pair of Sèvres dishes added to the bag, dishes that the dealer had almost drooled over. His mouth had watered at the sight of the contents of the bag but his tongue had been hard and dry when stating the price he was willing to pay. He had smiled while counting out twelve five pound notes, a smirk of triumph!

Sitting on the train which would carry her home from Wolverhampton, Ava's fingers tightened angrily about the empty bag. Every way a woman turned she was taken advantage of by men, business or bed it was all the same.

'Bilston . . .' the call of the conductor sounded from the train's corridor, '. . . next stop Bilston.'

Business or bed.

The thought returned with the fading of the conductor's call. Ava glanced through the window at the passing forest of smoking chimney stacks. Bilston was the same as Wednesbury, a depressing little town choked in its own soot. But Bilston held one pleasure!

Wheels clanking noisily over the points of the metal rails seemed to chant *Church . . . House . . . Church . . . House . . .*

Returning her glance to the bag resting in her lap she wrestled with feelings already hot and demanding.

She had told herself after that first visit there could be no more, but resolution had melted in the heat of desire and she had capitulated, not once but over and over again. Church House was designed to give its patrons complete privacy and total gratification, no matter their tastes.

But paradise came at a cost. Its fees were exorbitant; they had proved an extravagance she knew ate away what was left of the mortgage she had raised, yet still she had paid, indulging her passions until the money had virtually run out. But desire had not drained as those sovereigns had. Nights spent tormented by the thought of what Church House had supplied; those young bodies soft and perfumed, those willing skilful hands, had at last driven her to find a woman of the streets.

Distaste rose in her throat.

The odour of cheap perfume, the smell of gin on the breath, the exaggerated assurance of the delights to come, had all curdled until disgust had almost had her turn away; but, strong as aversion had been, the burning inside herself had been stronger, the desire so avid it had to be satisfied and she had gone with the woman.

But passion spent in a doorway of a darkened street!

The grind of metal on metal, the loud hiss of steam as the train slowed to the station, made no impression on the thoughts circling in Ava's mind.

It had lasted only a few minutes, every sound from that gloom-enshrouded street stinging her brain. To be discovered there! To be found with a common prostitute! That would be humiliation enough, but to be exposed a lesbian . . . that degradation could hound a woman to her grave! Warning had sung its harsh melody but lust had sung louder.

The woman had fumbled beneath her skirts. Ava's breath caught with the memory.

She had pulled away the bloomers her low laugh blown on a breath of gin as the touch of her fingers in that warm moist crevice had brought a gasp from her client's throat.

Then it was finished. The prostitute's hand had clawed the half sovereign she had demanded for 'special service' but then had demanded ten more.

Ava's glance travelled again to the window, the scene beyond invisible through the grey-white haze of steam floating back from the engine.

'*Ten more, dearie . . .*'

The words seemed to laugh from the curtain of steam.

'*. . . after all, we wouldn't want the 'ole town to be a' knowin' of your little fancies now, would we?*'

The woman's hand had reached forward.

'*. . . ten be all it'll tek to 'ave your secret kept safe . . . ten sovereigns can seal a woman's mouth, that be little enough, you does agree.*'

She had agreed.

The lurch of the train coming to a halt jolted Ava sharply forward, then back against her seat.

The prostitute had received her payment.

'Bilston!'

The call reached through the steam-misted window.

'Bilston town!'

Fingers closing on the carpet bag, Ava rose to her feet.

'He told you!'

Hands covered in flour, Eden looked up from the pastry she was mixing in a large bowl.

'But I said not to, the blame was mine and I should be the one taken to task not Davy!'

His tall figure blocking the light of the open doorway, Andrew Denby frowned.

'Why would you think David taken to task?'

A smudge of flour remaining where a finger had brushed her cheek, Eden watched the frown draw dark brows together.

'He thought should you hear of . . . of . . .'

'Of his finding you on that path? Oh yes, he told me.'

'Did he say it was my fault? I was not at the cottage when he called.'

Frown becoming a smile, Andrew Denby's smoke-dark eyes gleamed.

'That is not the way of David Melia. If there is blame to be taken then he thinks he should take it and he is fast proving himself man enough to shoulder what comes. But, as you say, fault did not lie with him; it lies with me for advising you take your cooking to market. Had I not done so you would not have suffered that fall.'

'Had I stopped to think instead of rushing off to the market? Isn't that what you really want to say?' Eden's own smile curving her mouth, she returned to her pastry.

'Maybe I should at that!'

'But seeing as the primary cause lies with you?'

'Truce? Let the matter rest?'

Their laughter joined together, Andrew watched the slender figure, the quick deft movements of her hands, the slight sideward tilt of a head that sunlight from the window gilded silver-gold. Had it been more than a fall . . . had she been injured in any way . . . Lord, what would he have done!

The thought a knife blade in his stomach, he forced it away. Eden Brent had suffered no serious effect and he thanked God for it.

'Then my rashness is to be forgiven?'

'This time yes, but Eden . . .'

Catching his glance as she looked to what she thought to be a question, Eden's pulses tripped.

'Don't . . . please don't put me through that again.'

It was there again, her imagination playing tricks! Unable to control the surge of colour to her cheeks, she turned to the oven checking food which needed no check. Why did this keep happening? Why did her mind insist on showing what was really not there? It had been a joke, he had teased her and she had placed an entirely different light on it. Heavens, what a fool he would think her, could he only read her mind. But that at least she was spared. Her thoughts would be her own; she would never share them, not with him, not with anybody.

'I will not have Davy walk me to market.' She turned a determined face.

Raising both hands in a gesture of surrender, Andrew Denby gave a slow shake of the head.

'Then you had best tell David that for he has already made up his mind that is what he is going to do.'

'Without asking me!'

'Or me.' Hands lowering, the smile in his dark eyes gave way to a serious look. 'Believe me, I had nothing to do with this, it is entirely the lad's own idea. He said he walked into Wednesbury every day so why not the two of you do so together.'

Turning pastry on to a floured board, rolling it lightly to a rectangle, the decision she had reached earlier came back to her mind. She had not thought to mention it just yet but, first or last, it would need be said some time.

'There will be no call for Davy to disrupt his working day by waiting to walk to the town with me,' she said, lining a dish with pastry. 'I will not be going there after today.'

'Not going?' Andrew Denby's frown returned. 'Might I ask your reason?'

She did not have to tell him anything, but then she had acted upon his suggestion so it seemed only good manners to explain the reason behind her decision.

'It is really very simple. I cannot make sufficient amounts of food to serve both a market stall and the canal folk; it is those people, the boatmen and their families, their friendship means more than . . .'

More than what? There had been the threat of tears behind those words. Andrew sat in silence. It seemed something she had set her heart on had been snatched from her . . . but what was that something?

'Eden.' He spoke her name softly. 'The reason you give, it is the only one? There is nothing else that has frightened or upset you?'

Having brushed the lid of the pie with milk she set it in the oven before answering.

'If you are referring to my fall that was simply an accident.'

'No accident is simple!' On his feet and beside her before the words were out, he grasped her arms, his fingers biting into tender flesh. 'Can't you see? You are important to David, you are important to . . .'

Staring into her eyes for a brief moment he loosed her arms then strode from the house.

One more second and he would have been unable to prevent the rest of that sentence leaving his tongue; one more second to say what throbbed even now . . . '*You are important to me!*'

Striding towards the boatyard, Andrew Denby's thoughts ran chaotically.

He had wanted to say it, wanted to tell her what was in his heart, that he loved her. But what effect would that have had except to have her turn from him completely, to lose the relationship they had developed. Yet what sort of relationship was friendship when it was her love he yearned for?

'. . . *their friendship means more than . . .*'

Those words not spoken, would they have said the friendship of the canal folk meant more to her than that of Andrew Denby? Could he honestly have wondered at the answer being yes? Those first encounters . . . He had hardly presented himself as other than disapproving, his every word had been condemnation of or a reprimand for her behaviour. All in all it was surprising she even bothered speaking to him . . . and now that she did, now that she showed warmth however small he would not risk the losing of it. What he felt for Eden Brent must remain where it rested now, buried in the depths of his heart.

But that would not ease the ache of it. Like David Melia, he cared for the girl scraping a living at Shipton

Cottage and, like that lad, he worried that one day she might leave for good.

'. . . *against my leaving* . . .'

That was what she had said regarding coins kept on that mantelshelf. To pay in part at least the rent which may have been asked of the owner.

'. . . *against my leaving* . . .'

It rang like a warning bell in his brain. Would telling her no rent would be required have her forego any idea of leaving? Should he tell her who owned the cottage she lived in, that its owner wanted nothing in respect of payment?

But pride was almost a fault with that young woman. Crossing the cobbled yard to the boatyard office he allowed himself a smile. Hard as life had been for her, hard as it still was, he knew she would not have passed one night beneath the roof of Shipton Cottage without gaining permission had she known its owner and having him accept a rent. And now . . . should she be told his name now, would that same pride have her accept or deny . . . would it have her remain in that house or set her feet on some other path?

That was one more risk he would not take!

Sitting at his desk he stared at the papers left by his clerk but his mind was still on Eden Brent.

She had sprung to the defence of the Melia lad. The fault, if fault there had been, was not his!

How those lovely eyes had blazed! A turquoise fire, they had proclaimed her ready to fight for the young-ster's good name. Defence of a friend . . . it was a quality not to be discredited. And when she had spoken of her accident on that path below The Coppice . . . it was the truth as told to David Melia, as she had told it again to himself, yet it was not all of the truth.

Rolling open the sheet of parchment he looked at it with unseeing eyes.

There were things Eden Brent chose not to share, either with himself or with David.

Through the glass partition, the clerk looked at his employer, his dark head tilted now against the leather of his high-backed chair. Deciding now may not be the most appropriate time to re-enter his office he returned his own attention to a blue-bound ledger.

She had given reason for not continuing to cook food for sale in the market, a sound and logical reason, but she had not revealed the disappointment he had sensed lay behind it. Andrew's eyelids closed, myriad questions dancing beneath them.

What could be so hurtful she could not speak of it, what so painful that thought of it brought the threat of tears? If only he could ask, but that would be to invade her privacy. She had chosen not to speak of whatever it was inside her and he must respect that decision . . . as he had respected that other decision, that other happening she had seen fit not to disclose.

Friendship! He stared at the ceiling. How much of what Eden Brent showed towards him was truly friendship and how much simply tolerance? Was her attitude towards him, her acceptance of his visiting Shipton Cottage, an indulgence designed for the benefit of

David Melia? Was she accepting one man merely to protect another? Was her friendship no more than a pretence . . . a pretence practised in order to safeguard the Melias' living?

No, he would not believe it!

Jerking upright in the chair, he snatched at the paper lying unread on his desk.

He was expecting too much of her, he was finding reasons simply in order to cover his own feelings, feelings that were absurd. So, she had not spoken of being asked to that house, of Sara Melia being sent to ask would she go to The Coppice. He had learned that from Sara's son . . . but even Sara's son did not know all!

32

He had asked her to live at The Coppice, to share that beautiful house with him.

Wooden shutters closed across living-room windows, Eden stoked the fire with sleck then doused the fine coal chippings with water so the burning embers would sleep through the night to wake with fresh life when she did.

Tobias Jevons . . . the elderly man she had held suspicion of being a murderer . . . She smiled to herself . . . How could she have entertained such a horrid idea! But *any* idea she might have had concerning him could not have been anywhere near as fantastic as the truth.

Familiarity born of months of living at Shipton Cottage, her hands reached down basins and bowls from the rickety dresser setting them alongside the dry ingredients she would need for next day's cooking.

Of all the notions she might have had, not one would have touched the reality of Tobias Jevons being owner of that house. Had anyone in Gospel Oak known that? Not Sara Melia, for she had gasped surprise loud as her own.

Checking the mutton which would simmer all night

in the side oven of the gleaming cast iron firegrate, she took a freshly laundered cloth from the length of finely twisted rope that ran above it.

And Andrew Denby, did he know? Her spine tickling with just the thought of the handsome man who offered her friendship, Eden flicked the snowy white cloth and draped it across the assembled articles on the well-scrubbed table.

She could have asked that question when he had called here earlier today. She could also have told him of her visit to The Coppice, of walking with Tobias Jevons through its gracious rooms, shared with him what that man had told her of his wife and newborn child; of the smile which had touched his mouth as he had spoken of feeling their presence, of a love waiting to be renewed. But she had said nothing of those things . . . nor had she told of that request that she go to live in that house.

What would Andrew Denby have made of that?

Baking tins and roasting pan set ready on the hob, she turned a glance about the room she had prettied with covers and curtains sewn from a length of honeysuckle-printed cloth found tucked away in a drawer. Cooking and needlework, skills bestowed more by the teaching of her grandmother than of school, they had stood her in good stead.

'. . . *she will never do any good . . .*'

Words, hurting now as they had when spoken, whispering shadows in her mind, she stood holding a cushion her gaze did not see.

'. . . *she will never amount to anything* . . .'

Sharp to the point of cruelty, pale eyes regarded a young girl, her petite figure seeming to draw back from the slash of a razor-keen tongue, her heart-shaped face lowered against a withering stare.

The headmistress who had ordered she strip away her clothes had intended the savagery of those words. In return for being disobeyed she had deliberately spat a malignance she had hoped would grow over the years, would become so deeply embedded that no amount of love would cure, that, like some hideous disease, would lie hidden deep within, eating away at a child's life.

'Once said never forgotten.' That had been Grandmother's gentle warning when either of her granddaughters had come close to speaking in temper . . . as it had seemed Myra had spoken that day she, Eden, had gone to Moorcroft to tell her of their grandmother's death.

But Myra had not spoken out of temper. Eden's hand gripped the soft cushion. The words had been hard only to drive a sister away in order to safeguard her from the evils of its mistress . . . an evil she, Eden Brent, must seek to redress.

She had been given that chance. Setting the cushion in its place on the wooden squab, a bench-like couch years of polishing now reflecting the pretty cloth like some dark mirror, she turned back to the table.

It was a heaven-sent chance! She would no longer need to count every penny, to scrimp and save on her own meagre living in order to put money from her cooking into the pot on the mantelshelf; she would have no landlord to pay . . . and with someone like Tobias Jevons on her side then the authorities would be bound to pay more attention to a complaint brought against Ava Russell.

But what complaint could she bring? A letter allegedly written by a dead girl . . . an accusation so terrible it would rock the whole town . . . Who would believe such of any woman, much less one of the social standing of Ava Russell! Would Tobias Jevons . . . would Andrew Denby? They would never be asked to believe . . . they would never be told of her sister's shame, of her persecution, nor would anyone; only Aunt Dora was privy to the degradation Myra had been forced to endure and she would not renege on that confidence.

Yet, if by the same chance she was offered now in being asked to make her home at The Coppice, its owner should believe the story of Myra's abuse it would be of no avail. She would not use his name in any attempt to avenge those wrongs, and most definitely not any financial assistance he might offer.

How then could she fulfil the promise of her heart? How could she ensure Ava Russell paid for her crimes?

The profit from her cooking would have grown at a faster rate by selling at the market and by following the further suggestion of Andrew Denby that his boats carry her food on to other towns to be sold in shops there; but no matter how quickly her savings amassed money alone was not enough. She could not buy justice. If she were to bring Ava Russell to book she would require evidence, but evidence of enforced lesbianism was something that woman would guard with her life.

Then how to keep the promise she had whispered at her sister's grave?

Taking the cup which had held her evening cocoa, she carried it to the scullery and washed it by the light of a candle in a jar.

How . . . unless she too asked for position of ladies' maid at Moorcroft House? Would she be strong enough to tolerate what Myra had lived through?

Hands which knew every inch of the tiny cottage reached for a cloth lying beyond the lemony perimeter of candlelight.

Would Ava Russell employ her?

The cup dried, that same inner knowledge of the space around her ensuring the cloth back in its place, she blew out the candle.

Given what she had read in Myra's letter, the truth she knew those words contained, then there was little doubt of the answer. A shiver ran needles along every vein. Why would there be? Becoming a partner in lasciviousness, no girl would own to willing acceptance, no girl would condemn herself to the years of imprisonment which would follow; of that the woman would be certain.

Stepping into the lighted warmth of the prettily curtained living-room, Eden's fingers tightened about the cup.

No, Ava Russell would not refuse . . . but then Ava Russell did not truly know Eden Brent!

Coming to the curve that led Lower High Street on to the rise which became Church Hill, Ava Russell slipped quickly through a low wooden gate set in high brick-built walls encompassing the grounds of Moorcroft House.

There had been no prostitute walking the street, no doxy stepping out to offer 'a good time for a sixpence'. It seemed any women selling those particular wares were parading them only in taverns, in well-lit premises where every potential customer could be seen and noted. The Wednesbury 'Ripper' had them all wary of taking a customer from the streets.

But she could not be seen entering an inn or tavern and, as for being observed speaking with a woman of the night! Crossing the darkened grounds made more gloomy by the absence of a moon, Ava hissed her irritation. The need which had driven her to look for ease among the local strumpets still burned and gnawed in her stomach. It was risky looking anywhere for her particular brand of pleasure, even more so when the search took her to the streets of her home town, but the visits to Church House had all but drained her purse. The money gained from the selling of figurines and dishes had gone into the coffers of that establishment and she had vowed to herself each visit would be the last.

But vows easily made had been the more easily

broken, and sovereigns had followed sovereigns down the same bottomless pit until once more little remained. Desire was a flame which refused the quenching. The heat of it grew, increasing with the days until it seemed it would burn her alive. That was how it had been for the past couple of weeks, a scorching red-hot flame feeding a craving so voracious as to have it burst into wild volcanic fire exploding along every nerve until it could no longer be controlled but became the stomach-twisting fervour which had tonight driven her first to the streets then on to the house of that schoolmistress.

The woman's sharp-featured face had exhibited no surprise. Ava's feet crunched the hard unkempt path which led to the rear of Moorcroft House. She had led the way to a vulgarly over-furnished front parlour where she had listened impassively. *A girl, one she was absolutely certain would utter no word of what she was made to do.* Ava had spoken quietly, the schoolmistress responding as she might the request for a joint of meat. She had such a girl, she was here in the house, Ava could take her pleasure. No money had exchanged hands, the unspoken fee being that of one woman's hold over another, the unspoken ransom of evil. Ava Russell would never be able to commit her accomplice to the hands of the judiciary without suffering the same fate herself.

The girl had been young, barely past her twelfth year. An orphan taken from the poorhouse, grateful to the woman who had rescued her from that life of poverty; but what of the life to which she must now resign herself, how long would she give herself to the slaking of another woman's lust before doing what Myra Brent had done? But no thought of that had interfered with the satisfying of Ava Russell's need.

Passing the line of bushes alongside the small outbuilding which had been home to her stablehand, Ava walked on, her thoughts unchecked.

Thin to the point of being all bone, the girl had shivered beneath the hands stroking her body. Her own fingers clumsy in performing lust-gasped instructions she had squeezed breasts larger than her own, trailed a tight-closed mouth over a stomach convulsing beneath its touch, then rubbed rather than caressed the warm, moist channel topping Ava's parted legs succeeding in bringing an explosive burst of passion which resulted in no real quenching of desire.

It had cost no money, but it had brought no relief. Maybe when she got to the Continent, maybe then she would once more train her own lover. Yes, she would train a girl of her choosing, teach her the art of making love, the skills necessary to satisfy another woman. The thought lancing a trail of heat from stomach to throat, a thrill of emotion that had breath a prisoner in her throat, Ava smiled her first smile of the evening.

'I've been a'waiting of you.'

Soft-spoken in the darkness, it made the breath burst free of the chains holding it in Ava's throat.

'I guessed you might come this way.'

'Who are you, what do you want!' Ava snapped,

anger at her private grounds being invaded overriding caution.

'Who I am will be seen once we be inside of the house.' The voice seemed to smile. 'As for what it be I wants then surely you don't need the tellin' of that, but in case I be wrong in presumin' then I will give the tellin'. What I be wanting is money . . . money to keep what I knows of you from being hawked all over this town.'

Blackmail! Ava's blood thickened to ice. Whoever was standing in the shadows carried the threat Alfred Birks had carried, was making the same demands he had made. But no one apart from him and his lady love had known of the liaison between herself and Lenor Medwin; and that dirty little stablehand and the pathetic maid were both dead. Yet here was someone else claiming that knowledge and its ill-gained reward . . . someone very much alive!

'Well, do we be goin' inside or do I take myself to that posh George Hotel along the street? I 'ave no doubts as to the attentions I'll get when I tells the doings of the mistress of Moorcroft House.'

'*The doings of the mistress of Moorcroft House.*'

Each word the loudness of a bell ringing in her brain, Ava tried to think. Had she been careless that first time of paying a woman of the street for her service? Had she been recognised while visiting the high-class brothel that was Church House? The first was a definite no . . . and the second? Any casual observer seeing her enter that house in Bilston could have no knowledge of its reason, and certainly one whose speech was as rough as that of this person would be no client there.

Encouraged by this, Ava returned sharply. 'You had best leave before I call for the constable.'

'Call him!' The reply no longer held the hint of a smile but an open sneer. 'I've no worries if you 'ave none.'

It was a challenge! Ava's thin mouth tightened. But one she could not take up. Should this intruder in her garden really have the knowledge claimed, then to risk it being voiced abroad was not to be dared.

Swallowing hard, hoping to clear all trace of supposition from her voice, she asked, 'What are these so-called doings you speak of and what on earth leads you to the belief I will give you money?'

'The 'doings' be that of brushin' the muff, and you'll give me what is asked 'cos you wants that secret kept tight as that little hole you likes fingered atwixt your legs.'

There could be no further doubt. Tight as bowstrings, Ava's nerves quivered. But how . . . how had she been found out? Birks? His lover? Myra? Impossible! The dead don't talk.

The dead don't talk! Breath hard in her lungs, teeth clenched so firm they hurt, the phrase sang in her brain. The dead didn't talk but a letter could. The letter Eden Brent claimed was written by her sister . . . Had it somehow been seen by the creature standing in the shadows, might it even now be in a pocket or a bag? Stolen! It had to have been . . . The other Brent girl would never have willingly allowed it to fall into the hands of anyone else.

'Well! You decide quick, I ain't about to stand 'ere all night.'

Sharp and demanding, each word vibrated along Ava's veins. How much would this one want? How regular would the demand be made? It would be no once-in-a-lifetime, of that she could be assured. Like Birks would have done, this blackmailer would come again and again . . . and when the last halfpenny was gone? Ava felt a laugh start low in her stomach . . . This one would no doubt do as she herself would do in their situation . . . Sell the letter to whoever was interested!

Thoughts darting like quicksilver, she searched for a way out then a rustling in the shadows warning of impatience, she said, 'I carry very little money with me. I will need to get more from the house, but first you will tell me how you came by your information.'

A loud sniff or a stifled laugh? Ava could not distinguish but the answer caused no doubt.

'I don't 'ave to tell you nothin' . . . but I ain't vindictive so I will. Not every woman at Church House earns her livin' by lyin' on her back for a man or by strokin' another woman's fanny. I be one who sees without bein' seen, one of them as cleans up the mess folk of your sort leaves behind. I seen you the times you come thinkin' a veil across your face to hide what your mouth watered for, then when you was done and left I heard the wenches laughin' and talkin'. Brushin' the muff was what they talked of. Now, I might be no more than a room maid, but that don't go to say as I 'ave no brain. I knows what a story like that could do to a woman should it get spilled . . . and I knowed the money could be earned by holdin' it the back of the teeth. That bein' so, I followed you, not once but three times, and on each you come here to this house. You be its owner, Missis Ava Russell. Oh yes, I found that out an' all . . . so if you wants to remain here playin' Lady Muck then you'll get me that which I be 'ere for. Ten sovereigns be the price. That don't be much to ask now do it? Ten sovereigns can seal a woman's mouth and you does want it sealed, don't you? Ten sovereigns and I'll be on my way, unless o' course you would like that muff of your'n brushed . . . Won't cost near so much as havin' it played with along of Church House.'

At Ava's back, soft enough not to be heard beyond the confines of the garden, a snigger seemed to scream contempt.

'What do you say? Shall we tek ourselves an hour in that bedroom of your'n, I could mebbes show you a few delights them there wenches along of Bilston ain't learned yet . . . I wouldn't be askin' of no extra payment. Call it showin' of satisfaction with our little arrangement. Ten sovereigns pleases me, a ticklin' of your fanny pleases you . . . we both be satisfied.'

Fingers clasped against the sibilant hiss of one more sniggering laugh, Ava's mind whirled.

'. . . I knows what a story like that could do . . .'

'I knowed the money could be earned by holdin' it the back of the teeth . . .'

'*Ten sovereigns can seal a woman's mouth . . .*'

But for how long? Paramount, that one thought rose above the others. Only so long as the sovereigns did, and then this creature would be back for more, threatening and sneering!

'Well!' The voice was louder, less patient. 'Do it be payment or do it be I teks my little titbit along of the George?'

'It will be payment.' Ava's whisper mingled with that of leaves dancing on the night air. Turning on the ball of one foot, a hand lifting to strike, she whispered again, 'Oh yes, you will get your payment!'

33

'The wife checked at the 'ouse afore we settled for the night; the wench were all right then, her said as her would be setting the things to readiness against the mornin' an' then would be gettin' herself to her bed.'

The operator of the narrowboat the *Gospel Maid* stood cap in hand in the office of Denby Boat Builders. He hadn't known why the owner had sent for him and now he waited nervously for the outcome of their meeting. Would it be the sack, would it mean his wife and family would be without home and the means of feeding themselves? Lord forbid the doing!

'The missis . . .' the boatman swallowed, an anxious, noisy movement of the throat which had his Adam's apple dancing, '. . . her had a look to that scullery an' also asked might her use the privy along of the backyard just so as to check all were as it should be . . . Her wouldn't never go leavin' lessen her were convinced the wench were safe. If only Old Nick hadn't died, that dog were true to his name if any dog was; he could hear a butterfly fart from a mile off and 'ave its throat out afore it got to settlin' its arse on a poppy . . . beggin' of your pardon for the sayin'.'

Behind the heavy mahogany desk, Andrew Denby nodded. He had known this man from boyhood and knew the simple honesty of him. What he had said, coarse as it may have been put, would be the truth.

'Old Nick was one on his own,' he answered, allowing a brief smile.

'He were that, Mister Andrew. Like I says he could hear, smell and see sharp and clear as the devil hisself and he'd 'ave the gizzard outta any man a' tryin' to do what oughtn't to be; wouldn't 'ave nothing untoward 'ave gone on 'ad Old Nick been wi' the boat. Reckon it'll be a year or two afore I gets another dog the like o' that one.'

'There was no boat moored alongside of your own?' The boatman shook his head. 'None but the *Maid* within sight, Mister Andrew, but if you be a' thinkin' that what were done were by the hand of one of we . . .'

The quick lift of a hand cut the sentence short and Andrew Denby's smile, though brief, was reassuring. 'No, Jed, I don't think any cutman would do what was done last night, and certainly not any who knew Miss Brent . . . But somebody attacked her, the question is why? For what reason?'

'You reckon it were done for money? That it were a thief lookin' for easy pickings?'

He had thought so himself when the Melia lad had come to tell him of finding Eden lying on her living-room floor, hands and feet trussed like market poultry her head and face streaked with dried blood. But though each room of that cottage appeared as if caught

by a whirlwind, the money kept in a pot on the
mantelshelf and that kept for the buying of ingredients
for her cooking were still in place. So, if not cash, then
what had any thief been looking for? There were no
valuables in Shipton Cottage; that meant only one
possible explanation. The girl herself! Whoever had
entered that house had done so not to rob but with the
express purpose of . . . his blood chilling, Andrew
Denby's hands closed into hard balls . . . of harming
Eden Brent . . . maybe of killing her!

'I brought the *Maid* from her moorings just as dawn
light touched the sky. The trip along of London being
a long one and the cargo I were hauling having to catch
the India boat, I thought best to sail soonest I could see
a stretch in front o' me. I never thought somebody to
break into the Shipton place. All looked to be as it
should afore we pulled away or we wouldn't never 'ave
left.'

The man was blaming himself for what had
happened. Recognising as much in the twisting of the
cap and the anxious look of the eyes, Andrew Denby
rose, circling the desk as he assured the other man no
blame was attached to him but, with the boatman's
leaving the office, he felt the cold fear hit his stomach
the way it had when the Melia lad had come running
in.

David had gone to Shipton Cottage in order to walk
with Eden into Wednesbury as he had stubbornly
declared he would. The shutters still closed across the
downstairs windows had alarmed him and he had

entered the house not bothering to knock. At first he could see almost nothing, the fire in the grate being all but dead. He had crossed to the window and opened the shutter and, as daylight poured in, he had seen the living-room scattered with the contents of every drawer and cupboard, then . . . the lad had gulped air before saying . . . *'Then I seen Eden, her were lying across the hearth, her d'ain't move when I called her name. I . . . I were feared her were dead.'*

So had he! Staring out across the busy boatyard, Andrew felt the chill of ice strike again at the pit of his stomach. His every nerve had jangled at the sound of David Melia's voice shouting to the clerk that he must see the gaffer 'now', but on seeing the stricken look on the lad's face it seemed his heart had stopped.

Leaving David to follow, he had galloped the distance to the cottage, his brain knowing only he might have lost the girl he had never told of his love, that Eden Brent might be dead and, through the pain of it all, had beaten one promise; the person responsible would suffer the same fate! That vow had been on his lips as he had strode into the tiny house and was silently renewed as he saw the girl lying asleep, one side of her pale face darkened with a purpling bruise.

'Shh!' Sara Melia's mouth had pursed the sound as he framed his question then she had slipped out of the room, leaving him alone with Eden.

He had wanted to lift that sleeping figure into his arms, hold it close against him, to whisper the love which had flowed like a fountain, the rush of it gathering in his veins hurtling into his throat until he felt he must choke on it. Then her eyes had opened and she had smiled at him.

Lord, what that smile had caused in him! Glance resting on the waters which ran beside the boatyard, he tried again to analyse the emotions which had raced with that smile but, if he lived a thousand years, he would still not name them all. Anger? Oh yes, there had been that, a whole burning river of anger . . . Desire for vengeance? That, too, in equal measure, but of all the sensations driving through him the overriding one had been love. It had risen from deep inside him, an all-embracing upsurge, a pulsing throb that was a drum in his brain, a pain in his heart that had him cry her name.

'Eden.' He whispered it now as he had then and, in his mind, saw again the swift look which had gleamed momentarily as those turquoise eyes had opened, a look which had been shut off but not so quickly that he had not caught it. But had it been what he thought . . . what he hoped? Albeit faint, could it have been a shadow, a semblance of the love he himself felt?

But then it was gone and she was thanking him for his concern but insisting there was no need and that he must not neglect his business on her account.

Not neglect his business. Andrew Denby laughed, a soft, hopeless laugh. He would bypass heaven itself if it meant a moment with her. Would he have told her as much, would he have spoken of that fierce longing chained inside him?

The moment had been snatched away with the

coming of Tobias Jevons. Turning from the window, Andrew returned to his desk, acid settling on his tongue; the acid he had tasted as Eden Brent's smiling words of welcome had met the other man. One man welcomed, the other politely told he must not neglect his business. The nib of a slender pen snapped against the surface of the desk. It had not been difficult to see which of the two Eden Brent preferred!

Which of the two she preferred . . . could it also be which of the two she loved? Unable to settle beneath the cloud of that question, Andrew Denby rode the path leading to The Coppice. It was not unknown for a young girl to take an older man, money was a powerful motive for such marriages. But what of love? Could Eden Brent love a man old enough to be her grandfather . . . be *in* love with him!

'That is a preposterous question.' Tobias Jevons laughed as it was put to him. 'You have no reason to think that. I am very fond of the girl, in fact I would say yes, I do love her, but not in the same way you do.'

An apologetic curve touching his mouth, Andrew met copper-coloured eyes. They were alive with a brightness they had not held in many years.

'No need to say what I can read for myself on your face,' Tobias waved a hand dismissively. 'You love the girl and I admire you for it,' he smiled widely, 'I'd call you a fool were you not to.'

'Won't do me any good.'

'It won't if you don't tell her! Though I don't take the girl to be blind, she can see for herself the feelings you have, they show clear on your face; but no maid takes it upon herself to speak the first words. That be up to you and I counsel you do it quick, my lad, or you be like to lose her to another.'

Sitting in a velvet-covered chair, the light from high-arched windows played across the tense line that was Andrew Denby's mouth. Was there someone in Eden's life, someone she loved?

Settled in his own matching chair, Tobias read the pain hovering on the face of a man he had watched grow from childhood, one who had known the true identity of an old man living in a cottage at the entrance to that long drive, and who had kept his secret.

'Andrew.' Hand resting on a malacca cane, he spoke gently. 'I was your father's friend as well as his partner in business and I claim that same privilege with you. I feel you to be the . . .' voice breaking, Tobias swallowed hard against the sting of his own pain, though the sheen of it gleamed a watery veil over his eyes, '. . . the son who was taken from me. That being so, I speak as I know your own father would speak. Go to her, tell her of your feelings . . .'

'But if there is someone else!'

'Then she will tell you.' Tobias answered the swift interruption. 'There will be hurt in it for you should she be given in love to another man, but that will be as the bite of a gnat compared to the anguish you could both suffer should you remain silent.'

'Both?' Andrew frowned.

Sunlight turning grey to silver, Tobias' head

nodded. 'Yes, Andrew, I say both, for it is my firm belief Eden loves you. We have talked several times since my returning to this house and whenever our conversation touched upon you a gentle flush would invade her cheeks and, though her eyes lowered, they could not hide what lay in their depths. She will not speak, though the holding back break her heart. That is a barrier that must be broken by you. Eden Brent has pride, pride to match your own, that much was shown by her refusal to accept my proposal she make The Coppice her home. It would have meant a life of ease for her but she declined, saying she had been taught to take only that which she had earned. It was gently said but the meaning of it rang clear; she would accept no man's charity.'

But would she accept his love? Andrew sat quietly, the thought reverberating in his mind.

'She told you of my asking her to share this house, to make her home here?'

Drawing his mind away from that one thought, Andrew shook his head. 'No, she did not.'

'Pride.' Tobias chuckled. 'I told you she had the same affliction you have. But Andrew . . . don't let pride get in the way of happiness. Regret sometimes comes so late that life has already passed by. Have the courage to take it in hand, to seek the thing you want most from it. Believe me, it is the only way. Sorrow is a bitter medicine and it brings no cure. I know for I drank it long and deep. Do not tread a path that leads nowhere except to heartbreak.'

'My father always said you were a wise bird, now I know what he meant.'

Pushing to his feet as his visitor rose to leave, Tobias Jevons leaned heavily on his cane. 'Eden Brent refused my offer to share my house as a daughter or even a housekeeper,' he said quietly. 'My hopes go with you she will not refuse to share yours as a wife.'

Share his home as a wife.

Andrew Denby's mind wrestled with the thought of what the asking might bring. It had been weeks before the friendship they had now developed. How could he expect it now to become love? Tobias Jevons was seeing things through different eyes. He did not know of the antagonism Eden had once held for the son of his old friend. Could he risk the return of those feelings, could he jeopardise that friendship on one slim hope? She had given him no cause to think him other than a casual acquaintance. Their meetings were pleasant, their conversation no longer spiked, but it was not the conversation of a man and his sweetheart.

Sweetheart! It was a word he might never hear from her lips.

'Evenin' Mister Denby, sir.'

Brought up by the call Andrew returned the greeting of the bargee mooring his narrowboat alongside Shipton Cottage.

'Be the young miss all right? Her ain't suffered no lastin' hurt I 'opes.'

'A cut to the head but thankfully no permanent injury.'

Jumping on to the towpath to where his own horse waited to be released from the tow line which pulled the boat, the man looked at Andrew. 'We thanks God for that, me and my missis both, but I'd be a' thankin' Him more should He grant me just two minutes with the swine as broke into that there cottage. I guarantees he wouldn't never stand on his legs again! And that don't just be a vow made by meself, Mister Andrew, but it be the word of every man jack o' we, every boatman as plies the canal be of the same mind . . . Find the bast . . . well, find the one attacked that wench and make him a bed at the bottom of the nearest lock. Don't suppose them there coppers have nabbed the varmint?'

'Not so far,' Andrew replied, swinging easily from his own mount.

'Bit too far for 'em to come likely, them chaps be too fond o' their comfort to trek across the 'eath looking for villains, but should I catch sight of the fellah I seen a' walkin' toward Wednesbury that night . . .'

'Which night?' The demand crackled on the quiet air, the force of it bringing the other man's attention from hobbling the horse.

'Why, the same night the young miss were broken in on. I left the wife and the lad to bring the boat to her mooring . . . They set for the night down around yon lock.' He pointed a callused hand in the direction from which he had come. 'I dropped off as we come through the town, I don't care for the missis to be walkin' across the 'eath after dark so I went for the supplies we was needing. To be truthful I had meself a taste o' the jug along of the Lea Brook tavern . . . keeps a good drop of ale does Thomas Challinor . . . but it were a clear 'ead I'd be needin' if it weren't a pit shaft I was to sleep in, so I took no more than two pints; that bein' the way of it I knows it were no trick of the mind when I seen that figure a' comin' towards me on the path, though from the look I could have been forgiven for thinkin' it a vision from hell. Old it looked, walked bent over a stick, and the jacket and trousers the colour of night.'

'The face,' Andrew urged as the telling ceased, 'did you recognise the face?'

'D'ain't see it.' The bargee swung his head slowly. 'Wore a flat cap low over the brow and the collar of the jacket were pulled up over the chin and though I wished the fellah goodnight he made no answer, just hobbled past like I wasn't there; but so sure I comes across him again he'll be glad to talk, he'll tell me did he see any other man a' walkin' of that path even if I 'as to choke it outta him!'

Walked bent over a stick!

The boatman, having tended the needs of his horse, had returned to the narrowboat, yet Andrew Denby stood, the blood in his veins chilled.

Those murders in Wednesbury . . . There had been talk of an old man being seen in the vicinity, a man needing the use of a stick to walk! Had that same man visited Shipton Cottage? Had the murderer widened his field in search of victims? Had he intended that next victim to be Eden Brent but had he been frightened away before he could finish the job?

Finish the job. The words were cannon fire in his brain. The bargee had seen no face . . . but Eden . . . He drew a long juddering breath . . . Eden must have seen, she could identify . . .

. . . *Finish the job* . . .

He would have to do exactly that to save himself . . . the man would be back!

34

A high moon painted the heath in shades of alabaster and pearl, the movement of wisps of baby cloud sprinkling the tussocky grass with spangles of silver while each outcrop of limestone was etched with light gleaming about it like a robe of pale silk. But none of the beauty of the night impressed itself upon the mind churning with questions.

Had the someone who had entered Shipton Cottage done so with the intention of murder? Why had Eden been bound hand and foot? What was it the intruder had ransacked the house in search of?

The first of those questions Andrew Denby could only guess at; perhaps something had startled the intruder causing him to leave the house with his task unfinished. The second of those questions he found simpler to answer. Unlike those poor unfortunates murdered in Wednesbury, Eden had been bound at wrist and ankle, but not been killed . . . That had to be because should whatever was searched for not be found then Eden would be needed alive, tortured maybe until she told what was necessary.

Tortured! Andrew's nerves jolted. Had that procedure already begun, was that the cause of Eden's bruises, the cut to her head? Had she known . . . been told of the fate she would suffer once the rogue had what he'd been looking for? Lord, it was a wonder she was still sane!

But the scaffold would see the one who had done that to Eden Brent, and it would see the one who no doubt had paid for it to be done. That was the answer he had for the third of his self-asked questions.

Shipton Cottage held nothing of value to anyone except a letter, a letter damning Ava Russell, and it could only be Ava Russell who had hired a man to burgle and possibly kill Eden. How the woman had found where she lived was unimportant now; all that mattered was going to Moorcroft House and facing her, of telling her should aught befall Eden then he himself would tell the authorities all that Dora Benson had confided to him.

Dora Benson had not wanted to tell him anything. Moonlight sketching shadows on the ground, stealing the pale shimmering robes from rocks dotted about the heath only to replace their silken glory moments later, went unheeded against the pictures filling Andrew's mind.

Thin, work-worn almost to a shadow, the woman had left the clamour of the small brick-built brewhouse which served for a nail-making workshop.

'*Yes, I knows Eden Brent but I don't know where her be living.*'

The woman had answered defensively, wanting to

shield Eden from anything which might result in trouble. It had taken some little while, Dora being convinced he meant no harm only when her husband came from the workshop and vouched for the honesty and fair dealing Andrew Denby practised with each man having the good fortune to work for him.

Dora had invited him into her home then, apologising for the frugality of it all, and after offering tea which he had accepted with thanks and listening to all he could tell of Eden, she had glanced at her husband and at his nod had told her own story.

Quietly, interrupted by the occasional pause as she searched for words in which to explain the more delicate situation Eden's sister had found herself in, it had all come out; all that Myra Brent herself had revealed and also of the letter she had written.

And it was that letter Shipton Cottage had been ransacked for. But it would do Ava Russell no good. If he could prove hers was the true hand behind the assault upon Eden, he would ensure the whole country learned of that woman's vile practices. Knowledge of what was being gossiped of while waiting to be sentenced would be Ava Russell's own torture.

. . . Ten sovereigns can seal a woman's mouth . . .

Ava Russell stared at the ceiling above her bed. That had been the payment demanded by that slut of a woman.

. . . I knows what a story like that could do . . .

Only there *would* be no story, for payment had been

given. But no sovereigns had changed hands. Ava's inner smile was pure hatred.

The woman's mouth had been wide beneath the leering grin, a brief shaft of clouded moonlight showing the gapped teeth. Ava's inward smile deepened. It had shown for one short moment before the mouth had opened to scream. But that scream had known no birth, nor would that mouth open again. She had waited there in the grounds of Moorcroft House, waited for money . . . but there was no profit in death. Nor had there been profit in her own journey.

Unmoving except for the glance playing over the ceiling, Ava recounted her doings of earlier that same evening. She had waited until after sunset before reaching deep into the wardrobe to extract a shoddy jacket, trousers and flat cap. Bought for a supposed fancy dress party, her cook had given no second thought to the procuring of them for her mistress, saying only they had come from a pawnshop so they needed hanging outside in the yard to air away the smell of damp. There had been no fancy dress, their use being that of making a woman look like a man . . . of making the mistress of Moorcroft appear as a working-class man worn out by his labours, and Samuel's cane had completed the illusion. Samuel had carried the cane every day since bringing it home from the Crimea, but it had never served him as it had served her.

Beyond the fringe of thought sounds echoed on the stillness but Ava remained with her memories.

Birks had thought to blackmail her. Poor stupid Birks!

'*Wait you there, old 'un.*'

The words he had spoken to a bent figure hobbling from the gloom, walking stick tapping the ground, came from the mouth of the man pictured so vividly by her brain.

'*I'll be passing that way in a minute or so . . .*'

And so he had. Alfred Birks had returned but not to pass, he had remained at the Church Steps, his chest and stomach slashed by the blade that 'old 'un' had drawn from the walking stick.

Her wit and Samuel's cane had saved her from the demands of a blackmailer as it had prevented Lenor's maid having the same idea.

It had happened as she had surmised. Ava's glance played on the white ceiling. Shoes that had most likely belonged to Lenor had tapped loudly, heralding the girl's approach. She had chosen the same route taken by Birks, coming by way of Ethelfleda Terrace, the way which brought her to that same alley where her lover had met his end.

'*Spare an old man tuppence for a bite o'supper.*'

The words she had called echoed now in Ava's head. Dilly Madely had gasped relief on seeing a bent old man grasping a walking stick in order to hold himself on his feet as he hobbled forward. But it had been no tuppence she had given, but her life! Samuel's cane had once more done its work and Ava Russell, disguised in the worn clothing of a working man, had simply walked away. But the clothes had not been disposed of, they had been stored in their hiding place, along with the cane. She had been sensible to keep them. Ava felt the smile spread in her chest. They had proved her salvation yet again.

She ought not to have sought the services of a woman of the streets, but the craving that was a flame in her stomach, desire lancing like blades, a hunger ravenous and consuming, a maelstrom of desire ripping away all common sense, had sent her in search of the only thing which would ease the longing . . . sent her in search of a woman. She had agreed, thinking to service an old man and be back at her trade in less time than it took to laugh over the doing; but there had been no return to the streets and the woman's payment had been the slashing of her chest and stomach. The Wednesbury Ripper was the term used to describe the perpetrator of those foul killings, but no one in Wednesbury had suspected the mistress of Moorcroft of being that killer.

Nor had the maid who cleaned the rooms of Church House! Above her head the shadows of evening began to inch across the ceiling. They would darken as those enveloping the garden of Moorcroft had darkened but these would hide no blackmailer.

The woman had played her game well. No morsel of regret, no trace of remorse or repentance for the murders she had committed, draped itself on Ava's conscience; only pictures fresh as if they had taken place but a minute since played clear in her mind.

'. . . *the doings be that of brushin' the muff* . . .'

Again a mouth seemed to move, to speak words only her mind could hear.

'. . . *you decide quick, I ain't about to stand 'ere all night.*'

Ava smiled at the echo in her brain.

The woman had not stood all night. She had stood only long enough for that blade to slice across her throat then she had collapsed, folding slowly, almost gently, from the knees as some player on the stage might curtsy to an audience. But there had been no audience and no applause, only a blade slashing and ripping at a body already beyond its feel.

She had laughed, a low exultant laugh of sheer triumph. Ava's eyes watched the encroaching gloom swallow the daylight. A feeling of exhilaration had swept like wildfire through her veins, had danced a wild dance of success, an exultation of victory. Once more she had defeated a challenge, destroyed the one who had made it and no other was witness. There was nothing and no one could call her to answer for what she had done. Ava Russell would never pay the price for murder.

She had laughed again but, as she had raised the blade to insert it into the body of the cane, the laugh had become a stranglehold, a choking blockage in her throat while her lungs had gripped convulsively on the handle of the swordstick. She had fallen there beside the door of her own house, fallen across the dead body, her own refusing to move. It had not moved since.

The smile which had spread so easily in her chest had died the same way.

The stroke had whipped across her brain taking with it the movement from arms and legs. But not the movement of her mind. Trapped where she lay, inert except for the flicker of eyelids, she had realised the truth and if she could have laughed one more time she would have done so then.

Nothing and no one could call her to answer for what she had done!

The thought had flashed.

Nothing and no one . . . except the will of heaven!

He had come immediately Davy had told him what had happened. Eden dressed slowly, pulling her clothes over aching limbs. Andrew Denby had called each day since . . . She pushed the thought away. Even now, a week from that awful night the memory of what had occurred brought fear to her throat.

Why had someone broken into this house? Eyes closing against the sting of moving her aching body, she sat on the side of the bed. She had come from the scullery, barely entered the living-room . . .

Pictures racing across inner vision, she drew a sharp breath.

. . . the light of the lamp had seemed strong after the pallid glow of a candle. Her spine had tingled, a strange feeling playing with her senses, the feeling of someone else being there in that empty room. She had made to draw back, instinct warning of something wrong and, in that same instant, from the corner of her eye, she had caught a movement, a dark shape lifting and in the seconds before it crashed down on her head she had glimpsed a pair of eyes.

Fingers twisting together, Eden tried to clear her mind, to erase the pictures from it; but, vivid in detail, hard and strong as reality, they clung on.

A coat collar turned up hid mouth and chin . . .

Relentlessly the memories returned, each demanding its moment in the theatre of her mind.

. . . a flat cap drawn low over the brow had held the rest of the face in shadow, but not the eyes . . .

Eden's whole body tensed.

Not those terrible glittering eyes! Her head had turned, drawn towards the shadow of movement at her side and, in that one fleeting second, her glance had locked with one spewing venom, a loathing so strong it had blazed like black fire, its message seeming to reach for her, wanting to pull her into itself, to destroy her in its own malevolence . . . and, more terrifying still, had been that awful conviction that the hatred came from someone she knew, someone she had met before!

But that was the result of shock. Gingerly, only too aware of the reaction of bruised flesh to any sudden move, she pushed herself to her feet. There was no one she knew who had eyes like those, no one in her life who had ever displayed the intensity of feeling, the hatred she had seen there.

Yet, tell herself what she did, tell herself a dozen times a day, that same feeling remained. Somewhere, sometime, she had seen those eyes before.

'You shouldn't be a' leaving of your bed . . . Mister Denby said you was to rest.'

Sara Melia turned to the figure coming slowly from the stairs, sympathy and anger mingling as she saw the bruising dark against pale skin. What no-good rogue could do such to a young wench? The cat were too good for the like of men like that, they should have the rope and so sure the culprit were caught then Andrew Denby would make certain that were what he'd get.

'Mister Denby is very kind but he is not my keeper.'

No, he ain't, but there is summat he would like to be. The thought kept safely inside, Sara tutted her disapproval as Eden settled thankfully to a chair.

'You have all been very kind,' Eden smiled, accepting freshly brewed tea, 'but now I am well enough to take care of myself.'

Sara's head shook slowly. 'That ain't what Mister Andrew will be sayin'. He cares about you, wench. You might not see but other folk does, Andrew Denby cares a great deal about you.'

Much as she wanted to follow Sara into the washhouse to help with the laundry, the ache in her limbs told Eden she would be more hindrance than enough.

'. . . *Andrew Denby cares a great deal about you.*'

Did he? Eden stared at the tea she had not tasted. She had dared to dream that that might be so, dared to hope . . . but hope, like dreams, had been fleeting.

'*Dreams does no harm, lessen you* mixes *them with the truth.*'

Another of Grandmother's sayings. Eden smiled ruefully. But was that not what she had done? She had allowed that which she longed for to become entangled with what was given, and that was wrong. She could not take friendship and weave it into love; Andrew Denby had offered her one, she could never expect to be offered the other.

Yet there had been moments. She took up the cup, gripping it tightly in an attempt to still the trembling that came with the thought. Moments she could not forget. Like the one when, the day following the assault upon her, she had wakened to find him standing beside her bed. There had been such a look of tenderness on his face, a depth in his dark eyes that she had felt her heart cry its own response. Then Tobias Jevons had been shown into her room and the look had vanished, replaced by one which could be read almost as anger.

How could real tenderness, even that of friendship, die so quickly unless it were simply imagined? Sipping the hot sweet liquid, Eden felt the same sadness which had risen at Andrew Denby's abrupt departure. He had seemed suddenly angry . . . but for what reason? And the evening he had called on his way to Wednesbury. She had glimpsed that same unreadable look deep in his eyes and for a heart-stopping moment she had thought he would take her in his arms . . . but then the moment was gone and so was Andrew Denby.

Replacing the cup on its saucer, she stared unseeingly at it.

He could not refuse what he did not know was his. He could not refuse her love.

Beyond the tiny living-room, the thump of the wooden maid beating linen in the heavy tub reverberated on the silence but Eden heard only the beat of her own turmoil.

And, if by some miracle, Andrew Denby were to love her? Nothing could come of it! Fingernails bit deep into the soft flesh of palms. She could never accept it, how could she? How could she ruin his life, for that was how it would be. A girl from Hobbins Street, a place so poor its inhabitants knew hunger from birth! That might be overcome. Andrew Denby did not give the impression of snobbery, of the possession of wealth being a dominant factor in his life. But lack of money was not the only thing made Eden Brent undesirable as a wife, not the only part of her background could give him cause to despise her . . . There was her sister!

But no . . . not Myra herself! Eden's mind revolted at the thought. Eden was not wicked . . . her sister was not dirty! It was what she had been forced to do, what Ava Russell had insisted upon, vile acts no girl should ever be made to partake in! But would Andrew Denby believe that? Would he believe Myra had done what she had in order to support her grandmother and sister? Or would he believe she had been a willing partner, one who enjoyed the games that were played . . . would he see Myra as no less a lesbian than her mistress?

But the test would not be put. Myra's past would

never be revealed. Andrew Denby would never learn her secret.

Myra's secret! A jolt ran the length of Eden's spine. The letter written by her sister . . . had whoever had ransacked this house found it . . . had it been stolen?

Pushing to her feet, she cried out as a shadow from the open doorway fell across her vision.

35

'I found her meself, out there in the garden, a' covered in blood and lyin' atop a corpse slashed almost to ribbons.'

Andrew Denby had listened to the woman who had cleaned at Moorcroft House.

'Whoever would 'ave thought it!' The woman had sobbed. 'Whoever would 'ave teken a murderer to be a woman.'

Who indeed!

Had Ava Russell been lying at the back of the house while he had knocked on the door at the front?

There had been no doubt in the minds of the constables the cleaning woman's screams had sent running to that house. The jacket and trousers Ava Russell was dressed in were splashed with blood, her hands were covered in it and the blade of the swordstick still clutched in her useless fingers was rust-brown where blood had dried on it. It was like a signed testimonial, an unspoken admittance to her being a murderess and one readily accepted by the magistrate.

'*All carry the same hallmark,*' The magistrate had declared. '*Each victim was despatched in the same manner, the throat being cut and the body ripped open by a blade. But with the accused being unable to answer to any questions the law can make no call for trial. The outcome, therefore, must be that until speech returns the woman, Ava Russell, will remain under medical supervision.'*

Medical supervision! Andrew Denby played a glance over the high walls and tall iron gates of the private sanatorium. That magistrate might just as well have acquitted the woman for, as things were, she could not be tried or sentenced; Ava Russell had got away with murder after all!

'Doctor is of the opinion that a major part of the paralysis is the result of shock.' The matron who had conducted Andrew to a small room holding only a narrow iron-framed bed, a chest of drawers and a bedside table with glass-topped lamp, touched a hand to the covers smoothing a non existent crease. 'Once that is gone he is convinced the use of the limbs, as the speech, will be restored. It should be remembered, however, that a stroke does often result in one side of the body being permanently affected. We should be aware of such a possibility. We should also be aware of visiting hours . . .' A sniff emphasising displeasure at having routine disrupted, the matron glared at Andrew. 'You may have one half hour . . . but future visits will be made at the regular time!'

With a swish of grey skirts beneath an apron whiter than God's own snow and starched stiff as cardboard, the woman had swept from the room, a whiff of carbolic circling after her.

Looking down at Ava Russell, Andrew felt the bile of distaste bite his throat. The woman could not speak with her tongue but her eyes said she knew the reason of his visit . . . They knew and they laughed.

'I know you can hear and I know you can understand.'

Almost black against the pristine pillow, the dark eyes gleamed.

'It was you, wasn't it?' he asked. 'You who went to Shipton Cottage, you who struck and bound Eden Brent?'

Ava's eyelids closed slowly, then opened.

'Is that your sign for agreement?'

The eyelids closed again, remaining so for a couple of seconds before lifting.

It was a yes. Ava Russell was answering.

'You were looking for something?'

Again the lowering of the eyelids.

'That something was a letter, a letter written by Myra Brent?'

Black against the pillow, the eyes regarded him. Would she answer again?

'I know there was such a letter. Dora Benson told me of it. Was that the reason of your going to that cottage?'

Slowly the lids dropped. She was hiding nothing but she would know that in the eyes of the law she had admitted nothing. What can't speak can't lie! The adage seemed to taunt in the stare once more fastening on his face.

'Did you find it? Do you have it?'

No movement of eyelids confirmed the answer, only that mocking laugh, that dark evil glittered in a coal-black gaze. Even now, malice was Ava Russell's master.

'If you will not answer that, then will you answer this.' He paused, feeling the acid of his throat spill on to his tongue. 'Did you intend to kill Eden Brent?'

There was no hesitation. With the last syllable not yet free of his lips the eyelids lowered, pressing hard against the eyeballs beneath. A swift intake of breath brought the next question. 'Were you disturbed? Is that the reason Eden Brent is still alive?'

The same sign telling him the assumption was correct, he glanced with exasperation at the door being opened. The half hour was not up yet!

'This is highly irregular!'

The voice of the matron cut shrilly across the room and, staring up from the pillow, Ava Russell's eyes laughed again.

She was aware all right! Andrew's teeth ground his frustration. Aware he could ask no more questions. But her being disturbed, and by whom, no longer mattered . . . It had meant the saving of Eden's life and that was all he cared about.

'Highly irregular!' Heels tapping on floors polished to a crystal shine, the woman swept into the room, her face flushed and angry beneath a wide starched cap. 'The time allowed for visiting patients is made very clear, and that time is not now!'

Dressed in a dark suit and tie, a tall thin-framed man

answered in the same acerbic tone which had addressed him. 'I am aware of that, as you should be aware, that being Missis Russell's solicitor, the law allows I speak with her whenever I deem it necessary; and the law, I might inform you, has precedence even over this establishment.'

A loud sniff her reply, the matron turned on her heel but could not resist one last curt rejoinder. 'Then I hope the law will take note a patient needs rest!'

'Please.' The solicitor touched a long finger to Andrew's sleeve as he, too, moved to leave. 'If you would not mind staying. What I have to disclose to my client I prefer to be said in the presence of a witness.'

Not waiting for an answer, the man drew a sheaf of papers from a leather Gladstone bag, his voice droning on.

'Missis Russell, the doctor assures me you are in possession of your hearing and that your ability to understand that which is said to you remains unimpaired.'

Andrew looked at the figure in the bed, at the eyes suddenly alert with apprehension. Ava Russell was no longer laughing!

'That being so,' the solicitor glanced briefly at his client, 'I have to inform you the bank has taken possession of Moorcroft House and the few items remaining within it. I am given by them to tell you the residue of the sum it sells for . . . if any residue there be . . . will be paid in due course. However, added to the amount of money found at Moorcroft House . . .' he flicked a page, running the tip of a finger over the next, until arriving halfway down, '. . . the sum of which amounted to . . . here is where I wish a witness present to testify my words should they be questioned at some future date . . . the sum of which amounted to eighteen pounds four shillings and threepence three farthings. I would add that of that sum ten pounds is due for legal services accruing over the past months and will be deducted, the rest will be given over to the sanatorium in order to cover the expense of the care you have received so far.'

Papers returned, the Gladstone bag snapped shut, the solicitor glanced once at Andrew before requesting an exchange of cards. Then, with a brief nod of the head, he was gone.

Ava Russell was destitute. Moorcroft House did not belong to her and what was left of her money was already spoken for. But private sanatoriums were expensive . . . and charity had no place in the running of them. Drawn again to glance at the face, white now almost as the pillow, Andrew could see she too was thinking that same thought.

The return of the matron, followed by two timid-looking nurses, seemed to fill the quiet room with a rush of sound, drawing Andrew's glance away from the bed.

'One moment!' He lifted a hand halting the order for him to leave immediately. 'Can you tell me, should this patient be unable to meet the cost incurred by remaining in this establishment then where will she be placed?'

A sarcastic laugh bedded in her throat, the matron sniffed. 'I can tell you that. She is to be given to the care of the parish. In other words she is to be sent to the place where all paupers are sent . . . she is to go into the poorhouse!'

The poorhouse! Andrew could almost feel pity as a glance caught the jerk of fingers scrabbling at the bedcover. No, Ava Russell was no longer laughing, the sneer and taunt had gone from those raven eyes. In their place gleamed panic, a dark silent scream of utter horror. She had felt the first tremor of her own returning ability to move, had heard the words of the matron and realised their full meaning.

Sentence had already been pronounced! Andrew walked from the sanatorium. Ava Russell had heard it proclaimed. She would hear, move and most likely speak, but only within the walls of the poorhouse; she was condemned to a fate more odious to her than death.

How many years would she live it? Climbing into his carriage, he turned the horse towards home.

Ava Russell was a true daughter of the devil and her evil had indeed reaped its own reward.

'Sara has her own home to care for as well as a living to earn. I will not take advantage of good nature.' Eden's determined look met the coppery smile of her visitor.

'Sara will be . . .'

'Paid . . . but not by me!' Sharper than was meant, it

was followed by a quick apologetic smile. 'Forgive me, but I will not take charity, though I thank you for your kindness.'

Determined as ever! Tobias Jevons smiled inwardly. It was an aspect of Eden Brent's character he had come to admire . . . even if sometimes he thought it to act not entirely in her best interests; but he could not blame her stubbornness; after all, did he not possess the same trait? Allowing the smile to show he said, 'You are a very independent young woman. A few weeks spent at The Coppice would see you fully recovered and it would afford myself great pleasure. Will you not give it some thought?'

From the towpath which ran before the small house the call of a boatman brought a horse to a standstill, then was followed by a second call asking permission to fill water pails from the well.

Sunlight gilding a slight frame, glistening on fair hair like golden fire, brought a tightening to Tobias Jevons' throat. The canvas in his bedroom . . . it might be a replica of what he was seeing now; but this was a living, breathing girl while his own dear wife . . .

'I have thought of it.' Eden turned from speaking with the boatman. 'I love The Coppice, it is regal and beautiful but at the same time gentle, filled with a love which seems to touch me whenever I enter. Your offer is tempting but I have to refuse.'

'But why?'

Eden's glance flicked to the window to where the narrowboat began to move. 'That is why. It is not only

Sara must make her living, I also must do the same. The people who work the canals buy the food I cook; without that I cannot feed myself or pay rent for this house.'

Bright as newly minted coins, Tobias Jevons' copper-coloured eyes narrowed, fingers gripping more tightly on the silver-topped malacca cane. 'Rent?' He frowned. 'You pay a rent for this cottage . . . to whom?'

'To nobody as yet, and I shouldn't really call what I put aside each day a rent for, not knowing the owner of the property, I could not agree a sum. I only hope that when someone does claim payment the money in that pot will prove sufficient.'

He had not been mistaken in his beliefs. Tobias watched the slip of a girl who had once left tuppence on his gatepost as payment for advice. She had the quick fire of pride, but she also had dignity. Andrew Denby was stupid not to ask her to wed with him, serve the young fool right if, as he had been warned, some other man scooped her from under his nose!

'I was afraid the person who . . .' Eden faltered, '. . . who came into the house that night might have taken the money in the pot but, thank heaven, it was not stolen.'

Thank heaven you were not severely injured. Tobias Jevons' own thanks were silently given while aloud he asked, 'Was *anything* stolen?'

'That is what is so difficult to understand.' Eden's brow wrinkled her glance showing puzzlement. 'Nothing was taken. I suppose I surprised him and that is the reason I was struck. Then, fearing I might run to the narrowboat moored at the bank, he bound my wrists and ankles.'

Then stayed long enough to turn the place upside down before making his getaway! As before, Tobias kept his reasoning to himself saying instead, 'Leads a man to ask, what would any thief expect to find in so tiny a house?'

'I don't know. I am only too glad he did not find the money in that pot . . . I really don't think I could have saved enough to replace that as well as the amount I already put aside. It would be a relief were the owner to come, to agree the amount he required in order for me to live here.'

Fingers relaxing, copper-hued eyes softening, Tobias answered. 'The owner has called here on several occasions and he tells you now: there is no rent required for Shipton Cottage.'

'You!' Eden stared. 'You own this house?'

'The land it is built on belonged to my father, the materials for its construction were provided by him, so yes the cottage belongs to me though it was built by Ezekial Shipton and lived in by himself and his wife from their marrying.'

'But you knew I was here! Why did you not ask for payment?'

'I needed none.' Tobias shrugged. 'Besides, the meal an old man was brought was asked no payment of.'

'I didn't want money!'

'Neither did I, my dear.' The lined face smiled. 'I

also thought I did not want friendship but, in that, I was wrong. Despite my sour ways you continued your visits until, in the end, I waited for them, wanting to see you, hoping you would come and you did, every evening without fail. That was your kindness. Allow my not speaking of rent to have been mine.'

The house in Hobbins Street was empty, the cramped brewhouse which had seen the making of the family's livelihood was empty, the fire in the forge dead and cold. Had that which had been feared for so long finally happened? Had the making of nails no longer brought money enough to feed them? That is what had to have happened; they had been near enough penniless when she had left Grandmother's house and now Aunt Dora and her family too were gone.

She ought to have called more often, maybe she could have helped. But she had told herself the pain of the past was still too great. Would Dora have acted that way . . . would the woman who had loved and comforted a motherless child have turned her back on that same girl, forgotten her as she had forgotten Aunt Dora?

But I did not forget! The thought was a cry of pure anguish but, as Eden walked quickly from the place of childhood, the feelings of guilt did not subside.

Where had the family gone? The sons were grown and capable of travelling to find work, but their mother . . . She had been so tired and worn, always sharing most of her own food between her boys until it seemed she was no more than one of the shadows which haunted the badly lighted house. Aunt Dora would need to find a home quickly, but where? Who would employ a woman so . . .

Striking so hard it rocked her on her heels, the answer slammed into Eden's mind. No one would give work to Dora Benson . . . and the only shelter she would find would be the poorhouse!

Clenched fingers pressed to her mouth holding the cries inside, Eden stared towards Meeting Street. Often with her hand clutching Grandmother's skirts a young child's feet had clattered to keep up as she was walked quickly past a building which even to so young a mind had appeared dark and forbidding. Was that where Aunt Dora was now . . . in that place so feared by the poor of Wednesbury? The institution spoken of as not breaking only the heart but destroying the very soul of those condemned to live within its walls.

But not Aunt Dora . . . she would not be left to such a life! Her grandmother's shawl propping a courage already threatening to fail, Eden crossed the Holyhead Road into Meeting Street.

36

'What the hell do you think you are doing, going off by yourself!'

Sobs which Eden had fought all the way home from that poorhouse flared into resentment as Andrew Denby's angry words met her. Stepping inside Shipton Cottage she retaliated, her whole frame throbbing with quick anger.

'And who do you think you are!' Green-blue eyes danced with fire. 'You have no right to speak to me that way.'

Already on his feet it took Andrew Denby only one stride to reach her. Hands fastening an iron grip on her elbows he glared down at her, his words coming hot and furious.

'I have every right, dammit . . . I'm in love with you!'

She had not heard right. The fire left Eden's eyes but she made no answer. She had thought he said . . . but that was her own foolish mind.

'I love you . . . you little fool!'

Dark eyes held the look she had seen before, the look she had told herself was yet one more trick of her mind.

'That gives me the right to worry over you, to want to protect you, to ask you to be my wife.'

She was not imagining, this was not a dream. Andrew Denby was real, he was here in this house . . . he was asking her to marry him!

'I have loved you from the very beginning,' his voice was softer now, husky with tenderness, 'from the moment I found you huddled against that bridge freezing to death.'

'You love me!'

A smile crossing his lips adding to the warm sable softness of his eyes, he drew her closer, his arms holding her against him. 'Is that so very difficult to believe?'

It was more than difficult, it was impossible. How could he feel love for her? She was from a different world, a world of poverty while he . . .

'I have wanted to tell you . . . to ask . . . but we seemed always to be at odds; then when I came here to find the place empty and you nowhere to be found, I realised just how much you truly meant to me, that without you my life is empty. I knew then I had to say what is in my heart: I love you and I want you to be my wife.'

They were words she had longed to hear, words she had dreamed of hearing. Held in that embrace Eden felt her heart crack. They were words she must refuse!

Pushing free she moved several paces away. Not daring to trust herself to look at him, knowing that what she must say would end any future relationship, that the friendship they had between them now would be broken for all time, but still she had to say it.

'I . . .' her voice trembled, '. . . I'm sorry but I . . . I cannot become your wife.'

Silence, breath-catchingly deep, seemed to Eden's agitated mind to go on for ever but at last Andrew Denby spoke, tension cracking his words.

'I beg your pardon, I have embarrassed you. It was presumptuous of me to think you could possibly entertain the idea of consenting to marry me, to believe . . . to hope you might return my love. I see now that cannot be.'

'That is not so!' Words she tried to hold inside swept past all resistance. 'It is not because I do not love you . . . I can't marry you because of . . .'

Not moving from the spot, only his glance moving across a face pale with emotion, Andrew demanded quietly.

'Because of what? Have you given your word to some other man?'

'No!' Eyes swimming with unshed tears lifted to his.

'Eden.' He moved close but did not touch her. 'Answer me honestly. Do you love me?'

How could she lie, how could she say words which would have him turn from her . . . how could she live without him? Yet how could she do otherwise when knowledge of what her life held would one day have him despise her!

'Andrew, I . . .'

'Don't!' He interrupted swiftly. 'I can read your answer for myself; you may wish to deny it but it is there in your eyes. You do love me Eden, refute it if you must but you cannot hide it.'

No, she could not hide it, but neither could she give way to it. His life must not be ruined as a result of hers.

'Say it.' His look gentle with love he reached for her, drawing her back into his arms. 'Say it, my darling, say you love me as I love you.'

Heaven could give her this one moment, a second of time to treasure. Breath held against the rapture of it, Eden let herself be held, allowed herself the bliss of lips closing on hers, the touch of his body strong and firm against her own. This was the paradise she had longed for, the desire of her soul; she could take it now, take the love he offered . . . But how long would love last . . . how long before paradise turned to ashes in her heart? To whisper the truth would be hard but, of all things, Andrew Denby deserved to hear that.

Taking one more moment, breathing the scent of him deep into her lungs, she whispered, 'I do love you, I love you with all my heart.'

Holding her even closer, Andrew laughed, a deep jubilant, thankful laugh. 'Then you will be my wife.'

Now for the pain! Knowing the moment must be broken, Eden pushed gently from his arms. 'No. . .' It trembled on the brink of tears but the storm did not break. 'No, Andrew, I cannot marry you and please . . . don't ask me why.'

'No, I won't ask you, instead I will tell you. You are refusing me because of Myra, because of what happened at Moorcroft House and the things Ava Russell forced her to do.'

In the quiet hush of the small cottage, his words calm

and unruffled, Andrew told of how on following her to Moorcroft, not finding her there he had gone to the house of Dora Benson and she had told him the whole of Myra's story.

'It was that letter the intruder searched this house for,' he took her hand, holding it between both of his own, 'a letter which could harm only one person: the mistress of Moorcroft.'

'Aunt Dora told you.'

'Yes, but don't hold that against her. She could see I loved you, that I wanted only to protect you.'

'The man who came, the one who struck me . . .'

'Was no man,' Andrew cut in. 'That was Ava Russell. It was she in men's clothing and it was she who committed those murders in Wednesbury, killed in order to protect the secret of her vile practices. But all of that is over, the woman will never walk the streets again.' Quietly as before he told of Ava's incarceration.

'But that changes nothing.' Eden pulled her hands free. 'What Myra did cannot be erased.'

'But it can be forgiven and forgotten.'

'Can it?' Eden rose to her feet. 'I went to Aunt Dora's today to ask that same thing but the family were not in the house in Hobbins Street. They were gone, driven out by hunger and want. Don't you see, Andrew, I failed Aunt Dora as I failed Myra. I did nothing to help either of them; I brought my sister only unhappiness and that is ultimately what I would bring you should knowledge of this ever become known. That is why I will never become your wife.' Taking an envelope from her pocket

Eden held it towards him. 'Read it,' she said, 'read what it was my sister suffered . . . suffered for me!'

'You need hold no grief for Dora Benson or her family.' Andrew watched the stricken face. 'They did not leave Hobbins Street for the reasons you think but in order to work for Tobias Jevons. He wanted reliable hard-working staff and I recommended the Bensons. Dora and her husband will care for the house whilst the sons do the same for the stables and grounds. As for this,' he took the letter and held it for a moment, 'I have no wish to read it. I know that what Myra did was done out of love, for the love of a sister. You know that, too. Myra loved you and your grandmother enough to go through hell in order to keep you safe. Honour that love, Eden, honour it by burning this letter and living the life she would have you live.'

For the love of a sister! Her heart twisting, Eden took the letter and tossed it into the fire, watching the corners of the envelope crisp and curl, then burst into orange flame. Myra *had* gone through hell for her sake and she would tread those same paths to shield Andrew Denby from shame.

Turning to tell him so, she was forestalled by a call from the towpath.

'That will be the trainee manager of the new boatyard I've had built along of Wiggins Pool. He is taking the first boat built there to pick up a load of glassware from Stourbridge. Would you like to see it?'

At her nod Andrew caught her hand, holding her back just long enough to say, 'I love you Eden, no matter how you decide to live your life, remember always that I love you.'

She wanted his kiss, wanted his arms to hold her but, in taking her own happiness, she would eventually rob him of his. This thought all that held her together, she walked out to the towpath. There, an immaculately painted hull reflected its deep blue and lemon colours in the smooth sun-kissed waters.

'. . . *honour that love, Eden . . .*'

The words burned in her mind as she looked at the sleek narrowboat, Davy Melia pointing smilingly to its white-painted name.

'. . . *honour it . . . by living the life she would have you live.*'

That was what Myra would want, that was the love of a sister.

Catching the look she turned to him, Andrew frowned. 'You don't like her?'

'The boat is beautiful.'

'But?'

'The name,' she answered.

Andrew frowned again, 'The *Eden Brent*, I thought you might like that!'

Pure happiness lighting her eyes, Eden stepped close to the man she loved.

'Eden Brent was a nice choice,' she whispered lifting her mouth to his, 'but would you make it the *Eden Denby.*'

If you enjoyed
FOR THE LOVE OF A SISTER,
here's a foretaste of
Meg Hutchinson's new novel,
THE WANTON RED-HEAD.

PROLOGUE

She had to do it!

This was a chance that would never come again! Auburn hair streaming in a breeze that pressed a thin cotton dress against long colt-like legs, the slight figure ran across the open heath.

But if she could not make it happen!

If she were saddled with a child!

Thoughts clanged like the passing bell, the impact of them bringing the flying figure to an abrupt halt.

That would mean the end of everything. If this one opportunity were lost, this one straw Fate was holding out to her was allowed to pass her by, it would condemn her to a life of misery, a life such as her mother had lived in a poky terraced house back to back with faceless rows of the same.

To live a lifetime as she lived now, sharing a yard with eight other houses, the families of four of them using the same wash-house, the same water pump . . . the one privy . . .

Looking to where the winding wheel of Spindrift Colliery rose black against the vermilion of a cloudless sky, Thea Maybury's pretty young face twisted with repugnance.

That wheel rode the sky like the chariot of death and that was what it brought to many of the people living in its shadow; death to men choking their days away in the black bowels of that coalmine, children sleeping top to toe in beds shoved into rooms whose very air was laden with the dust of the coal they were forced to help drag from the earth, children who coughed with the sickness of the lungs that digging also brought. A life of torment and grime was what she would have, a life many women of Darlaston lived working until they dropped, then every night asking the Lord to keep them from falling with yet another child.

Breath catching in her throat, Thea's nerves tightened. Spindrift Colliery! It was aptly named. Every dream dreamed by men who passed within its black mouth, every dream of women who toiled pulling coal-laden bogeys from the pit head soon spun away; drifting mists of dead hopes.

That was what the child would bring to her.

Staring at the spirals of smoke rising from the chimneys of the houses built simply to serve that colliery, Thea Maybury anxiously twisted the cloth of her cheap skirt.

It would ruin everything, bring an end to her own dreams; they too would be lost like spindrift melting in the first rays of a summer sun, taking with them all she had longed for every day of living in that hovel of a house, what she had prayed for every night - and now that prayer had been answered, the chance she yearned for was offered and to let it pass . . . !

Disturbed by her presence a bird flew up from among the rough tussocks of grass, its song spreading over the quiet evening as it rose to meet the sky. Watching it glide effortlessly, graceful wings etched dark against the brilliance of a setting sun, Thea felt her heart lift. Fate which had offered the dream now offered the solution.

Thea watched the bird, its wings feathering the air holding it where it wanted to be. As she must hold to what she wanted.

To let it pass . . . She smiled beginning to walk on. No, she would not let it pass, she would not lose the dream . . . not even if it meant dropping the child down a mineshaft!

'You've got to help me, 'Lyssa, you are the only one I can turn to.'

Thea Maybury watched incomprehension become disbelief on the face of the young woman sat on the edge of a narrow iron-framed bed.

'You've got to, you do see that, don't you, it's the only way.'

Stomach nerves taut, Thea broke her pretence of a sob, threading the void of silence. 'Lyssa was not going to agree . . . she would not . . . but she had to be made to agree!

Beneath the cover of another sob Thea Maybury's mind worked like quicksilver. The offer which had been made to her had come like a gift from heaven; it was all she had ever wanted, a new life in a new country. She would no longer live in near-poverty, no longer skivvy carrying things to market, making do with the cheapest of clothes. She would have her own fine house and all that went with it . . . Thea Maybury would live like a lady.

'No one will ever know.' Allowing yet another false sob she crossed to a corner of the tiny room where she rested her hand on a chest of drawers before proceeding. 'Nobody will think twice, it won't matter for you, after all it's not like you have . . .'

Not like you have anyone interested in you. Alyssa Maybury finished the sentence in her mind. Alyssa the older sister, Alyssa the dowdy sister, Alyssa the girl a man never looked at once he had seen the pretty Thea.

'You must see,' Thea persisted, paying no mind to the hurt she saw before those other eyes were lowered, 'this is the only way, the best way.'

Best for all of them or best for Thea? Alyssa could not prevent the thought rising beneath the hurt. Her sister had always been self centred, the world must not simply revolve around Thea, it must revolve *for* Thea.

'This way I can help more with Mother than I can by taking stuff into town.'

Stuff! Alyssa's fingers clutched the bed's cold iron frame. That was all it was to her sister. Not for Thea the stitching which helped keep a roof over their heads, not for her the back-breaking hours of tending vegetables they sold to the kitchens of Darlaston's wealthy and certainly not for her to assist in the caring of a sick mother.

Across the narrow space dividing the bed from the chest of drawers Thea felt the weight of hesitation. Alyssa had not answered, she hadn't uttered a single word . . . and when she did would that word be 'no'? But it couldn't be . . . she would not let it be; there were ways and there were means and if one failed then the other must be tried.

'Don't say no, 'Lyssa, please . . .'

Breaking long enough to force a fresh sob, she pleaded. 'This is what I've hoped and prayed for, you can't let me lose it now, you can't!'

You can't! Refusing to be held back thoughts ran wild in Alyssa's mind. This was the way it had ever been between them, Thea doing exactly as she wished, the blame for any mischief it might cause being left to lie heavily on her sister's shoulders. Always the responsibility had been placed with her. 'You should have watched her' . . . 'You should have taken more care of her.' That had been the way of their mother; she could never bring herself to accept there was any fault in her youngest child. But then Thea had always come first in their mother's affections; the delicate, pretty red-gold-haired Thea must have the new dress, Thea lifted to a mother's knee each evening, Thea who must not be burdened with any but the very lightest of chores, Thea who could do no wrong.

But Thea had done wrong and now in typical fashion looked to her older sister to take the blame, to carry the guilt. This though was too much. Alyssa's fingers clutched even tighter against the cold iron. She could not do what her sister was asking. It was morally wrong, a sin against a child and a sin against God; she would not help, not this time.

'No.' Looking to where the slight figure waited, Alyssa shook her head briefly. 'No, Thea, I can't . . .'

The scarlet-gold of the dying sun filtering through the small square window caught the blue lightning flash of Thea's eyes, her answer spitting the flame of anger.

'Can't!' she snapped. 'Can't or won't! Oh, I see why you refuse . . . you haven't been offered the chance so why should I have it! That's the truth of it, isn't it? Oh yes, that's the truth all right, you are jealous, you have always been jealous of me, admit it, Alyssa, you have always been jealous!'

Had she always been envious of her sister? Alyssa felt the mental slump as she acknowledged the grain of truth the answer to that accusation must contain. Yes, childhood had been a time of envy and so many times a sadness. Not so much an envy of the lovely red-gold curls and pretty face, not even of the new dresses with their ribbons and bows their mother had sewed. That she had learned to deal with but the sadness of not being shown that same love, that special love which had always been Thea's. Yes, it was the love their mother had lavished on her younger daughter which the plain Alyssa had longed to experience; her mother's love she had wept for in the dark hours of night, prayed for the length of each day, but when evening came it was Thea lifted to their mother's lap, Thea held close to have her head stroked, hers the face receiving the last gentle kiss when put to bed: it was that, only that. . .

'Admit it!' Anger bruised the silence. 'Admit it, Alyssa, give the devil his freedom!'

Sharp as a blast of cold wind stripping trees of the last of their leaves the outburst blew away the shadows of guilt and for the first time Alyssa faced that which she had known for so long, known yet refused to know: for Thea it was Thea, it would always be Thea and nobody but Thea; in her sister's eyes only self was of any consequence.

'Give the devil his freedom.' Calm despite the emotions churning her mind, Alyssa looked at her sister, at the pretty face twisted now with temper and frustration. Always in childhood and even to this very evening she had drawn back from that look, allowed Thea her own way, but now all of that was gone. Thea must face her problems, own to her responsibility, accept the results of her actions. 'Give the devil his freedom,' she repeated quietly, 'that is what you have always done, that is what you did a year ago . . .'

'That's not true, I was forced . . .'

'No.' Alyssa shook her head again. 'Mother may have believed your story but I never have. You behaved then as you have behaved all of your life. You fulfilled your own desires, took what you wanted, gave freedom to the devil that sits inside you, the devil of selfishness;

but you forgot that demon gives his own rewards and he has given you yours. You knew what you were doing that day just as you know what you are about now, what you are always about, Thea, getting your own way, making things suit you . . . but not this time. Yours was the sin and yours must be the carrying of it.'

Across the room a slant of sunset touched red-gold hair lending a halo of flame.

That was how saints had been portrayed in those pictures which as children she and Thea had been shown at Sunday school, holy men and women their heads crowned with haloes of gold.

For the briefest of moments Alyssa was back in the small rectory room of St Lawrence Church gazing in wide-eyed awe at the paintings of people spoken of as the Blessed Apostles, of Saint Anne and her daughter the Virgin Mother of Christ, their calm serene faces captivating her young mind.

'I should have known that would be your answer . . .'

A toss of bright head threw a thousand gold-tipped slivers of light showering the gathering shadows like tinder sparks. The accusation snapped harshly in the gentle quiet. It broke Alyssa's reverie and once again it was her sister she watched. No face of gentle saint, no tender loving smile painted those delicate features. The look of anger and aggravation which, from their earliest years, heralded a fit of the sulks should Thea be opposed in anything. Then as quickly as the storm of temper had threatened so it cleared.

But Alyssa had seen this same swift cessation of

anger many times and always it had proved a prelude to another of her sister's wiles. This was not an end of demanding; it was not in Thea's nature to give up before gaining the last little bit of what she had set her mind to.

Across from Alyssa a fresh cascading of light danced like fireflies in the tiny room, a last gift of the disappearing sun touching a blessing to her sister's head. Watching her now, the delicate features no longer wearing the mutinous look of aggravation, the tightness of temper no longer pulling at the pretty mouth, Alyssa thought again of the painted saints. Yes, her sister was beautiful but there was a saying about beauty being skin deep . . .

Alyssa caught the thought before it could go any further but she could not prevent the sudden rush of feeling in her heart, a feeling of pity. Why? She tried to reason the emotion; surely her sister, the strong-minded, beautiful Thea, needed no one's pity?

'I should have known . . .' Fireflies fluttered with Thea's brief shake of her head. 'I should have known what you would say but despite your reason being pure jealousy, of your wishing to see my life ruined, of wanting me to lead the same life you will always lead, a soul-destroying poverty-ruled existence, I realise that . . . yes, it is best I clear this matter myself.'

Lowering her hand to a half-opened drawer of the chest Thea looked at the sister she had always been able to manipulate. The hair was the same, maybe a shade or two darker, the gold glinting among the rich

heavy folds forever dragged back from the face which
though not as pretty as her own, yet held a certain
attractive quality; but it was the eyes, those dusky
winter-violet eyes that had the real beauty, a beauty
compelling enough to ensnare any man should her
sister but try. But 'Lyssa did not try. 'Lyssa was not
given to slipping away at every opportunity and she,
Thea, had never encouraged her to. It served very well
having her stay at home. Getting on with the business
of earning their living meant no encumbrance on
herself, instead it allowed that liberty which had ever
been indulged to its fullest. In the softening shadows
of approaching night the tightening of Thea's mouth
remained imperceptible. Liberty! That was the one
thing she craved over all else, release from the yoke of
living hand to mouth, to escape the smoke and dirt
of Darlaston . . . of the new fetters threatening to bind
her! Her hand closing on the edge of the drawer, she
breathed the sharp breath of resolution. She would
never wear those chains . . . never!

Alyssa had watched . . . was watching. Deep inside
Thea laughed. The sister she had always so easily
twisted round her finger would do her bidding yet
again.

'Thea!'

Edged with concern, the call merely had Thea's
inner smile deepen, yes, 'Lyssa would do as
demanded.

'Thea, what are you going to do?'

Lifting a blanket-wrapped bundle from the open

drawer, Thea faced her sister and now that inward smiled etched her lips. The battle was almost won!

Eyes brilliant as the minute lances of light sparkling in her hair, Thea shook her head in affected sadness. 'Do?' she echoed. 'Exactly as you said I should, face up to my responsibility.'

Concern becoming a needle-sharp prick of anxiety, Alyssa watched the smile, the cold glitter of eyes fastened on her own. This was a Thea she had not known before. A girl who had never accepted the results of her foolhardiness was now accepting consequence? No! A trip of nerves told Alyssa there was something else behind this sudden acquiescence, something infinitely alarming. Her sister had never tolerated denial and instinct warned she would not do so now.

'But you of all people, 'Lyssa, should know what I am *not* going to do!'

The very quietness with which it was said, the calm, even tone smooth as frozen ice added frissons of fear to Alyssa's tense nerves as she glanced at the bundle held in her sister's arms then at the face which gleamed an awful triumph.

'I am not going to allow this . . .' Thea gave a shake to the bundle, '. . . this mistake to ruin my life, so I shall get rid of it. You have no need to worry, no one will ever find it . . . but should you find yourself thinking in those hours when sleep refuses to come, then remember I told you . . . I told you nothing would take this chance from me. Remember also that you were as responsible as I, for you sat there knowing all the time I would throw this . . . this nuisance . . . down the first pit shaft I came to.'

JOIN
MEG'S CLUB!

Become a part of the Meg Hutchinson story
today by joining the

* * * * * * * * * * *

Meg Hutchinson Readers' Club

* * * * * * * * * * *

Membership of the club is free and, once you join,
you will automatically receive each new edition of
the club newsletter *THE YARN*.
Inside you will find special messages from Meg,
exclusive extracts, fellow readers' letters, the
chance to obtain collectable Meg merchandise,
competitions galore and price promotions
available only to club members.

* * * * * * * * * * *

To join the Meg Hutchinson Readers' Club and receive
the first edition of the club newsletter *THE YARN*,
simply send a postcard with your name and address to:
Margaret Hutchinson, Kadocourt Ltd,
The Gateway, Gatehouse Road, Aylesbury,
Bucks, HP19 8ED.